This book is a work of fiction.

This book is dedicated to my cousins

Jinx McCombs and Paul Nordstrand

who first introduced me to

the glorious Mendocino and Sonoma coast.

Contents

Part 1
The Summons

1

Gran was a trouble-maker. That's what my mom said; it was one of the nicer things my mom said about our Gran. Mom distanced herself from her mother at the first possible opportunity. Her sister did the same. Two very conventional women, the sisters Celine and Mandy. Sometimes that's how families shake out.

My cousin Scott and I had the luxury of treating Gran's purported eccentricities as entertaining, if we thought about her at all. She wasn't real to us. My mom huffed and said, "You didn't have to grow up in her house…" My Aunt Mandy lifted her glass, saying emphatically, "You two have no idea…" with unspoken memories left hanging in a shudder.

Mom and her sister grew up with their mother in Berkeley, California. According to our moms, their father, a man named Roger, occupation unknown, was the first in a string of men Gran went through over the years. Whether she still has a "swinging door" as they claim, Scott and I cannot verify because we have not seen Gran since we were small children. We know her last name is Templeton but only our moms' sporadic comments remind us that we even have a grandmother.

In fact, we have grown up without the benefit of any grandparents at all. Every one of them died young, with the exception of Gran. Our moms' father, who was never "in the picture" anyway, died mysteriously when our moms were young. On my Kuiper side of the family, my dad speaks sentimentally of his mother, Rosa, who, like my dad's father, died before I was born. Scott's paternal grandparents never left Ireland and died there before Scott was born. When we were teenagers trying to be coolly cynical, we used to talk about our Dead Grandparents Club or speculate that we had bad genes.

Since we were not dealt a good hand of grandparenting cards, it might seem a shame that we had no contact with the one grandparent who was still alive, but we didn't know any different way of life. Other than occasionally hearing other children's tales of Christmas gifts from a doting grandparent or being envious on Grandparents Day at school when we had no guests, we two really had no idea of what we were missing. All we have are the intermittent and vague stories about our Gran coming from the disapproving lips of our moms.

My name is Elizabeth. According to my dad and to the photo on the wall, I possess the same head of wild dark hair as my Grandma Rosa. I am on the short side of average whereas Scott—birthname Prescott Thomas Sullivan—who also is dark-haired and brown-eyed like me, is one long and lean fellow. Scott is my best friend. Scott and I are only children and that is probably why we are so close. We also share the same birthday although I am ten minutes older. This reinforces our observation that our moms do everything in synch. Our moms see each other every day, therefore from babyhood Scott and I were together daily as well. If our moms are their own kind of unit, the two of us are also one.

Our parents hired a nanny named Consuela when we were babies to take care of both of us while our parents were working or socializing. Consuela officially lived in the pool house in my back yard, but she spent most nights inside our house; she is the one I remember most often coming to my bedside when I woke with a nightmare or was sick. Thanks to my babyish mispronunciation, we all called her "Cozy."

Scott and I adored Cozy in the way little ones do without conscious thought, taking her for granted as the source of warmth, comfort, food, and attention. Scott and I vied for a center spot on her lap, sometimes pushing each other away until Cozy gently reminded us to share.

When she had to return to Florida to take care of her elderly Cuban parents, my heart was broken. I cried every day of second grade until my teacher suggested that I write Cozy a letter every week, as part of my Saturday morning routine. Cozy wrote back for a number of years, and then the letters came more infrequently until they stopped. By this time my letter writing was built into my routine and I kept writing. My parents eventually got a letter from a nursing home social worker informing them that Cozy had early dementia and was no longer able to read my letters, and at that point my parents told me I should stop writing. But I couldn't give it up and kept writing to my old nanny every week until one day the social worker wrote directly to me and told me that Cozy died. She thanked me for my letters saying they had brought Cozy real joy even as she faded away.

I kept that letter from the worker. I was fifteen at that point, and I think now it was the single best thing I ever did in my childhood.

My dad, Matthew Kuiper, spends his time either at work (he is an architect) or playing golf. He's a striking man with dark eyes and hair inherited from his Mexican mother and tall frame from his Dutch father, but he was a moving target in my childhood, nice enough but never around too much. Always hazy on details, unless it was about architecture or his golf game. When I cornered him to help me complete a school project, he explained that his father's family came from the Netherlands right before World War II and my dad's father met his mother—the enchanting Rosa—at her family's Mexican restaurant in Sacramento. They fell in love and scandalized both families by running away to get married. As a pre-teen I thought it was totally romantic. Why they died so young, is part of their mystery. My dad was an only child and is not interested in ancestry. But he did give me his mother's name for my middle name.

Scott's dad, Ryan Sullivan—boisterously proud of his Irish heritage—is an insurance broker and a sports nut. He came from a large Irish family but he was the only one to move to the United States, and his contacts with this family in Ireland were always limited. We heard rumors of a rift in the family. Grudges and shunning. But the story was not laid out for Scott in any definitive manner. Uncle Ryan never took Scott back to his mother country. I think sports took the place of Uncle Ryan's family. He took Scott and me to Giants and Athletics games and Warriors games. He also yelled a lot at our Little League and softball games. But Scott was never the athlete his dad wished him to be; Scott turned out to be a tech nerd who also loved to work on old cars. I still love sports, especially tennis and volleyball. I run several miles every day, but as Scott's lack of sports interest became apparent, Uncle Ryan also stopped inviting me to events. Scott says his dad divides his time now between work and hanging down at the sports bar with other like-minded folks, making a dutiful appearance at home only for happy hour. A few times a year the four of our parents travel someplace with a spa and golf course and maid service.

If you were dropped down into my childhood house or Scott's, you would have trouble telling them apart. Both are large sprawling homes with pools, located two blocks apart. The sisters work together. My mom buys and sells homes, and Scott's mother does the interior design work. My mom is the older of the two, however there is an aura that they are interchangeable. They dress impeccably as if always ready to go out the door and meet a client. And I've never heard or see them argue. (Perhaps by that I mean, I have never heard Aunt Mandy defy her older sister.) They appear to be of one mind. They are successful.

As for Scott and me, we made it through high school hanging with a reliable crowd of friends, not walking too close to danger and rebellion, having fun but still getting good enough grades to get into UC Davis, which is near the suburban town of Dixon, California where we grew up.

Now we are approaching thirty. I am a frugal woman with simple taste. The car in my driveway is the same 2008 burgundy Civic I bought for myself with my first job, and I live in the second story of an old Victorian house near downtown Davis. My parents keep pushing me to buy a house of my own. When I say I don't make enough money as a teacher, they laugh and say that of course they will help me out. The message is clear. Funky apartments are tolerated for college students but not for their daughter who is ready to exit her twenties. I have managed to resist their pressure. Scott gave in to the similar offer from his folks. He makes more money than I do, but he still took his parent's offer of a down payment. He shrugged. He wanted the three-car garage to work on his old cars and plug in his electric car, but why he needs four bedrooms, I can't imagine.

So, here I am, Elizabeth Rose Kuiper, eighth grade teacher. As long as Nellie my landlord and downstairs neighbor doesn't die or sell her house, I can be completely self-sufficient. I love my job and the hours I am with my middle schoolers are my happiest. Some folks—even teachers—don't like working with middle school-aged kids, but I do. And now with a few years under my belt I have a sense that I know what I am doing. Which doesn't mean there isn't a learning experience every day, but it does mean that I have some Velcro with which to handle the surprises that thirteen-year-olds throw at me.

My weeks have a flow: weekdays are strictly teaching and prep work done in my old upstairs apartment, then on Friday nights I have let-your-hair-down times with my colleagues, picking a pub far enough away from our school to reduce the risk one of our student's parent walking in on us. Saturdays, besides shopping and laundry, will find me outside jogging or hiking or playing tennis. Sometimes I get together with college friends who still live around Davis, going to just enough concerts to stay in touch with my generation's culture. Sunday morning, I might swing in to spend an hour or two with Mom and Dad if they happen to be in town. But Sunday night is saved for Scott and I to order pizza and watch the Warriors or an old movie, as well as deconstruct our latest encounter with our parents.

I'm not antisocial. Scott and I both date, from time to time. He dates women, and me, men. (Let me reconsider what I just said. To be honest, the dating happens less and less often as I move on through my twenties.)

It is a comfortable existence, if routine.

Recently I have been questioning that routineness, asking myself, is this what life is all about? Scott and I sometimes touch on that topic, but because it is too existentially huge, we tend to change the subject.

What does any of this have to do with my Gran and her trouble-making ways? Well, it does become relevant, eventually.

2

I was contemplating how to teach iPhone-addicted eighth graders the importance of Reconstruction after the Civil War. What new approach could I take to tie the textbook to their lives? I sat back on the deep orange Cost Plus rug that covers my living room floor and let my eyes browse over the bookshelves that line one wall. That wall is painted forest green; the opposite wall is gold. Two large, long multipaned windows look out over the tree-shaded street. My kitchen is yellow and my bedroom grayish blue. I love my apartment, and my landlady.

She is a gem, my landlady. Nellie Avon. Old, but spry. Every morning when I leave for work at 6:30 I see Nellie finishing up her morning walk. I worry about her in the winter when darkness prevails at that hour. She says not to worry, she has her Doberman named Fletcher by her side, and it is true he provides a formidable looking companion even though Nellie has trained him to be as sweet as a golden retriever. On the rare occasions when Nellie leaves town, usually to see her sister in Petaluma, Fletcher goes with her. She named him for her late husband who died in Vietnam a long time ago. Which is sort of weird—naming a dog for your husband—but obviously it doesn't strike her as an odd thing to do.

She has lived alone ever since the original Fletcher died. She spends her days in her own garden and doing volunteer work at the gardens on the Davis campus. She taught horticulture there, becoming a docent after she retired. I met her while doing my student teaching when I took a group of antsy sixth graders on a field trip to the campus gardens. She was able to engage those students like no one I ever met. I made a special trip over to thank her the next day and one thing led to another, and here I am; for eight years I've rented her upstairs apartment, accessed by stairs outside the house.

Nellie allows me to paint my walls whatever colors I want and I have brushed many different tints and shades and variations of colors onto my walls and ceilings. It suits me. It most definitely does not please Mom. I have heard a thousand times how jarring my colorful walls are, how much nicer it would be to have pale gray or off white everywhere. But I didn't understand why Mom was so bothered by my decorating style until one day when I overheard her tell my aunt that my apartment looked just like Gran's houses. That, apparently, was the kiss of bad taste.

I'll admit that comparison made me curious about Gran. Through my childhood, my mom made once-a-year duty visits to her mother, accompanied by Mandy, never by our fathers, and Scott and I were generally left behind. They returned from those visits as if they needed to take long showers to wash off their experience. For weeks afterward they would discuss the goings-on and misbehaviors of their mother. Since they spoke in generalities and innuendoes when

Scott and I were around, we never learned the nitty-gritty of my Gran's misbehavior.

On this evening, I sat on my living room floor, my lesson plan book laying open in front of me, an empty ice cream bowl next to the history text book. I jumped when my phone rang. I reached across to the table to grab it but when I saw Mom's name, I lay down on the floor to do some stretching exercises while I talked to her. I found it soothed me.

"Elizabeth."

"Hi, Mom. I thought you were on a cruise."

"We are, nearing Belize later tonight."

"Having fun?"

"Um. Well, there are a lot of people on board who…"

The connection broke up and I was glad to miss hearing the complaint about whatever low-class behavior my mom was forced to witness.

"Mom, you're breaking up. What's up? Is everything okay?"

"Elizabeth, you or Scott have to go check in on Gran."

"What?" I sat up.

"Gran sent me a text and said she had some sort of issue and needed to see Mandy and me immediately. Of course, we can't do that. If she has a health issue, she should go to her doctor and if it's emergency, they can fly her by helicopter to Santa Rosa. That's what they do with everyone who chooses to live way out there."

The North Coast was hardly the middle of Bolivia, but to my mom and Mandy, it was a world apart.

"Mom, I can't just drop my classes and take off in the middle of the week. What are you thinking?"

My mom has never been able to conceptualize the life of a teacher. Nor has she tried.

"Isn't that what they have substitutes for?"

"Yes, for when you get sick or have an emergency," I countered.

"This may be an emergency. Anyway, I want her to quit texting me. She won't stop, both Mandy and me. Just constant texting all night last night. Who taught her to text anyway?"

"So, you want me and Scott to drop everything and drive hours up the coast to check in on Gran whom we don't even know? And why? So you can carry on with your vacation and not feel guilty?"

To my astonishment, my admonishment sounded bold. Normally I just try to get along with my parents without any pushback.

There was a pause and finally Mom conceded. "I don't want to drop everything when it's probably for nothing. Gran can be dramatic."

"Has she ever done anything like this before?"

"Well, no, she mostly ignores us. Which is why this is strange and why I want you or Scott to go check it out, you know, just in case it is something, I don't want to be accused of neglecting my mother. It wouldn't look good, although few would blame me if they knew her."

While not surprised at my mom's callous attitude, I was blindsided by the strange request. But on second consideration, my curiosity was piqued. Maybe it would be a good change of pace. Maybe Scott would buy into it.

"Mom, I won't promise to do this, but there is a three-day weekend coming up, and if it can wait until Saturday, I'll think about it. Send me her address or phone number."

"Good for you, Elizabeth. I knew I could count on you." Mom sounded relieved and ready to move on to the black-jack table. "I'll text you her address."

"Uh, Mom, any advice? What can I expect?"

Her laugh could be heard all the way from the Caribbean. "Oh God, Elizabeth. Who knows? She's a mess." And then as if she didn't want me to change my mind, she added. "But, dear, she loves colors a lot. You might enjoy that."

I hung up the phone and sat there bemused. As sometimes happens after being distracted, when I looked back at my lesson plans, I had a sudden inspiration and furiously began jotting down ideas, focusing so intently that I almost forgot about visiting Gran. However, before going to bed, I called Scott.

"Hey, Scott, are you busy?"

"Just heading to the shower."

"Why don't you sit down, Cuz, cuz I am going to lay an idea on you and I hope you'll say yes."

"Okay," he said slowly. "I'm sitting here on the toilet. That work for you?"

Scott and I were toilet-trained together, so of course it didn't faze me. "I don't know what you have planned this weekend, Scotty, but it can't be more of a hoot than driving up to Gualala and checking in on our Gran."

The silence that followed was predictable. Scott was not one to lose his cool easily.

"Say what? Lizzie, I think I need you to repeat that. Have you been drinking?"

"You know I never drink during the week. No, you heard me right, and I know it's crazy but I'm so ready for a lark, and doesn't this sound like a real kick in the ass?"

"No, it just sounds bizarre. You're going to have to fill me in."

And I did, telling him what Mom had told me. Scott didn't sound convinced even after he knew the sketchy details.

I finished with "So don't tell me you have a hot date this weekend or tickets to a concert or something. Say you'll go with me."

Scott was silent, then weakly mentioned something about a woman he was thinking about asking out.

"Ah, but thinking about it isn't the same as doing it, Scott. Come on, you've been wanting to try out your little Karmann Ghia on the road. You said you wanted to try it on curves and I hear there are a lot of curves going up Highway One. I have AAA coverage, just in case."

Scott bristled a bit. "Hey, when I fix up a car it doesn't need towing." Then he added, and I could tell he was caving, "Why are you so gung-ho to do this? You haven't seen Gran since… maybe it was that summer when we were about second or third grade, after Cozy left and our moms couldn't find anyone to stay with us. We met Gran in Sonoma at that winery and our moms had a big fight with her. What makes this such a great idea? What's motivating you?" He sounded suspicious.

That made me stop. "I have no idea. None. A few hours

ago, I was here writing lesson plans and admiring my latest paint job, thinking how much Mom will hate it, and now I am ready to forgo a hike out along Tamales Bay with my hiking group this long weekend, all to drive up the coast to check in on our crazy Gran. I guess I'm just ready to do something different, something impromptu."

"Apparently," Scott agreed. "I'm mystified, but I'll consider it."

"Fantastic!"

"Can I take my shower now?"

"Go for it."

3

We got on the road early Saturday, figuring we'd stop along the way to take a hike and get some fish and chips in Bodega Bay. Scott had done a good job fixing up the sleek red Karmann Ghia, and for an old car it ran smoothly, first in and out of the Bay Area traffic and then on the rural roads that led to the coast. We talked as we usually did of sports and politics and work and concerts and hikes we wanted to take. Scott had always been intrigued with my teaching, treating it as something he could never do. And I in turn was properly impressed with his skills, both his old-school mechanical know-how and the technology career. I think that is what made our adult friendship work: a mutual respect and curiosity about the other's interests. That and the aforementioned reality that we were a comfortable unit to balance out our uncomfortable relationship with our parents. Unity based out of necessity you might say.

After an hour of driving, we stopped talking and just cruised along enjoying the hills with their lush spring greenery beginning to become summer golden, little lambs in the fields, cows munching and the occasional horses with tails whipping in the wind. The sky was blue with huge fluffy white clouds. A real stellar day, and we were old enough now to appreciate the beauty around us, driving through the bucolic rural landscape of western Sonoma County. It was a day to feel young and hopeful and alive. It was easy to shed news-gloom and work stress on such a day.

"What are we going to do when we get there? Have you thought about that?" Scott asked me as we crunched our fried fish and dipped our chips in vinegar and ketchup at our lunch stop in Bodega Bay.

I'm normally a planner but today didn't have any plan. "To be honest, I've been so busy doing my grades that I haven't given it much of any thought. I just thought we'd feel it out as we go. Wing it. I mean we have no idea what the issue is."

"Or who Gran really is and how she will react to us showing up when our moms bugger out," Scott replied with a mouthful of clam chowder.

"Well, I called her and she never answered. I left a message and just said that Scott and I were going to come because our moms were out of the country."

"And she never responded?"

"Nope. And the second time I called, her mailbox was full. Maybe she never got the message. Maybe she doesn't care. Maybe she's angry. Maybe she doesn't want us to come. Maybe she's sick. I don't know."

"Or maybe she's dead." Scott's voice was garbled by a gulp of soda.

I shot him a started look. "I hadn't thought of that. I don't know how I would feel about that."

"It's not like we really know her, or have any warm fuzzy Granny memories or feelings."

I nodded. "True. Although ever since we got this assignment from Mom, I find myself curious. So, I'd hate to find she has dropped dead or is really sick."

We both stood up then with the same impulse; perhaps we were wasting time eating lunch and watching the boats, when our Gran might be dying. We had planned one more hike along the way, but decided to nix it and just head north. It was a couple of hours of driving yet, on one of the most twisted and dazzling drives in the state. We thought perhaps we had been up this way once during our early childhood, but neither of us had a memory of this drive or of seeing Gran in her coastal home.

Scott drove on, heading up and over the steep grade at Jenner, leaving me time to take in the stunning view. From up high on the grade, we looked—well I looked, Scott kept his eyes on the road fortunately—out to the endless blue sea and horizon, a few fishing boats bobbing up and down and far out to sea a huge ocean freighter looking miniscule from this perspective. I gaped at the steep drop off down the rock cliffs to the ocean hundreds of feet below us. Looking straight down helped me understand vertigo but we were on the northbound side of the road, not the ocean side, and I trusted Scott's driving. I often spend time on coastal outings, beachy days, hiking and wine tasting south of Bodega, but this location farther north caused something to awaken in me; I'm sure it was a mix of our strange mission and the phenomenal view.

I told myself that when we got there, we would walk in on Gran and she would look at us in surprise, and we would have some sort of conversation, either a polite conversation, or, if you believed our moms, a very rude conversation, and then Scott and I would turn around and head home. Yet I found myself hoping that there was something we were supposed to find out or do. That we would be needed. We had packed for overnight, just in case.

When I expressed my thoughts to Scott, he wasn't so sure. "I think you've been reading too many mystery novels, Liz. This may be a trip of folly, but I am enjoying this drive. Nice to see what this car can do, and this road is so much more fun to drive than freeway driving. So, there's no harm in any of this. I'm happy to be right here!"

We stopped at a view spot, used the restroom and despite our urgency, decided we had to see where the path would take us. It led to a lookout point, old wooden decking and rails, surrounded by tall golden grasses waving in the breeze and impressive purple thistle flowers adding a bold color. Standing there and looking out was wondrous. I felt like I could fly out over the ocean like the vultures and hawks that soared below us; that's how high up we were, overlooking the blueness that stretched forever to meet the sky. When I was a kid, I had a favorite book called *Henry and Mudge and the Forever Sea*. This was it, the forever sea.

Ever so far below, we could hear the crashing of waves on rocks, but it was so remote that it felt like we were in the clouds. And the quiet! Oh, the quiet up where we stood took my breath away. I lived on a clattery town street, always something, a motorcycle, the garbage truck, a delivery van, music from a neighbor's house, Nellie on the phone (she was slightly hard of hearing), people out walking their dogs. I loved my little apartment but it was not quiet. And tell me when a middle school is ever quiet!! At my parents' house, generally they have the television on as background noise. Even when I go trail walking with my Saturday group, in the loveliest of places, we are most often engaged in conversation with each other. In this moment though, it hit me. This is silence. Only the wind added some texture to what entered my ears: the gentle sea wind and the far-below sound of those crashing waves. But in between, where Scott and I stood, it was simply silent. Scott must have felt it, too, because he didn't say a word.

Mutually, we turned and walked slowly back to the car, watching a bright yellow goldfinch dart in and out of bushes. Only back in the car did we continue our normal conversation. But something had altered. We didn't talk of it. It happened though.

Welcome to the North Coast. That's what I thought later.

The road went on, occasionally straight, most often curving in and out of gulches where creeks ran down the steep mountain side and into the ocean. Trees were thick and the air was lush with spring-time life including small waterfalls spilling water under the road and down to the sea. Spring in California is the best season all over the whole state, it is true. Nellie was always telling me that.

Sometimes the road passed through open meadows with cattle, a few old ranch houses, and just the occasional home, second home or first, who knows? There were no supermarkets or big box stores around, that's for sure. Living here would take a different kind of mentality. My mom called it the boondocks.

We passed some trailheads but, while tempted, felt we should stay on the road north. It was getting to be late afternoon when we crossed the Gualala River, kayakers' colorful boats on one side of the bridge and meandering water twisting around sandbars as it flowed to the ocean on the other. And, there was the town of Gualala.

Scott eased the car into a parking lot in front of a market. "What's her address, Lizbeth?"

I pulled out my phone and for the first time looked at what Mom had texted me. "Post Office Box 340." I looked at Scott and he looked back at me with annoyance.

"Post Office box? How are we supposed to find her if we don't have a real address? Is that all your mom sent you?"

"Apparently." I was kicking myself for not noticing that earlier.

"Well, you better call again and hope Gran answers this time, or… or we will have to call our moms back and get an address."

I called Gran but the result was the same, mailbox was full, and then without looking at Scott, who was staring out the window, I called my mom's cell, then Scott's mom. The signal was poor for both calls, and I honestly wasn't sure either went through. Anyway, there was no answer. Scott looked pissed. For someone who had just told me that the drive was worth it all regardless of what we found with Gran, he did not look so philosophical anymore.

"What the fuck, Liz? We drove all the way out here and now we have no way to find her?"

In an effort to redeem myself, I looked around and spotting the post office, I confidently answered. "I'll just go ask at the post office."

He didn't look convinced but started the car and drove across the street to the post office and turned the engine off.

I hopped out of the car. "Coming in?"

He shook his head. "I'll just stay here and check my messages. Go ahead."

I went in the door myself. But before I could get to the front of the line, Scott was beside me, phone in hand. "No signal out there. Maybe it will be stronger inside." He bent his head to his phone while I went up to the counter.

"Hi. I'm looking for Mrs. Templeton." (It hit me that I had no idea what Gran's first name was; talk about being totally unprepared.) "I'm her granddaughter and we've come to visit but the thing is, we don't have her address. All we have is a post office box. I'm wondering if you could tell me where she lives."

I realized it sounded lame, and sure enough the postal clerk's face told me I was right on that score. "Ma'am, I can't do that" is all she said. I don't think I am old enough to be called Ma'am. It caught me by surprise and I didn't know how to respond. Scott came to help.

"I'm Mrs. Templeton's grandson. We know she lives somewhere around Gualala, but we haven't been here in years and our mothers are not around. We think Gran may need some help."

The clerk was not moved. "Sir, I can't give out information like that."

"We can show you our IDs," I tried.

The woman just shook her head and turned to the next customer in line. Scott and I stood aside, trying to decide how to proceed. It was not like we knew the area, or the town. We wandered outside and stared around us.

A voice behind us made us both jump. "Uh, I overheard you talking to Susie. You'll never get any information from Susie. She's straight from the book."

The man speaking was dressed in old jeans and a work shirt. His gray hair was long and unruly, but piercing blue eyes were all you noticed within the first second of laying eyes on him.

We turned, eager for any enlightenment. He looked us over as if trying to vet us before divulging any information. We must have looked properly nerdy and totally witless, clearing doubt about any nefarious motives because he reached out his hand to first Scott and then me for a handshake.

"I'm Floyd Copper. I haven't seen your Gran for a while. I've been working up in Fort Bragg for the last year, just got back to town, getting my mail started up again. But we used to work over at the Art Center together and down at the theater. I know she has two daughters. She sometimes mentioned them." He started to say more, and an amused look crossed his face, and then he went on. "But I didn't know she had grandkids. What did you say your names were?"

"Elizabeth Kuiper and this is my cousin Scott Sullivan."

"Where you all from?"

"We live in Davis," we replied almost in unison. Floyd Copper smiled.

"Yeah. Davis. Took a wine class there once, many years ago. Tried getting some vineyards going up near Annapolis. Had a lot of fun on that venture, although in the long run it never worked out. But that's another story." Another pause as he seemed to let some memories play out like a movie in his mind before coming back to the blustery parking lot in Gualala where Scott and I stood getting colder by the moment.

"Would you be willing to let us know where Mrs. Templeton lives?" Scott was beguiling with a warm smile but direct. I admired his approach until he added, "My cousin Elizabeth seems to have overlooked the fact that we would need an actual address to find our grandmother since we have never been here. And it seems that our mothers forgot to give us that little bit of important information, too."

I glared at Scott but Floyd laughed. "Well, that does seem like an oversight, doesn't it?" I tried to smile, willing to be the brunt of the joke if he would help us out.

"Yeah, well, she lives up the road a bit. Head north up out of town and look for a grand old wooden place called St. Orres, then go a little farther on and you'll see a road, just a gravel thing, to the left, ocean side, and head down for a half mile, and fork to the right. Her place is kind of set back out of sight from the drive, but you can't miss it."

I doubted that. "Sounds a little hard to find. But you say we can't miss it?"

He grinned as if in on a joke. "Yep, you can't miss it." He

laughed again. "Good luck, and I hope everything is okay. She'll give you hell if she's just fine and you come fussing around her. She never did like anyone fussing about her. Drives her crazy. And when that woman is crazy, well, it is all sorts of fun to watch!"

Amused at his own speech, he gave us a salute, called out to a man walking across the parking lot, and ambled off to greet him. "Hey, Paul, good to see you. I'm back home and happy to be here!"

Scott and I looked at each other. "What do you think?" Scott asked me.

"I think we have no other options unless we just go on home. Do you remember what his directions were?"

"Pretty much." Scott sounded dubious. "North. Saint something or other. Turn left."

"Well, let's get going. It will be dark in about three hours and I don't want to get lost in the dark."

"Do you think it's true that Gran will be ticked off if we just show up?"

"Hey, she is the one who started this whole deal. I'll just throw it back at her," I said recklessly. "Besides, we are only doing this because our moms insisted."

Scott moved towards his car. "Perhaps we should not go that route. Maybe we should just tell her we took a whim and decided to come up to see her. No big deal, you know?"

I stopped and considered. "I get it and you may be right. If she doesn't want to be fussed over... and she does sound like someone who might appreciate a good lark...."

Scott grinned. "You keep using that word. Lark. Sounds old-fashioned and sort of British comedy-like."

"I think it sounds like a free and beautiful bird."

As we opened our car doors, a man walked by. "Like your car. That's a good year. How's it handling the roads up here?"

Ten minutes of animated conversation ensued. Scott could never resist engaging in stories of his car, where he had salvaged parts and how he had fixed up the old Karmann Ghia, all to the admiring ears of this stranger who had a few car stories of his own to tell—it was a hazard when hanging out with Scott. When he encountered another classic car fan, the stories could go on and on.

I cleared my throat. "Uh, Scott, we don't have all that much time."

Scott reluctantly drew himself away from the car conversation and said we had to move on. The man opened his wallet and handed Scott a card. "My business is car repair, but my true love is these old beauties. Let me know if you ever want to sell or need a part, or just want to drop by and see what I've got in my garage." And with that he gave a friendly wave and a nod to me, and made his way into the post office.

"Well," I said, "you gearheads always seem to find each other. Small town life."

"Yeah," Scott said. "I kind of like it."

4

Without any clear mileage directions to guide us, and feeling very historic without GPS or even a paper map to go by, we drove north. It was hard to imagine that not too long ago, no one had anything but maps or written or oral directions. Of course, we weren't on a dangerous journey, and there was no great problem if we got lost. If we didn't find Gran before dark or we got low on gas, we'd simply come back to Gualala, get pizza and beer and find a room for the night, then give Mom and Aunt Mandy another call and see what we could do. Still, we were out of our predictable routine and I was excited. I imagined telling my eighth graders about it when I got back to my classroom. They didn't believe people could function without cell phones.

Shortly after we left town, we saw on the right an onion shaped tower on a darkly wooded building with a sign naming it St. Orres. That sounded familiar from the man's description.

"Inn and restaurant. Let's keep that in mind in case we don't find Gran."

"Or we find her and she doesn't invite us to stay."

"Or we find her, and she invites us to stay, but we don't get a good feeling about it. Like if her house smells or something," Scott said.

"What? Why would her house smell?"

Scott looked embarrassed. "Well, you know sometimes old people don't smell good or maybe she cooks weird shit that stinks up the place. I don't know. Seems like once I heard my mom mention something about smelling funny."

I started laughing. "Well, maybe Gran is just very cool. You know, I remember Mom coming to my apartment when I was in college and wrinkling up her nose and saying it smelled funny. She never got used to the smell of weed. She always preferred the smell of cigarettes and gin!"

"Maybe," Scott conceded. "I know my mom was always telling me to take a shower, but I thought it was my stinky socks. Hey, does that look like our turn?"

"Seems like it could be. Left turn is what the man said, is that it?"

"Ocean side of the road." Scott slowed down and turned into a narrow paved road by a lone, leaning mailbox with no name perched on a wooden post. The road soon that turned into rough gravel about a hundred feet off the highway.

"Hate gravel for my tires," Scott grumbled but kept going.

I looked all around. Thick trees made the road darker than the time of day would warrant. Through the branches I could see glimpses of the ocean and realized we were quite close to the bluffs. We drove slowly north now, parallel to the ocean, our road separated from the crashing waves by a narrow forest of trees.

Just when we were sure we were heading down a trail to nowhere, we came upon a building with three bay doors sitting in the middle of the tall trees. We guessed it was a garage but there was no house in sight. A dusty four-wheel-drive SUV, vintage ten or fifteen years old, sat near the garage.

The road pretty much ended at the garage and Scott began to move the little Karmann Ghia back and forth to turn around. While he went forward and reversed, I studied the old garage. The trim was painted blue, a soft faded sea blue, but the walls were composed of round stones. The bay doors were closed tight with locks securing them. The building was two stories with smaller windows above the bays. Something caught my eye over the doorways.

"Hey, Scott. Stop. Look at that."

I pointed, and Scott stopped and twisted his head around to see where I was pointing. "Says something. Can you read it?"

I rolled the window down and concentrated. The letters were made of marbles or broken glass or something shiny and bluish embedded in the stone wall of the garage. Squinting, I read aloud, "Mackintosh and…" This next part of the wording was in the shade, so I hopped out of the car and went closer. "Templeton!" I shouted. "Templeton!"

"Gran!" Scott said and put the car into park.

I came back over to the car and leaned in. "This has got to be it, Scotty. Ready to go see?"

Scott got out of the car but then just stood there looking around. "What if, you know, it isn't Gran or she isn't home, or you know, what if there are dogs?"

I didn't laugh. Scott had a thing about dogs. Genuine terror after a bad experience when we were small.

"I'll go by myself. It's okay."

Scott bristled. "I can't let you do that." He reached down and picked up a branch the size of a small tree trunk. "Okay, let's go."

We turned towards the garage, but then he again hesitated. "Is there a house? All I see is this garage and it's all locked up."

We walked to the far side of the garage, and there we found a rustic archway made of smooth reddish-orange branches similar to the one Scott had picked up to protect himself. It opened on a semi-maintained path made of chipped wood pieces, winding and then curling out of sight. There was no gate, so it seemed like an invitation.

"Come on. We've come this far."

Scott looked like he wished he were back in his own garage with a wrench in his hand, but loyally he followed behind me. The path was heavily shaded by the trees but when we came around the bend in the path the sight was blinding. We both stopped short to let our eyes adjust.

Ahead of us, the path continued through an open meadow of waving grasses, golden in the late afternoon sun, like a wheat field on the prairies. In the distance the ocean was several different colors of blue from turquoise to deep navy blue, and far out the horizon was a straight line with a fog bank separating the sea from the blue sky above. It seemed to tell us to enjoy the bright sunshine and colors while we could because at its whim the fog would return to blanket us in grayness.

When we got our bearings, we saw a house and ventured on through the meadow towards it, Scott keeping a strong hand on his protective stick. It's not that I wasn't leery of encountering aggressive dogs rightly protecting their home turf from invaders, but I didn't harbor a visceral fear like Scott did. I was secretly glad he had his stick, and also glad that he had no macho desire to hide his fear behind bravado.

About half way across the meadow, the grasses were cut shorter and we began seeing human-made rock formations. They were everywhere, and not just rock formations but metal and wood sculptures. The meadow was covered in them, some tall and some shorter, some abstract and some clearly representing animal or human figures. We kept walking towards the house and as we approached closer, we stopped to absorb the sight.

I'm the daughter of an architect but... Never seen a house like this." I don't know why I was whispering.

"What would you call it?"

"A flying saucer house?"

"A ski slope house?"

"Well, that man was right in a way. He said we couldn't miss it. We could have easily missed the road, but this place is..." I didn't know how to describe it.

Scott laughed and finished my thought. "It is the absolutely most unlikely house you would ever find our moms living in!"

"Yes, that's it. This has to be Gran!"

Scott wondered, "She didn't live here the last time we visited her. We were pretty young. But I would have remembered this place."

"I think Gran lived in a town, and I remember it was

a tiny house, compared to our childhood Dixon houses." I scrunched up my face to remember. "In fact, didn't she live in a mobile home park?"

Scott grinned. "Must have; at one point I remember our moms talking about how Gran had turned into 'trailer trash.' Well, she sure doesn't live in a trailer now."

I paused. "If indeed this is actually her house. Come on, Scott. Someone may have binoculars on us right now. We better keep going."

"Hope like hell it is just binoculars." Scott swore. I tried to clear away images of an ambush, leaving our bloodied bodies strewn across the stone-filled meadow. My imagination was going wild. And… but… I was enjoying it.

"Don't be ridiculous. We're just looking for our Gran," I said bravely. But I'd never been a trespasser before.

As we walked on towards the house Scott motioned over to the bluff. "How far down do you think the water is?"

"What? You thinking of jumping?" I laughed equally nervously.

Then we were standing in front of the big house with a roof that looked like a skateboard ramp. It was covered with colored flags hanging from every post and window, all blowing in the wind, making it look like the whole house was a sailing ship at sea.

We stared up at the house for a minute, to take in the effect of it. Before we could make the final steps to the front porch, we became aware of someone watching us. Perhaps it was a low growl that brought this awareness. It focused our attention to a chair to the right of the front door where a woman sat, a medium-sized dog by her side. The dog appeared ready to leap at the slightest command from the woman.

"You've got no more than ten seconds to tell me your name before I release Johnny here to send you running." Her voice was gruff. She was in the shadows so we couldn't really make out her features. She didn't move from her chair.

Scott and I both started speaking at once. The woman raised a cane into the air like a scepter and silenced us. "For God's sake. Shut up." She then pointed to me. "You, girl. You first."

"I'm Elizabeth Kuiper, and this is my cousin Scott Sullivan. You are our Gran." I added the last in the hope that I was correct.

There was a silence. At least she had not unleashed the dog on us. Scott added, "Our moms are traveling and asked us to come and check on you. They said you asked them to come."

I could have kicked Scott. We had agreed, or so I thought, to just say we were on a lark and traveling around and wanted to stop by to get to know our Gran better. But now it was too late. So be it. We would see how she would take it. She had yet to admit she was our Gran anyway and certainly hadn't rushed down the stairs to embrace us and offer cookies and milk.

It was hard to define her silence; what did it mean? Finally, not wanting to continue to stand there any longer like a couple of fools at the foot of the stairs, I ventured. "Can we come up and see you? We've been driving all day, and I, well, I have to pee."

She snorted, almost a laugh. "Come up here. But you," and she pointed at Scott, "drop that stick. My friend here hates sticks."

Scott dropped the stick. I could see that he did so reluctantly, as it was the price of admission, but I'm sure he didn't trust the old woman. Don't think he really thought she was kin, not yet.

When we got up to the top of the porch, we could see her better. Her skin was weathered and a knitted cap covered her head. A bandage completely covered one of her eyes. Her shirt was purple plaid. A pair of binoculars lay on her lap and a walking stick was held firmly in her hand.

I figured this had to be our Gran. Surely she would have told us if she wasn't, unless she was completely bonkers.

"I'm not surprised your moms wouldn't come. I should have known they were too busy to bother. Just as well."

Then I knew it was our Gran. Her voice was disdainful yet matter-of-fact in tone.

She pointed to a door down the side of the porch. "In there is the john." At the word john, the dog perked up his ears and Gran smoothed down his fur and spoke to him in a tender voice, much different than how she had addressed us. "Sorry, Johnny boy, just a poorly named human slang term for the bathroom."

I was amused at her tone of speech talking to her dog, like he was a person. Very civilized. But I went on to the bathroom. I really did need to pee. Scott followed me but Gran stopped him. "Only room for one at a time in there, Prescott. Let me look at you."

It was not a request, it was an order, and Scott stopped and turned to look at her. I hurried as fast as I could to get back to him, so fast that I failed to take in much of my surroundings inside the house. It was just a mudroom anyway, with a small toilet, really not much more than a WC. On my way in and out of the bathroom, I remember seeing work boots, some tools, bird seed, a shovel, planting pots, some jackets on hooks by the door. The bathroom was sparsely furnished, just a closet with a toilet, but it was clean enough.

I was back to rescue Scott in a minute or two. "Your turn," I said to him cheerfully before Gran could say anything either way, and he strode off eagerly.

Gran turned her good eye to me and I saw her face more clearly. Shockingly, I saw my mother in this older face before me. My mother as she looked when recently she had been really sick and I had to come over and deliver a prescription for her. When Mom had opened the door to me and reached for the bag in my hand, I had been shocked to see her look so aged. Now I was seeing that same face in front of me in Gran.

"Prescott seems very nervous."

She said this as a statement. I didn't know if I was supposed to respond. Tentatively I covered for him. "He's more of a city boy, Gran, but he's a heck of a mechanic!"

She didn't comment, just nodded. In the silence that followed, as Gran stared out over the meadow to the sea, I asked her, "What's wrong with your eye?"

She jerked her head back to me. With one eye covered by a bandage she had to turn her head farther around to see me. "Had an accident. Should heal but I have to keep it covered, doctor said."

That's all she said.

I wondered if she would invite us in, or what our next step would be. Scott made his way back to us, walking slowly I could tell. I finally pressed. "Gran, is that what you wanted to tell our moms? That you hurt your eye? Can we do something for you?"

Gran wasn't helping things with so much silence. Her hands were moving even if her lips were not. She rubbed the knees of her jeans. Her hands were veined and darkly tanned, not pretty but looked strong, like someone who did a lot of physical work. Her feet were clad in slippers so she surely wasn't doing physical work today. Johnny the dog had relaxed at her feet, eyes almost closed but not asleep.

In this silence Scott tried to make conversation and he gestured to the ocean. "Really great view you have here."

Gran grunted and seemed to acknowledge this fact as obvious but not requiring comment.

It felt ridiculous to just be standing around, suspended. I thought it would have been better for her to have told us to leave. So ridiculous that I finally lost patience and putting on my teacher voice, I moved toward the front door and briskly said, "Gran, how about I make us a cup of tea? Will I find some in the kitchen? I'll bring it back outside for us." I put my hand on the door so as to make my point.

My bossy tone woke Gran up. She looked at me and I

almost thought I saw a smile. She nodded. "Lemon zinger," she said to my back. Scott started to follow me, but Gran told him, "Prescott, you can sit there." And she pointed to an old Adirondack chair to her left. Scott made a wide circle around Johnny and did as he was told. As I went in the front door and down the hallway, I heard her say to him, "So, where and when did you become afraid of dogs? What happened?"

I didn't hear Scott's reply. I found the kitchen but first I glanced quickly into the other rooms I passed by. A dining room held a huge table made out of a glorious redwood burl. Twisting and irregular, it gleamed as if polished daily. The table would have easily seated ten. A huge open cabinet of plates and platters lined one wall. The living room was more cluttered, with two sofas facing each other by a large fireplace, and a coffee table piled high with haphazardly stacked books. Two high-backed but comfortable chairs sat next to a lamp. The walls were thickly lined with art work, paintings, fabric wall hangings, quilts. Old photos sat next to wood carvings on a wooden beam that served as a shelf. The ceiling was a mass of beams crisscrossing the tall space with hangings of cloth and other artwork blowing gently in the ocean breeze from the open windows.

The kitchen needed some tidying. I like to cook and Gran's kitchen, once you looked past the mess, was fully outfitted with good-quality kitchenware, but clearly it was not used much. I jumped when I saw an empty mouse trap in the corner. The counters were piled with painting brushes, pots and soil, boxes of granola bars, more books, old mail, even clothes. The kitchen table was also full of items: pens, paints, paper tablets, smeared clothes, and as if misplaced, a bowl of fruit. The kitchen sink held plates and bowls from several days' meals, mostly looking like cereal bowls, and indeed the shelves were full of cereal boxes and the recycling bin in the corner held empty cereal boxes along with newspapers and wine bottles.

I did, however, find a full shelf of tea. Clearly Gran was a tea drinker like me. Scott was just going to have to make do, because I saw no coffee anywhere.

Looking for milk in the fridge, I saw a lineup of yogurt containers, no milk, some old cheese, and a bag of oranges. And a cloth bag of groceries, unopened, as if someone just placed the bag right in the fridge without unpacking it.

The tea pot was electric and there were several clean mugs so in no time I had a tray of three mugs and headed out the door, grabbing a jar of honey and a spoon on my way.

Scott looked more relaxed when I got out, and he took the cup of tea without comment. I handed one mug to Gran, who nodded her thanks after I offered the honey.

"Give you time to snoop around?" she said. I thought it was an uncharitable comment, but none of us was playing by any social etiquette rules here. Ever since I had gotten the request—the demand—from my mom to go check on Gran, it seemed like normal behavior was pushed aside, and so strangely it didn't seem that there was anything Gran could say that would offend me.

We settled into a little tableau there on the front porch. Gran who had yet to move from her chair, Scott, folded like a pretzel into the old Adirondack, and me perched on the top step, my back against the post. We sat there drinking tea, looking out over the ocean and watching that fog bank creep ever so slowly towards shore. None of us seemed in a hurry as we individually absorbed the fact that we seemed to be starting out on a new page of our family journey. All of this without a word spoken. It occurred to me later that night, that because Scott and I—for some unknown reason, maybe instinct—were able to sit comfortably in this holding pattern without breaking the spell, we passed some sort of test of Gran's, and that made everything going forward possible.

It was a tipping point. I didn't push to have my questions answered. Scott didn't wonder aloud about the safety of his car parked out on that gravel road by the old stone garage. Neither of us wondered what would happen in the next hour or that evening. As to what Gran was thinking, I don't have a clue. But we sat there until our cups were empty and long cold, until Johnny sighed in his sleep, until the fog bank finally covered the afternoon's sunshine and left us shivering in the damp, sunless air.

5

It was Gran who finally moved first. "I hope one of you knows how to cook. I haven't felt up to it these days so I'm not eating much besides yogurt and cereal. But Tibby brought me a real treat this morning—I think she was trying to motivate me to do something." She shook her thin body and made an effort to stand up, stalling the first time, then successful the second.

She looked at both of us. "Well? One of you know how to cook a fine fillet of fresh salmon just caught off these waters this morning?" She motioned to the vast expanse in front of us.

Scott spoke first. "Elizabeth's a good cook."

I nodded although I smiled inwardly. Throughout our lifetime, Scott called me many different names—Lizzie, Liz, Beth, Betsy, Lizbeth—rarely Elizabeth. He must have sensed some formality was required in the situation.

Cooking was something besides teaching where I felt confident, although Gran's piercing eyes—or in this case, eye—were intimidating.

"Who's Tibby?" I asked as we slowly followed Gran into the house and down the hall to the kitchen.

"Best friend. Best friend I ever had. And she knows me." Gran gave a crusty laugh. "She knows I am too frugal to waste such a glorious piece of fish. And somehow, she must have known I would have company tonight because it's a large piece. She's psychic that way."

The house was a strange mix of top-of-the-line equipment and economizing features, fine artwork displayed next to practical and necessary country items. Every room held an eclectic air as if it really didn't care what kind of statement it should make. In any case, it was not a bit boring and very colorful, and I looked forward to exploring it later if given an opportunity.

Fortunately, the kitchen was surprisingly well stocked and I was able to find an adequate pan to sauté the salmon and a steamer to cook the kale that Tibby had also brought. Gran pointed to a loaf of whole wheat bread. "From the local bakery," she said, and then pretty much ignored me after that, turning her attention to Scott, who looked a little uncomfortable with her one-eyed gaze.

"So, Prescott, what is it you do to afford fancy sports cars?"

Scott looked at me, bewildered, and behind Gran's back I just shrugged. Surprises were the name of the game obviously. He hesitated to respond and Gran impatiently informed him, "I may have one eye for the moment but there is nothing wrong with my hearing. The waves were calm this afternoon and I heard your car drive down the road and stop by my garage. I know a few things about cars myself, you know."

Scott replied bluntly, "No, actually I don't know much of anything about you, Gran."

"I see. What exactly do your mothers say about me?"

Scott squirmed but truthfulness seemed to be the theme

of the day. "They generally think of you as, well, as out of the mainstream." He seemed proud to have come up with a description that could be taken as positive or negative, depending upon context.

Gran gave that strange cackle of a laugh again. "Out of the mainstream?"

"You know, counter-culture, different, doing things your own way..." Scott floundered. He looked at me but I turned back to the stove quickly, my shoulders shaking.

"And all this counter-culture, beat-her-own-drum crap, is it said with admiration or derision?"

Scott thought and then said, "Let's just say your way would not be their way of doing things."

"Ha. Prescott, you could be a diplomat. However, in my presence, I would appreciate the straight-out facts, not any bullshit!"

"Well, Gran. Facts? What is one person's fact is another's illusion, don't you think?"

"Holy cow! You can talk up a slick one, young man." But Gran didn't seem angry, seemed more charmed than anything. Charmed despite herself. And I suspect Scott was having fun as well.

Scott leaned forward and repeated, "Wouldn't you agree, Gran? We don't all think the same, and our moms have a different way of thinking and living than you do, based on our short acquaintance."

"Okay, young man, I will agree with you on that topic. I know what my daughters have said to my face and can only imagine what they say behind my back, but I see they have not poisoned you two completely, not if you drove all the way out here to check up on me, as your mothers so carefully put it."

"Well, now, Gran, isn't that what you asked for? Didn't you ask for them to check up on you? They were concerned for your wellbeing and now we see you have an eye injury, so perhaps they were correct."

Scott was still agreeable and light voiced but he was not backing down and not mincing words. I finished marinating the gorgeous orange fish in some soy sauce and honey that I found in the cupboard and adjusted the stove burner, but my attention was with the two at the table.

"I most certainly did not ask Mandela and Cinnamon to come here to 'check on me.'" Her tone was affronted.

I turned around at this. "What? Who?" I shouted before Scott could.

"I take it you did not know your mothers' given names?"

"Mandela and what?" Scott stared at her and then at me.

"I gave your mothers significant and beautiful names as baby gifts, and from the time they went to school they refused to use those names." Gran seemed genuinely hurt.

Scott shook his head. "You named your daughters, our mothers, Mandela and Cinnamon. Who does that to their daughters? Whatever possessed you?"

I went back to my sizzling fish, the smell starting to permeate the room, and calmly said over my shoulder. "So that is why they called themselves Mandy and Celine." And to Scott I added, "Hey, Scott, you should work in the schools. I've seen every sort of name imaginable by now. Mandela is dignified and Cinnamon is a lovely spice that everyone likes. But they do sound more like Berkeley-type names, and honestly, I don't think our moms have the personalities to appreciate the exotic nature of those names. Was the Mandela for Nelson?"

"Of course. One of the true heroes in this world."

Scott got his composure back. "But Cinnamon, who can even say that much less spell it without stuttering?"

Gran paused. "I simply loved the sound of it. That's all. It was so beautiful. I never dreamed that my little girl would grow up to hate it so much." Her defiant tone softened a bit. "Of course, I was only eighteen at the time, so what did I know of the small-minded ways of the world then. I was an idealist."

She seemed genuinely sad now. I liked the defiant Gran better, and so I cheered her up.

"I like the sound of those names, too, Gran. It's just a shock to learn it now. I mean Scott and I are almost thirty and we didn't know our mothers' birth names. That's crazy."

Scott added. "I signed loan documents with my dad and mom and I'm sure she signed them 'Amanda.' I guess she legally changed her named. Well, Gran what other surprises do you have for us while we are at it?"

I drained the kale and added some butter and sesame seeds I found in the cupboard. The seeds were not fresh but hopefully would be okay. Someone around this house had once cooked.

"Almost ready to eat," I called out.

Gran pointed to the drawer and instructed Scott to get the cutlery and napkins. But she remained quiet.

I set the salmon and kale and sliced bread with some butter on the table and I admit it looked awfully good. Gran gave it a long look and then gave me the simplest of nods which rang with approval. Good.

As we took our first bites, we sat appreciative. I had to satisfy my curiosity. "Gran, you must be a good cook. Your cupboards are so well stocked, and your pans and knives are quality." I left the statement hanging out there.

She finally chose to answer my round-about question. "I don't cook, but Mac's a fabulous chef."

6

Were we supposed to know who Mac was? I was entertained by this bizarre conversation. I didn't have too much at stake. Yes, she was our Gran, but until this day, we had seen her only a few times in our lives, and what was the worst that could happen if this visit went sour?

Still, I felt a growing endearment toward this old woman.

When she offered no explanation, I ventured, "And Mac is?"

Before Gran could swallow and answer, Scott burst out, "MacIntosh! The name on the garage."

Gran nodded, subdued.

"Spelled in shells or stones or something," I remembered. "Your name was there too… Templeton. Right?"

"Mine too, yes."

Was she going to explain more or not? The silence was so loud I could hear Scott swallow. Gran got up slowly and went to the mudroom coming back with a bottle of wine which she dusted off with a towel, then fished around in a drawer, banging and clattering, before coming up with a bottle opener. Returning to the table she handed it to Scott.

Scott handed it to me. "Lizbeth's better. She worked at a bistro during college. She always opens our bottles. I can fix any car but can't open a wine bottle."

"Yeah, he does much better with beer bottles." I laughed and took the bottle and studied the label. "Nice, Gran. Really nice."

"It's not white, but I thought maybe we could handle red with our fish without having a conniption fit."

I've never seen anyone stall so long over questions that hung in the air, but this was worth it, this bottle of wine. I opened it carefully and let it sit there to breathe for a few minutes.

"Glasses?" I asked Gran and she motioned to the dining room.

"In the credenza."

I wandered into the dining room and walked around that stupendous wooden table I had seen earlier. The side board was dusty, and I picked out three wine glasses and blew off some dust. When I returned to the kitchen, Scott and Gran had taken a pause in eating to wait for me. I took a towel and polished up the glasses and set them on the table. It was a fabulous bottle of wine, more than my teacher's salary allowed. What next?

They both watched while I poured the wine and then we sniffed and sipped it.

"Good," said Gran. "One doesn't always know how a wine is going to keep over so many years."

Added to my mental list of questions was why did she have such a fine bottle of wine out in her mudroom and why did she open it on this particular occasion. But for the moment we commenced eating in a comfortable silence, just as our time in the afternoon gazing at the sea had been peaceful.

"Brought this one up from the cellar the other day and drinking it will save me from taking it back down again," Gran said as if reading my mind and partially answering my question.

"This wine is incredible," Scott finally said as he took another sip. "And the fish too." He nodded at me.

"Fresh from the sea is the best," Gran said. "Elizabeth, you did it credit."

Glowing with her praise, I reached for our empty plates and cleared the table, setting the dishes in the sink. Scott made an effort to stand up and help with the dishes but Gran stopped him.

"Let the dishes sit. They'll not bother anyone. Let's finish the bottle in the living room and I'm guessing you have some questions for me. I appreciate that you both had the sense not to bombard me with an inquisition while we were eating. One should never ruin a delicious meal and fine wine with demands and interrogation!"

Scott murmured, "Words to live by," and picked up the half full bottle and his glass.

"Elizabeth, carry my glass too," Gran demanded. "I may fall down, have done so a few times lately with this damn eye patch, and there is no sense taking a risk of wasting that wine."

Dutifully, I picked up her glass and mine, and followed her into the living room. There was a fireplace but it hadn't been cleaned for some time and there was no wood stacked nearby. Gran turned on a lamp instead, and the yellowish light glowed into the darkening room, casting shadows. Scott and I sat on the old overstuffed couch and Gran sat in what was obviously her chair. A large chair sat conspicuously empty next to her chair. Scott and I both had the intuition not to sit in it.

Gran spoke of falls, but she moved gracefully, if slowly, and sat in her chair as if they were old friends. We waited for her to open up the conversation. I'm sure Scott was as curious as I was about so many things. And the funny thing was—we compared notes on this later—the two of us felt completely present in the moment. I had no thought of whether my friends were enjoying the hike I was missing this weekend. Scott didn't even think about his car on the road—had he locked it?—or his latest work assignment. And neither of us really thought about our moms and how they fit in this family constellation.

Gran took a small sip, held her glass tenderly and familiarly in the fingers of both hands, then looked at us with that strange one-eyed stare. "Okay, what do you want to know first?"

Before I could ask, Scott broke in. "Do you have any questions for us, Gran?"

There was that laugh again. "Prescott, you could be on a negotiation team. But, yes, I do have questions, but I've learned a lot in the last hour. I know that Elizabeth can cook. I know you are a car whisperer. I know you both know when to be silent and when to be direct. I know that you have a different approach to life than either of your mothers. And sometime soon, I would like to know two things: what work you do to make a living and what are you doing to enjoy life. But for now, I think your questions are more pressing, because you don't know me at all."

We cousins absorbed this for a moment, and then I asked, "For starters, who is Mac, or MacIntosh? Is he more than the cook? And does he live here?"

Gran looked at Scott, who nodded.

"Sean MacIntosh, a true Scotsman, bigger than life, and yes, he was our cook, and a damn fine one. He was my…" and here she stopped, and I wasn't sure whether she needed to find the right descriptive word or whether she was choking up. "He was my only man, my only love for almost thirty years."

She looked up at the wall and our eyes followed. A large framed photo of a rugged-looking man in jeans and sweater with the wind blowing his hair and a grin so big that his large beard couldn't hide it. His eyes were squinting into the sun, but one could read the intensity and connection with the photographer. He stood with one foot on a wooden boat and both hands on his hips. Free and open and very attractive. That's what I thought.

"I took that photo during our first year together. He liked to take that little boat out into the surf, never could get used to a kayak. He loved every minute he was on that boat. He loved every minute he spent building this house. He loved every minute he was with me, in bed with me, in the kitchen with me, sitting in this chair next to me, or out by the waves with me…."

The shadows in the room held Gran's voice like a spell. I didn't want to break that spell by asking why our mothers only talked with disgust about a revolving door of men.

The silence stretched out as Gran seemed to be lost in time. Finally, Scott said quietly. "MacIntosh and Templeton." He said no more than that. Perhaps it was a tribute to a love affair.

Gran smiled. "Yes, he put that on the garage, abalone shells, he also was an abalone diver."

She cleared her throat and proceeded like a story teller. "I met Mac at the art center. We were taking a stone building class, learning to make artistic stone fences. He'd lived here on the North Coast only a short while. I'd never met him until that class. But we never separated after we met."

"When did you move to Gualala, Gran?" I was trying to get a timeline in my mind.

"Moved here from Benicia," she replied, not answering my question. "And never looked back. Best move I ever made."

"Mom said you lived in a trailer," Scott threw in.

"Yes, and I know what they thought. They were quite appalled. But it was all I could afford at the time and I met the nicest folks there. People who didn't care what I looked like or what I did. They just accepted me. That was a tremendous relief. I started working at the market you passed on your way through town, across from the post office, and when I could, I bought myself a little house in Point Arena. That's up the highway a bit. Great little house. I painted it twenty different colors. It was full of life."

Gran laughed and looked at us. "I don't have to tell you what your mothers thought of my taste. I felt liberated from their constant criticism. Free at last. I was in heaven!"

She turned to Scott. "Prescott, see that photo album over there on that table. Bring it here."

She took a colored picture out of the album and passed it to us. A small house with a by-luck-or-by-golly garden and porch with vines growing on it. The house was painted bright blue on the outside with purple and gold trim on the gingerbread molding.

"That was my home in the years between the mobile home park and meeting Mac and moving here. I was very happy there in Point Arena in my little Crayola box of colors, but when I met Mac and moved here, I was even happier."

I started to say something and stopped.

Gran looked at me, her one eye seeming to read my mind. "Okay, Elizabeth, what is it you started to say and then had too many good manners to go on? Say it."

I squirmed. "Well, okay. I don't quite know how to say this, but our moms would say things that they thought Scott and I didn't hear when we were younger. Things about how you had, well, you had a lot of men. I think the words they used were 'a revolving door.'"

"Lizzie!" Scott was mortified but somehow the moment seemed ripe for any question at all, even the most embarrassing.

Gran smiled and then started laughing, and as she laughed it seemed that her vocal cords were remembering how to do it again.

Finally, she wiped her uncovered eye with her napkin, still grasped in her hand. She took another sip of her wine before responding.

"A bit of an exaggeration I'm afraid, but I like the vision of that revolving door. I was full of life and appetite. I guess your moms were a bit overwhelmed and frightened by who I was in those days before I settled down with Mac."

Scott squirmed at this notion of our Gran being full of sexual desires, but I was having a blast listening to her openness, and perhaps a little jealous as well.

"Who were you? Who are you, Gran?" I asked at the same time as Scott threw in, "So tell us more about Mac and how you happened to be in this house now? And he built it by himself?"

"No, I helped him. And about twenty different friends and crafts people. You know the friend who knew the most about pouring concrete, and the friend who happened to be a plumber and another who was an electrician. And there are a lot of carpenters around here. Up here on the coast, people have to be more self-sufficient, know how to manage a septic tank and propane supply, watch out for mountain lions and keep the deer out of the garden, figure out where to take your trash and recycling, manage when there is a power outage and pull each other's car out of the mud when the rains are heavy. So yes, Mac and I had a lot of help building this place, sort of a community project, took about five years to finish."

"Where did you live while it was being built?"

"Mac and I lived in the garage. There's a couple of

rooms over the garage and we lived there together. I sold my little Point Arena house to help pay for the big house. We had an outhouse and an outdoor shower. We were in love, new love. We stayed in love always, but that new love knocks your socks off, so we were running on adrenalin night and day!"

Gran's face softened as she talked. I found myself able to look past the scruffy bandage that covered her left eye and see a woman in love.

"Did you and Mac design this place? It's a really interesting design."

Gran answered Scott honestly. "If you are trying to say that it is a hodge-podge of design, well, you are right. We had a lot of fun. Worked with a local architect and he shook his head sometimes at what Mac and I wanted, but he was creative and open and intrigued with basically a bunch of amateurs doing this build."

Gran stopped and turned to look at both of us still side by side on the couch, our wine glasses long empty. "Take it from me. Having a long-term, hands-on project you do as a team with someone you love passionately... well, it doesn't get any better in life. Those were five of the most exciting and meaningful years of my life. Not that it wasn't great to finally move in and live our days in this place, but sometimes the process is as important as the completion. I would wish that experience for both of you, and just remember I was in my forties when I had that privilege."

She raised her glass, took her last swig and put her glass on the table next to her and sighed, and was then silent. I figured she was lost in her memories. The biggest question that remained was what happened to Mac? Where was he? Had he left her? Had he died? Or was he traveling and would come home soon? And what did any of this fascinating history have to do with why Gran had called our mothers and asked them to come and see her?

We had a lot more to learn, but I felt my eyes getting heavy. Scott too looked drowsy, but Gran looked unchanged.

After all her passion-filled reminiscing, I wasn't about to throw out the big question, "So what happened to Mac?" Not yet.

I just couldn't do it. Instead, I yawned.

7

Gran noticed my yawn. "You too fancy to sleep on the couch? If so, you'll need to go back to town for a room, or St. Orres. My upstairs hasn't been dusted in years."

I looked at Scott and he shrugged, so I answered for us. "Couch would be fine, but we need our bags from the car."

Gran stood up stiffly but walked smoothly to the front hallway and returned with a heavy-duty flashlight which she handed to Scott who put away his cell phone flashlight without a word. To me she handed a stick with bells on it.

"What's this?"

"Wards off the critters."

I must have looked startled.

"Bears?" I said, the first thing to come into my mind.

"Not as likely as mountain lions or raccoons. But yes, I've seen bears here over the years a few times. Shake the bells. The animals are sensible and want to keep away from you."

I laughed nervously. "Thanks for the tip. You know we are urban people, Gran. Not used to the dangers of country life."

She eyeballed me. "I've lived in the city and I've lived in the suburbs, and I know the dangers there, night and day. I'll take the odd encounter with a perfectly reasonable wild critter any day over the human variety."

What could we do but head out the door? I never go to bed without brushing my teeth and my toiletry bag was in Scott's car. We went out the door, down the porch steps, across the wide meadow and down the dark path alongside the garage, out to the road where the quiet was everywhere.

A weak light shone from the eaves of the garage, and we could faintly read the MacIntosh & Templeton name embedded in the grouting of the stone. Scott checked out the car with a glance and opened the trunk to get out our two overnight bags and his computer. I grabbed my water bottle. On the way back the wind rustled the trees and bushes along the pathway. It was like a tunnel with walls of bushes that appeared impenetrable and yet felt porous, offering no escape for us while allowing all sorts of night creatures to come through. Our fears were giving us the jitters.

"What wimps we are," I murmured to give myself courage.

"Call it what you want, but this is giving me the creeps," Scott whispered back.

"Why are we whispering? Who is going to hear us? Gran said to make noise!" I ended with a shout and shook the bell stick over my head. Then I couldn't refrain from a giggle and gave Scott a sudden poke with the stick.

"Hey! Stop that!" He started running, and the flashlight he was carrying moved up and down so rapidly that it created a strange underwater effect on the trees around us. I followed, feeling about ten-years-old, laughing but not pausing until we entered the meadow and came face to face with a creature with shining eyes. We stopped in our tracks and stared.

The stare down lasted only a few seconds, but it calmed us because of the steadiness of the eyes. It wasn't big enough to be a bear or a puma, as Gran called the mountain lion ("such a much more poetic word I think!"). As it slowly turned and strolled away from us, I saw that it was a fox, a sleek and beautiful animal with more dignity than either of us possessed at that moment.

We looked at each other, then quietly turned toward the house and walked up the stairs and into the house. Gran was bringing blankets and pillows in to the living room.

"See any wild things out there?" she asked with a half-hidden smile.

"As a matter of fact, we did. A lovely fox. We had a little moment together and it went away," I replied, trying to act like it was no big deal.

"Didn't bother you?" She looked right at Scott.

He thought. "Funny, you know, it didn't. I guess I never had a bad experience with a fox before, just dogs."

Gran just nodded and handed him some blankets and a pillow. "In there." She motioned. "There's a longer sofa in the other room. Hope it's long enough for your tall frame. You know where the bathroom is. I'll see you in the morning. Oh, if you have any energy left, do the dishes."

That was that. Away she went without another word. I plopped the blankets on the couch and went back to the kitchen and Scott followed. We did the dishes and tried to clean up the clutter around the room, and by then I was more than ready to sleep.

Back in the living room, Scott stood for a moment looking at the photo on the wall, the one of Mac and then several others. Then he pointed to the bathroom. "You want first dibs?"

I nodded and when I got back to the couch, I turned off the light and was asleep in minutes.

In the middle of the night, I woke and didn't know where I was, feeling that strange disconcerting sense of displacement, until the waves outside reminded me. Before I could fall back into sleep though, I heard something between the rhythmic surge of wave on rock below the bluff… a wailing sound. I sat up, suddenly very awake and slipped my jeans back on and followed the sound. It stopped and then started again. I peeked into the room where Scott slept and he was snoring softly, undisturbed. The keening cry started up again before being covered by a thunderous wave but I could tell it came from outside.

The front door was ajar and I stepped out onto the porch. The fog was hovering over the meadow but it was thin and allowed the moon to shine through as if through a misty gauze curtain. It took a moment but I saw her, Gran standing in the meadow near the cliff in her nightclothes, the folds of her gown sticking out below the robe that was whipping in the night wind. She was facing the ocean, leaning on her walking stick, the kind adventurers use, tall and hand carved. Johnny was crouched on the ground next to her, motionless.

As I watched she raised the stick with one hand and shook it at the sea and cried out, an unearthly sound of rage or grief. Whatever was behind that noise was something so deep it was beyond my experience. I knew that I didn't know it. I understood what I didn't understand. That's the only way I could sum up what I was seeing and hearing.

Going out to her would be dishonoring, I felt sure of that, but I knew that the sound being absorbed by the trees and the pounding surf on the rocks below belonged to Gran and Gran alone.

I stepped back inside the door where I could observe Gran without being seen should she turn around. I thought I should stay and watch, just in case she went hurtling herself off the precipice. I stood guard in the doorway, shivering without a jacket, but not wanting to leave my post.

When at last, after about another ten minutes, she turned and trudged back up to the house, I quickly dodged back inside, leaving the door as she had left it, pulled off my jeans and jumped back under my blankets. Although I closed my eyes tightly, somehow, I sensed that Gran looked in at me before she made her way, padding softly on slippers, back to her downstairs bedroom.

In the morning I wondered if I dreamed the whole vision until I looked down at Gran's feet as she sat at the table drinking her tea. I saw that her slippers were wet and muddy and the carved walking stick lay where I had heard it be dropped across the front doorway.

8

I made scrambled eggs that had been in Tibby's grocery bag, adding leftover salmon and some onions I found in the fridge. I found some stale coffee and Scott was able to get his morning fix. Gran reached for her cereal box, but when I placed a plate of eggs in front of her and Scott, she ate with gusto. Scott did as well and then he picked up the plates and started the dishes.

Gran looked at me and asked, "Did you sleep alright on that old lumpy couch?"

I replied in the affirmative, and then she asked Scott and he agreed.

Gran muttered, "Youth!" and almost smiled as she stood up saying, "Tea on the porch. We have business to attend to."

She headed to the porch, and Scott threw up his sudsy hands in bewilderment behind her back. She called over her shoulder, "Leave the damn dishes, Prescott."

I grabbed my jacket. The morning was foggy and the porch was in the shade. On second thought I also grabbed the plaid wool blanket that I had wrapped myself in the night before. I took my hot tea and Scott grabbed his coffee and a jacket and we joined Gran where she and Johnny sat, in the same position we had first seen her yesterday.

"Questions?" she asked without any preamble.

When someone is so straightforward, it makes it easy to not beat around the bush in reply. I asked the question that had most puzzled me the night before, not that there weren't many more on the list.

"Where is Mac now?"

"Mac is gone."

Scott pursued this. "Gone as in left town, or gone as in…?" He left it dangling.

"He's gone from life on this earth. He's gone to the sea. He went one last time and didn't return. Hundreds of times he went out to sea and always returned. The last time, he did not. He joined the sea, and that is where he is today, at one with the waters."

We waited to hear more. Why did we care about someone we had never heard of before yesterday? We did, that's all. He was Gran's man. I suspect that her howling at the moon and waves the night before had everything to do with the mysterious Mac.

"He went out fishing as he had done so many times before, right off the point there." Gran pointed north vaguely. "He was alone in his boat, but his friend Jim was fishing nearby in his kayak. A sleeper wave came up, and Jim said Mac was just standing there in his boat, fishing pole in his hand, and staring away from the ocean, something we all know never to do. Jim tried to shout to Mac but Mac didn't turn to look; the wave washed over my Mac and pulled him out of the boat. His friends—oh, the whole damn Coast Guard, too—tried for weeks to find him, but they never did. Only his boat washed up on the rocks, piece by piece. Mac was gone."

My throat was tight. "Just like that?"

"Just like that," Gran said grimly.

"When did this happen, Gran?" Scott asked after a moment.

"Three and a half years ago, right before the biggest rain storm in twenty years. It rained every day, every night. All it did was rain and rain, and I took it personally as though the skies were weeping for my loss. The waves and the sky just blended into one big wet world. It was right before our roof leaked. Right before the road muddied over and the power went out for days. I was marooned here. It was such a time of bizarre happenings and I couldn't fathom what had happened. That life could be so empty. That he, my Mac, could be gone. I almost lost my mind."

What could we say, we two novices at love and grief? Our sheltered suburban upbringing glared utterly bland in the face of such pain and passion.

Gran shook herself as if from a trance and looked at both of us with a look out of that one good eye that dared us to ask more about the subject. "Well, is that the only question you have for me?"

Neither of us spoke for a moment so she led the way. "Elizabeth, what do you do for a living?"

This was easier ground. "I teach eighth grade history and art in Davis."

"How long?"

"Almost ten years."

"Then you like it." She said this as a statement not a question.

"I do."

"Absolutely you do or you wouldn't still be doing it. You wouldn't be stupid enough to spend all those years of your life doing something you didn't like, would you?" she queried me fiercely.

"Well, no, I mean I don't think so." I regrouped. "I do like it. In fact, I love it, Gran. I just never thought about it that way before."

"You should think about it that way, and think about it every day."

"Well, there are days, of course, where it is a challenge, and maybe I'm not loving every minute of it."

"Of course not. That's not what I meant. I think you're bright enough to understand what I meant."

I hoped so, too. Gran made me want to be that bright.

She had one more question for me. "Where do you live?"

"I have an apartment in Davis, downtown. Old house. My landlady lives downstairs. She's my friend. Nellie's her name. A retired horticulturalist." I didn't know why I was going on about Nellie, but it occurred to me that she and Gran might appreciate each other.

"Umm" is all Gran said and then, "No children? No lover?"

"No kids. No boyfriend now."

She turned her one eye to Scott. "And you, Prescott. Where do you live and what do you do with your hours and days?"

"I write software."

"For who? What purpose?"

Scott paused. Her questions were not the normal polite "what do you for a living?" questions. And he also clearly didn't know what Gran meant by "for what purpose?" It might mean more than just for what company and product. In our second day with Gran, we figured her comments and questions were loaded with deeper meaning. Therefore, he hesitated before answering.

"I design software for Ancestry.com. It is a website for..."

"I know what it is for." Gran had a sudden change in her voice. Her body became more erect. "So you know how it works? This ancestry tracing and tracking, or whatever you call it?"

He looked at her strangely. He even looked suspicious. "Well, of course I do."

We both expected more questions from her after this sudden interest, but instead she just got quiet for a moment before she turned the tables once again.

"What else do you want to know from me?"

I was ready this time. "You haven't told us yet why you called our moms and asked them to come see you. They haven't been here in ages, right? Over the last years they meet you in Santa Rosa once a year, but they don't drive up here anymore, right?"

Gran laughed. "Well, that was Mac's doing I suppose. He didn't have any use for my daughters, not because he didn't want to like my daughters. I tried to warn him ahead of time, and he honestly didn't have any preconceived ideas, but when he met them, he decided he didn't like them at all."

"Why was that?"

"He said it was because they didn't treat me with respect. Mac was big about respect. And the one time they came here and met Mac, they failed in that regard, and he had no use for them after that."

"So, after that you always met them in Santa Rosa without Mac?" I guessed.

"Yes. That's it. The last time we only made it an hour before we went our separate ways. Just long enough for our lunch to be served and eaten."

Scott redirected the conversation. "What is confusing is why you clearly haven't had any kind of relationship with our moms for years, and you tell us that you didn't need them to check up on you, so why did you called them to come? It seems, well, it seems not your MO, if you know what I mean. Not that Liz and I know you very well after less than twenty-four hours, but still, can you see why we are confused?"

Once again, Gran threw a question back at us. "And why did you drive all the way up here? You wouldn't have had to do it. You have busy lives. You don't know me. Your moms made sure I didn't have a chance to get to know you two. They always gave me a strong hands-off message when I mentioned my grandchildren."

I smiled. "I can't tell you exactly why I came other than to say, as Nellie sometimes says, 'I took a notion.' And then I talked Scott into coming with me. Something just clicked in me that said why not go get to know your Gran? If not now, when? I think it was a spur of the moment decision, but maybe not."

Gran pursed her lips. "Sometimes there is a swelling of momentum of which we are unaware that leads to a decision, true." She turned to Scott. "And, Prescott, why did you come along and leave your computer and your cars behind?"

"Lizzie tricked me." He laughed. "She convinced me that I should try out my Karmann Ghia on Hwy 1 and see if it was all I had bragged about. But how do you know I like cars?"

"By the sound of the car you were driving. I also like cars, old cars that is. And you have a mechanic's hands, like Mac's. I can see that your hands do more than make love to a keyboard all day."

Reflexively, Scott and I both looked at his hands. I wasn't sure what Gran saw. Maybe something. Maybe she was shining us on. We were intrigued with her, but did we trust her?

And she had yet to answer our question. She could be infuriating. For the second time—the first was when Gran told us our moms' given names—I felt a small twinge of pity for our moms, growing up with such a mother as Gran.

As if reading my mind, and once again dodging the basic question hanging out there in the misty morning coastal air, Gran settled back into her chair as if to begin a story.

"Do you know your moms' early life?" She went on before we could answer. "I was not even eighteen when I gave birth to Cinnamon, and she was barely out of the womb when I got pregnant with Mandela. I left their father before he could get me pregnant again. But he was going to leave anyway, so I just beat him to it. Gave me a bit of a lift to have that power! But there I was, not even twenty with a newborn and a toddler and not even a high school education. Their father left with no forwarding address and no child support in the mail, not once. My choice as I saw it was to go back to my parents or go live in the commune down the street in Berkeley. My parents were good folks, the Templetons, but they had opposed me marrying so young. Although they reluctantly gave me permission, they never trusted Roger Perry. They were right, but my pride wouldn't allow me to come crawling back to them. Oh my, I was proud in those days! Not helpful, but that's just who I was, maybe who I still am, and so I won't second-guess myself now.

"Therefore, to the commune I went and it suited me well, at least for a while. I was able to find a role in the commune, and it took care of our food and shelter needs for a few years, and the loose anything-goes philosophy was just down my line, at least for a while."

I was caught up in her story. "Did something go wrong?"

"Give humans an organization and it isn't long before power and ego issues will pop up, regardless of the utopian philosophy of the original creators. And after five years I had to get out and away. Had a run-in with the self-proclaimed leader, who was nothing more than a macho skunk in hippie gear wanting to keep all the women under his control. So I left with my girls and moved across the bridge to Benicia and got a job. Had more than a few boyfriends during that time but never let them give me a dime or move in. Perhaps that is where your moms got the revolving door theory. My daughters never liked one of them and made sure that the men knew it."

Gran looked a little grim at this memory. "I worked at that supermarket for thirteen more years until Cinnamon graduated from high school and then I couldn't stand it anymore. I told the girls they were on their own for college and that Cinnamon could be responsible for Mandela who was finishing high school early. I had started my adult life at eighteen, so they could too. At least there were two of them. I left them the house though, so it's not like I left them high and dry. I had bought a house in Benicia back before prices went through the roof, back when a clerk could buy a small house. I saved money for years so that when I left, I could give the girls a month of groceries, my car, and the mortgage paid up for three months, and told them to figure it out themselves. They wanted to distance themselves from me anyway. I embarrassed them. They were so damn conventional, always were and never changed. I figured they didn't want to be around me any more than I wanted to be around them by that point. I loved them but I didn't like them. I couldn't do or say anything without their criticism, and they always ganged up together. I had no ally in the family. And it is a horrible thing when you feel like you are in a war with your children."

Gran's face was sour. "And over what? Not just big things, but things like my hairstyle, the colors of my walls, the kind of car I drove, the clothes I liked, the friends I brought home, the kind of music I liked, my friggin' earrings even!" Gran smashed her fist on the arm of the chair.

"Gee, Gran, sounds like the roles were reversed. Usually, it is parents screaming at their children about their hair, clothes, friends, and music," Scott offered her, trying to get her good humor and equilibrium back.

Her face cleared. "That's the truth! But I knew I had to

create some distance between us. I was absolutely ready for a new beginning. My parents had moved to L.A. to be closer to my sister, and my brother moved into their old house in Piedmont. I didn't belong in L.A. or in Oakland. As luck would have it, I had a girlfriend from my workplace—Tibby, who brought us the salmon yesterday—who moved up to the north coast a few years earlier with her husband Jim and son. She invited me up to visit so I jumped on a bus and headed north. I fell in love with the place and moved into my trailer in Gualala and have never looked back."

"That must be the Benicia house that our moms sold to start their real-estate business," Scott mused.

"Eventually. Yes. They lived there a few years while they studied and got their licenses, then fixed the house up and sold it and that was the seed money for their business going forward. They met your dads somewhere along the line."

"I bet they painted your little house something neutral before selling it," I joked.

"They painted it all white within a week of me turning the mortgage over to them."

Before she could tell us any more stories, I tried to pin her down. "Gran, now will you tell us why you contacted our moms to come see you?"

"Simple. I wanted some help with a problem, and I had too much wine that night—Mac kept our basement well stocked and I am still going through some of his stash—and lost my normal brain functioning. During that inebriated state, I foolishly called, sent a text or maybe two, well, maybe more, to your moms. Under my normal mental acuity, it would never cross my mind to do that. I full well know that my daughters are not the ones to help me with a project that is near and dear to my heart. But I lost my head that night and made the call, and in the morning, I absolutely regretted it, and could only hope that they would forget about it, or think their mother was going even more crazy than ever. However, your mom did something I never would have dreamed; she called you two and pulled you into the picture."

Gran stopped and gave us the sharp look from that one eye. We returned her gaze, not knowing what we were supposed to say. She went on half to herself, "And now, son of a gun, I am trying to figure out what to do with you two."

Scott kind of bristled. "What *you* want to do with *us*? And we have no say in the matter?"

I added, "And we still have no idea what you are talking about. But Scott's right; it is your choice. I think you have three choices, actually. You can keep us in the dark and we will take some time to see the sights around here and then go home tomorrow. Or you can fill us in fully and let us decide if or how we can help you. Or you can fill us in and tell us you don't want our help. But it would really be helpful and less frustrating if you just quit being so mysterious."

Gran stiffly took this all in. Not sure if she was offended or relieved. I got up and asked if anyone wanted some more tea or coffee. Scott shook his head and Gran said nothing, so I went in to get a refill myself. When I got back out, Scott was sitting where I had left him, but Gran had moved over to deadhead a flower while Johnny was keeping a watchful eye on us all.

To make things a little lighter, I said to her, "Johnny sure is a sweet dog. Have you had him long?"

Gran turned around and looked affectionately at the dog who wagged his tail. "Ten years. Mac gave him to me as a companion when he was out fishing, so I wouldn't be alone. And now it is Johnny who keeps me sane."

Scott tentatively put his fingers down near where Johnny's nose was resting on his paws. The dog lifted his head and sniffed Scott's hands. I could see Scott stiffen and then relax. Soon Scott was petting the top of Johnny's head with amateur movement, but Johnny didn't complain and let himself be touched by the man who was afraid of dogs.

Gran threw some dead flower heads over the rail of the porch and turned to face us. She sounded more decisive, even though she threw us one more delay. "Here's a plan. You two need to see some local sights. Get out and hike around. I'll give you a map and some ideas. Be back by dinner and we'll go out to St. Orres with Tibby if I can track her down. I'll share everything with you tonight and then you can decide if you can help me or just go back to your life in Davis and I'll be glad for making your acquaintance at long last."

It was a directive not a question, but I think she knew we would be curious enough to handle one more stall in hearing the whole story. And there was nothing to lose. We'd get a day of sightseeing and a meal at that lovely place down the road, and tomorrow we could go home and have some new experiences under our belt.

9

It was as if Gran had ordered a perfect day for our exploration of her north coast. The sun sparkled on the ocean, where small white caps didn't keep us from spotting five whale spouts and seeing one whale that threw itself out of the water and landed with a smacking splash on the ocean surface before quickly disappearing from view, leaving only a foamy reminder of what had happened. We kept track like school children: Scott spotted three and me two of these spouts, but I got credit for grabbing his jacket sleeve and turning him to see the whale jumping out of the water.

The places Gran sent us hiking took us through woods and open meadows with grasses swaying just like in her meadow in front of the MacIntosh-Templeton abode.

(Not sure what to call her house. Certainly not a mansion, nor a cottage or a bungalow. It was nowhere near a sleek modern beach house, but it also was not an old-fashioned farm house, or a mountain-style cabin. It was impossible to find a label for the structure that Mac and Gran built.)

Wild flowers grew along the bluff trail where we went hiking and waves pounded against the rocks with a fierce boom that felt like an earthquake as its force went reverberating and traveling through our bodies.

After the bluff walk, we moved on, windblown faces, hair

a mess, and found a steep wooden staircase descending a steep rocky cliff to a pristine beach with large round rocks. Taking off our shoes we walked in the sand, leaving our prints in the wetness. We spent vacations during our childhood and teen years at Santa Cruz, Stinson Beach, and other beach towns, but when was the last time we'd been on a beach recently? Too long, we both decided. We felt like children again, and since we had known each other since babyhood, we were free to retreat to being those same kids building sand castles on the beach, using our hands and sticks and rocks, since we came ill-equipped with proper shovels and pails However, I doubt if we could have as much fun as we had on this day, even with the best digging tools.

We lost track of time, and when the waves started to approach our creation, we saw that the tide was rapidly coming in. The few people who had also been on the beach earlier in the afternoon were long gone, and we were the only ones left. We quickly grabbed the jackets we had flung off, grabbed our shoes and ran barefooted back to the staircase in time before the tide caused any danger.

We climbed halfway up and looked back at our sprawling sand creation, our magnificent castle, and saw the first wave hit it, rush over and back leaving it lumpy and soft, and the second wave smooth it almost back to level sand. And so it goes at the beach, and so it goes.

"It was a grand castle," Scott said.

"The best ever."

"The best until the next one." Scott finished our thoughts with a voice that sounded about ten years old. We turned and trudged up the stairs back to the little red car waiting patiently for us beside the road. We made a valiant attempt to get the sand out from between our toes and out of our ears and hair before getting into the car. We dug out our phones, checking the time, and figured it was time to head back to Gran's to get cleaned up for dinner.

"I don't have much else to wear." Scott shifted the car down to go around a tight hairpin in the road.

"Me either, just a different shirt. Will have to do. Hope it isn't a fancy place."

"It's the beach. If we aren't dressed appropriately, I would be surprised, and Gran will just have to deal with it."

"Speaking of Gran…" Strangely we really hadn't discussed her much all day. "What do you suppose she is going to lay on us this evening?"

Scott carefully motored around a corner and shrugged his shoulders. "Hard to say. I just hope she finally spits it out. We have to get home tomorrow." His tone did not sound like a ten-year-old anymore.

"What's your hurry?" I teased, although I, too, had lesson plans to work on before Monday's first period class.

Scott actually blushed. "Oh, ah, might have a date Sunday night, maybe anyway."

"Well, Prescott Sullivan, you little devil. Who is she? And where have you been hiding her?"

"It's a maybe, Liz. I don't want to spook it so I'd rather not discuss any details, but I don't want to be out of town and miss a chance with… with her," he finished lamely.

I backed off. I knew when things were tender.

"I agree, our drop-dead leave-town time should be about 10:00 a.m. so we get home in time for all possibilities. I have a date with my lesson plan book and PBS. Not as exciting as your night, perhaps."

"No more talk. Shit, Lizzie! I told you I don't want to put a hex on what's already only a possibility!"

"Okay, okay, so Gran's project…?" I changed the subject.

"Who knows?"

We found Gran's road without too much trouble, only had to flip a U and turn back once, and made our way down the gravel drive.

We got back to the house about 7:00 p.m. It was still light this time of year, and Gran was sitting in her familiar spot with Johnny by her side. The dog got up and greeted us with tail wagging. Scott put his hand down and petted Johnny's soft head, and he looked up at Scott with adoring eyes. I looked at Scott's face and I think he felt that canine love a little bit as well.

Gran wore her same jeans, but she had a different shirt on, one that looked like a fabric version of a stained-glass window, longish, covered her hips almost to her knees. A long, beaded necklace hung around her neck, and matching earrings dangled almost to her shoulders. Her feet were clad in leather clogs, her hair was combed, and it looked like she had a fresh bandage on her eye, one that covered less of her face. Gran was dressed up, we figured, coastal style.

"Hi, Gran, we had such a great day. I hope we aren't too late for dinner?" I cheerfully called out to her as we approached the steps to the porch.

"They'll hold the reservation for me," she said brusquely. "Tibby is there already waiting, I'm sure. She's always early."

"We're kind of sandy, so we need to wash off our feet and change shirts and that's about all we can do, didn't bring too many clothes."

"You'll be okay. People dress all sorts of ways here. No one turns up their nose at honest clothes."

"Honest clothes," I thought. That was a new phrase to me. Wonder what my mom would think of that expression. I doubt my mom had too many 'honest clothes' in her closet, whatever that meant specifically.

When we were ready, Gran asked if she could ride in Scott's car. I scrunched into the back, which could hardly be called a back seat, while Scott helped Gran sit in the passenger front seat. From the back seat I watched her as she kept her eyes on Scott's hands on the wheel and gear shift. She seemed to be taking in all the details of the old car.

Our drive to the restaurant was a short one, nice for me since I was uncomfortably crowded in the back of the Karmann Ghia. We parked and walked up to the soaring Russian-style wooden building, an onion-topped structure with windows around the top.

We walked up wooden stairs to the entrance. Inside, a massive fireplace with benches caught our attention first, and then a wooden staircase that went up and disappeared around a corner. The woman behind the desk greeted Gran with a hint of deference, and she took us into a large dining room. The tables were dwarfed by a massive ceiling, the inside of the tower we had seen from outside, with windows letting in the late evening light. Below the tables felt intimate and cozy, with candles flickering and people murmuring, with occasional bursts of laughter. About half the tables were taken. It was Saturday night and life was booming.

We felt totally comfortable in our jeans and clean shirts. Although the man at the table next to us was in suit and tie and the woman in a cashmere-looking sweater and dangling earrings, the table on the other side held a happy foursome of friends dressed in jeans and sweatshirts, hair as disheveled as ours had been on the beach, laughing and digging into their food with gusto. This was a very comfortable place.

We were starving and we didn't have to wait long. Tibby had ordered appetizers for us, scallops piled in a small tower and crab cakes with a delicious sauce that I couldn't quite figure out. I wondered if Gran would pay for it, but we had credit cards just in case.

But first, before we sat down and started tasting, we met Tibby, and she was a hoot. When Gran introduced us, Tibby came up to each of us in turn and gave us a hug that almost broke our ribs and then held us at arm's length and gave us a warm but interrogative look and proclaimed, "Hell's bells, how great to meet you two! Gran never told me she had such gorgeous grandchildren! This is a special occasion!"

Tibby had the outgoing warmth that Gran's crusty personality—or protective personality—couldn't muster for us, and I felt gratified to be warmly embraced, to be welcomed, and to be called young and beautiful, no, gorgeous! Who doesn't love that kind of welcome?

But Scott was looking puzzled. And after we sat down and

studied our menu and were clued in by the attentive waiter as to our choices and made our orders, Scott looked at Tibby and back at Gran.

Gran barked, "What's on your mind, Prescott?"

He thought for a moment and then said, "Tibby, you said... you called... you used Gran's name; I mean, our name for Gran of course is Gran... but you also called her Gran. I guess that just seems weird to me."

Something clicked in my mind. "Well, our moms always refer to Gran as Gran. I figured just like my mom always calls my dad 'Dad' when she is talking to me about my father, I just figured our moms called you Gran..." Now I was confused, too.

Tibby looked at Gran. "You mean your grandchildren don't know your first name, Grandin?"

Our mouths dropped.

Gran took a drink of water and sat her glass down. "It is possible that my daughters never told my grandchildren that my name is Gran, my full name, Grandin. My given name is Grandin Margaret Templeton. I was named for my grandmothers. But everyone always called me Gran."

I suppose it doesn't matter at all, but we were shaking our heads. Here was one more thing we didn't know about our grandmother, not even her name!

Scott said, "But why do our moms call you Gran instead of 'Mom'? That seems so strange. It's like if I would call my mom Mandy or Amanda."

Tibby looked at Gran, we all did. Gran shrugged her shoulders. "It's just the way we did it when they were little.

Didn't seem odd at the time. All the children at the commune called all the adults by their names, not their titles. Part of the equality philosophy that our leader promoted. I think it also kept children from having one real mom; we were supposed to consider all the children 'our' children and the kids were supposed to consider all the women as their mothers. The women even nursed each other's babies. Kids slept with different family groups. It was encouraged and it didn't bother me. It felt progressive. Of course, I left the commune under unpleasant circumstances, but I left not due to the commune concept, but just because Daryl was such a misogynist, such a narcissistic creep."

The tone of her voice, spitting with anger, made me wonder if there was something even more sinister to Gran's story, but I didn't pursue it.

"So, our moms always called you Gran." I shook my head. "And they never mentioned that it was your name, not your title. Either they let us think that you were called Gran because you were our grandmother or they just didn't care to enlighten us on the matter." I shook my head again and took a long drink of my wine, another good bottle ordered by Gran for the evening.

"Is it important?" Gran asked, seemingly honestly surprised by our surprise.

Before I could answer, Tibby intervened. "Gran Templeton, it is not important as in earthshaking important. But don't you think it is a damn enormous symbol of the lack of communication you have had with your family, lo these many years?"

She finished with verve, her face wobbling with emotion, and she looked Gran directly in the face. Tibby had two good eyes and could match Gran's one-eyed view with all the fervor of a very longtime friend.

The waiter brought our bread and dipping oil and gave Gran a chance to recover from this admonishment, and Scott and I to recover from our discovery. And the more I thought about it, the more I agreed with Tibby. It was not important at all, and yet it was significant on many levels.

Gran cleared her throat after the waiter left and cleared her mind with a sip of water. "You have a point, Tibby. A point well taken. And to the extent that I have disturbed you Elizabeth and Prescott, I apologize."

Spoken as a woman who rarely apologized, I'm guessing, but we appreciated it. The humanization of our Gran.

Emboldened by the wine and by Tibby's harmonizing presence, I reached out and actually touched Gran's hand and squeezed it. "You know what, Gran? I have to think about all the lack of information Scott and I have about your place in our life, and about our moms and so much more. Enough family baggage to take years to sort out. But heck," and I lifted my glass up to each of those around the table, "I'm having a hell of lot of fun here in Gualala. Surprises seem to be the name of the game here, and I'm ready for them."

Tibby joined me with gusto. "Good girl, Elizabeth!"

Scott stared at me, gave a wry smile, and then slowly lifted his glass up towards us.

Finally, Gran, too, lifted her glass and reached across

to clink mine. After she took a drink, she carefully placed her glass on the table, and we all four looked at each other. Tibby could have probably led the way with what discussion came next, but I sensed that she felt she had already done her friendship duties and now it was up to the rest of us.

"What's next?" I finally said directly to Gran.

She gathered herself together, you could actually see her resolve emerging across her face, her one good eye, her shoulders and hands. But before she could utter a word, the waiter came with our entrees. Tibby had a huge burger with all the accoutrements. Gran had a piece of lovely-looking halibut. Scott ordered the lamb chops and I had a roasted duck leg with orange confit sauce.

Given the distraction, Gran quickly and firmly said, "What's next is that we enjoy our dinner because the food here is excellent and..."

Before she could finish Scott murmured, "...never spoil a good meal with interrogations and inquisitions."

She gave him a look that tried to be fierce but then smiled, the warmest smile we had yet collected from our grandmother, this woman named Gran.

"Okay, Gran, let's eat first, but tell me, are we getting closer to finding out what is going on with you, and how we might be involved?" Scott entreated.

"Yes. We are," Gran said and then squeezed the lemon on her fish and picked up her fork. She looked at us and we did the same thing.

But she added, "Tibby is here to help me stay on task. Right, Tib?"

Tibby nodded and said with a mouthful of sandwich and a dribble of ketchup on her chin, "Yes, no one leaves this building tonight without being fully informed. I promise."

We had to accept that, and our dinner was delectable. The dark pressed gently in on us from way above through the round dome window, as we sat around the candles on our table and complimented the food and wine, and talked of our hike that day, and went on and on about our favorite movies and books and our work. Tibby did most of the questioning and feedback. We did most of the talking, and Gran ate with relish and quietly listened.

10

The unobtrusive waiter cleared the table of all our dishes, no leftovers among us, and brought us our after-dinner drinks. It was mint tea for Gran, decaf coffee for Tibby, full strength expresso for Scott, and a hearty chai tea for me. He left the check right beside Gran and before anyone else could make an attempt to pick it up, Gran put out her credit card and gave it back to the waiter who quickly processed it and returned it to her.

Gran cleared her throat and began. "I want no interruptions or questions. This is hard enough for me to talk about without having to go over and over it, and stop and start and repeat. So, listen up."

It sounded like an order but we read it more as a pleading, and simply nodded.

Staring somewhere between her cup of tea and the wall over our shoulders, Gran said, "Mac and I were married on the day we were to move into our house for the first night. I never thought I would get married again, after my first disastrous teenage marriage, but Mac thought it would be a great celebration and I came around to agree. It was a spectacular day, right, Tibby?"

Tibby nodded enthusiastically but didn't say a word.

"Tibby and Jim were our witnesses but a crowd gathered,

all the people who helped us build the house, friends from the art center, and all our friends from grocery clerks to the post office staff, friends I knew from my trailer park days. People brought food and spread picnic blankets. Even a bagpiper showed up, and Mac put on his kilt and danced for us. We had fiddlers and everyone danced all over the meadow. Mac had mowed the grasses himself with a hand-held scythe. It was a perfect day, even the fog and wind cooperated.

"We settled in to live our lives, doing what we needed to do to bring in income, this and that, making our art work, Mac fishing, me doing my thing, friends over for big dinners around our redwood table, nights at home by the fire, reading and talking, and Mac cooking up great food. Years passed. A good life.

"And then one day, Mac woke up distracted, almost crabby. When I asked him what was wrong, he growled at me. I won't forget his words. 'Get off my back, Grandin. Leave me be.' He'd never talked to me like that. I was stunned, but then he walked out the door and got his boat and went off fishing.

"And that was the day he never came back." Gran kept going without faltering. "Tibby's husband, Jim, was in the other boat, and he said that Mac was not himself that day, was not focused on the important thing when you are on the water, paying attention to the waves. Mac turned his back on the ocean and was fiddling with his line when the big wave hit him. Jim was nearby and was able to right his fishing kayak, but he saw Mac get swept over. Jim was the last one to see Mac.

"Jim was never quite the same. Tibby can attest to that."

Gran looked at Tibby who just nodded again, this time somberly.

"Jim died of a heart issue just six months later, so Tibby and I have sustained each other as widows for three years now." Gran paused. "But more than just as grieving widows, which we are, we are strong friends and women of independent ways, too. Always have been, and always will be."

A sip of tea and she went on. "That's just background. It was almost a whole year before I could force myself to clean out Mac's room. We each had our own private room upstairs in our house. Mac's room was a mess and it took me a time to get through it all, so it was about a month after I started that project that I came across this."

Gran pulled out a paper from a bag she was holding on her lap, and she presented it like evidence at a trial. It was handwritten in flowery handwriting on old fashioned stationary such as I had not seen since I was a school girl writing letters to Cozy.

Scott and I leaned our heads together to read it. Gran and Tibby sat silently and watched.

Dear Mr. MacIntosh, my name is Chelsea McGowan and I live in Ontario Canada. I was adopted as an infant and all I know about my origin is that I was born in Scotland and adopted there but grew up in Canada. My adoptive parents have recently moved to Vancouver and don't visit often. They were good to me but ever since I was a child, I have been curious who my birth parents might be. My (adoptive) parents had no information about my heritage because they worked with an agency with sealed adoption records. Recently my husband and I have had the sadness of three miscarriages. Desperate for possible explanation, I began to wonder more about my heritage and whether there is anything in my medical history that would lead to my tragedies. My DNA testing and ancestor tracing came up with nothing for my mother, but I had a match with a Richard MacIntosh of Edinburgh Scotland and in contacting him found out that he is not my father, but that you are most likely my birth father. He sent me your address. I would be very eager to meet you and learn more about my past. I hope you are a kind man and would consider being in touch with me. I promise I will not cause you any trouble but I yearn to know of my past for my sake as well as for the children I want so badly. My address is on the envelope. I hope you will write to me. Sincerely, Chelsea

Scott cleared his throat. I started to say something but then remembered and kept my mouth shut, just silently handed the letter back to Gran.

"The date the young woman wrote on the letter was two weeks before Mac was so surly with me. And the postmark from the Canadian postal service was smudged and unreadable. I had been in bed with the flu the day before we lost him, so Mac went to the post office to pick up our mail. Normally I picked up our mail on the way home from the market where I worked.

"In one way I was greatly relieved because finally I understood why Mac was overwhelmed that day. At least I knew it wasn't anything I had done to make him angry. On the other hand, I was disturbed that my husband, the man with whom I shared everything, would have this secret and not tell me. I brooded on that for quite some time. But when I finally told Tibby about it, she immediately pointed out to me that there was a far more important matter to consider, this young woman's desire to know who her father was. And of course, once I got over making it so personal, I knew she was right. The return address was neatly cut off the envelope, as if perhaps Mac had carefully removed it and taken it with him, and perhaps he was going to write to her. I had no way of knowing his exact intentions.

"I considered whether I should try to contact this Chelsea McGowen; however, I found myself reluctant to do anything. I began to talk myself out of it, finding excuses to avoid trying to find her. She never gave a town after all, just Ontario. That's a big province. And surely by now she would have given up ever finding her father. And what would Mac have wanted me to do? Maybe he knew he wasn't the father and this was a scam. Maybe he didn't want to acknowledge paternity. I found every excuse to not deal with this. I knew Tibby thought I should make an effort, but she didn't try to force me. I was still grieving Mac and then this information on top of it all made me out of sorts most of the time. I felt guilty about doing nothing, and absolutely reluctant to do anything. A horrible place to live, in the middle between guilt and inaction."

The waiter came back and started to ask us if we wanted more drink, but he must have sensed he shouldn't break the mood, so he quickly replenished Scott's coffee and disappeared.

"Then I made one more discovery." And here Gran brought

out display number two, a leather-bound journal, worn on the outside with the inside pages filled with inked writings. Reverently, Gran opened the journal to a page near the end of the book.

"Mac kept a journal. I knew that, but it was personal and I never gave it a thought, even didn't think to look for it after he was swept away. But then one day when I thought we had mice in his room I decided to vacuum his old chair and moved the cushions and found his journal which had slipped between the cushion and the chair.

"As you can imagine, I had a good long cry for a while when I found it. I took about another month—got the courage and sat down to read it. It was a heartache and a joy. It was like he was with me again. This journal started before we met, back when he left Scotland for the last time and traveled across the United States. But naturally the part that I relished was when he wrote of our meeting, confirming that our coming together was as magical for him as it was for me. He spent quite a bit of time talking about the building project, all the details of getting permits and pouring concrete and putting up studs, things that you might think were boring but since I was with him all the way, I relived all those creative hard-working years of my life. He talked about living above the garage in our sweet but cramped quarters—things I had forgotten and his writing brought it all back to me in vivid memories."

Gran paused. "I cried a lot, but it was healing to read it. He didn't write every day; this one book covers decades of living. But I soon realized that Mac was a great writer. He should have written a book.

"I sat there all day and into the night, and I read and re-read slowly. And around midnight that night, I read his last entry. And that is when I knew that I had to do something."

Gran opened the journal to that final page and held it out for us to read. The writing filled two full pages, in a small print, which even under the dim lights of the St. Orres dining room was legible. We read.

Some days stand out. In the middle of all our regular days here, me and Gran in our sweet crazy home with the waves crashing right over the bluff, our good, good loving, all our happy nights and days.... But some days life intervenes, history crops up its head and everything stops and takes your breath away.

Today I got a letter. Just a freak thing that I picked up the mail today. Usually, Gran does. But she's got some sort of flu, so I said I would go to town and get our mail. And there was this letter and it was addressed to me. Who do I know in Ontario, Canada? I didn't want to bother Gran, she's sleeping, so I brought the letter up to my room here and opened it.

Fuck it. A young woman claiming she is my daughter. DNA tells her this and Richard—ye wee sleekit!—he gave her my address and never let me know he did it. Fucker!

There was a space in the writing, and when the writing commenced it was now in blue ink instead of black.

Okay, had a drink, got to calm down and think. She didn't say how old she was, but the last time I was home in Edinburgh… God what a terrible time that was, the fight with Richard, the death of our mam, and then the whole thing with Marlena.

Trying to remember what happened. Spent two weeks with that woman. Screwed day and night. Did we take precautions? I don't remember. Probably did the male thing and assumed she would take care of it. Shame on me. Such a beautiful woman—all that dark hair—but hell, two more weeks with her would have put me in the looney bin. She was a roller coaster ride. Up and down. Happy and then weeping. Angry and then sweet as honey. Giving and then withholding. I didn't know where I stood with her. Wanting me desperately and then pushing me away. Accusing me of cheating on her when she wore me out so much, I didn't have the energy to get out of bed much less go out and find someone else to screw! It almost killed me to say goodbye to her, but it would have killed me eventually to stay. Like walking away from a scalding hot pot of gold. You want it so bad but you know it'll burn you. I almost thought the pain would be worth it, especially since things were so bad with Richard and my mam not being there anymore to keep the family peace. But some tiny scrap of self-preservation made me walk away at last and not give her any forwarding information. I didn't give Richard any either, not for ten years more!

So, the question is, did Marlena get pregnant? I don't know what else to say. Certainly, had many opportunities to do so those two weeks. We hardly left the bed! If it was just Marlena's word for it, I wouldn't trust her, but how do you hide from DNA? And this girl deserves to know who her bloody father is, doesn't she? I have to write her but what kind of can of worms does this open for me? For Gran? I'm sure Gran will understand. She had her own colorful past. But still, I need some time to think about this. Going fishing in the morning, good time to figure this all out. But I know in my gut, or is it in my soul, that I at least have to contact her, this Chelsea McGowen. It's the decent thing to do, to at least give her a response. Of course, I'll talk to Gran about it, but I need a day to myself. I won't even go out with Jim. He can take his own boat. I gotta be alone for a bit. So much history swirling around my head. All that crazy time, that time before I came to Gualala and met my beautiful feisty Grandin. I hardly want to think about that whole time, who I was then and all the ill will. I remember leaving town and saying to my mates, I never want to see Edinburgh again. It's my grand home country, Scotland, but between the ugliness with Richard and the craziness of Marlena, to say nothing of the sad memories of mam, I haven't been able to go back.

There was another space and then just this one sentence.

As to the thought of maybe having a daughter, I can't even begin to wrap my poor soggy mind around that amazing thought.

Naturally it took us a time to read through all of this, and I had to agree with Gran that Mac was a very readable writer, even in a personal journal like this expressing such emotional realizations and memories. I handed the book back to Gran, saw her face and realized that this was more than a fascinating story for her. It was her life.

Gran held the journal in both hands, and pushed on with her narrative, as if wanting to get it over with. "As you can imagine this filled in so many missing pieces. I can relate to Mac's long-ago passionate entanglement. No judgement there. People in glass houses after all! And I knew of his falling out with his brother and his grief at his mother's death, all a long time ago. It was his passion for life that first drew me to him. But I never heard of Marlena, only general stories of old loves and old relationships. I knew he had mixed feelings about not having had children. All in all, it didn't shock me that an unknown child might turn up. Life is full of such stories. Bottom line, I count his journal as a treasured gift, keeping Mac close to me, letting me get to know just a little more about him.

"But of course, the real question for me then was what to do. Unfortunately, with frustrating timing, right about the time I found the journal, I received word that Richard, Mac's brother had died several years earlier, and his wife and children no longer lived in Scotland, so that avenue of inquiry was useless. And there was a part of me that still wondered if it all could be a mistake, that perhaps the DNA test was wrong. I guess I was still not wanting to move on it. And I figured the young woman would have figured that her father didn't want to be in touch and would have given up after three years.

"But Mac kept coming back to haunt me. From his journal it was clear that he was going to do the right thing, so I should make the effort for him. But I still was stuck. Total inertia despite the reoccurring dreams I had of him telling me what to do.

"Then one day Mac came back to make me take him seriously. It's like he was saying, 'Gran, if you don't help me out and do what I can no longer do, I will have to come back in person and make you do it.' One day a clavicle bone was found on the beach about ten miles from here, washed up with a storm. It took a while but they did DNA testing on it and it was my Mac."

Gran sat totally still and stared at her hands; her one visible eye was wet. We modeled Tibby and just sat in silence with her. We looked into our empty cups clutched in our hands.

"I got the results of that test a week ago, and they gave me that bone so I could give Mac a decent burial. And I did. Tibby helped me. We had quite a drinking session afterwards, a good Scottish binge that Mac would have understood, until Tibby knew she had to go before she wouldn't be able to drive home safely. I stayed up and drank more. I don't know how much I drank, but the next day I found three empty bottles of Mac's good wine and I can't blame too much of that on Tibby. Then… well, first I should throw in one more matter that is the complicating factor in all of this… It's not this stupid eye infection that is the problem for me; that will heal soon, but I am having surgery soon. Odds are one for a gambler to contemplate. Fifty percent chance of full recovery, although it will take time, and fifty percent chance that I won't make it to be a really old woman. No matter the details, I will fill you in when you need to know."

Gran noticed the unspoken rustle in our attention to her story. "Don't let that bit distract you," she sternly warned us before going on.

"But the thing is I know that I cannot wait any longer to fulfill Mac's wish. I have already procrastinated long enough to make me ashamed of myself. I will never be able to face my future life or my imminent death if I don't try to fulfill Mac's last wish. But I have to accept that I cannot do it myself.

"So, the night we buried that small part of Mac that the waves returned to me, in this inebriated state of mind, in desperation and an overloaded, unrealistic sense of sentimentality, I called your moms and when my phone calls didn't go through, began texting them. Must have texted them five or ten times that night. What a fool thing to do! I have never had a relationship with my daughters that would call forth their help on any matter except maybe to bury me. And I admit that it wasn't all their fault. I am a stubborn and eccentric woman, and not a patient mother who tried to meet my girls halfway. They simply drove me mad, and I suppose I did the same to them. They became such completely opposite people from me, and I might have just been outrageous enough to egg them on."

At this point Tibby put her hand on Gran's arm and squeezed it but she still stayed silent.

"Well, not much I can do about that now, but then you two showed up yesterday. I have to admit that I had a heads up. Susie from the post office called me on my house phone to say that some young people were in the post office saying they were my grandchildren. She wanted to protect me so she put you off and then gave me a heads up. Apparently, she walked to the window and looked out and saw the car you were driving. She also saw you talking to my old buddy Floyd who was back in town, so I figured he would give you the scoop on me. He never could keep a secret if his life depended on it and he never did meet a stranger."

Scott ran his hand through his hair. "So you…" I kicked him under the table. Now that we knew the back story, I felt we were getting very close to knowing what Gran was going to ask us to do. I had an inkling but wanted to hear it from her lips.

"So no, I didn't actually hear your car drive up and then know what kind of car you were driving," Gran confessed, with a small smile playing across her face. "The waves are much too loud for that. Although the truth is that I do know a bit about cars, especially old classics. Right, Tibby?"

And Tibby once again nodded but still kept her mouth shut.

Gran turned to Scott. "And someday you and I can have a good car talk."

She doggedly got back to her story. "To cut to the chase, as you may have surmised by now, I need you two to fulfill my mission. Go to Ontario, find this Chelsea, and tell her about her father, or at least give her the DNA sample from Mac and have her do a match with her own. Take her a letter from me in which I will tell her everything I think she might want to know about her father. And you can tell her what Mac said about Marlena on the chance that she is her mother."

We looked at each other and back at her, our eyes and jaws open. Since Gran seemed finished with her narrative, I spoke, hopefully for both of us. "Well, Gran, don't you think this can be done by mail, I mean once you are able to track down her address? Why a personal visit? I mean we do have jobs and lives and… all."

I was having trouble remembering what was more fascinating about my life compared to the drama and passion Gran and Mac's lives and stories. My mind was jammed full of everything I had just heard, and being under the dome in this beautiful room here by the sea had transported me to a mystical reality. My daily life seemed like a different universe.

Scott nodded his head in solidarity, but Gran was dismissive. "This must be done in person. You must see that."

And she looked at us as if we were slow-witted. Like we were missing something so obvious that any functional adult would understand.

She looked at me. "Your teaching year will end very soon, right? And then you have the summer weeks. And you, Prescott, you can use some time and your skill to see if you can track down an address for Chelsea and then see what you can find about a Marlena in Edinburgh thirty years ago. And I'm guessing you are the kind of employee who never takes any vacation time, so you must have some due."

As an afterthought she added, "I'll finance your trip, of course."

Scott just sat; mouth slightly dropped. And I made an attempt. "Well, now, Gran, I usually teach some summer school and try to take a vacation and catch up on appointments and have lunch with friends…" I stopped. Even I wasn't impressed with my list of summer activities, especially since I had not got the summer school assignment this year because of a change in programs. But still, I resented the presumptive tone in Gran's voice.

Gran just looked at me without a word. I didn't know whether to shake her for her assumptions or hug her for her grief or try to find out more about her surgery or admire her for her clear-headed plan. And, damn it, despite myself, I had growing vibrations for something new and fascinating to do with my time.

She cleared her throat and started to stand up. "Time to head home. Tibby, will you drop me off so Elizabeth doesn't have to be hunched over in the back seat?"

Tibby's eyes gleamed with both amusement and sympathy for Scott and me. "Sure, but first a pitstop."

Gran and Tibby walked off to the bathroom and Scott and I followed and waited in the bar to see if there were any more comments we should hear.

As we stood there a friendly voice called out, "Hey, there you are. I saw your car in the lot and wondered if I would run into you again."

And sliding off the bar stool a man approached us. Scott immediately held out his hand and greeted him happily.

The man turned to me. "Jerry, from the auto shop in Gualala," he said to me as he saw I had no idea. "We met in the parking lot yesterday."

"Oh, sure, yes. Sorry. I tend to glaze over when my cousin runs into car people!" I laughed. I wasn't sure why I wanted this stranger to know that Scott was merely my cousin. The man smiled at me, and I found it was easy to smile back. He answered my smile with another of his. They seemed to be in bountiful supply. Then he turned back to Scott and talked more about the Karmann Ghia.

About then Gran and Tibby came out of the bathroom and when Jerry saw them, he greeted them. "Have you eaten yet? The halibut is really spectacular tonight. Caught off Point Arena today, chef told me."

Tibby answered, "We've eaten already and, yes, good as always here. In fact, we are on our way home. By the way, do you think you'll have time to work on my pickup this next week? No emergency, but a couple of maintenance jobs need doing."

"This week is jammed, Tib. Well, in truth I promised the guys I'd go fishing one day and have to run get supplies from Santa Rosa another, plus the Johnsons need their car for a trip coming up. But next week should work. Just call me at the shop and I'll set a day for you."

He said goodbye to us, but I sensed a longer look at me. Was I imagining or wishing? Scott didn't notice, but when I caught Gran's eye, she gave me a look and said nothing.

Scott just commented, "Small towns…" and left it hanging.

11

We followed Tibby through the darkness back to Gran's house. As soon as the Tibby's pickup stopped, Gran was out of the car and making her way into the tunnel to the house. We parked and walked up to the open driver window. Seemed like something should be said.

"It was really nice to meet you, Tibby," I said blandly at a loss for what else to murmur.

She looked at us squarely and said her piece, what she had probably been wanting to say all during Gran's story in the restaurant.

"You two, you have an opportunity here. If you are smart… well, all I want to say is to think about this carefully, or maybe what I want to say is to not think about this overly much, just take a chance. When you go back to your normal life tomorrow there's a good chance you'll wonder why bother with all of this, and it will be easier to just ignore or placate your Gran. And no one will know. Your life will just go on its way. I know that your Gran is not the easiest person to live with and surely, she was not the greatest mom to her difficult daughters, but she has been the greatest friend to me. We lived a unique lifestyle for years even before Mac and Jim. But then we celebrated having the greatest partners, both of us! Gran and I pulled each other out of shock when our husbands died, and last year she nursed me through major surgery, and now I will do the same for her. But this mission she is asking you to take on, neither she or I can do it. It's you two… or no one."

I interrupted, changing the subject a tad. "What kind of surgery does Gran need to have? And is it really fifty/fifty that she will come through?"

"More or less. Maybe more like 60/40. Tumor in her kidney. But don't tell her I told you, and don't you dare tell your moms. Let her do that afterwards or whenever she wants to do it."

She pulled out a business card, tattered from sitting in her car so long, and handed it to me. "Gadgets & More," it said, with a downtown Gualala shop address and her number on it. "Call me and I'll give you updates."

Scott opened his wallet and handed Tibby his card. I shrugged my shoulders. "I'm a middle school teacher. I don't carry business cards."

Tibby laughed. "And I don't own the shop anymore, but my number is the same."

I took out a pen and wrote my phone number on Scott's card and Tibby took it and tucked it into her shirt pocket.

Then she grasped the steering wheel tighter as if she were already on Highway One. But her eyes were on us. "You may never live the life your Gran has lived; yours may be a lot tidier. But it couldn't be as vital and exciting. We all make mistakes; life is messy and to think otherwise is to not be living authentically. Expect and accept that life is often complicated and challenging, even while it can also be simple and totally glorious. If that sounds like a paradox, well, it is. All truth is a paradox in my eyes. And you have an opportunity to step out of your normal routines and have a little adventure. I won't come right out and say that you will regret it if you don't because I don't know you well enough to have a full view of who you are. Of course, you can easily shrug this off and go for the practical solution, but I am challenging you to take some risks, have some fun. You would be doing it for your Gran of course, but more than that, I think you would be doing it for yourselves. Life is too short not to walk through doors when they open right in front of you."

She tapped her hands on the steering wheel, and grinned at us, a wicked yet warm smile. "Okay, that is my sermon for today. There's lots more I could say, but I need to get home to take care of my herd. They don't like it when I go out in the evening and scold me every time. When you live alone, it's good to know someone needs you!"

"Your herd?" Scott repeated.

Tibby held her hand out of the car. It was a worn but strong hand with the beginning of arthritis bending her joints. And she held up a finger for each animal. "Five chickens, four goats, three cats, two old dogs, and one very friendly donkey." She laughed again. "And that's why I never spent enough time in my shop to make a go of it! But I mostly opened my shop to gossip with the folks who came in to browse. Next time you get up the coast, you must come over and meet my critters. I'll give you some homemade bread and my goat's cheese and pour you a mean Manhattan!"

She put the car in gear to turn around on the dead-end

road and called out to us, "Now go in there and make sure your Gran gets to bed soon. This has worn her out completely, body and soul." And then she stopped and added, "And buy her some groceries in the morning before you leave. Once she gets that eye patch off, she can drive again, but that's not until Tuesday and then she has surgery a week from Monday, so she could use a few things."

She quickly flipped the U turn and was off down the gravel road into the dark shadows of the thick trees, bumping and raising dust as if she had driven this way thousands of times before.

We hurried after Gran and found her at the bottom of the porch steps contemplating them as if they were Half Dome to climb. Here in the opening of the meadow, the moon shone down from a clear sky loaded with stars, more than I had seen since a high school camping trip in the high Sierras. Scott grabbed Gran's arm and she accepted his help to mount the stairs. Johnny greeted her like she had been gone for a year.

In the hallway she headed without a word to her bedroom while we watched her silently. At the doorway of her bedroom she turned, her hand resting on the doorframe.

"Elizabeth, would you make me some breakfast in the morning?"

"Sure."

A nod. "It's good to have someone cook for me again. I miss it."

She went in her room and turned around. "And lock the

doors and give Johnny a treat for being alone all evening. I'll leave my door open for him. He always sleeps with me."

I was comforted by the thought that Gran had Johnny to sleep with, warming up her bed, and I hoped this was not one of those nights where she would find the need to go out and scream at the sky and waves. I had not yet mentioned what I had witnessed to Scott.

I was fairly sure I would not sleep well, so much whirling in my brain, but the hiking and the wind and waves and all the good food and wine must have told my body to take over my crazy mind, and I did fall asleep. The next thing I knew I was back in the kitchen making the best breakfast I could with the available ingredients. While Gran might like someone cooking for her, I was surprised how much I was enjoying cooking for her and for Scott in a kitchen pleasantly haunted by a man I never met. As I picked up the seasoned frying pan, I imagined Mac's large capable hands grasping this same pan as he made breakfast and dinner for a younger, laughing Gran. Maybe after a night of good sex, I thought with a smile.

After breakfast Scott drove to the store in Gualala and picked up some groceries. When he got home, he emptied out the groceries onto the counter for Gran to see.

"I saw Jerry's auto shop on the main drag coming home," he said.

"Jerry probably knows every car up and down the coast," Gran said. And then she added, "And all the car owners, too. Jerry could run for mayor and win by a landslide—if Gualala actually had a mayor—but I think he prefers to stay out of politics. It's safer. Even in a small town, or maybe especially in a small town, politics can be nasty."

Not that I had any direct experience, but I did put in my two cents, "Well, Gran someone has to do the work to run a city. Not every politician is corrupt if that is what you are saying."

She shrugged. "Not saying that. Just saying that it is hard to be in the crosshairs all the time when everyone knows their neighbors. Jerry is either smart enough to stay out of things or he is avoiding conflict. Probably a bit of each. Jerry's embedded in this town and perhaps feeling some obligation to remain neutral goes along with that."

I found this interesting. A bit of small-town sociology—or perhaps it was psychology—from Gran's viewpoint. But it was time to get on the road home.

I folded the blankets and put together my backpack. Scott and I found Gran on the porch in her usual spot. I handed her a cup of tea but she just set it on the table next to her chair.

I had no idea what to say or not say at this farewell. My thoughts were a scramble, tumbling without form or structure. But we couldn't just walk away without saying something! Couldn't give some mundane goodbye either. Too much had happened in less than forty-eight hours.

I don't know why I felt it was up to me to say or do the right thing, but it seems I often played that role. But it was Scott who came through.

He squatted and patted Johnny who was sitting by Gran's feet, and by so doing Scott was eye to eye with Gran. Scott tended to tower over people so it was a kindness to put himself and Gran on the same level.

"Gran, I have to ask you something before we go."

"Okay."

"No one calls me Prescott, although it is my legal name. Yet you do. I'm curious."

Gran took so long to answer I wondered if it was going to be another question she would pass on. "You were named for my father, Prescott Randall Templeton. He was a good man, and he was, I suppose, a stable male influence in your mom's life—both your moms—when their dad was gone and the men in the commune were a mixed bag. My parents would have wished I had come home to live with them when my first husband exited the scene, but they were not judgmental people and they knew I had to do things my way. They saw my girls as much as they could before they moved to L.A. to be near my sister. I was surprised but also elated when your parents named you Prescott. My father, your great-grandfather, was a good man, and I regret that I didn't tell him that more often. I was so full of myself, and it wasn't until after he and my mother moved south that I realized how much I had underappreciated him. I did see him a few times in his older years, and he was gracious and forgiving of me. He died much too young from my viewpoint. I love the name Prescott for that reason, even though I know everyone calls you Scott."

"Well, I'll be damned, Gran. Thanks for telling me that. I had no idea."

Gran looked wearily at him. "I can't believe your mom would not have told you for whom you were named."

"There are obviously lots of things this family has not talked about, Gran. Elizabeth and I have to go home now. We have work tomorrow. And, Gran, I have a date tonight too, to be perfectly honest. Who knows, maybe this will be the one I've been waiting for." Scott laughed but in a relaxed manner, as if he could trust talking to Gran about these relationship matters after all she had shared with us.

And Gran did relax and smile back at him, a softness coming over her face. "Have a safe drive down, keep your eyes on the road, and don't drive that little car too fast on the curves. I have high hopes of seeing you two again sooner than later. And whether you take on my mission or not, I don't want to lose you. I know you may need time to think about everything, but let me know your decision soon. Okay?"

She was not exactly begging, but it was the most vulnerable thing she had said to us all weekend.

I assured her, "Gran, of course we'll think about it, try to sort out all that we've learned. It's all kind of boggling, I hope you realize that!" I laughed, a bit nervously. "But I promise you we will get back to you soon. And Gran, you've told us you are having surgery, could be life changing. Do you expect us to not tell our moms? They might be angry at us later, if you, know if…"

"If I die? Don't tell them! Don't tell them anything. I don't need any flapping about on their part to interfere with my focus on what is to come next. Like I said, I am very sorry I contacted them about coming here to help me with Mac's daughter. I claim temporary insanity, but then again it did bring you two into my life.

"As for the surgery, it's a week from tomorrow. I will most likely survive the surgery itself, although I know people do go south during surgery. The odds I told you about are what the docs will find from the surgery. And if the verdict is benign, then holy cow, I recover and go on with my life here in this sweet house that Mac and I built. If I am told I have a limited time to live, then I will find a way to contact your moms and have a little time with them, but it has to be on my terms as long as I am able, you understand?"

She glared at us. We both nodded, Scott still crouching down beside her and me leaning against the porch railing. After another moment of intensity, her face relaxed, and she put her hand on Scott's shoulder.

"Help me up, you tall, handsome grandson. I'll say goodbye right here and now."

She first gave Scott a hug, her face folded into his chest, and then she reached up and tousled his hair like a little boy. Then she came over to me and grabbed me into a hug I can only describe as fierce. I was surprised at her strength, but I didn't resist. When had I ever been hugged so fully? Somehow all Tibby's words of the night before came back to me, all expressed in that hug by Gran.

"Bye, Gran," I said, and then I looked at her eye-to-eye. Her one good eye conveyed so much that I wondered if I could handle being in the gaze of Gran's two eyes when the patch came off.

"Thanks for the cooking, Elizabeth. It meant a lot to me. And you, you… you take care of yourself."

We went down the stairs, backpacks bouncing on our shoulders. When we got to the bottom, I looked back up at her and called out, "Bye for now, Gran. We promise to let you know."

She waved once, her face stoic now, but I felt her looking at us until we disappeared into the tunnel by the garage.

The drive home was quiet as we motored through forests and on cliff roads offering the dazzling blue vistas of ocean and sky and finally carefully powered up the Jenner Grade and down again into the town where we saw the Russian River release its waters into the ocean. We didn't really talk. I had to hope that Scott was at least partially thinking of his date that evening. Me? I was trying to get myself to focus on eighth grade history curriculum, but it was hard to compete with getting to know our Gran and her life stories.

Part 2
Beginning the Journey

12

The truth of the matter is that despite having been completely caught up in Gran's engaging story while we were with her, there is a high likelihood that that if two separate things hadn't happened once we were back in Davis, both Scott and I might have settled back into our daily lives, and not heeded the bizarre charge from our gran-named-Gran to go off across the country on a strange mission we did not yet fully understand.

We were both adults with jobs and lives. And when we got back to Davis, we would very quickly feel that whole structured life drift over us like an invisible but encapsulating net.

However, before we dropped back into normal life, two separate things happened.

Scott's date with the graduate student that Sunday night—Gina was her name—turned out to be gold. I learned of this the next evening when I called him to get a report. For whatever reason, Scott's dates rarely mustered more than a bronze in the dating medal success. Scott admits that he is usually the stumbling block. But his enthusiastic response to my question was an unabashed outpouring of satisfaction. And he claimed to be very certain that it was a mutual reaction.

That would lead one to believe that Scott would be very

inclined to stay put in Davis for the summer and not go traipsing all over the continent at the behest of Gran.

However, in a serendipitous turn of events, the golden Gina was leaving in one week's time for a summer in northern Ontario—yes, Ontario, Canada—to do research on beavers in the French River region of that province for her doctoral thesis in Animal Science.

"Ontario, Canada, Cousin Lizzie," Scott chortled.

"Yes, I hear you. Ontario, Canada. It is quite a coincidence," I had to admit, but I added, "You know, Ontario is an extremely large province, Scott. It's huge!" Leaving him to come to his own conclusion.

He just kept saying, "Lizzie, Ontario, Canada. I mean what are the odds?"

And then he repeated, "Ontario, Canada!"

And I could see that in his mind he was already there.

That was well and good for Scott, and admittedly it was a truly amazing coincidence. But it was a second occurrence on that Sunday that kept me from sliding back into my familiar and fulfilling day-to-day reality and letting Gran's crazy mission die on the vine.

What happened is that when Scott dropped me off Sunday afternoon in front of my place, Nellie was in her garden working. The garden that surrounds her house is a masterpiece as you might imagine with Nellie in charge, a fertile abundance of fruit trees, vegetables, and flowers.

She straightened up to greet me and pressed her hands into the small of her back—her back talked to her when she bent over too long. Waving a goodbye hand to Scott who drove away anxious to get ready for his date, Nellie called out to me, "Welcome back, dear girl. Come on in and have a cup of tea and cookies. Just made some peanut butter oatmeal."

Didn't take much to persuade me. I needed a transition from the weekend before hitting the text book, and I dropped my bag at the bottom of the stairs to my apartment and followed Nellie into her familiar kitchen. How often had I sat at her table and watched her bake or make me tea, all the while appearing to give me her full attention while I talked my head off?

She put on the kettle and pulled out two mugs and some tea bags.

When she brought the mugs to the table, she stopped and looked intently at me. The force of Nellie's two bright eyes drilled into me. I reached for my mug to break her study of me.

"Elizabeth, something has changed about you."

This was getting weird. In the last few days, I had experienced the scrutiny of three older women, Gran, Tibby, and now Nellie; I don't recall when I had received that much close attention. Certainly, my mom never looked at me with such an extended gaze, unless she was critiquing my hair. But Nellie was not looking at my clothes or hair. She was looking far deeper.

"What are you talking about?"

Nellie sat down, leaned forward, picked up her mug, and ritualistically blew on the hot liquid. "I've spent my life studying plants and can tell the difference between a healthy plant and a sick plant. I can also tell when a plant is bursting with eminent bloom, full of energy and life, one that is spreading roots and reaching for the sun. And you, dear, at this moment, are reaching for the sun. So, what's up?"

Embarrassed, I changed my facial expression and shifted my body language, but Nellie just laughed at me and lifted her mug in my direction and then put it to her lips. "Can't fool me. Maybe you fell in love this weekend, or maybe something else."

I stood up and motioned to her bathroom. "I've got to pee, that's it. I am bursting with pee!" And I left her sitting there at the table with a smile on her face.

When I returned, she just looked at me, and before you know it, I was telling her the story of the entire weekend, meeting Gran, her amazing house, learning about Mac, hiking along the ocean trails, and even about Gran's screaming at the night sky and ocean waves. I didn't mean to tell her about that last story, but it came out and Nellie was the best of listeners. She just nodded as if that was the most sensible thing in the world for someone to do.

Finally, I explained that Gran had a wild idea that Scott and I must go in person to find and contact Mac's daughter in Canada. Nellie asked a few questions, details, but when I couldn't answer most of them, she stopped and spoke. "Okay, I can see that you don't have all the pieces of the puzzle yet. But that will come with time."

She spoke so confidently that I looked at her sharply. "You act like we are going to do it, no question asked."

"Oh, but, Elizabeth, of course you must. This kind of fascinating opportunity comes along so rarely. It is not the normal offering one gets in life, the chance to make a clear choice to follow a certain path. Usually, these forks in the road are much more subtle, and sometimes you don't even realize you have changed course until later. What a gift, for you and for Scott."

I just shook my head. What was happening to my predictable, steady life? Teaching, prepping, laundry, walks and lunches with friends, occasional dates…? It was a good life, wasn't it? Why shake it up? But here was Nellie acting as though Gran's mission was not to be ignored.

Nellie read my face and laughed. "You're confused. I understand, but think about it this way and it might help. When you are my age, ancient!" she laughed, "and you look back at your life, will you regret taking a chance to do something completely different? Something that will add color to your life in one way or another?"

I picked up on her last comment. "See, Nellie, that's what I'm thinking. I like color as much as anyone, but the kind of color that might come from this venture could be, well, could be not so great."

"Phooey, Elizabeth. It's not like you are giving up your job. It's summer break. It's not like you are losing your home. I will save your apartment for you, and as an added bonus I'll even reduce your rent while you are gone! You'll still have friends when you come back. In fact, as I see it, it's kind of a cushy bit of risk taking. But it most definitely has the potential to be a life-enhancing experience. You've been handed a gift, my girl!"

I was still dragging my feet. "It is so bizarre. Not sure

how to explain this whole mission to anyone," I conceded. "Maybe I am thinking of explaining it to my mom," I admitted.

Nellie didn't answer right away. Finally, "When I met my Fletcher, I had a gut feeling that it was a good thing. Everyone told me I was nuts. The nicest thing anyone said to me was 'I'm so terribly worried for you.' I almost walked away from him. But what a mistake that would have been.

"You see, Elizabeth, he wasn't perfect. He was edgy sometimes, and had outrageous taste in music, and his background was quite a contrast to mine. But what we shared was so good. He was always respectful and caring to me, encouraged me to do what I wanted to do. And so, I took a risk, lost a few friends, made my parents furious. Of course, who knows how our lives would have unfurled over decades of a long marriage, but then, no one ever knows the future. And for those three years we were married, before he was drafted and sent to Vietnam, those years were the best of my life. Being with him opened me up, gave me new perspectives, and, oh my, Elizabeth, to be loved like that…." Here Nellie stopped abruptly for a moment.

"And though he never came home to me, I had those three years, and if I had not taken that risk, my life would never have been the same. It would have been different, of course. Would have saved myself horrible grief, at least the losing-Fletcher grief, but maybe I would have some other kind of grief. And I'm sure I would've made some good stuff happen for myself, but I wouldn't have had what I had with Fletcher, such an overwhelming knowledge that everything was right. So much fun too. That time we had together has sustained me in many ways all these years. I'm just telling you that saying yes to life with Fletcher is something I will never regret."

She stood up and came over to me and pulled me up by my hands. Her arms and hands were strong after a lifetime of garden work. She hugged me and turned me to the door, handing me a bag of cookies.

"Go up and settle in. I'll be so interested to hear what you decide to do."

As I walked slowly up the outside stairs to my door and fumbled for my key, it occurred to me that I should talk to someone my age, a friend who wasn't old and wise like Nellie, or old and outrageous, which perhaps described Gran; it would be good to talk to someone more my own age, someone besides Scott who was too close to this strange idea, someone my age who looked at things sensibly with a similar world view. But something held me back that evening. I thought such a peer simply wouldn't understand.

Or maybe I worried such a peer would be able to talk me out of it.

13

Two weeks passed and my school year finished. I was too busy during those weeks to think about much of anything other than school. But Scott was all in for the trip thanks to his new infatuation. I met Gina ever so briefly before she left for Canada and found her likeable; she was exuberantly passionate about animals, which was an interesting matchup for Scott. She even had a rescue dog of indeterminate breed who was going to live with her sister while she was in Canada.

I must have been leaning towards buying into Gran's venture myself, because I turned down a much sought-after summer art job for kids at the University, which had popped up at the last minute. It should have posed a real dilemma to turn it down, but it didn't. I can only say that I was under some kind of old woman-spell, between Gran and Nellie. Nellie laughed at me when I said that and she called it the Power of the Crone! She said it would be good karma for when I got to be a crone myself.

Lately it seemed like my best companions were thirteen-year-olds or eighty-year-olds. My same-age friends didn't stay focused long enough to listen to my vague new summer plans. As if they had not heard me, they wanted to know if I could sign up for the summer tennis tournament, or schedule some East Bay hikes, a weekend in Carmel, the Outside

Lands music festival or lunch in the City. And when I backed out of all those possibilities, not knowing the breadth and scope of our summer adventure, they seemed to lose interest, with a quick "Oh, that's too bad, let us know when you're back." I was beginning to wonder whether my friends lacked a basic sense of curiosity or if the truth was that I was not very important to them.

Tibby sent an email when Gran got the eye patch off and said Gran's eye looked as good as new and Gran was really happy to have that "damn thing off my face." And then when Gran was safely out of surgery, Tibby called us with the news that it had all gone well. As to whether the growth was malignant or not, that would take weeks for results. Meanwhile Gran was home and Tibby had moved in to help her out for a time. And Gran sent us a message through Tibby—threatened us—to remember not to tell our moms about her surgery, promising that she would do so in her own time.

When Tibby put Gran on the phone to hear that we agreed to carry out her mission, Gran acted as if she was not surprised. Before she hung up, Tibby quietly assured us that Gran was very relieved.

As for Mom and Dad, and Aunt Mandy and Uncle Ryan, they got back from their big Caribbean adventure and were full of talk and photos about that, and full of plans for the upcoming golf tournament at their club. When they invited Scott and me to join them for a dinner three days after they got home and four days before our planned departure and we managed to get a word in edgewise with our very unclear plan to help Gran, they kind of looked at us blankly. It was like they had forgotten that it was my mom who had called me in the first place to tell me to go up to Gualala and check in on Gran. And they never asked about Gran's health, so we didn't have to skirt around that subject with a white lie as a procrastination tactic.

This may give the impression that Scott and I don't love our parents. We do, at some level, of course. We had an easy childhood, lacked for nothing, and it was all pleasant enough. I think our moms did their best to do the right thing as moms, going to school events, making sure we did our homework, and not letting us stay up too late, as teens telling us about the dangers of drugs, and for me there were explanations about sex. My mom always made sure to include me in "Take Your Daughter to Work Day." And our dads were not abusive and provided for our needs without overly indulging us. On the surface, we grew up in model families.

It was the atmosphere of family that we were familiar with, and Scott and I provided a family within a family for each other, and that is where our strongest connection lay. But here's the truth: I felt more emotional kinship after two days with Gran than I ever had with my own parents. The stark contrast between my parents' home and Gran's was not just in appearances and style, but in something I had trouble putting into words. The difference was one of genuine connection. I think it had something to do with feeling seen and acknowledged by Gran, whereas my own parents didn't have a clue who I was. This was eye-opening to me.

When they finally absorbed what we told them of the upcoming trip we were going to take for Gran, our moms looked at each other and my mom said to her sister, "Oh God, she's got them hooked."

And Aunt Mandy spoke very seriously to us, like we were twelve-years-old and needed to be protected. "I don't know what Gran has going on now, kids, but you don't need to get sucked into her drama. That was so very sweet of you two to drive all the way up there on that horrible road to check on her, but if she is not sick then there is no need to be involved any further. We'd love for you two to be part of the fundraiser for the junior golf team, and I'm hoping you will be able to coach the middle school tennis club this summer, Liz."

Scott and I looked at each other, and I could see the condescending tone had gotten to him. He briskly laid it out. "Too late for that talk, Mom. We had a great weekend up on the coast, and we are all set to go back up there next Monday and then hit the road. We're excited about the trip."

I was super proud of him for speaking up, because generally it is either me talking back or us both doing the passive-aggressive work-around tactic with our parents.

My mom started to interrupt, and I could hear the deluge of 'Gran is just a troublemaker' stories ready to pour down on our heads when, of all amazing things, my dad intervened. Perhaps he, too, was tired of hearing our moms complain about Gran's strange proclivities.

"That's a long drive across country. What car are you taking?"

Scott and I looked at him gratefully for the diversion.

"We're going to take Lizzie's Civic. Good mileage. I'm not confident enough of finding charging stations for my Volt, and my old cars make for a great drive but not so sure what we might run into on this road trip, so we thought hers would be a better choice."

Dad nodded, and before my mom tried to interject her disapproval again, he stood up and motioned Scott and me to the window overlooking the driveway. He pointed to a silver SUV with Nevada license plates, sitting in the driveway.

"My Explorer is only a year old; I just bought it in Reno and plan on leaving it in Reno next fall when I open my new office there. It will be a company car for my Reno staff so I'm not taking off the Nevada license plates. Take it and you can handle rough roads and even sleep in it if you need to."

Dad smiled. "I spent a few months in my early twenties on the road in my old Mustang and have lots of memories. You two went right to work after college, but it's not too late for an adventure."

He added to Scott, "And as a tall man myself, I know you will appreciate having more room to stretch your legs and your back after hours on the road."

I wasn't sure how to take this loaner. The big vehicle was not my idea of ecological transportation and I started to say something about gas mileage, but Scott reached out and sealed the deal with my dad with a handshake.

"Uncle Matt, that's a great offer. I can't promise it will come back as clean and new-looking as it is now, fair warning. But I will drive it as carefully as I do my cars."

My dad just looked at Scott seriously. "It's only a vehicle. Just take care of my daughter."

Scott looked kind of surprised at this old-fashioned male

talk, and I was not liking it myself, but then again, I didn't get a lot of attention from my dad and was kind of touched by his concern and so kept my mouth shut. Scott didn't know what to say, but my dad did not relinquish his hand until Scott finally said, "Of course I will. We always look out for each other."

Dad released his grip and took me by the shoulders and gave me a hug, an awkward unpracticed move, but I loved it and slipped in a little kiss on his cheek, which seemed to surprise him and reduce him to a gruff try at the same, missing my forehead and landing a kiss in my hair. It was the sweetest moment ever with my father.

That was about it. Uncle Ryan gave his son a formal handshake and pat on the back. Our moms' faces were stiff, but they were silent as they gave us each a light hug and an air kiss. The memory of my father's embrace stayed warm within my memory.

We were essentially on our way.

14

Our next drive up the coast was a different experience in the Explorer. I asked Scott how he liked driving it, and he just smiled and said, "Very different from my Karmann Ghia or my Volt, but I like all driving, and your dad is right, this car is going to give me much better leg room for the long drive. How do you like it?"

"I admit it's fun to be sitting up high and looking out on things. I feel like I'm in a truck or something, except the drive is very smooth." I added, "Of course the gas mileage is going to kill us. That will be something to get used to after my Civic."

He shrugged. "I'm just feeling on top of the world, driving up this coastline and not knowing a thing about what tomorrow or next week will bring."

I teased him, "But you are hoping that somewhere along this dusty trail you'll find Gina and her beavers up in the French River."

We both started laughing at the same moment at my unintentional risqué language.

My grades had been turned in. Nellie would keep an eye on my apartment. Scott had a friend living his place for the month and had four weeks of vacation saved up for his use, and after that, he was remarkably cavalier about what he would do although he mentioned that Ancestry.com might compensate him for travel that involved a satisfying family history search. "It's worth a try," he laughed.

We pulled into Gualala like we were old-timers, stopping first at Jerry's shop. I looked at Scott and he said, "I promised to drop off some car parts for him."

Apparently, he and Jerry were in regular communication now.

At the garage, Jerry came out of the bay wiping his hands carefully before shaking Scott's hand. He waved to me casually and then turned to see what Scott had brought them. As usual with car talk, I zoned out and looked at people walking and driving by on Main Street. It was a cloudy day, and people wore sweaters and stocking caps. Early summer weather on the North Coast. I liked it.

Then Scott stuck his head in the car window and told me, "I'm going to make a call and Jerry says the best cell coverage is up by the road. Back in a minute." And he walked fifty feet away to the highway.

Jerry came around to my side of the car and smiled at me. "How ya doing, Elizabeth? Great to see you back up this way. Did you miss the cold?" He laughed and waved his hand at the overcast sky. His dark hair was pulled back into a ponytail and he wore a baseball cap that said Gualala Art Center. Despite the chill, he wore a tee-shirt, and when he lifted his hand to push back his cap, my eyes left his face and I could see a simple tattoo of a bird on the upper biceps of his right arm; perhaps an eagle. I brought my eyes back under my control and didn't stare at his arms, although I wanted to do so.

"Actually, I love this kind of weather. We don't get cool summer weather in Davis." I smiled back. And I added, "This place suits me very well."

Jerry's smile widened. "Glad to hear that. Some folks only want sunshine, sunshine, sunshine. Me? I like the weather here, the fog and the ever-changing temps, and when we do have sunshine it's like God dropped a day of heaven on us."

"Pretty poetic for a mechanic," I said and then bit my tongue because I thought it sounded snippy or teasing when in fact, I had loved what he said.

He threw back at me. "Yep, up here we are Jack-of-all-trades. I fix cars, do some welding, hold up my end of the bar at St. Orres, and also take a painting class at the art center. What's life like for you in Davis?"

Was that a bit of a friendly challenge, or even a defensive comment? I answered truthfully. "I teach eighth-graders so I'm a bit of a Jacklyn-of-all trades myself." I looked straight at him.

His look didn't waver and he shot right back at me. "Would you like to grab a cup of coffee while you are here? I also know coffee shops, not just bars."

"I don't like coffee." Why was I being rude?

He looked away; his face puzzled then protective. "Okay. Well, I've never been turned down by that comment before."

"I'm sure you have lots of practice asking women out." What was possessing me? I liked this man and I was acting like an asshole.

Amazingly, he didn't run away. He stood where he was and said steadily, "I don't, in fact. This is the first time since my girlfriend moved out on me four years ago. Perhaps I need more practice. But at least I know where you stand on the matter."

I felt like I was in the middle of the pond treading water, and what I really wanted was to come on shore, but I kept pushing myself away from shore at the same time.

I took a breath. "Jerry, I'm sorry. I'm sorry about your girlfriend leaving, and I'm sorry I'm sounding so rude. Can I regroup and start again? The truth of the matter is that I do hate coffee, but I would like to get together. Would you be willing to buy me a cup of tea and I'll buy you a cup of coffee?"

That smile. Like he couldn't help but show what he was feeling. At least I hoped that was true, because his smile was an image I would remember all summer long.

"You pick when and I'll pick where."

"Ah, here's the thing. We're here to see Gran and start off on a mission for her, and I think she wants us to get started as soon as possible, maybe tomorrow. Can we take a rain check? I'd really look forward to it."

"I'll accept that and have to hope you won't forget once you get out on the road. Scott told me that you two were driving across country. I've never taken the time to do a road trip myself, too busy fixing other people's cars for their road trips." Jerry stood back and eyed the Explorer. "Does Scott know how to work on new cars, I wonder?"

He didn't expect an answer, I could tell. I could see Scott

finishing up his phone call and starting to walk back to the car, still looking at his phone. I quickly said, "So, what happened to her, your girlfriend? Did she not like the weather up here?"

I was trying to be light-hearted, although I was curious. He answered, "Well, the weather and most everything that I love about the North Coast was not to her liking. She went to San Diego. Apparently, she is very happy."

Scott was almost in earshot, and Jerry just finished with, "Over our coffee/tea, I'll tell you more if you really want to know that sad saga. Frankly I can think of better things to talk about. Her leaving was a gift to me." And then with his smile returning, he backed away from my window and added, "You know where to find me, right here on Highway One. Hope you'll find your way back here."

Scott got back to us and opened the driver door. We all said a friendly goodbye and Jerry sent good wishes to Gran on her recovery (seems the whole town knew everyone else's business) and we were off to Gran's house, now confident of our directions and ready for whatever would happen next. I tucked Jerry's smile back into my backpack for future contemplation. We had business to attend to.

15

Gran was resting on the couch when we arrived, an open book face down on her lap. After letting us in with a warm hug, Tibby sat back down on a chair pulled right near Gran for easier conversation. She picked up a basket and took out a knife and a piece of wood and went back to her carving.

We dropped our bags, and going to the couch, Scott lifted Gran's hand and gave it a kiss, like a gentleman of the court. Gran loved it, you could tell.

"Prescott, you dashing man, you. I'm glad you came back."

"But of course, Gran. Did you doubt it?"

She looked at him intently, and then to me. Two functional eyes doubled the force of her looks. "I hoped you would come back. I knew you had the heart for it, but I understand the lure of your jobs and everyday life."

I had to smile. She made our daily lives sound like an evil distraction from her unconventional wishes.

Gran caught my smile and answered it by holding her arms out to me as I bent over her for a hug. After I settled in on the floor beside her reclining figure, Scott plopped down next to me, and Gran cleared her throat as if to make a rehearsed announcement as quickly as possible.

"I realize that over the years, I have been rather one-sided in my view of people and how they choose to live. I have stereotyped everyone who lives a more conventional life as boring people caving in to bourgeoisie or spirit-crushing routines; I have judged them to be people who don't think about the deeper matters of life or don't have any creativity. And in reverse, I gave the people who lived a counter-culture lifestyle the credit for being creative and superior. It pains me to admit that I have been wrong more than once over the years. I have come to discover that life and people are far more nuanced than my simplified version."

Tibby must have given her a smirk because Gran gave her a glare over our heads, the glare only two close friends can exchange.

Gran continued. "As I say, I have come to realize that there are many good people with brains and even creativity among those who follow a more conventional lifestyle and work. And there are those who look like they live outside the box, but their thinking is limited or close-minded, or even meanspirited despite their colorful outward appearance and language."

She continued doggedly. "I am going to go out on a limb and give your mothers credit for being gutsy in pursuing the path they wanted to live, no matter how different than mine. And they have done one important thing very right and that is raise you two."

Perhaps a brush with death, from her surgery, had jarred our Gran.

Gran finished her little speech; I guessed she had been planning what to say to us ever since we left her two weeks ago. "So, did I doubt whether you would come back? I accept and understand that your lives are important to you. You have created them carefully over the last ten years and they are not trivial—in fact they are important—and I have no right to demand that you drop everything at my bequest. Therefore, if you had chosen to stay back in Davis and live your lives, I would have accepted that you had very good reasons."

As scripted and un-Gran as this sounded, it was good to hear.

She brightened up as if thankful that her dutiful pronouncement was over. "But here you are, and I'm gratified you are here."

"We're excited to be here, Gran. But we are in the dark about exactly what you expect us to do."

Gran motioned to Tibby. "Tib, where is the list we made the other day?"

Tibby put her woodcarving down on her lap, searched under some papers and books on the little table, pulled out a yellow legal pad and handed it to Gran. Then she said to us, "You just got off the road. How about some tea or wine or nibbles?"

Tibby and I went into the kitchen, and as we worked together to set up a tray, I thanked her for keeping us in the loop on Gran's health.

"It was a pleasure to have someone to call, Elizabeth. To think that less than a month ago, Gran had no idea her grandchildren could be part of her life! Of course, she knew of your existence, but she lumped all of you, your moms, dads, and you two in one bucket. Since Mac died, it has been a lonely life for Gran. She and I keep each other going, she has the art community here, and she sees people at the grocery store where she works, or worked, not sure if she will go back or not. But there was a huge hole in her heart without Mac; her misery was often intense."

I thought of Gran out howling at the night sky. Maybe that was a good way to let it all out, and healthier than drugs or drinking.

I stood there watching the pot, waiting for it to boil, and considered. "Three weeks ago, the only thing I knew about my Gran was that she was an odd duck, living up here remotely on the coast, doing her own thing and not interested in us. If I had any image of Gran, it was that which our moms put in our heads through the years when they talked of Gran's misbehaviors or oddities. She definitely was not real for us, not flesh and blood reality. I had long accepted that Scott and I did not have a grandparent in our lives."

The teapot squealed and I jumped to grab it. "And now, now, things have changed so much. I think that is why I need to do this mission, whatever it is that Gran has in mind. It is so much out of the ordinary for me. I'm almost thirty and I'm ready for something different. I need to take a risk or two."

Tibby smiled at me. "Elizabeth, I've worked in the schools. And as I reminded your Gran, you took a big risk deciding to be a teacher and you put yourself in the position every day of influencing children and never knowing what might happen in your classroom. In my opinion you should definitely own that being a teacher was the risk-taking decision of your twenties. You'll always be a teacher, but perhaps there is another level of risk taking, doing something unknown for someone you are kin to but don't really know yet. Maybe this is the risk taking to start out your thirties."

I thought about this. "Why did you get out of teaching, Tibby?" Before she could answer I added the second thought that had crossed my mind. "And was it you who inspired Gran to make that little speech out there?"

Tibby's lined face broke into a conspiratorial smile.

"Caught me at my meddling! I just prod Gran to express things she is also thinking but maybe too stubborn to admit. Because you know Gran would never say anything she didn't believe. But yes, I convinced her that you and Scott deserved some respect for how you have built your lives, in order to start off this mission of mercy in a healthy way."

She grabbed the plate of humus and crackers, and I brought the tea tray, and as we walked through the door, she answered my first question. "I was a classroom aide, but I had to leave that work when our teenage son, our only child, was paralyzed in a motorcycle accident and I was needed at home to care for him. I was his caretaker for eight years until he died of an infection. Since then, I have worked part time as an aide in the schools. Still do. Until recently I was very busy with my little shop, my part-time school work, my animals, and being with Gran."

I looked at this kind woman. What heartache she had endured, yet she spoke in matter-of-fact tones, not lightly but not making it too horribly tragic.

Tibby patted my arm. "It's okay, dear. Geoffrey's loss is

always with me, as is Jim's. But I carry on and the sun comes up and goes down, and the waves crash on, and the children at school need someone to listen to them read, and so life goes on and I am a part of it. And I have Gran for my friend. I can cry with her. But you… you must make the most of your days."

We drank our tea, except for Scott who brought out a beer he had stuck in his travel bag, and we talked in general terms about what was next. Gran had a list, and the first thing on the list was to make a recording for Chelsea, Mac's daughter. She wanted to explain in her own voice what kind of man Sean MacIntosh was.

"I want her to get a flavor of him, what she would have felt and seen had he been able to get to know her." Gran's eyes filled with tears, which she brushed away impatiently. "It's so important. So important."

She turned to Scott. "You can do that for me, Prescott? You know how to make that happen?"

"Yes, Gran, we can figure out how to make that happen. Don't worry. Right now?" He looked around.

Tibby intervened. "No, Gran is wasted. She's been up more today than any day since she's been home from Santa Rosa. Gran, how about a pain pill and bed. Tomorrow's another day."

Tibby was brisk and I could see now that she had years of home nursing under her belt and Gran meekly acquiesced. "Scott, can you help me?"

So, they helped her to bed, with Gran murmuring, "Tomorrow. We'll make the recording tomorrow. That's the most important thing, that Chelsea knows what kind of man her father was."

When Tibby finished helping Gran get settled for night, she came back to us in the living room, put away her wood carving and told us she too needed to head to bed. "I never know when Gran is going to need something, although she is getting stronger and having less pain, so we are moving in the right direction. But I need to get my sleep. I've cleared out two bedrooms upstairs and put clean sheets on the beds for you two. There are towels in the upstairs bathroom. I'll stay down here with Gran."

She looked tired so I offered, "Can we take a night to help, Tibby? Give you a break?"

She smiled at me. "Elizabeth, that is very thoughtful of you, but it is getting easier every day. Last year, when I had my surgery, your Gran took care of me for several weeks, so now it's my turn and as long as I get enough sleep, I have no problem. But if you want to make breakfast, I would love not to have to do that. Cooking is not my favorite activity although I enjoy it more than Gran. Our men loved to cook. I love to bake but I have always been a 'duty cook,' and Gran simply doesn't cook at all."

Scott asked, deferentially, as if he shouldn't perhaps bring it up, "And you have no idea whether Gran's tumor is cancerous or not?"

"No. No word yet. They said it could be a while until the results are ready. Until then, we have to keep going forward as if…"

We weren't sure if she meant as if Gran was going to be

just fine, or as if Gran had little time left to live. Most likely it was just 'as if' either potential reality was right around the bend.

We slept upstairs in bedrooms that were a tad dusty, but full of interesting bits and pieces of tools, art pieces, books, and other items that I could not easily categorize. The bed was comfy enough for a good night's sleep.

The next day while I washed breakfast dishes, Scott set Gran up to record what she wanted to say. She insisted upon using an old video camera. Scott tried to get her to make something that could be easily transmitted digitally, but she felt that Mac's old camera was more concrete, giving Chelsea something tangible. Scott tried to say that most people no longer had access to equipment to view old movies, but Gran was firm. Scott shrugged and let her have her way.

She had a script in her hand, something penned out over the last weeks, but soon after Scott gave her the go ahead, she lifted her eyes off the page and gazing out the window, just started talking. We didn't interrupt.

She told Chelsea of Mac's upbringing, his move from his native Edinburgh to the coast of Maine, and then his return to Scotland for a few years to be there for his mother in her last decline. She mentioned Mac's brother Richard and that they were estranged, and that even after Chelsea had tracked down Mac's brother, Richard had not bothered to let Mac know. Then Gran told of Mac's return to the US and how he made his way across country in his old VW bus, working as a migrant carpenter, heading west slowly but surely, taking time to visit many places along the way. Gran told of his work and of his art and of his love of wine, women, and song, and she colored it so lovingly that instead of sounding wanton or irresponsible, Mac sounded like a gregarious man who drew people into his colorful world.

When she got to the part where she and Mac met, she signaled to Scott to stop the recording for a moment while she took a sip of tea and regrouped, and then she proceeded, her voice light and happy.

I enjoyed listening to the love story she laid out. I didn't stop to critique if it was all too rosy, I just savored hearing the story of our Gran and her Mac—Templeton and MacIntosh. I understood that Gran was describing the man she adored, presenting it as a gift to this man's daughter.

Gran asked for another pause before she launched into telling of the last two days of Mac's life, how he received Chelsea's letter. How he had written of it in his journal and after reading what he wrote, how Gran was convinced that Mac fully planned to be in contact with Chelsea, how he had carefully clipped out her address and no doubt put it in his pocket of the pants he wore fishing that day, or perhaps in his wallet, but neither pants nor wallet were ever given back by the sea. Gran described how Mac was washed overboard that day, despite his vast experience with the waves and the tides.

Gran spared only a few sentences to describe her own grief. Enough to let this daughter know how much he was loved and missed by his wife, but not so much as to distract Chelsea from the story of her father. Gran was a class act during all of this, that is what I saw.

Finally, Gran laid out the discoveries and the time frame. Discovering the letter and envelope from Chelsea, discovering the journal under the cushion, and finally, Mac's clavicle bone washing up on shore, confirming DNA evidence.

After another pause while Gran composed herself, she came to the conclusion of her sharing.

"As for his health, your father was the only person our age I ever met who needed no medications. I contacted his personal physician to see if Mac had shared any medical history that he may not have thought to tell me, and the doctor agreed with me that your father was exceptionally healthy. I was very sorry to hear of your misfortune in your pregnancies and will hope that..." and here Gran paused as if not quite sure what to say.

"I hope that life has treated you with more kindness than sadness."

She finished, "And so, Chelsea, this is the story of your father, a man who was more alive than anyone I ever met, well-loved, a skilled carpenter and a creative artist, and also loyal to me and to all his many friends. I swear on my own life and my knowledge of my beloved husband, that if your father had known of your existence, it would have completed his happiness beyond words, and if that wave had not washed him overboard, he would have contacted you that very day. I'm only sorry that in a cruel twist of circumstances and fate, this information did not come to me sooner, but it is my wish that you will receive this news with relief and not with bitterness that it didn't happen in a timelier manner."

Gran stopped, and Scott started to turn off the recording but she waved him on and continued.

"I am sending this message through my grandson Prescott Sullivan and my granddaughter Elizabeth Kuiper. They are doing me the honor of delivering this recording and this package of photos and mementos of your father to you in person. I myself am unable to travel anymore. I send you good wishes from the Mendocino Coast of California."

When Gran finished, she looked drained and Tibby quickly hurried her off to rest. When I watched them walking together down the hallway, their backs to us, I was imagining those two friends as wild young women, dancing and building houses, and making love to the men in their life.

I felt an upwelling urge to protect them, these two aging women. I had that same feeling sometimes when I was giving a test in my classroom and I saw all the young heads bent over their pages, pencils in hand, some faces smooth and composed, some scrunched up in agony and uncertainty, some faking boredom while staring out the window as if they didn't care. I would gaze at them all with a tremendous protectiveness, regardless that earlier that period some had been nothing but irritating.

Scott looked up at me and grinned. "Well, seems like Gran was married to a saint, Saint Mac! Wonder how Chelsea will receive this oral missive?"

I was jarred out of my lovely reflection by Scott's more cynical take. But I staunchly defended. "I thought it was a beautiful reflection on the man Gran loved, and remember this video is for a woman who never knew her father. Can you imagine? And why not give her something she can hang on to and admire?"

Scott shrugged. "You're probably right, but we are all making a big assumption here, you know. We don't know if this Chelsea is all sweet and philosophical, or if she is madder than hell at her old man for never acknowledging her and for her mother for giving her away. Or," and here he looked over his shoulder to see if Gran and Tibby had truly disappeared. "...we don't know whether she might want to come after any assets Gran might have inherited from Mac as his wife. These legal things can crop up with DNA upheavals."

I stared at him. I guess I had been living in a dream world as much as Gran. I had not thought of these unpleasant possibilities.

I put it to Scott, "So if these shitty reactions are so possible, why are you so eager to take this trek?"

He looked at me for a moment and then said, "Lizzie, sometimes you have to follow through on things, even if you don't know what the outcome will be. I think Gran is doing the right thing, but I'm sure that no matter what a gem Mac was, he was not perfect. And I also want us to be prepared that Chelsea McGowan may have all sorts of mixed feelings about our arrival."

"Yet you are still committed to go?"

"Oh, hell yeah. I'm ready for an adventure, haven't seen any of what they call the fly-over country, only been to DC and New York and Chicago, all by plane. I've been in a rut of working and fixing up cars, and as long as we are prepared for anything when we get there, I'm totally up for it!"

I must have looked disillusioned because he came over and lightly punched me in the shoulder as he did when we were preadolescents, and comforted me. "Hey Lizzie, it'll be a blast. I just want us to be prepared for anything, and we can always be the buffer between any bad reaction on Chelsea's part and Gran's tender feelings."

I thought about it and saw his point. "You know Chelsea may react one way and then come to different conclusions after she sits with it for a time. You and I have always known who our parents are so it's hard to imagine what it would be like to not know, and then find out, and then reach out and not have that parent respond. And she must have loyalty to her adoptive parents. Yeah, it has to be a little overwhelming. Her life has been very different than ours."

"Other than we have only now discovered our Gran."

"We always knew of her existence."

"Yes, but we didn't know her until a few weeks ago."

"But at least our parents didn't hide her existence from us!"

Tibby returned and motioned us to a side table with some packages on it. "Your Gran is too tired to go over this with you now, but she wanted me to show you what else goes with you tomorrow when you take off."

I looked at Scott. So, tomorrow was the day.

Tibby picked up a slender latched wooden box. Like everything in Gran's possession, it was not an ordinary nondescript box. It was painted with an elaborate design. "Inside are the photos Gran picked out to send to Chelsea. She wanted them in this box because Mac painted it, but I thought just in case it might get wet, it should be in something waterproof so here is my Jim's kayak bag to put all of these things in for travel.

I laughed out loud, "Tibby we don't plan on swimming many rivers with this in our arms."

She nodded. "Most likely, I'm being over cautious, but things happen you know, things out of our control."

Tibby went on to the next package. "These are a few tools from Mac's workshop, just some of the smaller ones."

The tools, a hammer with a well-used wooden handle, a Phillips head screwdriver, a small level, and measuring tape, and a few other items were held in a leather bag, embossed with Mac's name and a design of trees and what looked like deer or elk.

"That's beautiful!" Scott was impressed.

Tibby nodded as she put the tool bag inside the kayak bag, too. "Yes, Mac was very talented, half carpenter and half artist."

The next package was larger and Tibby carefully unwrapped the cloth that surrounded a kilt.

"Mac's family plaid?" I asked.

"Yes, and so Chelsea's too."

"Did Mac ever wear it?"

"Yep, on special occasions and I hear occasionally for wild times with Gran." Tibby grinned and then went on to the next item.

A woven basket with a lid and latch held a variety of smaller items, including a wooden pipe, a coffee mug, a flask, a silver belt buckle with a fishing man engraved on it, and a hand-knitted stocking cap. The basket also went inside the kayak bag.

Then Tibby stopped before going on to the last two items on the table. "Gran's instructions are very specific for the rest of this." We nodded dutifully.

She picked up an envelope. "Inside here are two photos which may or may not be pictures of Marlena who may or may not be Chelsea's mother. Gran searched through boxes of Mac's things, things he hadn't looked at since their marriage, boxes that had been moved many times over the years. Judging by the date printed on one, we thought it was a reasonable but by no means sure bet that this is Chelsea's mom. Gran is relying on your judgement, your intuition about Chelsea when you meet her as to whether she is capable of handling the lack of surety about who these pictures may be. It would be helpful if perhaps Chelsea resembles her mother, so study these photos carefully. There's a third photo of Mac with this same woman taken about that same time period."

"That's all pretty unscientific," Scott protested.

"Yes, Gran is aware," Tibby scolded him. "But sometimes that's all we have to go on, intuition."

"And observation," I added. "I get it, Tibby. I'll do my best for Gran."

"And for Chelsea," Tibby added. "This young woman apparently has no idea who her mother is or what she might look like."

Tibby moved to the last item. It was another beautiful bag. This one was fabric with colorful needlepoint embroidery; I thought it looked like an Eastern European quilt exhibit I saw at a museum once. Tibby opened the bag's draw strings and carefully extracted a leather-bound book.

I realized what it was. "Mac's journal! My God, I'm shocked Gran would give it away!"

"It was not an easy decision," Tibby agreed. "But she told me that she knew it should go to Mac's daughter, well… she said it should go to Mac's daughter if she seemed worthy of it. Those were Gran's words, 'worthy,' and that is why she wants you two to go in person so you can discern her…" Tibby seemed self-conscious about using the word… "worthiness."

"You are telling me that we have to decide if Chelsea gets Mac's journal?" Scott was incredulous.

"That's a fair amount of responsibility on us," I added.

Tibby patted my arm. "I know it sounds big, doesn't it? But listen, you can only do what you can do, and whatever decision you make will be the right one. Gran couldn't decide herself, felt she was too close to the situation, so she wants you to help her."

I spelled it out. "We are to meet Chelsea, deliver all the other items, let her listen to Gran's message, and then whatever our intuition tells us, we decide whether to gift Chelsea with these photos and her father's journal or bring them back home to Gran?"

"That's about the long and the short of it, Elizabeth. Are you up for it?" Tibby looked at both of us.

At some level I could understand where Gran was coming from. "I think I do get it. But I am still surprised that Gran would give up the book that holds Mac's life and thoughts in his own handwriting! Seems like that would be something she would take to the grave with her!"

Tibby put the journal back in the decorative bag which she slid into the kayak bag with the other items. "I was very surprised myself, at first. However, Gran explained that besides her memories, she has everything of Mac that she needs in the house and in all his artwork. Even the waves that took him, she feels are something she shares with him. She felt it was time to give his words to his daughter, 'if she is worthy!' I guess she reread the journal several times and realizes there are references to Mac's home in Scotland and his upbringing that might give Chelsea a sense of her heritage. And frankly it will also give Chelsea an idea of her father's humanness, flaws and all. Despite all that Gran said in her tape message, it would be an insult to Mac to portray him as a paragon of virtue! He'd hate that, even to his daughter!"

"If she is worthy," I mused. Interesting.

Tibby suddenly looked brisk. "Okay, that is done. Gran may want to go over it with you in the morning, but I think mostly she wants you to get off on the road as soon as possible."

I was suspicious that perhaps these two were hiding something from us. "Tibby, is Gran sicker than she is telling us? Is that why she wants us to get going? And if that is so, why don't we just fly? Why this insistence that we drive all the way to Ontario?"

"The docs still say she should make a full recovery from the surgery. They are not saying anything about the malignancy, but Gran wants to be prepared for anything, so that is part of her urgency. The other part is that this has hung over her for too long, knowing that Mac's wishes have not been carried out, and that Mac's daughter has not had the connection with her father she was seeking three years ago.

"And as for the driving instead of flying? It has to do with Mac's drive from Maine to California all those years ago. He always went on about how his experiences transformed him. I think it may be Gran's one regret in life, that she never did a big road trip, so I believe this driving part of the plan is something she concocted for you two. She wants her grandkids to not miss out because now she knows that she waited too long for herself. She will never leave the North Coast. This house is hers and Mac's. The ocean is her companion, despite all it took from her; it gives her comfort and renews her vitality every day. It's exactly what she got from Mac, comfort and excitement, stability and passion. She couldn't wait to leave the hospital in Santa Rosa after surgery, believe me! I could not drive her home fast enough!" Tibby chuckled.

Sitting on the floor around the coffee table that night after the older women had gone to bed, Scott and I studied the maps, both our phone and the paper maps that Gran had laid out for us. We made some rough jabs at our itinerary but decided to keep it loose and flexible.

When Scott checked his email for the tenth time in the last hour, I figured it must be Gina, but no. When he saw the message he had been looking for, he shouted, "Whew!"

I looked at him quizzically.

"Chelsea. She finally responded to my email from two

weeks ago. She will be home and when we get there she will let us know where we can meet."

"You mean, you are just now hearing from her?" I never asked, assuming it was all arranged. "You were willing to set off tomorrow not knowing if she even wanted to see us, or in fact, if she still lived where she was living...? And where does she live by the way? Would be nice to know where we are going."

"Relax, Liz! True I had not heard back from her and this could have all fizzled, or she might have moved to Florida or back to Scotland. And that would have made this mission a lot more complicated!" He laughed. I was astonished at how relaxed he was about all of this. I, on the other hand, felt unsure.

"I had an email address I got through her ancestry research, and I wrote to her to tell her that we have information about her father that we think she would like to hear and we will be coming to Canada soon, hoping she will be willing to meet us. I just figured in time she would get back to me."

"Unless it was an old email address? Or unless she has no interest in seeing us? Unless she's moved? Or..." I was sputtering.

"Sorry. I don't mean to upset you. I've been a little worried too, but somehow it seemed part of the adventure to have to figure something out when we got closer."

"What will Gran think if we have no way to get in touch with Chelsea?" I demanded.

"Listen," he said and leaned in to me. "Gran needs us to take off and go try to find Mac's daughter. If we can do so, that will be awesome for all of us, hopefully Chelsea too. But if we can't connect with her, Gran will still know she did her best to track her down and I will keep working on it, too. It's all for the best that we take off tomorrow and see what happens. And you and I get a road trip across North America."

I wasn't entirely convinced, but Scott was as certain as I have ever seen him. Then again, he had Gina at the other end of the drive. I was going to have to take a big swallow of letting go and get in the car in the morning.

I asked one more thing. "Do we at least know where she lives, what city?"

He looked back at his phone. "Peterborough, Ontario."

Now I breathed easier. We had a real place. A city we were going to put in our GPS for the end of our mission, the end of our road. It was this moment that our mission began to feel real to me, not to be defined as a lark anymore.

16

After breakfast, Gran walked slowly but determinedly to the front porch before we did. Instead of sitting in her familiar chair, she stood by the railing and looked out to sea. We hauled our bags out; ready for an early start.

"You have all of my gifts to Chelsea?" she queried.

"We do, Gran. All of them."

"And Tibby gave you the instructions?"

"Yes, and we fully understand, Gran."

Gran was silent then and her hands grasped the railing, as if squeezing something vital out of the old wood.

Then she reached in her pocket and handed Scott a credit card. "Here, take this. I said I wanted to fund this trip, so you can use my card for gas and hotels and food."

Scott put it back in her hand. "No, Gran. If we take your card, which you only use around here, and suddenly we are charging food and gas and more, day after day, your bank is going to contact you about fraud, and they will bug you, as they should, and even if you tell them that we are authorized, it will take time and energy. Plus, if we do happen to lose your card or have it stolen, then your bank will not know it wasn't just us, the authorized users, making charges."

Gran stared at him as if he were a genius, but she was disturbed. She wanted to fund the trip, she insisted.

I jumped in. "Okay, Gran, how about this. Scott and I will use our credit cards, and when this trip all done and we are home again, we can settle up with you."

She agreed reluctantly, and with that matter cleared up, we came to the interesting moment of saying goodbye. We each gave her a gentle post-surgery hug, exchanging a more robust one with Tibby. Then we stood on the grass in front of the porch. Gran stayed on the porch and looked down at us. It was fitting. She only needed a scepter like an old-fashioned queen bidding her explorers to sail off on a grand adventure in her name. We would be driving in an aptly named vehicle, Explorer!

While we would have cell phones and credit cards and modern interstate highways on which to drive our almost brand-new vehicle for this mission, standing there looking up into Gran's face, my imaginative mind enjoyed the fantasy of being sent off to the dangerous high seas facing unknown experiences, all inspired by loyalty to the queen.

Her imperious demeaner was belied by the quaver in her voice. "Elizabeth, you have the journal? You'll take good care of it? You understand what to do?"

"Yes, Gran. I understand completely. I will guard it every day."

"Good."

And as we finally turned, bags jostling from our shoulders and clutched in our hands, and walked across the meadow to the garage tunnel, Gran called out one more time, apropos of nothing except perhaps to entice Scott to come back when it was all over. "Prescott?"

Scott turned. "Yes, Gran?"

"When you get back, I will show you what's in my garage."

We stood there, expecting more, but Gran suddenly looked tired and turned to go sit in her chair. Only Tibby stood on the stairs waving goodbye. We gave a final wave before turning down the branch-covered path, then headed to the silver Explorer with the Nevada license plates, loaded up our baggage into the pristinely clean storage space, and jumped in.

On impulse, Scott ran back and putting his hands up to the windows of the garage, he tried to see what was inside. He came back to the car, and when I said, "Well?" he shrugged. "Can't tell, the windows are covered with paper. Guess I'll have to wait until we get home. Gran is a tease!"

The gravel crunched under our wheels as we drove away from the abalone shell MacIntosh & Templeton lettering on the old stone garage, paused at the crossroads of Gran's gravel road and Highway One, looked at each other and then turned north. We were truly off.

Part 3
Crossing America

17

The first day was easy. Gran had given us no time table, no preferred route. I'll hand it to her; she did not at any point try to micromanage our journey. Whether she was too tired to do so, whether she had trust in us, or whether she felt her part of the whole venture—her responsibility—was absolved once she sent us on our way, I'm not sure.

We wanted to explore along the coast before we traveled across the country. Heading north, we stopped to climb the picturesque Point Arena light house that towered a hundred feet or more over our heads. It was foggy below when we started up the steep winding stairs encased in the slim white tower but when we got to the top, the fog had lifted, and from the balcony that circled the top, our view was as spectacular as we could have hoped. We stood there looking out at the forever sea, sharing the sky with gulls and pelicans, breathing in the ocean air, and we took the sunshine to be a good omen for our trip.

On we went up the coast around hairpin turns with sharp drop-offs to the crashing waves. Finally, we arrived in Mendocino Village where we had lunch surrounded by flowers at a garden café and then walked along the bluffs. At one point we stopped to study the sea, thinking the timeless thoughts that millions of people have done before us when faced with so much grand power. Scott turned around and faced the town, resting his elbows on a fence post, seemingly still caught up in thought. I turned and tried to follow his gaze but all I saw beyond the village itself were charming homes with white picket fences and tall brown water towers with nasturtiums flowing like orange waterfalls. The forests made a lovely backdrop to the town. It was a very appealing sight, but Scott was not one to wax eloquent on charming scenes.

I bumped his elbow, causing his head to drop off his hand support. He pushed me gently in response.

"Okay, Prescott," I said, imitating Gran. "What's going on in your mind?"

He shrugged. "Lizzie, no offense to you whatsoever, but this is a town for lovers, not cousins."

He seemed about to say more but stopped.

"No offense taken, Scotty," I responded and patted his arm sympathetically.

He kept staring towards the town, where not too far in front of us, the breeze made a young woman's hair and skirt fly out behind her, and even from a distance we could hear her laugh as she grabbed for her hat with the help of attentive young man who laughed with her as their bodies melted into a kiss.

I grabbed Scott's hand and pulled him on down the path. "Let's hit the road, I promised Nellie we'd stop at the botanical gardens in Fort Bragg. That'll be less romantic so you will have nothing to groan about!"

Scott, released from his funk, challenged me to a race like

when we were kids, and we ran back to where we had left our car. (I won, but then again, I am a good runner.)

The gardens were every bit as lovely as Nellie had told me. Scott dutifully accompanied me walking around the well-kept inner flower beds and lawn, but when we pushed open the artfully crooked wooden gates created to separate the outer wilder gardens from the inner deer-protected areas, he led the way exploring narrow paths, through huge rhododendron trees and bushes (many in pink, red, and white bloom), and crossing bridges over small but rushing creeks. We found a little protected shelter with views out to a cove where thundering waves smashed on the rocks below us, and we soaked in the multi-sensory experience. It had been mostly an obligation stop, to appease Nellie the horticulturalist, but we were hooked and afterwards in the gift shop I bought a long-sleeved tee shirt with bright golden poppies and a quail, topknot shining. Scott bought a small ceramic harbor seal. I looked at him. "Really?" I challenged his sentimentality.

He actually blushed. "Well, it's not a beaver, but…" And left it at that.

We stayed at an inn over the harbor, starting off our journey with a degree of luxury, separate rooms with views over the fishing boats and sea lions who barked us awake in the morning. The waiter gave us an idea for a hike, which we did, and then we drove down the coast back past Mendocino to head inland, away from the ocean. I wondered when we would be back by the Pacific. But it was time to start heading east.

Inland through massively tall redwoods and then rolling farmland, some apple orchards and mostly wine grapes. We stopped in Booneville where Scott went into a brewery and I enjoyed a pleasant sit out in a garden with a book.

I was lost in my book when Scott was standing over me grinning and looking light-headed. "Scott Sullivan, it's not even noon and you're blasted. What's got into you?"

He shrugged. "Really good beer" is all he offered.

I stood up and held out my hand. "I'm driving, buddy."

He hesitated only a moment and then pulled the keys out of his pocket and handed them to me. "You know how to drive this big car? It's not your little Civic, you know."

"Don't have much choice, Cuz. I'll take it slow until I get used to it."

I got behind the wheel and Scott sat in the passenger seat making unnecessarily elaborate efforts to adjust the space for his long frame. It felt like a passive-aggressive slap at me for being responsible. I decided I didn't like it, but then again, knew that this was not the time to argue or reason with all the good beer fuzzing his brain.

And off we went, me driving cautiously at first, especially with Scott watching, but soon the effects of our morning hike coupled with the beer and lack of food put my cousin into slumber land. I relaxed and started to enjoy the drive down a nice open highway, with just enough curves to make it interesting but not so many as to make it work. More wineries eventually gave way to more twists in the road accompanied by scrub oak trees and typical California hills and ravines. Traffic was enjoyably light.

I was just getting into the rhythm of the drive, Scott snoring beside me, music on the radio, when as I came around a corner, I saw a small car in front of me veer right and almost go off the road, then sharply shoot left and then right again, this time disappearing out of sight over the side of the road, as if threading a needle between two sets of guardrails.

"Oh my God!" I said under my breath, and repeated over and over and over as I slowed our car and found a place to pull off the road just past where the car had flown out of sight.

When I stopped, I set our parking brake and emergency flashers with trembling hands, and I started to wake Scott but thought better of it. I didn't need my tipsy cousin to fall off the cliff, too.

My heart was pushing my pulse so hard I thought my head would explode with the noise. I looked both ways up and down the road but no cars were coming in either direction. I was alone. As I pulled out my phone, I gazed down into the ravine and fingers shaking punched in 911.

At first, I saw nothing down the steep hillside. I told myself to try to remember what kind of car it was. Surely someone would want to know that, and as witness—the only witness apparently—I should be an accurate reporter. It had all happened so quickly. What had I seen? I focused harder to remember.

Then I spotted a bright blue color far below me. Ah, that was it, a blue sedan, and as my Giants-fan uncle would have pointed out with a degree of disdain, a Dodger-blue car. (I could see only a bit of the blue and I finally realized why.

The car was upside down, leaning sideways, wheels facing the sky like an upside-down turtle. My stomach heaved but just then the 911 operator answered. That was a relief, cell phone coverage out here was spotty but in between breakups in the coverage I was able to give the information, although I wasn't entirely sure where we were in relation to towns, but at least I knew the road and knew how long ago we left Booneville.

The operator said she would call back to check. Scott had not emerged from our car, so I sat down on the guardrail to wait for help. I figured it could be a while but I didn't know what else to do. I was in no way capable of climbing down the hillside to check for life. But I couldn't sit, I jumped up and paced back and forth, my eyes never leaving the upside-down Dodger-blue car.

Soon I heard the cry. Made my hair stand on end which is something I always thought was a literary expression. I'm here to tell you it is real. I peered down and saw someone pulling themselves out of the car window. I waved my arms and willed that person to look up at me so they would know that help was coming. I focused my gaze with an intensity that left me with a headache. I was rewarded when a face turned skyward. I waved again and now shouted.

I was transformed into a magnetic force. I was sure that those eyes below locked onto mine as the person climbed slowly out of the open car window to drop to the ground and then stand upright, stagger, fall, get up, crawl on hands and knees, hold onto a branch of the scrub brush next to the car, put their arms around the oak tree that had stopped the car's farther descent down the embankment. She—for it was a she, I thought—had long black hair, jeans, a multi-color shirt, and made noises like a wounded animal that carried all the way up to me, haunting and clear. She moved, upward, then slid back down in the dirt, then upward again.

My mind went through what was in the back of our Explorer that might be helpful. I wanted my cousin beside me, not sleeping off a stupid mid-day beer binge. I wanted to do something, but I came up empty of anything helpful. I thought briefly of tying my clothes together to throw to the woman but that wouldn't make it remotely close to her. So, all I could do was keep my eyes on her to will her up that hill.

When would help arrive? The 911 operator called me back and told me help was on the way. "Hurry!" I almost screamed at the poor woman. "There's someone trying to climb up the hill!"

"They'll be there as soon as they can," the operator told me in her professionally calm manner. I wanted this woman to be hysterical like me and move mountains to get help to arrive, send helicopters or the national guard or something. Instead, she asked me informational questions about what I was seeing below me. Below me, the woman was making slow progress, falling down as often as she pulled herself up the hillside grabbing branches and pushing against rocks. I gestured wildly to encourage her, calling out to her, straining my own shoulders and arms, imploring her to make it to the top where I could at least give her a last helping hand to join me on the roadside shoulder.

An eternity passed. Or perhaps time stood still. Or maybe it all happened in a blink.

I stood there, leaning forward over the guardrail. My whole life had come down to this spot and this woman. She lay down once and didn't move for a few seconds. I came unglued and screamed at her, "Get up, get up, get up, don't stop, don't give up! Help is coming!"

I don't know if she heard me screaming, but Scott must have because suddenly he was beside me looking completely alert. I took my eyes off the woman and turned to my cousin, thankful to see him. I pointed wildly down the hill until he saw what I had been screaming about.

At that moment the woman lurched upright and stood as well as she could on that steep hillside, hands resting on a large boulder and she looked up to us, both Scott and me now, and her face was what I can only describe as demented. She called out something we couldn't decipher.

"My God, she's all bloody!" Scott said under his breath.

I looked again, and he was right. What I had taken to be a colorful shirt was a white shirt with spreading red coloring, now mixed with dirt from the hillside as she fell. There was blood on her face, too. I suppose the good news is that she was making enough progress climbing up the hill that we could see her better.

"You called 911?"

I nodded. "Someone is supposed to be on the way. Feels like it was hours ago, but I've lost track of time."

Scott ran back to our car and returned with a rope.

"Where did you get that?"

Scott began tying the rope around the guardrail post. "Jerry."

"Jerry? Jerry from Gualala?"

"Yes. He gave it to me the other day. Said no one should be driving around the north coast or across country without a few supplies just for emergency."

Scott gave it a tug to make sure it was secure, leaning his body away from the knot to make sure it would hold.

"What are you doing?"

"Going down to see if I can help her."

"Is the rope long enough?"

"Probably not to where she is now, but if I can get closer, I can at least talk to her and find out who else is in the car."

"Maybe I should go, Scott." I don't know why I said that, but somehow, I felt this was my encounter, this woman was mine to help, although what had I been able to do thus far?

Scott just gave me a look, all the while tightening the rope. "Maybe you'll not make fun of me with my weight lifting. While you are out hiking and jogging, I'm lifting weights, Lizbeth."

I grabbed his arm. "Hey, Scott, I'm glad you're here."

He nodded and looked over the side of the embankment where the woman had stopped her ascent. Was she resting? Or unable to exert any more effort? I wondered where she got the strength to make it as far as she had, especially while injured.

I glanced at Scott again and looked for any fear in his face but saw only concentration. A few hours ago, he had been drinking happily in a bar, talking with the bartender, and now he was heading over a railing at a vertical drop. This was not in his normal routine, weight lifting or no weight lifting. I took a moment to look up and down the road but saw and heard nothing.

Scott jumped over the guard rail, positioned his feet and gripped the rope in his hands, tugging it once again to check his knot. I instinctively, if not realistically, grabbed my hands over the rope too as if I could hold him if it slipped loose.

He looked at me and asked, "Lizzie, what do I say to her when I get down there?" It felt like a strange question under the circumstances and before I could answer he added, "You would be so much better at this."

Out of my teaching experience came the answer. "Just get her to talk, and listen to her. Let her know you are there but don't try to tell her what to do. Just be with her so she knows she's not alone." I was thinking of certain students, who when they lost control of themselves, needed just a listening ear for a time.

Scott nodded, turned his phone on by his ear pods, and then started letting himself down the embankment, holding the rope like a rope climber rappelling down a rock face. This wasn't Yosemite, but it was steep enough that gravity would be hard to battle against. I held my breath and hoped Jerry's rope was a new one.

He inched his way down, gravel and dirt sometimes pushed downhill by his hiking shoes, which fortunately he had not taken off since our morning hike back in Fort Bragg. The woman lifted her head to watch, and now I could see how young she looked. She didn't cry out anymore. Scott's rope let him get down twenty-five or thirty feet or so, but not all the way to her. But it was close enough that he began to talk to her. I couldn't understand what she said, her voice was weak and the wind was picking up.

Then I heard my phone ring. There must have been a cell tower somewhere close by in this wild land! Scott was calling me. He murmured to me, "She keeps saying her babies are in the car. That's all she can say. She's getting very worked up."

Oh God. Children! "Scott," I said urgently. "If she talks about them now, she'll waste all her energy getting hysterical again. Tell her help is coming, and then start talking to her about something you've done recently, just get her to listen to a story, get her mind somewhere else, talk about… I don't know, cars or sports or something."

And I hung over the guard rail and watched my cousin hang on to his rope, resting one boot on a large rock and the other he pushed into the slippery dirt, and I heard him over the phone begin to talk to her. This stranger lay prone on the dirt, blood flowing down from a head wound and her scratched arms, her torso showing a large gash in her chest when she propped herself up on her elbows, face stricken, eyes closed, sometimes fluttering open. In a calm voice, somewhere between compelling and boring, Scott first told her that he would stay down there with her until help arrived and then he began to describe how he installed a new carburetor on one of his vintage cars.

It was so bizarre; I can't begin to describe it. But I could see the woman relax, and even open her eyes from time to time and look at Scott. In the middle of his recitation, I whispered into my phone, "Scott, ask her what her name is, just in case she passes out before help gets here."

Scott put his thumb up to me and I heard him say to the woman, "By the way, that's my cousin up there on the road. She's called 911 to help. Her name is Elizabeth. I'm Scott. What's your name?"

She said something, I could see her lips moving. Scott said to me over the phone, "Her name is Angelica." A minute later she said something else, and Scott added to me, "Angelica Fontane, or something like that."

And at that moment came the most beautiful sound in the world, the sound of a siren fading in and out as it approached.

"Scott! I hear a siren! They're coming! They're coming!"

I jumped up and left my post, only remembering later that I had been holding the rope for emotional support for Scott. Apparently, Jerry's rope and Scott's muscles were more than up for the task. I turned to the road and looked both left and right, not being sure at first from which direction our deliverance would come.

And then it was upon me, bursting around the corner and pulling up into a hasty stop as I waved the first vehicle down, a CHP car followed soon thereafter by a fire truck, and then another one more. The troops had arrived. Something huge relaxed inside my chest.

Two officers came out of the CHP car and one walked towards me. I tried to be coherent. When the rescuers arrived, Scott turned to climb back up the hillside but it was tough and he didn't scorn the help of the first climbers on the scene who assisted him.

When he got to the top and put his leg over the guard rail, I grabbed him mid-climb and hugged him harder than ever before in my life. He hugged back and I could feel him shaking, or perhaps that was me. To be occupied, he pulled put the rope—Jerry's rope—and wound it around and around, his eyes watching his hands as if to make sure his hands did this menial task correctly.

The team of responders worked as if this kind of accident was all in a day's work, as it was. And one of the officers took my report, asking questions while writing down my information and name, etc. My eyes stayed on the action. It didn't take long for the woman to be lifted up the remaining fifty feet on a stretcher and put in the ambulance that had arrived. With her last remaining strength, the woman was resisting going into the ambulance. She looked at me, beseechingly. I left the officer and ran over to her.

Up close I saw how young she was, between the bruising, cuts, blood, and dirt, her face was probably unrecognizable to anyone who knew her, only her eyes blazed clear. As the medics worked on her vitals, I said to the officer who was trying to get me away from the stretcher. "She won't want to leave her babies down there. Can't she wait to see if they are okay?"

The medic turned to me. "She needs to get to a hospital right away. They are going down now to search the car." He turned and leaned in to the woman, "Don't worry. We'll take care of your kids. But we have to take care of you first."

Impulsively, because I felt such a bond with young Angelica over the last harrowing hour, I touched her hand gently, and said to her, "I'll stay here until your babies are out of the car, Angelica. I'll stay here."

The woman closed her eyes and gave me the slightest squeeze back on my hand and did not protest anymore. She was put into the ambulance, which soon raced off, back the way it came.

"Where will they take her?" I asked the officer.

"Cloverdale probably, unless she needs more help, and if so, they'll airlift her to Santa Rosa." The officer looked at me. "We don't need you to stick around. This could take a while, that car is pretty far down, and well..." The officer cleared her throat and looked away for a minute. "...Well, sometimes these things don't work out well."

Scott had joined me by then. The officer looked at him as though perhaps he could talk some reason into me. "If you just finish telling me what you saw, I can write my report and I will have your names and numbers and will get in touch if we need more information."

I stubbornly shook my head. "I promised." And I had, but the truth was I needed to know for myself whether Angelica's 'babies' were okay. And I needed to know if they were not okay, too.

The officer started to force us to leave, but then stopped and went out to direct traffic because suddenly there were cars again—rubberneckers now—and she never got back to us. Scott and I stood to the side, silently watching what was going on down the steep canyon. Some of the adrenaline had left me, perhaps Scott too, but he didn't try to get me back in the car. All signs of his alcoholic buzz had long disappeared. We both leaned against our Explorer and watched.

I could hear some of the discussion among the rescue team. Apparently, they often used helicopters during this kind of rescue, but the terrain and the trees didn't lend itself well for a helicopter to come in. Instead, the climbers rappelled down past where Scott had been, and on down the steep ravine Angelica had climbed up. As they looked into the car, I heard a shout and the veteran 911 team broke into cheers. My gut relaxed just a bit.

We kept our distance, afraid that the officer would chase us on our way if we interfered. But now she strode over to us and said, "They tell us that the children are strapped in their car seats still and at least at first appearance are okay."

I wanted to weep. "How will they bring them up?"

"Depends upon how big the kids are. We'll see." And she walked away, but she didn't tell us to leave. Scott put his arm around me and squeezed my shoulder.

They got those little ones up the mountain. In their innocence the kids probably thought it was all fun, each attached to the back of a climber who clambered up the steep ravine by rope, making it look easy. What muscles these climbers must have under their protective clothing! When the little ones arrived at the top and the medics swooped in to take them to the ambulance, I got a glimpse of the little faces, big eyes, snotty noses, and all.

If only Angelica could recover fully, I thought, she and her babies could be together again. My muscles lost the tension that had held me so tightly and, in its place, a huge fatigue began to creep in.

A happy ending to a terrible event.

Then we heard shouting, loud enough that everyone at the top of the hillside walked over and looked down the steep embankment. There one rescuer remained, and he had gone down farther than the upside-down car. His partners up on the road turned on their radios and listened to him. Then they shared the news. "There's a body down there. Looks like he was thrown from the car."

A silence fell on everyone except the responders who jumped back into action, only this time instead of search and rescue, they were doing a retrieval. Their whole demeanor changed. It was palpable.

Now the officer walked over to me once again. "Can you tell me again what happened when the car went off the side?"

I closed my eyes to bring back the memory and slowly recited. "As best I can remember, and it was just a fleeting look when I came around that bend…" and I motioned back to the curve in the road, "…the car swerved right as if it would go off the road suddenly, and then over-corrected to the left, crossed the center line, and then veered back sharply right directly off the road and disappeared, right there where there is no guard rail."

I know that memory is often unreliable. Still, it had just happened and it was so vivid. I hoped I was accurate.

The officer took notes. "And did you see that also, sir?" She turned to Scott.

He had the decency to blush. "No, I was sleeping. Elizabeth was driving and I was taking a break." He added as if it mattered, "We're on a road trip."

The officer looked at him and decided he had nothing to offer, so she turned back to me one more time. "Do you think there was another person in the car, male or female?"

That I could answer. "I had no chance to see anyone in the car."

She had nothing more to ask me. I figured what she was trying to ascertain for her report was whether someone had grabbed the wheel and forced the car off the road. She'd have to ask Angelica that question.

Scott called after the officer. "I talked to Angelica on the hillside before you all got here. She only talked about her babies; she was scared for them. She didn't mention anyone else in the car with her."

I chimed in. "When she climbed out of the window of the car, she was crying so loud that I could hear her all the way up here, and it was..." I paused, remembering, "it was awful, haunting, you know?" I looked at the officer to see if she might understand what I meant. "She climbed a mountain to get help for her babies."

The officer's stern business-only eyes looked at me for a minute and then she surprised me by saying, "Yes, that is what we parents do when our children are in danger." Then she resumed her official professional demeanor and turned back to where the crew was lowering a stretcher and a body bag down the hillside for a retrieval. But she stopped one more time and said over her shoulder. "You know, if you hadn't seen the car go over the side, it's possible that no one would have known to look for them. We can see where the car went off the road but it didn't damage the guard rail or any kind of fence, and it is quite out of sight. You probably saved several lives today. Judging by her injuries, I don't think she could have crawled any farther. It could have been days or even weeks before they would have been found."

My mouth dropped. I had not thought of that. But then I thought of Angelica's determined effort to make it to the top and I said to the officer, "I think Angelica would have made it. She was that determined."

The CHP officer gave what approached a smile. "Go get something to eat, stop for the night and rest yourself up. These traumas can come back to hit you hard later."

Scott led me to the passenger side door and opened it for me. I allowed myself to be led. He shut the door firmly and came around and took the wheel. As we drove off, the rescue crew were all busy at the grim task at hand.

Ten miles down the road I asked Scott, "Do you think we will ever know what happened to her?"

He shrugged. "We can watch the local news, I suppose."

I nodded. It all felt so strange, such intimacy and then such detachment. I had to practice a little of that as a teacher, but this life and death stuff, well, that was beyond my experience.

"Don't you think it would take a toll on you, to do this kind of work?" I asked Scott, another rhetorical question but he answered.

"Yes, of course, dumb question, Lizzie, but I also think

it is a relief to actively help, and salvage a bad human situation."

I looked at his familiar profile. "Do you feel that relief for having gone down to be with her for that time?"

He thought about it for a time. "Yeah, I do. I mean it was pretty silly, what did I do anyway? But it felt like I was doing something."

"You were amazing, Scott. That whole long story of rebuilding a carburetor. At any party you would have bored most people to death, but I was watching her and your voice really calmed her. Good work."

"Heck, I never would have thought of that if you hadn't instructed me. I was at a total loss, but then I just did what you said and that is the first thing that popped into my head."

"Scott, I'm starving. Stop at the first place you see, please!!"

There had been nothing but trees and hills for miles, but then we rounded a curve in road and there near the entrance to the town of Cloverdale was a restaurant advertising pie.

I pointed. "There, now, stop!"

We did, and two burgers and two huge pieces of pie later, we staggered out and drove through town, back on the freeway until we got to Healdsburg where we admitted we were ready to stay for the night. That night in our hotel room (on this night we got a room with two queen beds—I think we both wanted to have company) we watched the local news sitting on our beds. A brief news item told of a car going off the road on Hwy 128. Witnesses—that would be me and only me—said a blue Hyundai sedan went over the side of the cliff. One woman was rescued and her children in the car seats were found safe. An unnamed man in his twenties was found dead nearby after being ejected from the car. The woman was listed in serious condition but expected to recover. The children, a one-year-old and a two-year-old, had no apparent injuries and were being cared for by family.

I turned off the television as the news shifted to sports. In the silence we both sat thinking of it all. I finally spoke, "All that, all that drama and life and death, the dirt, the blood, the struggle, all of that, including someone's life being snuffed out, all of that just in those few words. It's weird, isn't it?"

All Scott could say was "Yep." And he opened his computer, not so much as to shut out my meandering words, but as if to say, "Well, what can we do about it? Tomorrow is another day, and we have things to do, places to go, a mission to accomplish." See how well I know him? I know just what he was thinking. As if to verify that, he turned and looked at me and gave me a thumbs up.

"Hey, we did good today, Lizzie. And I'm glad you were driving." He cleared his throat. "Tell me when you are ready to talk about tomorrow."

I nodded and was a quiet for a long time. Eventually, I said softly, "Just one more thing, Scott. Thank goodness for Jerry's rope. What else did he give you to put in the back of our car?"

"A blanket, a first aid kit, a couple of rain ponchos, a container of nuts, and a water bottle, oh and some car stuff."

I thought about this. "Why would he do that?" I wondered aloud.

"He's a good man. And a fellow gearhead." That's all Scott said.

I opened my book and tried to get away from daily life but I had not read more than one page when I fell asleep. First thing I knew, Scott was bringing me a cup of morning tea from the lobby of the hotel. Good guy, Scott.

18

After that drama, all we hoped for the next day was to have a smooth drive and enjoy some touristy experiences.

The direct route east from Healdsburg would take us right past our home in Davis, and that felt like a regression on this mission. So instead, we found back roads to get to Sacramento and on over the Sierras. For the first dozen curves in the road, I found myself holding my breath expecting to see a car shooting off the road and down a cliff. But after we rounded more and more curves with no such calamity, I began to relax back into the drive.

Once on Interstate 80 in the Sierras, we stopped at 7,000 feet of elevation for a good hike at Donner Lake. We'd both been here before and had good memories of this place. The air was crisp and cool with huge, white cumulous clouds moving around the blue above us. The mountain midday sun let us know we were at high elevation and we kept chugging at our water bottles. We had a wade in the deep blue lake, the waters of melted snow making us catch our breath, but it felt so refreshing we had to resist the urge to jump in fully since as usual we were hungry for dinner. We ate in an outdoor café overlooking the river in the mountain town of Truckee, then still energized, we crossed the border and into Reno for the night. Scott went off to observe some casino life.

I chose to stay in my hotel room and read. Maybe Nellie is right. Maybe I am an old soul in a young body.

Instead of opening my book though, I found myself eyeing the bag that held Mac's journal. I brought all of Gran's artifacts destined for Chelsea inside our hotel room every night, not wanting to risk a car break-in. Now my curiosity got the best of me.

Gran never said not to look at it. And I wanted to know a few things. I wanted to know what we were handing over to Chelsea, should I deem her worthy enough, and I wanted to know more about Mac's cross-country travel, over thirty years ago. If we were doing a similar trek, only in reverse, to fulfill Gran's wish for us, then I figured we should learn more about what Mac's experience had been.

Fortunately, Mac was disciplined about dating his entries with not just month, but year. How helpful. He wrote using very small printing but it was legible to my teacher-trained eyes. He'd crammed a lot of living into that one journal. He didn't write every day, sometimes weeks would go by without an entry. I tried to backtrack to figure out the timing for his trip. It took a bit of figuring but I finally narrowed it down and by trial and error managed to find the entries made during his venture from east to west across the country. I began to read.

The duration of Mac's travels was a lot longer than ours would be. No way around that. Mac took the better part of a year to arrive in Mendocino County where he settled into his coastal habitat and never moved on. Scotland and the east coast and other travels were behind him. Gran and their house, plus the sea, his art, and his carpentry became everything, and he never left for more than for an occasional short vacation.

But first, his trip. Mac didn't just travel across the United States. At times he stayed to work and live for a week here, a month there; one time he spent two months working on a construction job in Wyoming, leaving only when the snow came. I found that the route he took wove north and south of Interstate 80. He crisscrossed the interstate route like a snaking vine all the way to California. His journey west followed the old Lincoln Highway, now I-80, although parts of the interstate were barely open when he drove his VW bus west, unknowingly towards what would ultimately become his Mendocino coastal home. Although headed east, we, too, were going to take this highway; just like Mac, we would drive this route for experience and expedience.

I opened up the big paper map Gran had provided for us and studied it with new eyes. I've always been fascinated with geography. We were going to have to trace his journey backwards, so when Mac arrived in Reno, where we were just starting out, he would have had many months of travel and experiences. By the time he got to Reno, he knew he was near the end of his trip. Maybe he had many more journeys in mind for himself, but then met Gran, saw the Northern California coast, and fell in love with both.

I decided to try to read Mac's journal starting in our current location since it would take too much time to go back and read his east to west notes. It was a little awkward but would have to do. I looked up when Scott came into my room with a bottle of wine and two glasses.

"So, how's casino life?" I asked him.

He shrugged. "Not as much fun as I once imagined when our parents used to come over here and leave us home with Cozy. I hate to say it, but maybe I'm getting too old for this sort of thing."

I laughed. "Did you take a look at the average age of the people gambling, Scott? I think you either love to gamble from a young age and never lose it, or you don't have a taste for it. Maybe because our parents loved it, we don't."

"Maybe. We have always had an inclination to do and like the opposite of our parents. I just keep thinking about what car parts I could buy with the money I would put down on the blackjack table."

He handed me a glass. I took a deep drink.

"Pinot?" I guessed.

"Hey, you are getting good at this. You're right."

He sprawled out in the one chair in the room. I sat on the bed. "What've you been up to? You're reading Mac's journal?"

"Yep. I decided that if I'm supposed to make this big decision about whether to trust Chelsea with Mac's journal, then I better find out what's in it. How else can I make that decision?"

"Seems reasonable," Scott agreed easily. "What have you found?"

"I'm trying to find his thoughts on what we are seeing tomorrow, going through Nevada. But it seems he cut through

Nevada pretty fast. He'd spent two months in Wyoming so maybe he was trying to get west fast before the winter snows."

I picked up the journal and paged through. Scott came over and looked over my shoulder. "How do you read his writing? It's so small."

I laughed. "Hey if I can decipher eighth grade handwriting, I can make out anyone's writing. Mac's writing is actually pretty neat, although sometimes I wonder if he's been smoking something."

Scott grinned. "Well, I have a feeling that guy would have a lot of stories to tell us. I'm sorry we never got to meet him."

"That's another reason I'm reading this journal. I want to get to know him. I mean after all, he was Gran's husband, the love of her life, someone who made her..." I started to say, "make her howl at the night sky," but that was still my secret, so I finished lamely, "...made her grieve so deeply."

Scott went back to the chair with his glass and waved to me. "So read me some."

I leaned back against the pillows of my hotel bed and flipped through the pages. "This is about it for Nevada; he must have zipped on through but I like this passage.

Just want to get to the Sierras. Ready to see Tahoe, heard so much about that lake, and see the place the Donner Party lost their luck. Putting lots of miles on Mr. Mac today. Having good car luck ever since I got that new transmission back in Des Moines. Sure, set me back a shit load of $$! But so far, it has paid off. Do want to get to California sooner than later because storms are expected to hit within a week. Not sure my old bus will make it. Don't have chains or snow tires. But I *had to make one stop today to see the wild mustangs. I've always heard about Nevada's wild horses, remember hearing about them back when I was a boy in Scotland.... Revved up my imagination of the Wild West. Christ, my time just spent in Wyoming has kind of undone my childhood fantasies about the Wild West but when I saw the horses today, way off in a distance, I had to stop and watch them. Stayed off the road for an hour just watching. The concept of being wild and free just kept dancing around in my head. What's best for a horse, to be wild and free, to run without boundaries and duties or to be cared for by a competent and kind master, if a horse can be so lucky? And how about me? What's best for me or any man? Any woman, I should add. I've thought so much about that question all my life, and seeing these free-running wild horses today just gets me thinking more about the whole dance of life.*

Scott stopped me. "Any chance we could be so lucky to see wild horses tomorrow? I wonder if they are still around these days. We gotta remember, Mac was through here, what, about thirty years ago?"

"I don't know about the horses, but why don't you Google it before you go to sleep. Thanks for the night cap."

Scott got the hint, and as I carefully put the journal back in its bag, he put our glasses on the table, corked up the wine bottle and put it in our travel cooler. With his hand on the door, he turned to me. "Hey, you doing okay with yesterday's trauma?"

I thought about it a moment. "Yeah, I think so. I mean we know the babies are okay, and we think that Angelica is going to heal, although I can't imagine how she will get past the nightmare of driving off a cliff! And we never knew there was a man down there, never saw his face, so while that is sad to know, I don't feel any connection with him."

I thought some more and added, "You know what I keep dwelling on, Scott? That hour or so, while I was single-mindedly focused on that woman as she climbed up the ravine, was overwhelmingly intense and… and personal. It was such an interconnected experience, and yet now, it is over, we move on, we have no follow-up. We just detach, and move on. I'm not saying that isn't how it should be, but it kind of blows my mind. Not that I deserve to know all the sordid details, but it's just that I'm not sure life should be so disconnected. Do you know what I mean? Shouldn't we humans have more on-going knowledge of each other?"

Scott nodded but was silent. I thought of it in another way. "It's a little like in teaching. I'm closely involved with my students for a whole year. I think about them all the time, and I know their strengths, weaknesses, their home lives, their silliness and sadness, all of that. And then they move on and for most of them I never see or hear anything about them again. Oh, a few I do, like the ones who go to prestigious schools or get signed by the Houston Astros, or have an art opening at a gallery in Marin. And on the other hand, there was one former student of mine who was arrested for murder, the negative kind of newsworthy. But mostly, as a teacher I have to detach and let my students go off into the universe hoping I have done the best for them in my small role in their life. I don't expect them to write me thank you letters. It's more like I hope I have become a good part of the unseen fabric of their life.

"I know something about detachment, but not like that CHP officer, who sees so much real-life catastrophe and somehow has to detach each time. So, to answer your question, I think I'm okay, just lots to think about."

Scott looked at me. "Lizzie, you sure can talk up a shitload of good stuff! I admire that about you." He laughed at himself. "I understand what you are saying, but I simply don't know how to talk about it."

Interrupted by a text message, he changed gear. "Okay, that's it. See you no later than 7:00 for breakfast. Let's get an early start."

19

The contents of Scott's wallet spilled across our breakfast table the next day as he searched for his credit card. I picked up a business card to save it from a large drop of hot sauce spilled on the table. I turned it around to read "Jerry Garcia Mechanic Services Hwy One Gualala California."

I held it up to Scott. "Jerry Garcia? Are you kidding me? That's Jerry's last name?"

Scott looked up. "Yeah, you didn't know?"

"No, everyone just referred to him as Jerry, and I never asked further. What a great name to go through life with."

"Possibly," Scott said gathering up his loose papers and cards and replacing them in his overstuffed wallet. "Then again, it could have been a pain in the ass to take the teasing, depending upon your personality."

I thought about this, still holding the card. "Somehow I think Jerry has the personality to handle such things," I said, thinking of his smile.

Scott put his wallet away and when I belatedly handed him Jerry's card, he waved it away. "Keep it. I have his number in my phone. You never know, you might need it someday."

I started to push back but then had a thought. "You know, I was thinking we should thank him for giving us the rope and other safety stuff."

"Go for it. His phone number is on the card." He stood up. "Time to get going."

I slip the card into my bag, already thinking of what I might write to him. I'd do it that night after I settled into my own room and right before I opened up Mac's journal. Both writing to Jerry and reading Mac's journal gave me a sense of anticipation.

Now we just had to have a smooth drive across Nevada and spot some wild mustangs, and the day would be complete.

And lucky enough, we did both. We had a smooth drive and got to see some wild horses not held within the confines of a rancher's fence or corral. Seeing them caused me to think about Mac's musings on the subject of freedom versus being part of a community, both for horses and for people. I wonder how Mac would classify his years with Gran on the north coast. Had he found the best of both, belonging to the community of his marriage and his town, but one that didn't curtail his freedom to be himself? Had he found his answer?

Besides the horses, what impressed both Scott and me about Nevada was the openness. I'm not sure whether this was a desirable impression, or simply an undeniable impression. But it was an overwhelming feature of our drive. We drove and drove, and the hills laddered with snow fences were mostly absent of trees and stretched out as far as you could see, which was a long way. But whether you found that openness tedious, or whether you found it calming—I could make a case for either—the empty-looking landscape was topped off by the most beautiful skies, ever-changing gray and white clouds that were suspended magically in the pure air, floating in invisible oxygen. Sitting in the passenger seat gazing out the window, I watched them all day long.

I imagined being above or in those clouds looking down at our silver Explorer as we moved steadily down that interstate highway, passing trucks and being passed by drivers who apparently weren't worried about speed limits: an American West version of the Autobahn. We saw no accidents, however, so the open roads of Nevada were probably as good a place as anywhere to drive fast. The name Winnemucca intrigued me in an historical and linguistic sense, but we rolled right through the little town, not being hungry or in need of a rest stop, feeling the rhythm of being on the road, music playing, in a zone. We didn't stop at any of the gambling opportunities offered along the roadway. We just kept zipping along on I-80 East, as if we knew where we were going.

And by darkness, we exited Nevada, marking the wild horses as the high point of our day, and spent the night at a non-descript interstate highway motel right after entering Utah.

That night, tucked into my bed, I spent way too much time wordsmithing the simple text to Jerry, dialing my effusiveness up and down the scale, trying to get it right. Finally, I just sent it out—deciding on a very short text—trusting it would be received in the spirit in which I sent it, although I didn't really know what that spirit was. Oh well, the day was done and sleep was needed, so after finally sending out three separate texts to Jerry, back tracking to the beginning of our trip, I put Mac's journal safely away in the bag, and went to sleep.

(What I wrote to Jerry:

Day one on top of the world at the lighthouse at PA looking down at your ocean waves and rocks and horizon, sun came out above the fog; I'm taking that as an omen.

Highway drama on day two, your rope made a difference, your kindness and preparedness saved the day and won our hearts.

Wild horses today in Nevada: question, what's best, to be wildly free or to be safely wrapped up in the confines and comfort of community? Your thoughts?

I didn't have a clue whether he would answer, this auto mechanic named Jerry Garcia, or what he might think. Had I been too effusive? Even flirtatious? But somehow, I felt liberated, out on the road, no obligations, and I thought it was a minor but enticing risk.)

(He responded to my texts the next day, briefly but luxuriously.

Sunshine from the lighthouse always makes it worth the climb, and sheds light on your path.

And to my second text:

If I could win hearts with a rope, I'd join the rodeo. I feel fairly sure it doesn't work that way with you, but I'm glad the rope came in handy.

And to the third text he said,

Your wild horse quandary is a good topic for an in-person conversation. I anticipate.)

20

Scott and I had spent very little time preparing for our trip across the USA. This trek was a spur-of-the-moment adventure taken on for Gran, and in the weeks between first meeting Gran and when we drove off, we had been madly finishing up work and preparing to be gone for an indeterminate period of time. The last thing we had time for was to learn about the land we would be driving through and the people and places we might find along the way. But we were not traveling in a covered wagon encountering natural forces that would be life or death on the journey. We had cell phones, credit cards, a new vehicle, and gas stations, cafes, towns interspersed along the way. And it was America where everyone spoke English. Therefore, we weren't too worried, the confidence of the young and the naïve perhaps.

When we drove by the Welcome to Utah sign, I asked Scott. "Quick! What can you tell me about Utah, Cousin?

He said immediately, "Salt Lake City, Mormons, Great Salt Lake...." And then he ran out of information. "You? Ms. American History teacher, you must know something about every state."

"You covered the obvious. Let's see, Brigham Young University—I had a dorm buddy who transferred from BYU. Beautiful national parks, Zion and other names I can't remember, oh, yeah, Bryce Canyon, and I think you can float in the Salt Lake." I paused, "And the Mormons came from St Louis to stake out their spot, to build their own religious community led by, I think, Joseph Smith. Oh, and the Mormon Tabernacle Choir."

I was running out of ideas before we both said at the same time, "Skiing."

And then Scott added, "Sundance Film Festival."

It is perhaps kind of pathetic that that's all we know about Utah, but I have a feeling most Americans don't know much about their own state much less about other states.

But I made up for the factoids I didn't know about Utah, by knowing exactly where it was situated in the country and the shape of the state. When I was a young girl, my dad gave me a USA puzzle, and I was obsessed with that puzzle for a long time. I put it together over and over again. I remember the shape of every state, which ones were curved or jagged along the edges following rivers to define their boundaries, and which were almost straight-lined rectangles, and which ones, like Utah had a notch out of the top so it stood out like the buttes we would see driving through Utah. I also knew all the state capitals. I just have this thing for geography. I'm honestly surprised when people glaze over when I talk about it.

But even I was surprised to discover that the western part of Utah is covered with salt flats: flat land that shimmers into the distance on all sides, white and barren. As we drove and drove through this seemingly endless scene, Scott hit his hand on the steering wheel. "Hell, of course, the Salt Flat

Land Speed races are here. I never put it together that this is where they do those races! It's here!"

I looked around at the bleached landscape, flat and straight to forever. "Well, it's a good place to do it."

After another half hour of staring out at the landscape as we sped by, I found myself sighing. "This is just such a strange place, Scotty. I've seen a thousand nature documentaries, but to be right here in the middle of this weird white world is somewhere between amazing and spooky. Wouldn't want to be stranded out here on a hot summer day, that's for sure."

Scott put on some music and said, "Relax. We were smart enough to get gas this morning, and I saw a sign for Salt Lake City so at least we know there is something ahead of us."

But my mind was in the past. "Just think of the immigrants in their covered wagons traveling about two to three miles an hour behind an ox, passing through this land. They had no road signs. No hotel or Taco Bell to look forward to. They must have wondered what kind of strange land they had found."

Scott looked around again as if he might see something new and then nodded. "Yeah, it sure was a different world for our ancestors."

"I don't know how many of our actual mutual ancestors traveled this way. Let's see, my dad's mother came from Mexico so I am one quarter Mexican, and who knows what that means because you must divide that further into part Spanish and part Indigenous, right? And my dad's father is the Kuiper, and his family came from Holland right before

World War II; thank goodness they left when they did but their immigration did not involve covered wagons! My mom thinks that Templeton is Scottish. My mom's biological dad was named Perry, and she doesn't know anything about him, so either of those families may have been covered wagon travelers. But who knows?" I thought a moment, "Maybe Gran would know more. I'll ask her."

Scott looked at me for a moment before turning his eyes back to the long straight stretch of Interstate 80. "Here I am working for Ancestry and I don't know anything about my own family other than that my dad always says "Irish, Irish, Irish." It seems obvious that I would investigate. Guess I never asked my parents."

"We had to do a project in fifth grade on our heritage. Don't you remember that? We had to ask our parents all sorts of questions, and my dad was the one who helped me. He knew some family history. Maybe because his family was a mixed-ethnic family, the story was more interesting. Mom couldn't help me out much—she was pretty vague as I recall—but with everything my dad told me I could put together my poster board and got an A. Truthfully, I might have elaborated to make it more interesting."

Scott was quiet. "I do remember that assignment now. I asked my parents to help me complete the project and they weren't interested. My dad just said, what he always said, '100% Irish! 100% Irish.'" Scott imitated Uncle Ryan's voice perfectly and I laughed.

"Bet you didn't get an A," I taunted him.

"Oh, but I did. The teacher let me do another assignment when I told her that my parents were too busy working to help me with the ancestry project."

"That's weird," I said. "Just weird. Your parents always wanted you to do well in school. Weird that they didn't help you out."

"Yeah, well, Lizzie, sometimes they were weird like that. It was a long time ago. How did we get on this topic anyway?"

"I have no idea." I considered. "Oh yeah, wondering if our great-great-whatever-grandparents crossed the Utah salt flats in a wagon. Your Irish dad didn't, not in the 1980s or whenever he arrived. Maybe the Scottish ones did. I wonder if we have indigenous blood in us, or even African blood? Who knows? I can't believe you haven't checked out our family on Ancestry, Scott."

But I think I wasn't all that surprised, actually. Scott is more interested in the technology side of things than the history of anything, except maybe classic old cars.

Soon we were talking about something else. But that's the way conversations go while moving along at 75 miles an hour, driving on the ribbon of highway that crosses through the very striking, very strange salt flats of Utah.

We did make it to the Great Salt Lake, and had to take a quick try at floating in the water. Then checked into a hotel, showered, and walked around the downtown Salt Lake City area.

I had read in Mac's journal that "just to be a wee bit onery" he had made a flirtatious pass at the young Mormon women who were passing out information in front of the Tabernacle. It wasn't appreciated, and he was ushered out of the area by some Mormon men who didn't bother to try to evangelize him. Seems like perhaps Mac had a bit of the troublemaker in his personality, too. A good match for Gran.

By contrast, Scott and I were well-behaved tourists. We admired the Tabernacle and smiled politely to the missionaries out in front of the building and then headed off to dinner.

When I got to my hotel room, I sent a text to Jerry, too sleepy to spend much time wordsmithing or worrying about what meaning I might be conveying. I just wrote,

New day, new state, straight road, templed city, not much to say so why am I writing?

Before I slipped off to sleep, my phone pinged, and thinking it was Scott, I reached over slowly but when I saw it was Jerry sending a return text, I opened my eyes wider and lifted up on one elbow to read it. And I smiled.

No reason needed, please keep writing. I'm enjoying being on the road with you, Elizabeth."

He said nothing about Scott. I liked that.

21

The rest of Utah didn't disappoint. Buttes, red cliffs, clumps of bright green trees. Rivers winding through it all. We stopped and got out to breathe it in, hike around, take some photos, and didn't feel at all bad about spending an entire day in this region.

Angelica's plummet from the road back in California seemed long ago already. That is what happens with travel where there is something new to be seen every day. But we did see our second bad traffic accident of the trip while in Utah.

The accident we came across in Utah was much more removed from us than our very personal encounter back in that California ravine, although it also involved a vehicle leaving the road and tumbling down a huge embankment. The actual event was over before we happened by, but the aftermath was dramatic to witness. We saw a semi-truck sprawled out over the rocks and trees far down the mountainside. It was a moving van, and the truck's contents of furniture and boxes were scattered everywhere.

Although clearly the fate of the driver was paramount and it was hard to imagine any person could have survived such a horrendous crash, oddly what stayed with me for hours and days was the sight of all that furniture scattered, most of it battered and broken by the truck's long dive so far down the mountainside, but some of it amazingly had kept its shape.

A family was moving across country, I thought. They put their possessions confidently inside that truck expecting to unpack Grandmother's antique desk and all their dishes and their children's favorite toys and a library of books and everything that constituted their possessions. And now most of those possessions would not be salvageable. I know they were just things, and not on par with the life of the drivers in that doomed truck, but for me the pathos of the scene was symbolized by the possessions spread across the mountainside. Like a photograph that captures a terrifying event to freeze it in time forever, the sight of that accident imprinted itself on my mind.

But otherwise, we loved our drive through Utah and at nightfall we pulled into a hotel feeling very full of a quiet beauty, a day so full of the earth's colors that it satisfied my artistic senses!

I continued what was becoming my evening routine; every night I would curl up in bed, read a little more in Mac's journal, send a quick text to our parents and to Tibby as to our whereabouts without any real news of the day, and then I would indulge in sending a short but expressive text to Jerry, trying to encapsulate my thoughts and impressions into a few words. He always responded in kind, mostly about my text, only occasionally slipping in any news from Gualala.

In the morning we headed into a new state, and the skies just got even more interesting in Wyoming.

The day started off great with fresh air and a gorgeous sunrise. We checked out the breakfast offerings, standard roadside chain-hotel fare, including biscuits and gravy. Neither of us was up for a heavy breakfast so we picked at some suspiciously yellow scrambled eggs, small cylindrical sausages, bland looking English muffins, yogurt, under-ripe bananas and rather aged oranges. Surprisingly the buffet line offered a very good brand of tea, so to make up for the mediocre breakfast, I had more cups of tea than normal, not taking into account the obvious fact that we would be on the road all day. I would come to rue that decision.

We hadn't been on the road long when I saw a sign for an exit to a town that I had read about in Mac's journal the night before. It was the place he had stayed for several months to work on a big project constructing some sort of barn or processing plant. It was a place Mac left quickly for reasons he didn't mention at least as far as I had read.

"Scott, Scott, take that exit, quick!"

Scott did so but when we got off the road, he looked at me. "Okay. What was that all about?"

Looking around, we seemed to be pretty much in the middle of nowhere, other than a gas station and a tiny run-down café.

"Are you hungry, or what?"

"No, no, this is the exit to Eagleton and that is where Mac worked for two months. We should go see where it is. After all, he spent a lot of time there."

Scott, not having read any of the journal, was not nearly as keen on following Mac's footsteps as I was, but he is an agreeable sort of guy, especially first thing in the morning with sleep behind him and a second cup of coffee resting in the cupholder beside him. With seemingly endless hours stretching out in the day ahead, he obliged me.

Just to set things clear, this whole impromptu side jaunt was entirely my doing. I take full responsibility. It was not a mutually discussed plan.

It wasn't long before the interstate disappeared behind us and we headed over some rolling hills into the wild open lands of Wyoming, far removed from anything, no buildings, no traffic, just open land; the quiet was drowned out by the sound of the wind steadily blowing. These hills were bare, very few trees to be found. Occasionally we would see deer, and a fair number of cattle grazing, but mostly it was empty grassland.

It was beautiful. It was also a little unsettling to my eyes. But I felt experiencing new environments was part of what this trip was all about.

The other thing I was feeling was a very pressured bladder. All my morning tea was coming back to haunt me.

"Hey, Scott, keep your eye open for a gas station. I gotta pee. Bad."

"Give me a break. Do you see a single building, a barn, or a shed? Much less a gas station? Hold it in, Lizzie."

After another fifteen minutes, I had to admit, "Scott, I cannot hold it any longer. I'm going to burst or worst, leak all over the car if I can't pee soon."

Scott looked disgusted. "Elizabeth, you and your peeing. Just hold it! I don't even see any signs for a town. Didn't you say there was a town, the one that Mac worked at out here? Maybe it doesn't exist anymore. That was over thirty years ago."

"Scott. I'm desperate!"

"Okay, I'll pull over. You can just pee by the road."

"I can't do that, Scott. I need at least a bush to squat behind. Remember you men can stand up but I have to squat. Someone might see me."

"Damn it, Liz, there isn't a person in fifty miles. And the cows are not likely to be offended."

"Scott, look!" I pointed. Coming up ahead, there was a clump of trees off the road about fifty yards. "There, go in there."

Scott slowed down to look. "That's a private road."

Sure enough, beside the open gate to the gravel road, a sign was posted, faded but clearly stating Private Road No Trespassing.

My need to pee chased all rational thought out of my head. I was no longer Elizabeth the Unflappable. "Doesn't matter, Scott. No one is around. We'll just drive in, I'll pee, and then we'll be out of here before even a cow or a vulture notices."

I grabbed Scott's arm and squeezed hard. "Ouch, okay, okay!" He turned onto the gravel and drove through the open gate until we reached the clump of trees. I took a handful of paper napkins out of the glove compartment, opened the door and hobbled—couldn't dash with such a full bladder—as fast as I could to the privacy of the small trees.

Ah, such a relief. I let it all out, then pulled my jeans back up. The wind was whipping my hair and filling my ears and my senses. For a moment I was simply happy. Happy with the wind, the landscape, the sense of being on a road adventure. And mostly happy with the good feeling of an empty bladder.

When I turned to leave the shelter of the trees, I stopped short. Scott stood about half way between me and our Land Rover. Obviously, he had decided to relieve himself as well as long as we were stopped. He was in process of turning around, zipping up his pants. But between where Scott stood and our silver Explorer, a menacingly large pickup was parked. How had we not heard it? The wind, I guess. Scott stopped short, looking as surprised as I was.

I figured we would just have to make our apologies for trespassing and get away as quickly as possible.

Then I saw the dogs. And I heard the dogs. Both the sight and sound were terrifying to me, and I am normally comfortable around dogs. I moved to stand next to Scott, protective as I always have been when dogs are around. I have been doing it ever since we were four years old and Scott was attacked by a dog.

It happened in suburban Dixon when he and I were playing outside in front of Scott's house. Our moms were up on the front steps discussing a landscape project. Cozy had the day off. I had run into the house to get a cape so Scott could be Super Man and was begging my mom for a popsicle. Where the dog came from, no one ever figured out. He wasn't from our neighborhood. He attacked Scott before our moms knew what was happening. They ran out to the front of the yard and Scott's mom punched the dog with her bare hands and pulled it away from Scott. Immediately the dog turned and bit my Aunt Mandy before my mom managed to grab a stick and hit the dog over and over until it finally ran away.

It was a scene of horror. And I have never forgotten it. Scott was lying on the ground screaming with blood running down his legs and arms, his shorts and tee-shirt soaked red, with puncture wounds ripping up his arm, and large chunks of flesh exposed. My Aunt Mandy was trying to take care of him, while her own hand was bleeding. My mom was tearing off her shirt to stop Scott's bleeding.

Those are the images I remember when I think about that day. Scott screaming. My mom in her bra bending over Scott using her shirt to stanch his blood. My Aunt Mandy grabbing her own hand and watching it bleed. I did the only thing I knew, as a kid, to do. I gave Scott the Super Man cape to make him feel better, but my Aunt Mandy grabbed it to help stop the bleeding on her hand.

Aunt Mandy to this day still can't fully use her hand. Both Scott and his mom needed to get rabies shots because no one could track down the dog. For me, the trauma of that day was to see all the important people in my four-year-old life being attacked and everyone screaming and so much blood. For Scott, the trauma of the day was the surprise of the snarling dog, the sensation of being "eaten alive," followed by the painful rabies shots… all wrapped into one vicious memory. Not that we talked about it much. It was too tender a topic. Once in college after many beers, Scott got expansive and talked to me and a couple of other friends about this event. But mostly the door was shut on that discussion.

Since then, dogs have always made Scott nervous at best, terrified at worst. His experience with Gran's dog Johnny was the closest I had ever seen to seeing Scott relax around a canine creature.

But out here on this windswept beautiful setting—home, home on the range—was a situation from hell for my poor cousin, and while it frightened me to the core, I still found my first instinct was to protect him.

In the back of the pickup were three large dogs. All barking, snarling with wild frenzy, jumping and twirling in circles in eagerness to jump out of the pickup and come at us. A man climbed out of the cab of the pickup, a gun in his hands. I do not know guns, couldn't identify a type of gun if my life depended upon it, which is a very bad use of language to describe that moment. But the man seemed very comfortable with that gun. I guess it was a rifle because it was a long gun, not a hand gun.

He looked at us, and spat a very long trajectory of brown tobacco. If it wasn't for that gun and those dogs, I might have laughed. He seemed like such a walking cliché of a western bad guy.

I kind of brushed my shoulder against Scott's so he would know I was with him. I could smell the fear in him.

The walking cliché could also talk. "This here is private land. Can't you motherfuckers read? What the hell do you think you're doing?"

Although I wasn't convinced he was interested in our

answer, I tried. It was hard to talk loud enough to be heard over the wind and the barking of the dogs. My voice sounded like someone else's. "We're so sorry. It's all my fault. I needed to pee and wanted some cover so we came in. We'll get back on the road and won't bother you anymore. We're really sorry."

The man spat again. There is something about spitting that shows ultimate disdain and dehumanization. I've witnessed students in school-fights who will spit. It is an aggressive act of defensiveness and reactive hatred. It is the behavior of an unimaginative human trying to save their self-esteem.

Of course, I didn't actually think any of those thoughts in the moment. Standing there by the spitting man and snarling dogs, I only wondered if our time was up.

The man sneered at us and then looked casually at his dogs who hyped up the frenzy even more with his look at them. Then he lifted his gun.

"I don't like trespassers. I don't give no second chances, not even to pretty girls. And what's your story, faggot?" He addressed this to Scott.

Scott was having trouble breathing, because of the dogs I think, even more than the gun or the slurs. But he managed to reply, "We didn't mean to bother anyone. We'll get out of here. Our apologies."

I wondered later if we were too apologetic. Would this man have responded better if we had been defiant? Well, when one is at the end of a rifle barrel with dogs slobbering in anticipation of attack, I really don't know what else we could have done. Besides we had trespassed. And I realized as I stood there beside my cousin, that it would be all my fault if Scott was mauled by those dogs, or if we were shot and left under the endless Wyoming sky to bleed to death on the blowing green and golden grasses.

Was this man's goal to intimidate the hell out of us? He was doing a first-rate job of it. We were scared to death, and if I hadn't just peed, I would be wetting my pants or worse. Or was his intent even more evil? As we stood there, side-by-side, we had no way of knowing if this was it or not. I had never been held at gunpoint before, nor had I ever been afraid that I would be torn to pieces by dogs eager to do just that.

I wish I could say that I thought of my family or of my students in those moments, or that I had regrets that I would never know a great love relationship, or never stand by the ocean again. No, instead the thoughts going through my head were not grand thoughts, but rather they were of anger; anger that my life and Scott's life could end in such a stupid way for such a stupid reason. What was screaming through my brain was "Stupid! Stupid! Stupid! Elizabeth, this is Stupid!"

But I didn't say anything more. I was at a loss. My great gift for knowing the right thing to say at the right time, simply failed me. This was beyond my experience. Scott too was frozen into silence. The man raised his rifle again to his eye, pointed right at us. The dogs' barking filled my ears as they circled in the tight confines of the pickup bed, a small barrier which in no way would have impeded their leap at the word of their owner. I found myself wondering how many seconds it would take for them to get to us. Would the bullet kill us first? Could the dogs be faster than a bullet?

I don't know how long this standoff would have gone on, but suddenly there was another pickup. I never heard the second truck drive up either. Too mesmerized by the gun and dogs? Or was it that damn wind? I was beginning to hate the wind with a passion.

Compared to the first man who held the gun on us, it was a distinguished-looking rancher who stepped out of the pickup and took a moment to take in the picture. His boots looked like they never stepped in shit, his shirt was immaculate. His looks were pristine, but his presence was also ominous. The dogs stopped barking quite so ferociously and seemed not to know what to do. Wag their tails in friendship with the obviously familiar man, or continue to menace the intruders?

With the barking somewhat subsided, we could hear the second man more clearly. First, he said to the dogs, "Down!" The three dogs instantly dropped to the floor of the pickup, and silence reigned. He took off his hat to reveal pure white hair that ruffled in the wind. He looked around, looked at us, and then replaced his hat. It felt like we were watching an old movie. The effect seemed deliberate.

"Rusty, whatcha got?"

"Got some trespassers, Parker." The first man was still threatening, the gun still held pointing towards us, but something had shifted. He was no longer first in command here.

"I see." The second man turned to us. "What do you have to say for yourselves?"

I spoke up first. "Sir, we are so sorry. We did intrude but meant no harm. Honestly it was all my fault. I had to pee and wanted some privacy and this was the only bush I could see anywhere, and so I insisted we turn in. My cousin didn't want to because it was marked Private…"

I felt like an errant sixth grader making a case for herself in the principal's office. But this was no place for pride. I had to try to get us out of here since I had got us into this situation.

The second man muttered something that sounded like "Fucking tourists." Then he turned to the other man. "Rusty, put that damn gun away. I can't afford any more trouble."

And he turned to us and pointed to our Explorer. "I don't know where you were trying to go, but get out of here now and next time don't cross into private land." He looked at our car. "If you know what's good for you, stay in Nevada."

I nudged Scott and we walked to our car. Not wanting to walk right by Rusty, we had to walk between the dogs and the second man. I took a quick glance out of the side of my eyes at Rusty, and he actually looked rusty with reddish hair sticking out under the sides of his hat, ruddy face, big reddish nose, scrawny shoulders and skinny legs with a small pot of a stomach. His earlier hateful look of a bully swathed in bravado had altered. He now looked like a weasel.

We tried not to dash to our car, but rather walk calmly by the second man. I wasn't sure who was the one to fear the most in the long run, but in the short run, I had to be grateful to the late-comer. As we walked by him, I dared to say, "Thank you."

He didn't even nod, but with a steely voice replied, "You should be damn happy that I came along. Rusty is a good shot and his dogs would make you wish he'd used the rifle on you."

We just kept walking. As we passed the dogs, I could hear their panting and the growl deep in their throats, and I felt their wish to resume their aggression. It took all our self-possession to walk to our car, open the doors, sit down and put on our seat belts. Scott started the car and did a U turn, with all moderation and self-control. He maintained that composure until we pulled out of the gates and got back on the paved road.

Then he hit the gas and we took off, back the way we came, back to the interstate. Neither of us had any further interest in pursuing the life and times of Mac in Wyoming.

We had nothing to say for miles, even after getting to the interstate. But instead of getting on the freeway, Scott said to me, "I feel sick to my stomach. I have to stop."

So we stopped at the tiny café we had seen earlier, parked in front and walked in. I got a booth by the window, facing the door, and Scott went to the bathroom. The waitress, as friendly as Rusty and his brother had been unfriendly, brought a glass of water and stayed by the table, hoping to engage in conversation. Looking around the café I could see that there weren't a lot of people for a gregarious soul to talk to.

She asked where we were from, and having just swallowed a large sip of water and starting to cough a little, I just pointed out the window to our Explorer with the Nevada plates. She chatted on about this and that, about how the new truck stop down the road fifty miles had taken all the trucker business and things were so slow she was bored to death.

I don't know what possessed me, but I found myself telling her about what we had just experienced. Her eyes rolled. "Oh shit, you didn't cross into Rusty and Parker Brookings' property, did you?"

She went on before I could answer. "Those are the two meanest bastards in this whole county. Think they are the big bosses around here just because their grandpa owned the big Brookings Company all those years ago. It's gone under now, but they still think they are big shots. Parker is mean and crafty, stays just this side of trouble, keeps himself looking clean but does his dirty work behind the scenes, you know? But Rusty, he's so dumb he's outright dangerous. Last year, he shot two men who were cross-country skiing and wandered on to his property. Didn't kill the guys but sent them to the hospital for weeks. They sued him but his brother got him a slick lawyer, pulled some strings, paid them off. The local sheriff and DA were not going to go out on a limb to stand up for some guys from California caught on private property no matter how lost they said they were, not against our local guys. Just the way it is. Good thing you are from Nevada. Parker really hates Californians."

She talked on and on, but I had heard enough to cause my heart to start pounding again. Scott was still in the john. Then the waitress, Sandy her name tag said, added, "I went to school with those boys, Parker and Rusty, and all of us girls had to learn to stay out of their way. They had a reputation of doing just whatever they wanted with the girls around here, especially the Indian girls, but us white girls, too. Mean and nasty men. I got married as soon as I could to a big strong guy." She gestured back to the kitchen where a burly man in a white apron nodded to her. Looking past him, I saw Scott emerge from the bathroom, looking like he had taken a shower in the sink, his hair slicked back and his face still showing some droplets.

Suddenly I just wanted to get on the road. I turned to the waitress. "We'd like our order to go, please. Two burgers with all the works, fries, and two chocolate milkshakes."

She nodded and hurried back to place the order before Scott got to the table. He looked at me. "Getting our food to go, Scott. I just want to get some mileage behind us."

"I'm not hungry."

"Don't say anything. I learned some more about the guys we just met." I grimaced bitterly. "I want to give these folks some business and get out of here. You can throw it all out for all I care."

Scott looked at me but was quiet.

Then I added, "In fact, why don't you go wait in the car and check out where we can stay tonight. I'll wait for the food, and lunch is on me."

Scott and me, we have this kind of communication we can do even without words. Scott did not question my bossiness and just got up and walked out to the car. I could see him in the driver's seat looking at his phone and setting the GPS.

Our waitress brought our food, and I handed her cash including a hefty tip, smiled as best I could, and thanked her all while walking out the door and jumping in the car.

"Let's go."

And we did.

We drove all the rest of that day without talking much. As the day progressed, I had to pee again but was afraid to say anything. But soon Scott pulled into a rest stop, an attractive, well-appointed rest stop, one of the best of our trip thus far.

At the rest stop we ate the food from the café, and what hadn't appealed to us earlier in the morning, immediately post-trauma, turned out to meet our hunger by afternoon: a cold hamburger and fries, and a lukewarm milkshake beginning to separate. Crazy, how we had recovered to a certain degree. I would have told you that morning that I never would have an appetite again.

It wasn't until almost all the way across Wyoming, the sun setting in stunning glory with its light coming into our car from behind us in the west, that I finally was able to say aloud what I had been thinking all day. "Scott. If anything had happened to us besides having the shit scared out of us, it would have been all my fault. I'll never get over being sorry for putting you through that, especially with the dogs. I am just so, so sorry. I don't know how to make it up to you."

He looked at me for a moment and then back to the road. The thing about Scott is that he exudes calmness when he is driving. He didn't speak for a time and finally said, "I don't even know how to talk about it. It sure brought back my old fears with those dogs. But, Lizbeth, no need to apologize, really. We both do dumb things, and here's the deal. We just got unlucky. Ninety-nine percent of the time, you pull fifty yards into private property out in the middle of nowhere for five minutes, and you'd never get caught, or no one would mind when they see you are not up to trouble. We just got completely unlucky. I'm only relieved neither of us got hurt. And just for the record, if anyone had tried to touch you, I would have thrown my body at those dogs or that gun. If something happened to you, I wouldn't care if I lived or died or how badly I was hurt. I could never have faced your dad again."

I was moved by his heroic comments, given my role in getting us into that mess. Before I could say more, he finished. "But, next time, don't drink so much tea and make sure you pee before we leave anywhere. I'm going to have to start treating you like a child, young woman!" He looked at me in a stern expression, and then our nerves unleashed and we laughed, hard and long. Scott somehow managed to keep driving.

Another hour and we were crossing out of Wyoming. Few would blame us for being happy to leave that state behind, no matter its beautiful skies and first-class rest stops. Maybe another time we'd discover all that Wyoming has to offer that is beautiful and exciting, but for this trip, we were glad to be moving on.

22

On my childhood puzzle of the United States, I learned Nebraska's overhang on the western side of the state. I would make Scott turn all the puzzle pieces upside down and mix them up. Then I would pick up the pieces and hold them up so he could see the front, and I would name the state and tell him the capital. He dutifully played along with me, although he never had the geography obsession that I did. But I would barter: two games of map quiz and then I would play Legos or transformers with him. We had other friends who might play these games with us, but only in my little world with Scott did I trust that he would let me be the champion of the map world, and then in turn I would let him be the unrivaled king of the Lego world. It's how we stayed balanced, sharing the spot light. Once we got to school, we experienced plenty of competition, so I guess we both enjoyed the moments of being the star.

Nebraska was an easy state to identify by shape. But Scott and I both knew less about Nebraska than we did Utah. I didn't even put us to the test, knowing that both of us would come up empty. Instead, I pulled out my phone and googled Nebraska and read off a few facts so we could know that Nebraska was more than just corn fields, although we sure saw a lot of those.

We'd been rolling along for a while, when we passed the town of Ogallala. At the same moment we both said something to the effect of "Ogalala, a cousin to Gualala!" We were almost a week into our road trip and conversation had hit a comfortable lull.

When we could drive no farther, we pulled up into a cluster of hotels just off the interstate. So far, we had never had a problem getting a room and didn't make reservations ahead of time. We thought reservations were for old people.

We parked by the first hotel and unloaded our luggage, me hauling my suitcase and all of Mac's things in the kayak bag. The lobby of the hotel was abuzz with people, mostly high-school girls and some boys, and a mingling of folks who looked like parents. In the parking lot we had noticed a great many buses. Some kind of school trip?

We waited in line for a while and when we got to the counter, the young woman asked us for our reservation number.

"We don't have reservations," Scott said wearily. This had been a long day.

"I'm so sorry. We are full up."

Scott looked around as if surveying the region and then he said without much tact, "We are in the middle of nowhere, and you have no vacancy?"

The woman seemed perpetually pleasant and didn't take offense. "I'm so sorry. You see, it's the statewide cheerleading competition, and this year we are hosting it here in our region. It's so exciting!"

She appeared to have been a cheerleader herself, and to cover up whatever was going to come next out of Scott's mouth, which I don't think would have been kind, I interjected, "A cheerleading competition! That must be amazing. Do you compete yourself?"

She beamed. "Oh, yes. My team won second prize in the small-school category five years ago."

"That's remarkable. I see kids doing cheerleading and they are very athletic. Kind of terrifies me."

The woman, with a name tag that said Harmony, began to tell me all about her experiences. I engaged her for a few more minutes but I could sense Scott's impatience so I found a momentary break in her narration of how she was the one they tossed into the air, and asked her whether she knew if the other hotels might have a vacancy.

"I'm so sorry," she repeated her refrain without looking at all contrite, "but in fact, they have been calling over here to see if we had any rooms because they are all full too. This competition is a really big deal."

"I can see that," I said feeling more exhausted every moment, worn out by her enthusiasm. "You see we've had a long drive today, and we really need to find a place to sleep."

Scott asked wearily, "How about campgrounds? We have a tent."

She, the forever-cheerleader, thought hard. This apparently was a difficult question for her. Then the young woman from the next computer, who must have overheard our conversation, leaned over and helped her out. Smiling at us, she said, "The nearest campground is fifty miles back west on the river. They almost always have empty sites, although it is a weekend."

I groaned. "Fifty miles."

Then the desk clerk—the second one, not the cheerleader—looked at us for a moment and said, "Here's an idea. My mom runs a B&B five miles from here on our farm. She wasn't going to be open this weekend, but why don't I call her and see if she'd be okay with some guests?"

I eagerly turned to her. "Would you do that? We'd pay whatever. We are just so tired."

"Sure." She got her phone out of her pocket. "I need to tell you that it is my parents' working farm. My mom runs what she calls a Farm Bed and Breakfast. Guests come and stay in the farm house and help on the farm, learn about farming." She must have seen Scott's face because she laughed. "You wouldn't be pressed into hard labor, since you didn't sign up for that. Believe it or not, people sign up because they want to learn about farming, and then they find out it is hard work. But my mom has made a pretty good business of the nostalgia people have to go back to their farming roots or whatever."

She laughed and as she waited for her mother to answer the phone, she stuck out her hand and said, "I'm Jessica Anderson."

"I'm Elizabeth Kuiper and this is my cousin Scott Sullivan."

She put her attention back on the phone, had only a short conversation, put her phone down and said to us, "All set."

"That was quick."

"My mom is very adaptable. Raising four kids and being a farmer makes you that way!" She pulled out a map and drew some lines. "Here are the directions. I'd head out there right away if I were you because it is getting dark and finding the driveway is difficult in the dark, easy during the day."

Scott hesitated. "We haven't had dinner, perhaps we should find a place around here to eat first."

"Oh, don't bother, all the cafes and diners are full of cheerleaders tonight, and my mom always has food. I'll let her know that you haven't eaten, and she'll take care of you."

She sent us on our way, just like that. No further questions.

We hauled our bags back out to the car.

"I don't know about this, Lizzie. This is weird. What are you getting us into anyway?"

"Got a better idea?"

No response.

"That's what I thought. I also thought Jessica was very rational sounding. Better than Candy the cheerleader."

"Harmony was her name."

"That's even more precious," I replied.

Scott shoved his suitcase in the back of the Explorer. "We're ones to talk. Our moms are named Cinnamon and Mandela!"

"Good point." I laughed. "Come on, Scott. Where is your adventurous spirit? Let's go see. When in Nebraska, go stay on a farm. Maybe it will be fun. But at least it is a bed and hopefully something to eat."

One or the other of us was always starving it seemed.

It was a fairly short drive through several miles of corn fields, half grown, that lined the straight road, but it was getting dark and we almost missed the mailbox and gate. Scott spotted it at the last minute and pulled up to the gate. Then stopped abruptly.

I looked at him. "What?"

He pointed. There was a Private Property sign. He looked at me. I could hear him thinking, "Twice in one day?"

I hesitated too until I saw another sign. "Anderson Acres Farm Bed and Breakfast." I pointed.

And so, Scott slowly crunched down the gravel driveway, a quarter mile to where a farm house was aglow with lights pouring out the windows upstairs and down.

Scott stopped the car and muttered to me, "There better not be any dogs."

"Scott, it's a farm. Of course, there are going to be dogs." I almost added, "Duh, Dude." But then I felt sorry for him and said, "Hey, we'll wait until the owner comes out just to be safe."

23

A woman came out of the front door and waved as she walked down the steps, two dogs cheerfully bouncing along by her side. I jumped out and walked towards her, Scott following more slowly, and before we could say a thing, she called out as if our arrival was the most expected occurrence in the world. "Welcome! I'm Susan Anderson. Welcome to Anderson Acres."

When we got close, she held out her hand first to me and then Scott. The dogs were well-trained and stayed right by her side, tails wagging. We introduced ourselves and she in turn introduced us to the dogs. "This is Ralston and the one with the interesting eye is Patches."

Susan Anderson was a tall woman, large but comfortable in her body. I couldn't have placed her age—the mother of the young woman at the hotel desk would have to be in her forties at the youngest—but she was strong and earthy. She wore a faded tee-shirt with a once-bright rainbow on the front over the word "Imagine." Her jeans were also well worn. Long light-colored hair was pulled into a ponytail at the back of her neck, and her face was unadorned, plain and beautiful all at the same time, with a smile that warmed me instantly. After the day we had had, I felt that we had come home to comfort. I felt that all in the first seconds of meeting Susan Anderson.

"Thank you for taking us in," I told her. "I understand this is your day off, so we really appreciate it."

She laughed. "Days off are sort of a moving target around a farm and certainly in the B&B business. I'm happy to help you out. That silly cheerleading competition has thrown our whole county into a tizzy. You'd think the queen of England herself was coming to town. Let me help you with your bags."

She grabbed my suitcase and let me carry Mac's bag of memorabilia while Scott got his suitcase and tech case and we followed her to the house and up the stairs. We walked into an entry way with a typical farm house layout, living room to the left and dining room to the right and the kitchen down the hallway. As she went along, Susan turned off the lights.

"Just wanted to light things up so you could find us. But I don't want to blow out the electricity bill."

She took us upstairs and stopped before an open doorway. "Here you go."

She stood aside and let us walk into a mid-size bedroom with one queen-sized bed.

I looked at Scott and then back to our friendly host. "Oh, uh, Mrs. Anderson?"

"Susan," she corrected me.

"Susan, here's the thing. Scott and I are cousins, and well, we haven't slept in the same bed since we were probably eight years old…"

Throwing her head back, Susan laughed. "Oh, I guess I got that wrong. Jessica said you were such 'a nice-looking couple and looked so tired,' so I made an assumption. No problem. Scott, you take this room. The bed is better for a long, tall man like you."

She grabbed my suitcase and took me next door to a room with a double bed covered by an old-fashioned quilt with a star pattern. "Here you go, Elizabeth. You can have the Star room. It's my personal favorite with my grandma's quilts and my books and the best view of the garden."

"Thanks so much, Susan. Please let us know your rates so we can pay you."

She waved her hand. "Information is on that brochure on the table, but don't worry. We have lots of time. First you need a chance to freshen up. The bathroom's across the hall, and then Jessica said you hadn't eaten, so come on down and I'll give you the leftovers from our dinner. Lasagna, okay?"

"That would be awesome!" It was Scott, who was walking to the bathroom.

Susan grinned. "Well, I am glad to know you talk, young man. I guess you just needed to hear about food."

Scott smiled a sheepish grin. "Yeah, well, I usually let Elizabeth do the talking for me. She's so much better at it." He added as I threw him a dart of a glance, "And I mean that with all admiration and respect!" Then he disappeared into the bathroom.

I turned to Susan and rolled my eyes. "Sorry. We've been together in that car for a lot of hours!"

Susan laughed. "We have four kids so I know siblings.

And I suppose cousins can have the same dynamics! If you are open to sharing, I'd love to hear where you are headed. I spend most of my time at home. No place else I would rather be. But sometimes when I listen to people telling of their travels, I get vicarious thrills!"

She headed down stairs. "Just give me ten minutes to get dinner going. But come down anytime. We'll eat in the kitchen tonight. Jacob and our sons will be in from the barn soon. They've already eaten but they'll join us for rhubarb pie."

Scott came out of the bathroom just in time to hear "rhubarb pie." He gave a little fist pump and another grin and headed straight down to the kitchen. I got caught up looking through Susan's bookshelves. A good collection of books, many overlapping the books on my shelves at home in Davis. I suddenly realized it had been almost fifteen minutes, so I stopped in the bathroom, splashed some water on my face, ran a brush through my tangled hair and looked in the mirror; what a mess. Oh well, I was hungry and Susan did not look like someone who would be critical of messy hair and a crumpled shirt.

Scott was sitting at the table, and a beer had been placed in his hand. He looked as happy as I had seen him in days. I sat down and Susan pulled a pan of lasagna out of the oven. She was pouring me some wine when there was a commotion at the door and in walked two teenage boys and a man who had to be their father. They had taken off their shoes in the proverbial mud room.

Susan introduced us. "This is my husband Jacob, and our sons Ozzie and Ethan."

Jacob reached out a hand to shake, and Scott half rose to grab it. And then I followed. The boys just sort of nodded in that teenage manner very familiar to me. I smiled at them both and Susan encouraged us to start eating.

Jacob grabbed a beer and sat down at the table. He seemed a calm presence. The boys started to disappear, but Susan called after them, "If you want some pie, wash your hands and join us."

That brought them back. They washed up and came back into the room, jostling and shoving each other in the way Scott and I had interacted when younger. Now we did an adult version of that. I never felt sorry for myself not having a sibling. I had Scott.

Dinner was hearty and the pie was divine. Scott allowed himself to be talked into a second piece of pie by Susan and a second beer by the host, who also enjoyed one himself. The boys stayed with us, obviously used to strangers at their table, although the older boy Ethan blushed furiously every time I spoke to him.

The Andersons asked us about our trip and we filled them in. When one of us mentioned that we were from California, they said, "Oh, another surprise. Your car has Nevada license plates." So, we had to explain that quirk. And then when one of us said we lived in Davis, Ethan blurted, "Best vet school around!"

We stopped and looked at him. Ethan looked embarrassed. Jacob explained for him. "Ethan has one goal in life. To work with animals and he wants to go to vet school."

"So, will you come to Davis?" I asked.

"Nah. Out of state. Kind of expensive." He paused. "But it would be a dream to go there. Do you know anything about it?"

"I know the vet school is a big department at the university and one of our friends got his vet degree there. My degree is in history and art, and Scott has an engineering degree with a computer tech minor."

Ethan looked at us as if we had just been elevated a notch in his mind. I never felt so highly regarded just by virtue of my Davis degree, so I added, "You can even study wine making and agriculture."

Ethan interjected, "And they have a good performing arts department, too."

Susan smiled fondly at her son. "Ethan has studied the manuals of several universities and probably knows more about them than many of their alumni."

Jacob added dryly, "And window shopping doesn't cost anything."

Ethan became subdued at his father's remark so I consoled him. "I'm sure there are fantastic schools around Nebraska for studying to be a vet."

He nodded, seemingly a kid who already had a grip on the reality of his situation. "Yeah. I'll be okay. Just seemed like a cool school."

I couldn't help myself at that point and stifled a yawn. Susan laughed and urged us to get to bed.

"I have to admit this long day has caught up with me," I confessed and picked up my plate to take to the sink.

Susan took it from me. "You can help me tomorrow, but tonight, you need to hit the sheets. As for tomorrow, we are not on the usual guest farm schedule where we warn people that we will get them up early to eat and get out on to their assigned chores. So, you can sleep as long as you like and I'll have some breakfast here in the kitchen for you."

We thanked her and said our goodnights. I was in bed quickly, sent a few quick text updates, deliberately not mentioning anything about our scary Wyoming experience. I was too sleepy to open up Mac's journal. I plugged in my phone and was about to turn off the lights and drop into sleep when I noticed a title on a book in the shelf across the room and ended up reading for another hour despite my fatigue. Nodding off at last, I reached up turned out the light and lay there listening to the silence. No urban noises for sure, and not even any wind. I got out of bed one more time and went to the open window (screened for summer bugs) and knelt down so my face was level with the window sill. Outside it was not as completely quiet as I had thought. The sound of frogs carried up to my ears. I heard the soft sound of a cow mooing then. And after more silence, an owl was answered by another owl. Another five minutes and a dog barked, just once or twice, then silence again. Before I at last gave up the day and went to bed, I could hear the breeze rustling some tree branches.

I nestled my cheek into the pillow and had yet one more thought before oblivion hit me: this might be a hard-working farm, but the linens were first quality. Susan knew what she was doing!

I slept solidly and woke to the sun streaming into the window where I had crouched the night before. I could hear voices downstairs and an engine in the yard. And I smelled coffee and perhaps bacon. I jumped up and grabbed my phone. Nine o'clock. Holy cow! A record.

I threw on my clothes, stopped in the bathroom to brush my teeth and splash some water on my face, ran my hands through my hair, and bounded down the stairs.

Susan turned from the stove and greeted me with a smile. She had the same tee shirt on this morning, and that comforted me because I had pulled on yesterday's shirt as well.

"I can't believe I slept so late," I apologized. "Such a comfy bed and those sheets are lovely!"

"You noticed! Jessica and I decided that we might be a farm where we make people get their hands dirty, but people will forget their achy muscles if we have good food and nice linens! Little trick of the trade!"

She smiled as if I were in on the secret.

"Something to eat? You can have a light breakfast or a more substantial one. Your choice."

"Well, I should have a light one, I'm sure, but what smells so good? I'll have that whatever it is."

"I made a quiche using our own pork sausage and our own eggs. Plus, some early spinach from our garden. I'll get yours hot. Scott seemed to like it earlier. He ate two slices plus some toast and blackberry jam."

"Scott." I looked around. "I guess he beat me up this morning. Where is he?"

"He's out in the barn with Jacob, looking at some engines. Jacob has a tractor problem and Scott agreed to help." Susan gave me a smile. "Apparently, you are spending another night with us. Scott said he's calling this one and that is what you get for sleeping in so late. I think those were his words."

I laughed, "That sounds like Scott. Well, will you have us another night?"

"Of course."

I took a bite of the quiche, which was as good as it smelled. Then a long sip of my tea.

"Susan, I need to stay out of my bedroom because otherwise I will curl up all day just reading the books on your shelves. You are a temptress. Either that or we just happen to have the same taste in reading. Have you read all of those?"

"Most but not all." She added with a laugh, "Yet."

"I'm surprised you have any time at all to read with all that you do here."

"Sundays." Susan said as she efficiently cleaned the counter and put away the leftovers. "Sunday is our day of rest, and for us that means reading. We quit going to church a long time ago for reasons that, well, maybe later I can share with you, but we still liked the idea of a day of rest since we work so long and hard around here, especially in the summer. I intentionally put my books into your room, so I'm not tempted during the week, and then on Sunday when we shoo the last of our paying guests out at 11:00, we do the dishes, put in a load of laundry, and sit down and read."

"All of you?"

"All of us. Family rule. Well, family tradition at least."

"Reminds me of being a kid. In school we had something called 'Drop everything and read.' I loved it, but I always have been a bit of a nerd."

Susan smiled at me. "I've been getting this sense that you and I have a lot in common."

I smiled at her and drained my tea cup.

"Want more tea?"

"No, Susan, if Scott is out working, I think you should put me to work too. What was on your list of chores today. I can help."

Folding the tea towel, Susan said. "Okay. Today I was going to make some bread and weed out the new garden before the weeds get taller and stronger than the baby carrots and lettuces. Do you mind if your shoes get a little dirty?"

"Nope, I'm fine."

I spent the morning with Susan in the garden, while Scott was helping fix a tractor. I never saw him all day. About eleven, Susan texted Ethan who was hanging out in the barn (happy to have Scott to relieve him of helping his dad with a machine) and Ozzie who was supposedly putting the latest expenditures and income into a Quicken file. (Ozzie, being the family computer expert, was in charge of keeping financial records.)

Susan instructed the boys to go inside (and "wash your hands, with soap") and "make tuna sandwiches with chips, enough for everyone and have them ready by noon." Remarkably—given my experience with kids—they didn't complain, although Susan said they might get sidetracked. That had been known to happen. Still, it was clear that the Anderson kids had a real buy-in for the family businesses, both the farm and the B&B.

My conversation with Susan went back and forth as we got to know each other. She was fascinated with my story of Gran and our mission. Then I asked her about her story.

"Jacob and I were high school sweethearts who went off to college in Madison, Wisconsin, high on life and each other, full of plans for our future. We were both going to be teachers. We were going to move somewhere beautiful and exciting, maybe even overseas, and I was going to teach English. Jacob wanted to be a mechanics teacher. So, despite the lack of enthusiasm from our parents, we went to Madison, all bright-eyed at age eighteen, our dream come true! We were together all the time, loving the college life—make no bones about it—we were high on being away from home for the first time."

Susan's smile was warm with memory. "Such heady times! We loved our freedom so much we forgot that you need to have some smarts to manage the freedom! I was pregnant within a few months! We finished the first semester because it was paid for, then came home for good.

"I like to say that I got straight As in my college career, because for that semester I did! I laugh about that; it's my bitter attempt at humor about losing my college dream."

"So how did your parents handle it?"

"Oh Lord, they sat us down and read us the riot act about what was now expected of us, after first doing some bashing of the whole liberal academic and political culture. Yeah, that was quite a talk."

Susan looked at me wryly. "I can laugh about it now, but then it was humiliating. Jacob never faltered. He just calmly sat through the interrogation and said that he and I would get married and he'd help his dad on the farm, which is what his dad wanted him to do before Jacob insisted on going to college. And so, we did exactly that.

"We lived in a little house on his dad's farm. Luke was born and there we were, two teenagers and a baby, a family of three, not what we planned at all. We were both disappointed, of course, but we both loved Luke so much that we couldn't wish him away. We made the best of it and at least we were together. But let's just say we have handled things differently with our kids."

I thought about this. The huge disappointment made doable because of love. That was a great and mature love for two teenagers. I felt a stab of admiration, bordering on envy.

"We had Jessica a year later—it seems I get pregnant very easily—and then three years later we had Ethan and finally Ozzie, whose real name is Charles, but somehow when Ethan as a toddler kept calling him 'Ozzie,' it just stuck."

"And how did this farm and this house come about for you?"

"When Jacob's dad was killed unexpectedly in a tractor accident, the farm was divided between Jacob and his brother. His mom moved to town, and his sisters were left out completely, which was not really fair but that is the way things were done in his family. Both his sisters married farmers, and

I guess they're doing okay. The family is not very close, not since we dropped out of church."

"Oh, that sounds like a story," I said sympathetically.

"I guess it is." Susan jerked up a stubborn weed a little harder than necessary and grimaced as she tossed it into the bucket. "Despite our families being long-time members, we were treated like second-class citizens at that church after we came home from Madison, and it rankled us enough that we decided to not attend anymore."

"Susan, you can't have been the first young woman in this town or that church to have gotten pregnant before you got married!"

"Oh, you got that right. Happens all the time of course, here like everywhere. Some folks are proud as punch of their fecundity! But you see most folks are either repentant, or just so much part of the local culture that, I don't know, it doesn't matter for them, they just stay right in line with the church's expectations. So, what was different about Jacob and me? I guess people thought we were snooty because we wanted not just go to college, but we wanted to go to Madison! Isn't that crazy? Madison has a reputation as a liberal bastion here in this part of the world. To be fair, I'll admit to some aloofness that flourished in my younger self as well. I guess there was just something about us that got everyone's goat.

"Jacob and I had had a long talk and decided to just stop going to church. That made our parents even more upset. But they never disowned us; they adored their grandchildren and of course they cared about us despite our differences. We went for dinner once a month instead of once a week like our siblings all did, and that was just selfish on my part because I didn't want to give up my Reading Sunday time!"

Susan put her head back and laughed. "Isn't it the silliest thing that little old bookworm me would be considered counter-culture! I've learned to be more sociable with folks I grew up with. I can talk jams and quilts and child raising and gardening, and I love all of that, but when I want to get a deeper discussion going, I still get suspicious stares. And politics is a very dicey topic with some folks but with others, we can find common ground and agree to disagree on some issues."

"So, when Jacob's father died, you got half his farmland. And how about this house? Was this the house he was raised in?"

"No, this house had been his grandparents'. Jacob's brother got the house Jacob had been raised in. We moved in here, and almost as soon as we took over this property, Jacob and I started to follow a dream he had been nurturing for many years, ever since he gave up the dream of being a teacher. He began to farm organically. Not overnight but little by little."

"So how does that compare to how others are farming around here?"

"Pretty different, especially with corporate farming changing the way family farming looks all over the Midwest. But now more people are wising up to the mixed bag that chemical pesticides produce for crops and humans and animals. I won't lie to you, it is hard even for farmers who want to do so to diversify their crops and grow more organically. To make the break from conventional farming is very difficult, for financial reasons."

"But you and Jacob have been able to do it?"

"Not easily. It helped that Jacob's dad was able to avoid getting into the deep debt that is common for farmers. We didn't have to start off in a big hole. Everyone works hard around Nebraska farms. But to make a go of it with organic farming is different. We have been frugal and Jacob is a very good farmer, and I am very good manager. That all helps. Farmer's markets. Being connected to educational institutions, that's helped too. But when we looked at our four children, we had to take a long thought about how it was going to work. One thing is to make your kids be frugal along with you. Easier when they are young, but through high school there are so many expenses. Fortunately, our kids did not beg to participate in any of the more expensive activities. They probably just knew it wouldn't work for our family. I mean, we couldn't take off to drive them all over the state for swim meets, and contests. They basically had to do their school stuff locally as much as possible. They didn't complain much."

"You've raised very good kids, not entitled at all."

Susan smiled. "I think they're the best, but our farm has required many sacrifices on their part."

She took off her gloves and sent Ozzie a text to make sure the boys were not goofing off and were making the sandwiches. Not missing a beat, she put her gloves back on and continued her conversation.

"Luke is the one who is least connected to the farm,

and that's okay. He has a niche. Loves business, thinking of real estate. Not my thing but he's happy. He's at college in Omaha now and is talking about moving to Chicago after he graduates next June. He likes to visit, but I expect he will never come back here.

"And Jessica, whom you met, goes to the community college and works part time at the hotel. Her goal is to graduate with her degree in hospitality and then come back and help me run the B&B and save up her money. Then when Ozzie is out of college, and we won't need the B&B income for tuition anymore, Jessica will head out to purchase her own B&B near the water somewhere. She hasn't settled where that might be. Maybe along Lake Michigan or one of the other lakes. We'll see. I won't hold her to any of that. It is her life."

"Is that why you started the B&B? To fund their education?"

"Absolutely. One day when Jacob and I were brainstorming how to hang onto our organic way of life and still help our kids get to college, I had this thought: what if we combined our farming with educating people about growing organic? And how do you educate people best? Hands-on work. And how do you entice people to come and work? By making it appealing, romantic, and comfortable enough so that urban folks who know nothing about farming but who are foodies can learn where their food comes from. We tried to take advantage of the 'eating organic' popularity."

"Brilliant, Susan. And it looks like it is working, two kids almost through college, and two more to go!" I studied her.

"And it looks to me that you and Jacob still love working together."

Susan stood up as Ethan and Ozzie appeared with lunch. "That is the constant in our life, Elizabeth. Love and work, both but in that order. It has not been easy. And it is not always fun. Sometimes we get guests who are obnoxious. Who don't want to work. Who complain about everything and want their money back. And some who do the work so badly it causes us to work harder to fix the damage. But we also get some of the best folks. And we have made some connections that have helped. Yeah, it's been a good enterprise. I do plan on quitting the day Ozzie gets his degree though! I need more time to read!"

Scott and Jacob had not left the barn all morning, and Ethan took some lunch in to them. This was fine with me; talking with Susan made me feel like I had a new best friend.

If the scariness of the day before had shown us the worst of humanity, this time with the Andersons was showing us the very best.

We took off our gloves and sat on the blanket on the ground to eat. I asked her if there was a creek nearby because I had heard frogs the night before and Susan pointed to the south. "That's our pond. Lovely sound, isn't it? Very peaceful. We can walk over there after lunch."

Ethan came back and said he wanted to go back and see how one of the goats was doing. Apparently, she had been off her food that morning.

I thanked Ethan for the sandwiches and told him that

I particularly liked the cheese. "From my goats," he said proudly, "We make our own goat cheese."

After lunch we went inside and made bread. After we put the bread dough into the oven to rise, we sat down at the table with a cup of tea. We talked on and on. Susan told me she had recently turned forty, only ten years older than me, but I was humbly aware that her life experiences were ages beyond mine. Still, she wanted to know all about my life, particularly about teaching, and listened carefully and even asked my opinion on several matters.

Interrupting herself in the middle of her own sentence, Susan jumped up and hit her forehead in pretend angst. "Holy cow, Elizabeth! I've had so much fun talking to you that I forgot all my duties!"

Ozzie walked in the kitchen in time to hear his mom. "Elizabeth, you must be very special. My mom never forgets her duties!" A huge grin covered his freckled face.

Susan grabbed him and gave him a tight hug. "Take that sarcasm out of your voice, young man, or I'm going to make you and Ethan trade chores for a month!"

Ozzie wiggled out of her grasp. "But, Mom, that would punish both of us, and what did Ethan do wrong?"

She stuck a cookie in his hand and pushed him away lovingly. "Seriously, Elizabeth, I've got to scoot. I need to make your beds and get the green beans snapped and sweep the front porch and…" Her voice trailed off.

"Well, forget the beds. Scott and I are fully capable of making our beds. And I'll help you with the green beans, and anything else."

And so, we got back to work, and by the time the men finally emerged from the barn and washed up in the mud room, the house smelled yeasty and mouthwateringly of fresh baked bread.

Scott came in. He looked thoroughly content.

I observed, "Must have been a day spent with engines that is making you so full of smiles."

"Just what the doctor ordered after yesterday," he replied with a light punch to my shoulder. "Jacob has an old pickup he is restoring, an '83 Chevy C-10."

Susan looked at Jacob. "I thought you were fixing the tractor today," she said gently.

Scott quickly covered for Jacob. "Oh, we did, got that fixed in good shape, and then had some fun with the Chevy."

Susan relaxed. "Sorry to nag. Jacob deserves some fun. Glad you had a good day talking motors. He doesn't get much excitement generated among the rest of the family."

"I've got his number, so if I find parts for his pickup, I can let him know." Scott was jazzed about having expanded his classic car aficionado club.

It was a happy group that sat around the kitchen table that night and ate vegetable soup with fresh bread. If I hadn't spent the day learning how difficult this life often was, I would have believed we were in a fairy tale of rural nirvana, all fresh baked bread, happy kids, and the American dream. But what stuck in my mind from my day with Susan Anderson was that she and Jacob started with love, and they finished with love, each day, each hour, and each decision, and each event that came their way, bad or good. These two young Nebraska farm kids had found their soulmates early in life and forever after had shared dreams, disappointments, and hard work. They belonged together and to their land.

Jacob was the more low-key of the two, although Scott said he had enough to say while they worked together. That night, after we finished our dessert, the boys drifted into the other room to play a video game, and finally, with my urging, the quiet husband talked of their life.

"You know that old adage, well-used but so true, 'the whole is greater than the sum of the parts'? Susan and I try not to neglect the parts, each of us, but there is no way any of this could happen without the both of us."

Susan leaned forward and squeezed Jacob's hand; for once she was silent. Even Scott got a little teary-eyed. Then Ozzie walked back into the room and rolled his eyes. "What's going on here? This afternoon Mom is forgetting to do her work, and now you are both sitting here all starry-eyed like you are in love. Yuck. You two are old, you shouldn't act like teenagers!"

Jacob threw his napkin at his son and said, "Ozzie, you should be so lucky when you are ancient like your mom and me."

This time Susan let Scott and me both help with the dishes. And while doing so, we talked about our next day. I promised to not sleep in late so we could have an early departure. Jacob went over directions for us, although our plan was basically to get on good old Interstate 80 and head to Iowa.

That night I kept myself from reading any more of Susan's library, still didn't open Mac's journal, saving that for being on the road again, and instead filled in Tibby with a brief email of our location, sent a quick text to my mom and dad saying we were fine in Nebraska, and then, like dessert, spent some time writing Jerry the perfect text, keeping it short with well-chosen words, trying to sum up what we had experienced since Friday night:

This will need further explanation… but… we have new best friends on a Nebraska farm made possible by a cheerleading competition.

After breakfast, Jacob gave us both handshakes, formal but genuine. As he made his way out to his newly functional tractor. Susan handed Scott a snack bag and gave him a hug, and then she walked us out to the Explorer. With her arm around me, she quietly gave me a farewell blessing I would long remember. "Elizabeth, I'll be thanking Jessica for sending you. I love your openness and compassion and curiosity. I feel I have new friend. I'm kind of on a high and I hope we can stay connected." She squeezed my shoulders and added, "Now don't be afraid to take a chance at love when it comes to you, but never forget to find happiness in your own self, too."

I didn't know what to say. No one had ever been so unabashedly and vocally appreciative of me. Not that I'd had any verbal abuse in my life, but this affirmation was so freely given without a trace of embarrassment: it was definitely not the communication I had grown up with. I gave Susan a long warm hug as a thank you. Susan Anderson was the most self-secure person I had ever met, and at that moment I wanted only to live up to her description of me. I would never have guessed that the secret to life was really so simple. Or maybe that what was so simple needed such careful nurturing.

I wondered if Scott had been similarly moved by our experience. When we exited the gate and entered the road, he honked our horn three times. With the windows open to the morning air, we heard a responding honk of the farm tractor. We turned and grinned at each other.

"Have we just been in paradise?" he asked me.

"Who would have guessed that we would find such kinship on a farm in Nebraska?"

Scott nodded and then he proclaimed, "Okay, Cousin, let's get this mission back on track, on the road again!"

"Here we come, Iowa!" I shouted out the window and surprising a cow who was sticking his neck under a fence to reach some particularly juicy grass.

24

I confess that by afternoon of that same day, our initial enthusiasm for our drive began to dim as we drove through mile after mile of corn fields and truck stops, Nebraska blending on into Iowa.

Before I could do my usual "What do you know about Iowa?" Scott spoke up: "University of Iowa Medical School."

"What?"

"One of my roommates, Chris, went there."

"You sure have had a lot of roommates." At one time I had known them all.

"Yep, and most of us stay in touch. I remember when Chris went to University of Iowa."

"Where is he now?"

Scott shrugged. "Seems to have dropped out of sight… which I guess means he is not on Facebook. But I know that he went to University of Iowa."

I thought for a moment. "I have another University of Iowa connection: the Writer's Workshop. World renowned. In fact, I…."

I left the sentence hanging. My desire to attend the Writers Workshop is something I hadn't discussed with anyone, not even Scott. He looked at me now as if waiting for me to finish the sentence. "Yes? In fact, I…."

"In fact, I just read a book by a woman who teaches there. Marilyn Robinson."

Scott looked at me funny. He always knew when I was covering something up, but he didn't press me. I don't know why I was secretive about this little dream I had of someday writing something, something that would satisfy my craving to set down a story in print.

At midday, we decided to get off the freeway for an hour and followed an exit that showed a town five miles off the interstate. Taking a chance, we drove to the only café in this little Iowa town, aside from the usual fast-food restaurants. Cathy's Corner sounded like a place where a little local color might be found.

Scott's sandwich looked appetizing. Pulled pork barbecue. Scott is tall and lanky, and he can eat like a horse and not put on a pound. When I'm home and running daily, I can eat my share, but here on the road my exercise program was shot, and I knew I needed to be more careful. Sitting in the car all afternoon would not burn off many calories, so I ignored the Rueben sandwich with chips, and even decided against the minestrone soup, and instead ordered a salad. Mistake; a fake wooden bowl filled with a bunch of sad lettuce, and a lot of it, as if volume could make up for quality. It was topped with pale, tasteless tomato slices that would have appalled Susan Anderson.

This was a farm town in summer, so where were the luscious home-grown tomatoes like Nellie grew in Davis? When the waitress came back to refill our iced tea glasses, I asked her, politely I thought, whether the tomatoes were locally grown, and she sniffed, "Oh no, these are from Kroger's. Our tomatoes won't be ripe until well into July." She looked at me sharply. "You don't like them?"

I smiled and said, "They are fine, thank you. Could I have an English muffin to go with my salad?" I had to have something that crunched for lunch!

I decided that I would walk the straight and narrow on food until we got to Chicago. Scott promised me that when we stayed with another one of his old roommates in Chicago, Nick would make sure we ate and drank only the best. And I hoped, being in the city for almost a week, we should have plenty of opportunities to walk and jog.

I forced myself to look the other way when Scott offered me one of the two donuts he bought at the cash register. So strong was my junk food mood, I gazed longingly at the Wendy's as we drove by on our way back to the Interstate.

When we approached Iowa City, Scott suggested we stop for night there. "College town, should be some good beer."

I rolled my eyes. "Maybe you can relive your old college drinking days."

"You exaggerate our partying, Lizbeth. And besides you were with us most of the time, with or without Aiden."

I don't know if Scott regretted bringing up my college boyfriend. We didn't talk about those past days often. Ah, Aiden. More hot times per minute than any other time of my life. From the day I first met him in Scott's module during the middle of our sophomore year, my involvement with Aiden defined not just my social life, but my whole life for twenty-four months. I had a hard time focusing on anything else besides him, but fortunately I was a good student, and despite spending most of my time with Aiden engaged in non-studious activities, I miraculously managed to keep my head just above water academically.

Before I met Aiden, we were all a gang: Scott and his friends and roommates, and me and my friends and roommates, a big gang of good-natured college students who had fun but never forgot to study, who hung out together night and day. In the midst of all that shared companionship, when Aiden and I got together we buzzed in a little bubble that the others put up with, although I'm not quite sure why; we were, I am absolutely certain, obnoxious in our displays of affection as well as our frequent fights. Never before or since have I been a person prone to either displays of public affection or public verbal battles complete with dramatic and very temporary breakups. I asked Scott later—in total humiliation—why they all put up with Aiden and me, and he just said briefly, "We figured it was temporary insanity, and would pass."

And of course, it did pass. One day, I had one of those epiphany moments when I knew that the relationship was not good for me. In fact, it was just plain shit, this great passion of mine. Laughable. It became obvious to me after Aiden started drinking more frequently, plus smoking, and pills, and more. But with sudden clarity (that had probably been building for some time), I realized how ridiculous it all was. So, I broke up with him midway through our senior year, on our two-year anniversary, as a matter of fact. Aiden decided to drop out of school, went home to Sacramento and disappeared from our lives. Scott told me once that Aiden had entered a substance abuse program but had dropped out of that too before going into his father's insurance business, where his too-frequent binges and lack of follow-through were ignored or covered up by his indulgent parents. I don't know if he continued to be the charming and charismatic guy he had been during our college years. No one gave me an update on that.

"You know, you got out of that just in time," Scott quietly told me after we broke up. But he rarely mentioned Aiden again after that. And I didn't ask. I felt embarrassed at my behavior and astonished at my raging emotions for those two years. I wasn't myself. (That's what I thought, without understanding at the time that the person I was when hooked on Aiden was a part of the whole constellation of myself, and it was not without its pleasure. I may not have been proud of myself afterward, but I should at least acknowledge that it really was me. A me who changed over time. But that wise big-picture realization didn't come to me until much later.)

Post-Aiden, I spent the last semester of my university life madly recalculating myself academically and socially. I got my equilibrium back and pushed on to my graduation, got my teaching credential, and soon there I was living in Nellie's upstairs apartment, as steady and rock solid as I thought I should be. This is who I really am, I thought.

When Gran entered my life, it hit me that perhaps my steady Rock of Gibraltar persona—while healthier than that crazy college version of Elizabeth Kuiper—was not necessarily the final version of myself. Over the last few months, I had felt a vaguely unspecified restlessness. I had no idea what any of this was about or where it would lead but being on the road seemed to fit my state of mind.

I looked at Scott as he drove along and said gratefully, "Hey, Cuz. Thanks for sticking with me."

He looked confused. Clearly his thoughts had traveled on from his casual mention of Aiden, and it took him a moment to understand what I had been dwelling on for the last twenty-five miles.

Then his face cleared. "Wasn't just me, Elizabeth. All of our friends wanted you to come out of that relationship intact! Of course, you were good entertainment in the meantime, kind of a vicarious thrill for the rest of us nerdy creatures who never smoothly mastered relationships, much less high drama and erotica!"

He grinned at me and then began humming a sexy old song, which I recognized from our college days. I was not embarrassed, not with Scott, just grateful for his constant companionship and lack of judgement. That college girl Elizabeth seemed like she existed in another reality.

And so, we drove on, lost in our own thoughts, found a hotel in Iowa City, enjoyed exploring the university, and after considerable walking, we settled into a booth in a college bar and enjoyed a beer and pizza while crowds of University of Iowa students scrummed around us, voices periodically erupting in fevered laughter. I had memories of being in the middle of an attractive, hormone-driven group of young people, but now these kids seemed so much younger than us. Were we old at age twenty-nine?

We got back on the road in the morning, and when I knew we were getting close to the Mississippi, I decided that this icon of America should have more celebration than just crossing over it on a long bridge at Davenport, so after some quick Googling, I directed us north to the town of Dubuque.

Dubuque. How many names have the letter 'U' in it three times? This part of Iowa along the Mississippi was scenic, with broad stretches of river with sand banks and impressive white cliffs across the river. It felt like a long way from the rest of Iowa with its endless miles of corn fields. From my studies reinforced by a quick internet search, I was able to tell Scott how the ice age had formed this whole midwestern portion of the country and brought the rich dark brown soil. And the Mississippi—what a force! How integral it has been to the history of North America from long before Europeans came to the land. I found it humbling to think about. I told Scott that we couldn't just zoom across it on the interstate and told him why it was so important to go north to Dubuque to visit the Mississippi museum and see how the locks worked to process the huge barges and other boats.

Scott looked at me funny after a while, and crossed his eyes comically, even while driving. "You know you've been jawing on about geography and history ever since we got close to the river."

"Well, it's a big deal, Scott. Do you know…?"

Scott cut me off. "How about some music, Lizzie? You can even pick. Just stop with the history and geography lesson. I know, I know, the Mississippi River is a big fucking deal!"

But he grinned to soften his words. I accept that I can

be annoying with my enthusiasm to lecture and ramble on a given topic that is fascinating to me.

When we arrived at the museum and Scott saw the locks at work, however, the engineer/mechanic in him was intrigued and during our meal, a picnic dinner eaten in a park by the river, he talked enthusiastically about what he had seen.

As he finished his cheese and bread and flicked the last crumb out for a nearby bird, Scott said, "Okay, now are we ready to move on to Chicago? I'm going to text Nick and give him an ETA."

"I'm so ready. I've always wanted to see Chicago, and I liked Nick so much back in the day. What's his partner's name?"

But Scott wasn't listening, he was watching a young woman jogging by, with leggings on and a blond ponytail swinging behind her as she ran.

I let him enjoy watching her, and then poked him. "She looks a little like Gina, doesn't she?"

He jerked. "Well, maybe so. It's the ponytail. I find ponytails very sexy," he confessed.

"I'm sure that is all you were looking at!" I challenged him and he tried to look insulted.

I started giggling. Scott frowned at me and then grabbed my head and gave me a nooggie, something he hadn't done since middle school.

When he stopped harassing me, I said to him, "Seriously, Scott. You must be excited to be seeing Gina soon."

He tried to look nonchalant. "Well, we have a lot of miles to cover and things to do first. I'm just trying to be cool about it. I mean who knows how it will turn out, once I get up there. But, yeah, I do hope it works out."

"And she does have a nice ponytail, Gina does, among other parts." I patted Scott's arm and then said, "Okay, let's find a place to stay and then on to Chicago tomorrow. I'm ready for city life."

"Nick and Arturo live in a cool part of the city. Should be lots of places to go without having to drive. Give the old Explorer a rest. Nick told me a good place to park that's not too expensive."

"Where did Nick meet Arturo?"

"I don't know. It's a new relationship, I guess about a year old. I think they met in San Francisco when he was living there for a couple of years after he finished vet school. You can ask them. We'll be with them as long as we want, maybe a week?"

"Excellent!" I was excited to have an open-ended time with an old friend. And then I felt a pang. "But after that, then we really should push on to Canada. I'm getting excited about meeting Chelsea. And scared, too, about her reaction."

I also found myself worrying about Gran. Having heard no results from the surgery, I wondered if that meant the worst. And then I felt a little guilty about not spending more time thinking about Gran while we had been on the road. I couldn't let go of that line of thinking.

That night in my room, I sent my update to Tibby and Gran and made it a little more descriptive than usual, out of guilt no doubt. Finally, I began my nightly text to Jerry. It was like writing a poem or a haiku, where I tried to put all the things that, in person I would have spent hours talking about, into as few but well-chosen words I could muster. I had never done anything like this before, but I found Jerry to be a responsive and appreciative participant. Who would have expected this from a small-town mechanic? It was a lesson in making assumptions about people! Writing to him in this manner was satisfying to my creative spirit, but I had to be honest, it satisfied something deeper beyond just an English lesson. I was careful not to analyze anything about Jerry, however. No conclusions. Not now. Not while on the road, on our mission for Gran.

And dear Gran. I missed her. It was genuine affection but I felt that until our mission was complete, I didn't know what to say to her. All Tibby ever reported was to say that she and Gran were doing fine together and that results from the surgery were delayed but she would be in touch when she heard. It seemed to me that this was taking a long time, but what did I know about such matters? I was a novice about hospitals and surgeries and illnesses. And Tibby always ended her message with "You kids, enjoy your trip!"

After I sent off my text to Jerry and while I waited (hoped) for his return text, I pulled out Mac's journal. I hadn't read for a while and so there in Dubuque, Iowa, going back to read parts I had missed earlier, I once again sank into this man's story of crossing the United States before I was even born.

I got an eyeful!

When we met for breakfast in the morning, I wouldn't let

Scott take a bite. I was almost shouting. "You are not going to believe this! Do you know that Mac left Wyoming in a hurry because of what he called a 'grave misunderstanding' between him and another guy about a woman? And, listen to me, listen to this… that he also left because he hated the rancher whose barn they were building… a creepy rancher named—get this—Brookings! Only Mac's descriptive word was far more obscene than creepy! And it was this Brookings' brother whom he had the fight with about the woman!"

Scott looked at me blankly, and I almost screeched at him. "Scott! Do you hear what I am saying? According to that waitress back in Wyoming, that's the name of the guys with the dogs who scared the shit out of us! It must have been Rusty or his brother that Mac fought with. What a coincidence! I almost woke you up last night to tell you! So damn amazing! Gran is going to not believe it! I can't believe it!"

"Lizzie, you're talking in exclamation marks," Scott told me, his way of telling me to cool it and calm down. But he admitted that it was an extraordinary coincidence. And he shuddered. "I've tried to shut that whole experience out of my mind, certainly the name of that jerk. But I won't ever forget those dogs."

"I wasn't too fond of having a gun pointed at us, either, Scott."

"Pick your nightmare," he said grimly. "I think I would pick being shot and killed quickly over being torn apart by dogs." His voice was shaky.

I quickly changed the subject. "I'm so excited to see Nick again. I think he was my favorite of all your roommates."

Scott looked relieved to talk about something else. "I'm really glad that he is happy and settled now. Do you know that back in the day, Nick was the only one of my friends who didn't want to date you? And now we know why." He laughed and turned the car towards Chicago.

25

We lay, sprawled like seals on rocks, around Nick and Arturo's small living room. Their apartment consisted of four rooms plus a bathroom: two small bedrooms, a living room not much bigger, and a mini-sized kitchen. It felt somewhat like our college days except you could see they were making a start at getting some real furniture, and the artwork on the walls was certainly a step up from that to be found in our college digs. The guys served us a meal of homemade Chicago-style pizza made in a good quality pan and placed on real matching sets of dishes. But Nick apologized that the apartment was not yet fixed up as they planned.

"How long have you lived here?" I asked.

"Back in Chicago thirteen months, but in this apartment only a month. We wanted to live closer to Boys Town or Wicker Park neighborhood, but this was as close as we could afford right now," Nick explained as he grabbed another beer for all of us. Even I was drinking beer tonight. When with old college friends....

Arturo smiled up at Nick as he accepted his beer. Nick was radiating. He had always been the nicest guy, a super study mate, museum friend, and great buddy, forever kind to me and ready to listen to my raging laments during my frequent breakups with the aforementioned Aiden, offering consolation and even advice. But now my former college nice guy was a truly happy man, settled and vibrating both.

"Scott tells me you two met in San Francisco. And now you're here in Chicago. What's the story?"

Nick and Arturo exchanged a tender glance.

Nick began. "After I finished vet school I decided to try living in San Francisco. I had no money and lots of student loan debt, so when I got a job at a clinic, I decided not to get an apartment which would have taken most of any salary I made as a newbie. For the most part what I was doing was treating dogs and cats, being a city clinic, although one time my clinic got to treat an injured mountain lion, hit by a car while roaming around the city, poor thing. I really enjoyed that job and living in the City for the first time. While Davis is a great school and we all had a lot of fun, it was not San Francisco and I needed to experience it all!

"In short, my plan was to house-sit and pet-sit for rich people. It worked out great. I got to stay in some of the best places in the City. I just had to be portable about my belongings and ready to move frequently. Eventually I got a six-month job pet sitting and housesitting for some people in the Marina who were sailing around the world. What a great gig that was. Nice house, near Chrissy Field. One day when I was out walking their two Irish Wolfhounds… great big dogs and so sweet, even you would have liked them, Scott… suddenly one of my hounds wanted amorous adventures with a little pug dog, and after I managed to get my big fellow to leave the little pup alone, I noticed who was at the other end of the pug's leash!"

Nick grinned and poked Arturo's foot with his own and finished his story, "And it was this handsome man!"

Arturo grinned and then completed the story. "And it was truly love at first sight. I never believed in that idea before, but now I sure do!"

I prodded the two. "Okay, so you met in the park at Chrissy Field, and yada, yada, yada you are settled in Chicago together. There must be more to tell."

"Oh Lizzie, if you must know, I'll finish the story." Nick acted as though he wasn't dying to fill us in. "We walked together for hours until the little pug's legs were tired, and even my big guys were pulling me towards home. But Arturo and I agreed to get together the next night after work."

Arturo picked it up. "Turns out we were doing the exact same thing: house and pet sitting!" From the look on their faces, I could envision their excitement when they first realized this coincidence. I grinned at them.

Nick added, "And not only that, we soon found out that Arturo was raised in Chicago just like me!"

"Although I grew up in a very different part of town," Arturo added.

"Nonetheless, we both took our first breaths in this city!" Nick staunchly claimed.

"With one thing and another, in our daily conversations after that first day, we kept talking about Chicago. Arturo had come out to San Francisco after finishing college just to try something different and see where Harvey Milk had lived. We loved San Francisco. We both were having a great time there. But every time we were together, we kept talking about Chicago."

"A few months after we met Arturo got hired by a tech company and they wanted him in their branch in Chicago since he knew the town. Then my mom had to start chemo for cancer and my dad had hip surgery and couldn't get her to the treatments. And at that point, we quit discussing it and said, 'Why not?' We moved just like that. My pet-sitting gig was up, and neither of us had anything to tie us down, so we just did it!"

I laughed. "And then, and then, and then, and here you are!"

Scott asked, "How's your mom, and your dad?" I remembered how much Scott had liked Nick's parents.

"All good now! Worried about them a lot. Hard to see your parents have problems. I always saw my parents as invincible. It was scary, but my mom is in remission, and my dad is back on the tennis court. We lived with them when we first moved out here. I helped with Mom, Arturo commuted to his job, and it gave us a chance to save up some money and for me to find work. I'm back at an urban vet office, not too far from here, and I like it almost as much as I liked the job in San Francisco. I will admit we both had gotten used to Bay Area weather, and we suffered through our Chicago winter as if we had never lived here before. We moved out of my parents' house a month ago and here we are, enjoying the good life of the Chicago. Tomorrow we will give you a flavor of our city, music, beer, clubs, beer, music, beer…!" Nick laughed.

I pushed at them, "Please slip in a few museums! I know there are some good ones here. And someplace I can run. I need to get out on the trail! Life is not all beer, boys!"

They all lifted a toast to that, and Nick promised to show me some museums and Arturo told me where the best place was to go jogging. And with that, we ate more pizza, drank more beer, laughed our heads off at old stories, and perhaps had the music up a little loud, because about one in the morning there was a pounding at the door.

Arturo pulled himself off the floor, got up and went to the door with a little stagger and without looking through the peek hole, opened the door wide enough that we could see a young woman in a robe, hair disheveled, and a look on her face that could have frozen a forest fire. She was fiercely angry.

Arturo shrank a little and stood aside as if to get out of the way. The woman—on closer inspection, a very young woman—took a step inside the doorframe and swept her eyes over the four of us. Her voice held implied spittle.

"Turn down the fucking music! I don't know what you lazy bastards do all day, but some of us have to go to work in the morning, and some of us have babies that can't sleep because of your noise, and some of us have trains to catch and bosses that will piss if we are late. And if we lose our jobs, some of us will be out on the street because we can't pay the rent."

Nick jumped up and fumbled for his phone to turn the music down and then stood by Arturo to give him courage.

Following the sudden silence, Nick and the rest of us let our voices pile up all over each other in apologies.

The woman sniffed, "Some of us can't afford to party all night. Must be nice." And she turned around and started to walk down the hallway.

I jumped up and ran after her. "Wait!" I called. She slowly stopped and even more slowly turned around to look at me, ready for battle.

I stopped about ten feet from her and we looked at each for a moment without word. Then I ran my hand through my hair. "Listen, I am sorry. We were having a flashback at being college students again, and I guess we thought it was Saturday night and..." I let it go at that and stopped trying to get undeserved sympathy.

"We were rude and wrong and I really am sorry. My cousin and I are visiting from out of state, but Arturo and Nick just moved in here, and I don't want our fuckup tonight to get them off on a wrong foot with their neighbors. Give them another chance, and if they screw up, well... make them babysit for you or do your kids' homework or something," I finished lamely.

She stood there looking at me, a deadly stare-down. Then remarkably, she nodded. "Okay. They seemed like nice boys when they moved in, and I am wasted from work and the baby's teething and my ten-year old's having nightmares. So, I'll let it go this time, but there are twenty bars and clubs within two blocks of here. Take your good times out of the apartment so the rest of us who have to work can get some sleep."

I thought of defending Nick and Arturo since they obviously worked as well, although they had taken the week off work to play with us while we were in town. But I could smell the fatigue in this woman.

I called after her as she shuffled on back up the stairs to her apartment. "What's your name?"

She stopped at the first step and gave me another very long look. Finally, staring at me with a defensive look that reminded me of the face-saving countenance of some of my students, she said, "Myrtle."

"Hello, Myrtle. I'm Elizabeth."

She gave me yet another long, dead-looking look, but then, "College friends? Don't suppose they know anything about algebra...."

"They should, what they haven't forgotten." I added, "Why?"

"I'm taking a night class, every Tuesday night, trying to get my diploma. I didn't figure out algebra when I was in high school and I still don't get it."

She didn't directly ask, but I answered anyway. "I'll talk to Nick and Arturo and find out who did the best in algebra and tell them to be in touch with you."

She grunted and didn't say thanks or okay or great or anything. She just said, "Apartment 301, just overhead."

And then she was gone and I went back to the now-quiet apartment where Scott was picking up beer bottles, and Nick and Arturo were getting out blankets for us. All were suppressing nervous laughter.

They looked at me as I came walking back in. "What

did you do now, Lizbeth?" Scott and Nick asked at the same time.

"Just getting to know your neighbor Myrtle a little bit better. She, who has a horrible boss and a baby who is teething and a daughter who has nightmares, would appreciate if you boys would keep your partying to the bars from now on. And, oh, yeah, one of you is going to tutor her in algebra. Flip a coin and start reviewing your old text books!"

I laughed at their faces, grabbed my toiletries and called out, "Dibs on the bathroom, but I won't be long. And you can thank me for possibly saving your good neighbor award."

They gave me the sofa in their office and Scott slept on the floor in the living room since the couch was not long enough. We were soon all headed to sleep—I barely managed my nightly texts—when I heard the sound of a baby crying from above. It didn't last long fortunately, for poor Myrtle's sake. Then a dog barked nearby followed by a siren a few blocks away. A tom cat yowled and a kitchen worker dumped a bin of empty bottles, sending them crashing into a dumpster outside a nearby restaurant. I heard voices of people passing by on the street, laughter, a few choice swear words. And right before I finally slipped away to sleep, a truck noisily applied its brakes on the street and then revved its engine as it made an early morning delivery somewhere. We weren't in rural Nebraska anymore.

26

I never could drink as much as the guys who were fanatical about their beer. Not surprisingly, I was up earlier than any of them and this gave me time to take a shower and then open Mac's journal. Mac had enjoyed some good times in Chicago. He found Lake Michigan fascinatingly large and ocean-like and worked for a time on a boat that took people out on the lake. He spent his spare time at clubs listening to jazz and blues and soul. He also mentioned exploring some Frank Lloyd Wright houses, which perhaps gave him thoughts about the house he would one day build with Gran on the Pacific shores of Northern California.

It was clear that Mac became restless with city life, however, and after two months, he took off like a rolling stone, moving westward once again.

Finishing up that portion of his writing, I tucked the journal back into its bag and put the bag back in the large bag with all of Mac's stuff we were taking to Chelsea. As I did that, I heard the others waking up. I went out to join them. Scott was still stretched out on the floor but he was checking his phone and grunted a good morning to me. I could see he was nursing a hangover.

Nick came in looking worse for the wear as well. He looked at me with affectionate disgust. "Liz Kuiper, how the hell do you look so peppy and adorable this morning?" (You can see why I love Nick.)

Scott answered for me, "She just fakes that she's drinking. She doesn't do her share at all. She's gloating right now."

"Oh boys, oh boys, how can you think I have nefarious intent? I was just saving you money by not drinking all your stash. And I'm happy to make you all a big breakfast right now, if there is anything in your fridge but leftover pizza and beer."

They all groaned in unison. "Could not eat anything now." Arturo politely added, "But maybe later."

I laughed. "No problem. Tell me where I can go running and I'll get some exercise and be back here in an hour to cook up some breakfast. Do you have eggs and toast or anything else?"

Arturo took me into the kitchen and opened a well-stocked fridge to show me, then said to me politely but definitely setting the record straight, "Elizabeth, we are not obnoxious college students. We are grownup, employed, reliable, competent, adult men, who can even cook, you know."

I gave him a hug. I liked this guy already. Nick stuck his head in the kitchen doorway. "Lizzie, do I recall you saying something last night about tutoring someone in algebra? Or am I hallucinating about that?"

"No, you're right. One of you two is going to become the algebra tutor to your upstairs neighbor, Myrtle, who will probably never thank you, but if she passes the course, she may name her next baby after you. You just never know."

"And exactly why are we supposedly doing this?"

"Because we obnoxiously disturbed an exhausted woman with a horrible boss, who's taking night classes, and raising a cranky baby as well as a troubled ten-year-old. Who knows what else? I'm guessing single mother since she is the one who came down and didn't send some big mean man to beat you up! So, if you can help her, you might be back in good graces with your neighbor, which is a very desirable thing."

"Okay," Nick said, still confused. "And algebra? Where does that fit in?"

"Simple. She is taking a night class and is finding algebra to be a real challenge. She needs help and she figures if you two are college boys, the least you could do is to help her so she can be a college girl!"

They both looked at me, and Scott who had come into the kitchen, just laughed. "That's my cousin. Elizabeth, the organizer. You two have just been Lizzie-sized. I'd follow her advice if I were you, because it is no doubt for your own good!"

I stuck my tongue out at Scott, then finished filling up my water bottle, picked up the little map and I was off on my first Chicago adventure.

All week, Nick and Arturo gave us the royal Chicago tour (including museums). We walked miles along Lake Michigan and they regaled me with stories of the famous Hawk, the wind that could tear your breath away. During our visit, the summer weather featured a fair share of sticky warm humidity to make us know we weren't in California anymore. The heat didn't dampen our spirits though, and I got in enough museums and galleries to make me happy. We also visited more music clubs and bars than I can remember. It was a fantastic week.

On the last night of our visit, Tibby called. I could not hear in the bar, and by the time I saw the call and tried to answer, she had hung up. I motioned to Scott across the table from me. "It's Tibby," I mouthed and showed him my phone.

I slid out of the booth and headed outside to call her back. Scott started to get up to join me, but I waved him back. "I've got it covered. I'll fill you in."

I found a ledge to sit on outside the front door of the bar and while a steady stream of people entered and exited the place, cars rushed by on the street, the El train rattled by a few blocks away, and all the noise of the city rumbled around me, I called Tibby back and imagined her there with Gran in the house that Mac and Gran had created, with the only sound inside the house being the music playing on Gran's speakers, and outside, the wind and the waves and the occasional call of a raven flying overhead.

I had been drinking up my week in Chicago, embracing the urban ambiance, and living in the moment, but just like that, thinking of the North Coast, I found myself aching to be there, to sit and watch the waves, feel the wind in my hair, talk with Gran, feel Tibby's warm friendship, and, yes, see Jerry again. It was another type of wave that hit me, not oceanic, but emotional.

As the phone was ringing at Tibby's end, I calmed myself.

"Tibby!" I said to her answering voice. "I'm sorry I missed your call; we were in a club and the music was loud. What's up? How are you? How's Gran?"

Tibby's voice was steady.

"I'm fine, dear. And sounds like you and Scott are having a grand time. I've never been to Chicago and look forward to hearing all about it."

I pressed. "And Gran? I've been worried because we haven't heard the results of her surgery or how she is doing."

"Well, up to now, there hasn't been anything definitive to tell you, Elizabeth. And Gran has been adamant about not interrupting your trip. Once she sent you off, she was determined to let you two have the trip you wanted; to let the road take you where it will take you, is how she puts it."

It was true. Gran had shown great restraint. She had not interfered.

I persisted. "Tibby, hasn't Gran heard anything from those doctors?"

"There was apparently some mix-up with the biopsy. We never got the whole story, however there was some kind of snafu at the lab. It wasn't until this morning that Gran finally had a talk with her doctor. The news is a bit of good and a bit of not so good.

"The cancer is definitely in evidence and is expected to grow and eventually take her from us."

I gasped. And Tibby heard across the miles because she went on quickly, "Elizabeth, they said they feel the tumor is growing slower than they first suspected, and so Gran could very well have quite a lot more time before she gets sicker. Maybe considerable time, although they can't really say."

I wanted to scream. It was all so nebulous.

"But, Tibby, is there anything they can do? Medication?

Chemo? Radiation? Something to stop it or make it go away?" Of course, we had known this was a possibility, but why did it hit me so hard now? Had I maintained hope that things would be fine, that this was a scare but not for real? Or maybe all these weeks I had been thinking no news is good news. But now? I choked up.

Tibby behaved as if she expected my reaction. "My dear, that is exactly what goes through our heads, and I will be honest, despite knowing your Gran so well, I found myself wanting her to do everything possible to hold this off. But knowing your Gran as I know her, I was not surprised when she told the doctor no, she didn't want any treatments."

"But why not? Doesn't she want to do everything she can do? What about the rest of us? Don't our wishes count?" I sounded plaintive, whining like a little child. A man leaving the bar, gave me a double take when my voice carried to him.

Tibby was patient. I could almost feel her arms around me. "Elizabeth, there are so many things over which we have no control in this life, and then there are some times when we can make choices. Gran didn't choose to get this cancer. She didn't choose these results. But she can choose how to live; she has always done so, and now she will choose how to live out her life and how to die, and where to die, and to a degree when, although that is also mostly out of our hands. The doctors admitted that they don't know for sure how this cancer is going to proceed. Every person is different, and every cancer grows a little bit differently. So the doctors cannot predict one hundred percent the course that lies before us."

In the middle of my concern, as Tibby talked longer,

I felt that Tibby was using an implied "we" when she spoke of Gran.

"I'm not telling you this to upset you or Scott, or to alter the course of your trip. You are doing exactly what your Gran wanted you to do: get out of your normal routine, have a trip, maybe some adventures, have time together, and of course then fulfill the mission that is so important for your Gran. Gran would have been happier if I never called and told you about this medical news because she does not want to interrupt your traveling. But I convinced her that, for one thing, you have been asking me, and two, life is not just one long party and adventure. Life is complicated and I reminded her that Elizabeth and Scott are old enough to understand. They will figure out how to mix their pleasure and their exploring, along with learning about the nuances of tough times. Life is just that way, and you don't throw out the good times because of the bad times."

I listened silently.

"Therefore, your task now, Elizabeth, is to make that adjustment; hold your Gran and her health in your heart but keep having new adventures and discoveries along the way."

I was quiet for a minute thinking about what Tibby was saying. Seems like Nellie had told me something like this a while ago. She had been very serious and then she had laughed, those wonderful crinkly lines around her eyes and mouth doing a dance around her face as she told me, lightheartedly, "Wisdom from the crone, dear, wisdom from the crone!"

"Okay, Tibby," I eventually said. "Okay." And then I added, "Can I talk with Gran?"

"For her own reasons, she says she will talk to you when you get back. I'm sorry, Elizabeth. She wants me to do the talking now. I hope you don't take that personally." Tibby sounded apologetic.

But strangely, as much as I longed to hear Gran's voice, I did understand Gran's decision not to talk to us while we were on the road, although I was not sure I could articulate it. Gran and I were in synch.

Tibby then added, "Just this thought, Elizabeth. I know that Scott is heading off to meet up with his Gina after you two see Chelsea. We wish him all happiness. Obviously, we won't lay expectations on him for a return to see us. But I don't know what your plans might be…" Tibby paused and for once she didn't seem confident.

"I plan on returning home shortly after we see Chelsea. I have a few things to do before the school year starts. Then I want to come to Gualala as soon as I can!"

Tibby seemed relieved. But then she added, "Don't tell Gran I am saying this to you. She doesn't want to put any pressure on you, well…" Tibby laughed, "…no more pressure than she already put on you to take Mac's things to Chelsea! But once you left, she had faith in you. There is no way she wants to squash your independence. Be clear that encouraging you to come back soon to see us soon is not Gran talking, this is me."

Tibby paused. "When you make the connection with Chelsea, it will relieve Gran's mind. She'll sleep better and be able to feel like a mission has been accomplished, and a great debt to Mac will be complete. But she doesn't want to put pressure on you and Scott to come see her because you are doing a great favor for her. Know what I mean?"

Tibby seemed anxious, not philosophical anymore. What was obvious was her love for Gran. I realized that's what this was all about. Tibby and Gran loved each other. Call it what you will. Perhaps just friendship, but there was no "just" about it. It was solid gold love and it made me even more weepy to think about it.

I swallowed the lump in my throat. "We'll get on the road tomorrow and except for nights, we won't stop again until we see Chelsea. Please give Gran my love, and Scott's too. He's inside having another beer, but I know Scott would not be here if it wasn't for Gran. He could easily have flown out to be with Gina. This is us, both of us, doing this for Gran."

Tibby gave a noncommitted affirmative "hmm" but then she ended our call with this. "Scott is doing it for Gran, I agree. But he is doing it for you, too, Elizabeth. And he is doing it for reasons he can't even imagine. There are many nuances and meanings to the things we do. It's both simple and complex. It's being human."

I didn't have a clue what Tibby meant, but as I stood there looking out at the cars and people, I could feel her connection to me. I could feel her caring for me. It was incredibly personal and heart-grabbing. She certainly knew me far better already than my own mom did, even after a lifetime of parenthood.

I hadn't noticed the intensifying atmosphere around me,

being so wrapped up with the inner workings of my mind and heart. The first raindrops made me jump. A big plop hit my head and more followed. I moved under the shelter of the awning over the doorway.

"Tibby, it's starting to rain, and I need to go inside." And then for some reason I told her, "I've been reading Mac's journal. I hope that's okay."

Tibby laughed. "No rules about that. I can tell you one thing from my years knowing Sean MacIntosh. You could learn a lot from Mac, even back in his young roaming days! A lot of wisdom came out of that good-hearted wild man. It's been lovely talking to you, Elizabeth. Please give Scott my greetings."

I stood there only another moment, slipping my phone back into my pocket, before the rain began pouring down. I dashed back into the bar and found our table of friends, the scene just as I had left it. Scott looked at me intently from across the table. I just put my hands across my heart and he nodded, knowing that we would unpack it all as soon as the night was done. I noticed that he was nursing the same beer he had been drinking when I left. I could tell because he had peeled most of the label off the bottle.

"Raining like crazy outside," I announced to the table in general.

"Good old Midwestern downpour," Nick said gleefully. "Won't last long and it will clear the air, cool us off, and give you two a great getaway day tomorrow to head up to the UP."

Scott looked at him. "UP?"

"Upper Peninsula, of Michigan," Nick explained.

And in my mind, I flashed back to my USA puzzle where that little surprise add-on to the state of Michigan had perplexed me. Now the next day we would be heading that way. I thought of Gran and how she had never done this trip across America and now most likely never would. I figured there were a whole lot of things I hadn't done yet in life—bigger adventures than driving across America—and some I would do if I freed myself up to do so, and some perhaps I would never get around to doing. But I was doing this now. And it was all because of Gran stirring up the pot, shaking up my mind, giving me possibilities and strange missions to accomplish. Indeed, Gran was a trouble-maker and I was very grateful for it. Teeming with sentimentality, brushing away a tear, I lifted my glass of Chicago beer and took my last warm sip.

I had had enough beer for a while, and thought longingly of a nice glass of red wine and of someone special to share it with. I'm not sure where that last thought came from.

27

We got away the next morning reasonably early. But I first insisted Nick and Arturo go upstairs and leave a note with their phone number by Myrtle's doormat offering to tutor her in algebra. I felt absurdly hopeful that Myrtle would reach out for the help and that my friends would follow through themselves. Maybe I am naïve matchmaker. Or perhaps it is the teacher in me.

What with packing up and sharing last-minute farewells with Nick and Arturo, I told Scott that there was nothing that wouldn't wait until we were on the road in terms of sharing Tibby's news.

It was after we got out of Chicago traffic heading north, on the way up into Wisconsin, that I laid out Tibby's message. Scott was quiet until I finished with the substance I remembered from the conversation. Then he tapped a little rhythm on the steering wheel, and said, "Well, Lizbeth, I don't know about you, but I say let's not make any more sidetrack stops. We can even skip Milwaukee. Let's just drive until we are tired, spend the night somewhere, and then keep going. I'm ready to meet Chelsea and move forward. And you must be tired of schlepping that big bag of Mac's stuff in and out of hotels every night."

"I'm ready to keep going. But I'm surprised you want to

skip Milwaukee. I thought that town was famous for beer." I was teasing, just a little.

He shook his head. "Even I am ready for a break from the beer scene for a while."

And that's what we did, just kept pushing on to Canada, enjoying the lovely verdant scenery of this part of America. We passed through small towns, some rundown and some cute and homey, and more strip malls than we cared to see. We saw political signs that disturbed us. And we saw scenes that intrigued and awed us. But we kept moving on. Our sense of mission weighed upon us strongly in the aftermath of Gran's ambiguous news, and we plowed onward ever northeast, through northern Wisconsin, along the mammoth Lake Superior (whose deep waters begged us for a return visit) and through the Upper Peninsula of Michigan with all the forests of thick green trees and waterfalls.

On the morning of what we hoped would be our next to the last day before entering Canada, Scott had an idea at breakfast. "We hauled our camping gear all this way and haven't used it yet. We really haven't done this trip right if we don't camp out at least once. All this wild space here in the UP, there's bound to be some camping sites. Let's camp tonight."

It was a beautiful day, although a little sultry, and it did seem like we had been fairly indulgent by staying in hotels all along the way. I readily agreed.

I pulled out my phone and began to look for a camp site for our last night in the States. I found one in reasonable proximity to the border crossing. But it said first come, first serve.

Scott wasn't worried. "It's a week day, and we aren't in Yosemite so there's bound to be room for us."

So far on this trip we had been going with the flow with pretty good luck, so we trusted fate.

The main highway was beautiful, but we kept getting enticed to venture down back roads. We had committed to no stops but we thought surely these short side jaunts wouldn't take much time, however, they did add up. Our final stop was for dinner and the service was painfully slow. We began to get antsy to get back on the road, but we also wanted to eat first since we weren't equipped to make a camping dinner. We stuffed our food down quickly, then dashed out of the diner after paying our bill and jumped into the Explorer. Despite the long summer days, by the time we found our campground, it was well past twilight with no rising moon to be seen.

We pulled into the ranger kiosk and saw the window was boarded up for night. A sign said, "One campsite left. #32, pay in the morning on your way out."

A gravel road meandered through the campsites, each containing a tent or a camper. Most had a campfire burning and we could see families gathering around, roasting s'mores no doubt. Here and there children were racing around playing tag before bedtime. It took some searching, but finally around several more curves among the trees we peered through what was now certifiable dusk, rapidly turning to darkness, and saw a small painted sign: a faded 32.

We parked, grateful to finally have a place to stop. There was an outhouse nearby so we both relieved ourselves and then, figuring the campsite was just down the path by the sign, we put on our headlamps and grabbed our tent, sleeping bags, back packs and some water. I, of course, hauled out Mac's bag and threw it across my shoulder. We started down the path expecting around every turn to find an open space for our tent, but ever turn just revealed more curves in the path.

Scott looked at me. "Don't you think you could leave Mac's bag in the car, just this once? Who is going to come rip us off in the middle of the woods?"

I stubbornly refused to answer. We'd been through this before. Mac's belongings—Chelsea's inheritance—had become a talisman, entrusted to my care, and we were so close to meeting her that I couldn't relax my vigilance, no matter how sensible my cousin was. I didn't bother to answer, adjusted the bag on my shoulder, and kept trudging.

The campsite turned out to be about a quarter mile away from our car and it was completely dark by the time the path ended in a nice open area, flat and perfect for a tent, with a campfire pit, a bear box, and nearby the babbling of a creek. We couldn't really see much, but as we turned our heads from side to side, the light from our headgear lit up the features of this pristine little campsite.

For one moment, maybe three or four, we were very content. We dropped all our gear onto the picnic table, and rubbed our shoulders and arms, looking around for the most level spot to set up our tent.

And then out of the blue, the first thunder clap rolled through the trees and through our bodies, making us both jump and yelp. Perhaps if we were more seasoned Midwesterners or hadn't been so tired and busy pursuing our camp site, we would have smelled the storm coming. Nick claimed he always could predict a storm coming by the smell in the air. But we were just two nerdy Californians, not completely unfamiliar with camping, but definitely not ready for what was to come.

The rain began and it began without foreplay, just hit us like someone had turned on a fire hose straight down from the sky. The thunder continued and the rain fell so thickly that we could hardly see each other's head lamps. We both jumped to the table, grabbed our gear and began running wildly back to the car, hoping we were still on the path, occasionally almost running into the trees that lined the path. It took no time to be soaked to the skin, but on we ran of one accord.

And when we burst out of the trees and were back to our Explorer, we shoved our gear into the back hatch and tore open our doors to jump in.

And then I remembered.

"Scott!" I screeched and I turned around to dash back into the woods.

"What the hell are you doing?" He shouted at me.

"Mac's bag!" I turned for just a second to yell back at him, not knowing if my voice would carry over the roar of the rain and the claps of thunder that kept assaulting the air. Occasional flashes of lightning lit up the sky and in one of those illuminated seconds, I saw Scott looking at me with a look that told me he thought I had lost my mind.

I could read his lips as he screamed, "Let it go! Stay here."

But of course, I couldn't do that and I turned around and between the lightning and the light of my head lamp reentered the path and stumbled down the weaving path back to the world's best campsite.

When I arrived, the campsite was like a river, with water running across the ground, my shoes splashing with each step. I looked at the picnic table and it was empty. My first thought was that someone had stolen it but quickly realized that was ridiculous. Then I wondered if in my panic I had picked it up and pushed it back in the Explorer after all, but when I lurched around the table, there it was, having fallen down into the river of water that covered the ground behind the table, the bag looking like a dark log immersed in the creek.

I grabbed the bag out of the water about the time Scott came running up behind me, breathing hard. We almost collided in the dark, and without saying anything, I grabbed his hand and we began running back again, that same quarter mile, sliding in the now muddy path but managing to right each other so we never actually hit the mud, although I could feel it splattering up my legs. At some point, Scott took the bag from me and we kept running.

In retrospect, why did we run? We were drenched within minutes after the rain began. We couldn't possibly get any wetter than we had been at that point. Running was only instinct. I wanted to protect Mac's bag although by now I feared it was too late; in my mind I was picturing that magnificent journal as a sodden mass of pulp, with all the writing, the story—the story, for God's sake—washed into inky ruin.

My heart was broken. Mac's tools would survive, the kilt might, but the ever-so-important photographs and the journal would be lost forever. Gran had entrusted it to me, and I had failed because of a stupid decision to haul it with me at all times. What a ridiculous obsession! I cursed myself as I ran. "You idiot!" I shouted inside my head. And perhaps I actually screamed it out loud because Scott turned to look at me. I could see that even as we ran.

We dove into the car, dripping water from head to toe. Breathing hard, Scott handed me the bag and I held that wet rubbery slick mass to my breast and cried harder.

But I had to face the worse. I opened it and pulled out the first thing I felt. It was the bag that contained the journal. And then, I felt a little light-headed.

To make a long story short, the wettest thing in that bag was my hand when I plunged it shakily inside.

Then I really started crying, big gulps. Scott looked at me, I'm sure fearing the worst, and then he leaned over to look inside the bag himself. When he realized that everything in that bag was as dry as when Gran and Tibby had handed it to us back in Gualala, he started laughing! And after a moment I started laughing, too.

"It's a miracle!" was all I could say.

"No, not exactly," said my practically-minded cousin. "It's Tibby. Her kayak bag did the trick!"

And that was right. As we sat there with the rain pounding down on my dad's silver Explorer, in the middle of a campsite in the woods of Upper Michigan, just me and Scott, together as we had been all our lives, I mentally telegraphed Tibby my undying gratitude.

Scott laughed more. "And we thought it was so funny when she gave it to us, remember? We told her we sure weren't going to be fording any rivers or swimming any creeks."

"Little did we know!"

Scott looked at me. "Hey, Lizzie, I'm sorry I had this shitty notion to go camping. We could be nice and dry in a hotel room. Now look at us!"

And that's when I understood that we were drenched to the skin, and after the euphoria settled down, I now felt shaky with a damp chill.

Scott leaned back into the back seat and brought out a towel and handed it to me. "Dry up and take those clothes off."

I didn't argue. Scott was discreet and crawled back into the back seat to locate my suitcase, but it was buried under our wet tent, so instead he pulled out a tee-shirt from his bag and handed it up to me. It is hard to peel wet clothes off a wet body, but I did so, all while sitting in the passenger seat, first outer and then under clothing, toweled off, and naked and shivering, pulled Scott's shirt over my head, leaving my wet clothes in little soaked bundles on the floor under my feet.

Then Scott handed me a blanket.

"My gosh, Scottie, where did you get this?"

"It was in the bag of stuff Jerry gave us, you know, the rope and other emergency supplies?"

"Jerry?" I wrapped the blanket around me, its warmth and weight immediately comforting, and put the seat back into a semi-reclined position. Feeling overwhelmed and exhausted, I closed my eyes.

"Scott?"

"What?" came his voice from back in the back of the vehicle.

"I think I love that guy."

"Who?" he mumbled, distracted by trying to get his own wet clothes off his tall body in the confined setting.

"Jerry. Jerry Garcia," I murmured, almost asleep, certainly a sleep of shock as much as fatigue.

Scott paused a moment as if to figure out if my comment was serious or just grateful. "Lizzie, he's a good man."

I wanted to ask if there was another blanket for him, but in my drowsiness, I couldn't formulate the words.

The rain kept pouring, the Explorer stood solid, Mac's bag and his things were safe and dry. And I slept a very deep sleep. I believe sleep is my escape mechanism.

28

I woke up as it was beginning to be light, very early dawn. The rain had stopped, the sky was misty-morning lovely. We were still in the same spot but Scott was not in the driver's seat. I heard his soft snoring coming from the back of the car. Turning to look I saw his long frame spread out in the back of the vehicle, with our luggage and things pushed to one side to make room. He had his jacket pulled over his shoulders—clearly no blanket for him—and although sound asleep, he didn't look at all comfortable.

I pushed the blanket near where he could grab it if he woke up and quietly opened my car door to step out into the glistening world. It appeared so peaceful after the fury of the night. Looking around I saw not a soul and so I maneuvered to pee behind a tree, getting my bare feet wet and my bottom too. Wearing just an oversized tee shirt it was easy to make the camping squat.

As I re-entered the car, I noticed that my clothes, including my underwear and socks, were spread out over the front of the car, and Scott's were as well. Obviously, he had been up after the rain stopped and taken the wet things out from under my feet. I felt well cared-for. I was glad not to be alone that morning.

I sat there with the car door open, letting the fresh summer air into our steamy space, rethinking the day before. Reliving the moment when I realized I had left Mac's bag in the downpour brought a shiver to my spine even though I could also relive the overwhelming relief that the bag had kept the contents dry. "Bless you, Tibby!" I said again.

After a time of sitting there, I grew increasingly hungry and thirsty. Thinking of the utter satisfaction of a steaming hot cup of tea, I began to then imagine all sorts of breakfast delights: scrambled eggs, fried potatoes, toast with butter dripping and jam spread across the top. Or maybe a bacon omelet with cheese on top? I could almost taste the decadence of a chocolate croissant or a gooey apple fritter. And when my mind flashed on a bear claw with almond paste, I could hardly keep myself from making some noise to wake up Scott so we could get on the road. But then I saw my clothes carefully spread out across the hood to dry and contained myself, instead searching through the many compartments in the front seat, finding only a half-eaten granola bar, and a small bag of almonds. The rest of our food was in the back and would require waking Scott to retrieve.

I swallowed my hunger pangs and let my thoughts fill with human kindness towards my cousin. I worked unsuccessfully to make that meager granola bar breakfast satisfy me, along with a swallow of water from my water bottle. To distract myself, I slipped out the door and walked around the car, pulling the tee shirt down to cover my bare thighs just in case there were any peeping Toms lurking.

"Lizbeth?"

I came around to my open door and poked my head in. "Scott!"

He sat up and pulled his body through the opening between the seats and twisting, he crawled outside the car, stood up and stretched. I started to thank him for everything, but instead I couldn't stop a grin at the sight of him.

"Having fun this morning?" he peered at me, grumpy.

"It's just…" I stopped and then started laughing again. "It's just that you look, well, you look kind of like you got caught in a rainstorm and then slept all night in the back of a car. Your hair is all…" And I motioned this way and that.

"And you, you are not exactly a dreamboat. Your hair could use a bit of work too, and is that mud on your legs?"

I looked down at myself and then smiled at him. I was a mess. "I owe you, Scott. Thanks for taking care of me last night. I slept like a baby! Go figure!"

He stretched and rubbed his hand through his hair, further standing it on end. "I think I could have set a bomb off next to you and you wouldn't have moved! The last thing you said was 'I love him.' You remember that?"

That embarrassed me, but don't we always say that about someone who does us a good turn? And Jerry had done us several now.

Scott disappeared into the woods a few minutes and I managed to locate my suitcase (and didn't complain that he had piled all the wet camping gear on top of my bag). I pulled out some clothes and got dressed. Fortunately, it was summer time so all I would need that day was shorts and tee-shirt. I found a plastic bag and took my still-damp clothes and Scott's, too, off the front of the Explorer and shoved them inside, then dropped the bag into the mess that was now the back of our traveling home. I verified that Mac's bag was securely located right behind the front seat. It would be good to get that bag into Chelsea's hands. The responsibility was beginning to weigh on me. Perhaps Scott was right and I was taking it too seriously, but I thought of Gran and how these items were symbolic of her love for Mac and her gift to Mac's child in lieu of Mac himself, and I sighed, thankful again that they had made it through the deluge.

Scott came back to join me looking at the mess in the back. "We should probably straighten this all out now, but there is nothing but mud around us, and I'm starving and most of all I need some coffee. I'm guessing our camp stove is too wet or piled under everything else. Let's get going and find a place to get some hot drink and breakfast. Then we can look for gas, and decide if we go straight into Canada or clean ourselves up first, us and our car." He motioned to both of us, mostly our hair, and then to the back of the car.

"Breakfast first."

We both jumped into our familiar places, Scott driving because, well, Scott wouldn't know what to do if he wasn't driving, and I was quite happy to look at the scenery. I had rarely driven since that day early in our trip when I saw Angelica's car go off the side of the cliff.

We drove through the area of the campground that had been so populated the night before. Now it was deserted, with only a few camper vans remaining. One man was out trying to make a campfire out of the wet wood. We slowed and Scott rolled down the window to ask the man if he knew of a breakfast spot or coffee shop heading east on the highway. He looked us over curiously, vaguely mentioning a café about ten miles down the road and turned right back to his sodden firepit. It wasn't very helpful, but we wished him well building his fire with the wet wood, and left the campground. The ranger had not yet arrived and we decided to stiff the Michigan State Parks and not pay for our wet night, rationalizing that we hadn't actually camped there. Somewhere between our wet campsite and Canada, there would surely be a place to feed our stomachs. We didn't even care how good it was. We'd had so much good food in Chicago that we could certainly slum it for a while.

We found the café pretty much where the fire builder had tried to tell us it would be. Scott went in. I stayed in the car, ashamed of my muddy legs and weird hair. Scott took his brush and said he'd go into the bathroom first and try to clean himself up before ordering.

He didn't take long and soon he was back out to the car with a paper cup of steaming hot Lipton tea. What it lacked in flavor it made up for by being satisfyingly hot. Scott stood by my open window and sipped his coffee with satisfaction. "Ah, now I'm starting to feel human again. I ordered a ton of food. Might take a while the waitress said."

I sat there in the car and Scott stood there and we didn't say much, just enjoying our brew and thinking about the day before and the day ahead. Before too long, a young woman sporting thick blond braids and wide mascaraed eyes came out of the café with two bags in one hand and a coffee pot in the other. She smiled at Scot, refilled his coffee cup, and handed him the bag and with a flirty smile saying, "Enjoy your breakfast, and come back any time you are out this way!"

Scott looked embarrassed so I thanked the woman profusely and made sure she knew that Scott was my cousin, which made Scott turn and scowl at me. We had been known to protect each other by hiding behind the presumption that we were boyfriend and girlfriend to avoid unwanted advances. But this morning, since we would soon be on our way, I thought why not let Scott receive the attention of this young woman.

The waitress was called back into the café by the cook, and with an inviting glance over her shoulders, she returned to the café, swinging the coffee pot and her bottom with an equal slow verve. We drove on down the road to a pull off near a creek. I opened the bag and stuck my head in to inhale. "Ah. Food. What did you get? Actually, I don't even care. I can just eat the fumes."

"You can have the fumes, give me the egg and sausage sandwich first."

Happily, we sat there and I'm not ashamed to admit that we each ate a large egg and sausage on English muffin sandwich, and an even larger cheeseburger with fries. We ate all of it. Every bit. Then we drove on to a gas station where I went in and tried to wash the mud off my legs and brush out my crazy rain-washed hair.

When we both jumped in the car again, I said optimistically, "Let's head to Canada. We're so close now." Then I added, "Do I look presentable?"

Scott looked at me. "As long as no one looks too closely. Keep smiling."

I punched him on the arm, and he started the engine. "Okay, that's our last USA gas for now. Wonder what gas costs in Canada? And we'll have to figure out liters and meters and all of that."

"Hopefully we are bright enough to do so," I replied. "It will be good for our brains to expand our thinking."

We were on our way, and I will admit that I was jazzed. Finally, we would be out of the country. It's not like I haven't traveled outside the US; I lived abroad in college as I've mentioned and taken other vacations to Mexico and Costa Rica and Jamaica. But this was the first time I had driven across the border, and certainly the first time I had come to another country on a mission.

At the border, the car in front of ours was stopped for a very long time. The driver had to get out and open the trunk of his car. The guard went through everything very carefully and eventually made the driver pull his car to the side for further checking. Scott and I looked at each other and for the first time I wondered if we might not have all our border-crossing ducks in line. Scott looked behind us at the mess that had taken over our rear space. He raised his eyebrows to me.

"I hope that the condition of this car doesn't make us look suspicious. I don't think we have anything illegal with us, do you? And do you have your identification and all of that handy?"

I wracked my memory. "Do you have any beer in the car? I wonder how much alcohol you can bring into another country?"

"Just a few bottles, and there's a bottle of wine that we bought back somewhere along the way that you were going to save for whenever."

"But no cannabis, right?" I asked him. I didn't smoke but knew occasionally Scott did. I had become accustomed to California laws and I hadn't even thought about other states, much less another country.

Scott shook his head.

We were motioned forward, and despite a clean conscience, I began to sweat. Scott moved the car ever so carefully forward, and the guard seemed irritated by our slow progress and motioned with more annoyance.

The guard leaned into Scott's window and looked at him and then across to me and gruffly asked for our IDs. We handed them over and I thought my hand was shaking a little. I was suddenly conscious that my hair really did look awful, as if I hadn't washed it in weeks. I felt foolish that I had thought my quick gas station clean-up was sufficient to enter a new country.

The guard checked our ID on his computer, and then asked us why we were entering Canada, what was the purpose of our visit. Both Scott and I started to talk at once and then stopped and started again together, at which point I found myself stifling a nervous giggle. The guard glared at me, or so I thought, or maybe he just looked indifferent. After a pause during which I was quiet, Scott told the guard that we were coming for a visit to see a Canadian citizen, and then briefly to be tourists in Ontario.

"And how long is your stay and when will you be returning?" the guard asked with no expression on his face. I couldn't tell whether he was bored or just being stern. Then I realized this man and all the other agents I could see at other stations were responsible for guarding a country against terrorists and criminals and all sorts of illegal activity that I couldn't even imagine in my sheltered existence.

I spoke up and said, "Only a week or two."

I wondered what Scott would have said if the guard had pressed him. But all the guard said was "Do you have return tickets? Or will you drive back?"

Before I could speak again, trying to explain our uncertain plans, Scott answered with confidence. "Driving back after we see our family in Peterborough."

That level of confidence and specificity in Scott's voice must have done the trick, and the guard, who upon closer inspection was barely into his twenties, handed us back our IDs, then motioned us on with a neutral "Welcome to Canada."

We were in. We drove across a bridge and into the town of Sault Saint Marie, Ontario Canada, driving straight to our hotel, noticing the K signs instead of the M signs along the roadside but mostly thinking about a shower. Fortunately, our room was ready and the hotel let us check in early.

We flipped coins for first shower and I won. The feel of the water running over me was heavenly. Funny, I thought, last night I had water running over me, too. But I hadn't appreciated it. Maybe we should have just stood out in the rain and let ourselves get soaked. What was the harm of that? A few wet clothes and then the storm would have been over. I began to think we had over-reacted. I had a vision of Gran and Mac being caught in a rain storm. It hit me that they would have laughed and danced and opened up to be soaked.

As I dried off, I humbly thought that I had a lot to learn still about letting go of control and inhibitions. I couldn't even blame it on my concern for Mac's bag because when I first started running back to the car, I just felt like we had to run to get shelter, and it was only when I got back to the car that I remembered that special bag of items.

Oh, Lizzie, I said to myself. You are such an uptight woman!

But when I mentioned this revolutionary thought to Scott as our paths crossed leaving and going to the bathroom, he rolled his eyes. "Yeah, that might be fun if we were standing right outside our own back door and could enjoy the thrill and then go in and get dry and warm. But for God's sake, we are on the road out in a muddy campsite in the dark, with a cramped car to sleep in. And you may have slept like a baby last night under your comfy blanket with visions of Jerry Garcia dancing in your head, but I had a very uncomfortable night, and all I want now is to get some food for dinner and get to sleep early tonight. So, if you want to write a different script for last night's adventures, go ahead, but don't give me a part in it!"

With that lecture, he marched into the bathroom. Soon I

heard the shower and I didn't see him again for a long time. We were sharing a room again, not something we had had to do often on this trip, but it was the only room available at this hotel on a Friday night with a big railroad gathering in town. Apparently, there is a scenic old railroad excursion people come from far and near to enjoy. Sounded very interesting. I put that on the "next time" list, which was growing longer all the time.

Post clean-up, we spent our first night in Ontario ordering some Chinese food and eating sitting on our beds, cross-legged, only vaguely looking at maps on our phones while Scott tried to get Chelsea to respond to his text messages. Her lack of response worried me, but Scott just shrugged, apparently not concerned.

Scott dropped off to sleep very early, and I huddled under a weak bed light to read Mac's journal. He didn't write about Canada because he had gone straight from Maine across the United States, never venturing north of the border. But I had grown to love his writing style and not just about what he did each day, but also his side talk exploring what he was feeling and his ideas about life. I began to think I was in love with this man, too. Is it possible to be in love with two men you don't really know much at all, one man because he provided ropes and a blanket and liked my attempts at semi-poetic text messages, and one man having been your grandmother's husband, dead now over three years, who happened to write really, really well? It crossed my mind that perhaps I wasn't quite normal.

No wonder, I mused, that all the girlfriends I shared my

time with over the last decade, hiking, wining, lunching, book clubbing even, had disappeared from my life this summer. Was it my doing, not engaging with them, saving my brief communicating time for my texts to Jerry and Tibby or Nellie? Or had they lost all interest in me because we were so different in our preferences? I was willing to believe that I was not completely normal, although what that word meant was a little hard to explain. I was surprised how little it bothered me. One thing I had noticed on this trip was that Scott spent more time than I did on his phone communicating with others. Some of that was with Gina, obviously, but many times he mentioned texting with one friend or another. You might have thought I was the gregarious one, but in fact, at least this summer, I would give Scott that award.

Part 4
Oh Canada!

29

Early the next morning, we stopped to watch the boats going through the locks that connect Lake Superior and Lake Huron. It was fascinating, but we could taste that we were near completing our mission and so pushed on, determined to arrive in Peterborough for the night, hoping for a chance to meet with Chelsea the next day.

It was a long day of driving, stopping only to get gas for our gas guzzler (I missed my little Civic every time at the gas pump).

The end of our quest was so close. How would it go? Chelsea had been distant and not always responsive. She had never out-and-out said, "Don't come," however.

Jerry sent me a text.

It will be what it will be.

I was still anxious.

All day we drove. We set the GPS and I left the map tucked next to the seat of the car. Not sightseeing today, not even interested in geography, I stared out the window at Ontario blurring by, thinking only of meeting Chelsea. Scott was quiet. I suspected he was thinking of Gina and what might unfold. Here he was, actually in the same province at last. I didn't push him about Gina anymore. He only mentioned her occasionally. His original enthusiasm was less overt now that he was on the cusp of finding out if she was more than a fantasy.

Then it appeared, big and bold beside the road on Canadian Highway 69: the sign read "French River Provincial Park."

"Scott!" I pointed wildly. "Did you see that? We are here! The French River!"

He was much calmer than I was. "Yep. Saw that last night when I was checking out our route. I thought maybe you, being the great geography expert, might have figured out that we would drive along the outskirts of the park on our way to Peterborough."

I was a little chagrined at my own ignorance. I admit that while I could name most of the provinces of Canada, I do not know the perspectives and details. Clearly I should have been playing with a Canada puzzle along with the United States puzzle as a kid. I looked now at the GPS screen on the dash and saw mostly blue—so much water—with dots of land masses scattered like confetti. It didn't look at all like a conventional river to me.

"Are we close to Gina?" I threw at him. "Do you want to stop first?"

He didn't look at me. "First of all, the French River region is huge, and Gina's headquartered inland from here and this week she is out on a big lake. Lake Nip something. So, no. But even if she was a few kilometers away from us right now, I can only think of one thing at a time. We are going to see Chelsea, and when we are done, then I can easily drive back up here."

I understood. "But I still think this is kind of amazing, to be so close."

I was now keenly alert to the lush scenery. "Scott, it is really pretty here. Maybe you will stay here and never come home." I said it playfully but he scowled and repeated.

"Liz. I am focused on one thing right now. I think you should be, too."

I got his message and shut up. I didn't believe for a moment that it was just Chelsea and Gran's mission that were causing his singlemindedness. I'm sure it was complicated for him to think of Gina. I am sure he was nervous. I let it be and went back to staring out the window.

We did have a plan. I had bought a ticket to fly home from Toronto. Not knowing how long it would take to deal with Chelsea—five minutes or five days—I had built in some buffer time, figuring we could always enjoy exploring the area before my flight. Then Scott would drop me off at the Toronto airport and he'd head north to Gina. Scott was committed to driving the car back to California, with or without Gina. When he would return to California was a big unknown.

Scott didn't say any more to me about Jerry, either. I appreciated that. Jerry had accompanied me on this trip, via text messages, and through his kindness in providing us with safety supplies. I could not forget his warm smile as well as his appealing physical presence. It all caused a stir deep in my gut or my heart or my mind—wherever such sensations reside—but none of that amounts to a relationship, and I was not ready to make any conclusions about Gualala's Jerry Garcia.

Our meeting with Chelsea came before anything else now. We were driving at full speed and arrived at our hotel road-weary but without incident, checked into separate rooms, said goodnight and agreed to meet in the morning for breakfast before meeting up with Chelsea, should she be willing to do so. I gave Mac's journal one more reading, went through the bag of items and made sure everything was in good condition: the video tape that Gran had made, the box of photos of Mac, the family kilt, the bag of tools, the journal, and the photo of Marlena, Chelsea's possible mother. All there and accounted for.

Scott told me the next morning that Chelsea had agreed to meet us at a coffee shop that day. That was a good sign, but she had been vague about the time. I was at a loss as to why she would be so reluctant. By this time, being heavily invested in this venture, I told Scott that Chelsea should be overjoyed and thankful to get this information. I guess I sounded indignant.

Scott looked at me as we sat in the sunshine with our drinks, waiting for her. "Liz, you are usually smarter than I am about understanding people. But the way I read it, this is super complex for her. Imagine how you would feel if you didn't know who your parents were, your birth parents? You and I have no concept of that. We know who our parents are and always have, but she has to have all sorts of mixed feelings, wanting to know so badly, and yet feeling resentment towards Mac and her birth mother, and guilt when she thinks of the people who raised her. I get it. I bet she finds it weird and confusing."

Everything Scott said was true. Be patient, I told myself.

But I only had to practice patience for another five minutes until a woman in a sunhat and sunglasses, wearing leggings and a big over-shirt, walked up to us pushing a stroller with a sleeping baby in it. She stopped in front of us and we both looked up at her.

"Chelsea?" Scott asked, standing up.

"Yes," she said softly.

I stood up too and stretched out my hand to her. "I'm Elizabeth, and this is Scott. We're so happy to meet you."

She shook my hand and then Scott's. He motioned for her to sit down and offered to buy her something to drink, but she declined. "Thank you, but I brought my water bottle. I need to keep rocking the stroller so Robbie doesn't wake up, he just fell asleep."

She sat down but kept moving the stroller back and forth to keep the motion going for the baby. I found this a little distracting, but I haven't been a mother. I guess that when parents finally get a baby to sleep, they want a break.

Chelsea was average height, round cheeks, pleasantly round all over actually, with light clear skin, and when she eventually took her sunglasses off, we saw her eyes were blue or gray with long dark lashes and noticeable dark circles under her eyes. Her hair that tumbled down her back was very dark, naturally dark I thought and beautiful. She was striking in appearance if you could get past the fatigue or stress on her face. I had never formulated an impression of

Chelsea in the flesh; she had simply been a mysterious figure in my mind.

We three sat there for a suspended moment; none of us knew who should speak first and what we should say. Neither Scott nor I had formulated a strategy or considered if there was a right or wrong way to go about this discussion.

So as often happens, I just plunged ahead. "Chelsea, we have so much to share with you, and you may have tons of questions, but I don't know how to start or whether we should let you begin. Do you have a preference?"

A weak smile appeared on her face. "I'm so nervous, I don't really know what to ask or what to think. So maybe you should start talking and let's see what happens."

After that it was easy. I just started talking. I told her that although we had known we had a grandmother and had met her a few times when we were little children, we had no contact with her. Then I explained how we had met up with her at long last and how she had a mission for us to carry out for her, how it seemed bizarre to us in the beginning, but how eventually we understood that our Gran had a reason for wanting to do things this way.

I told her about Gran and Mac's long, loving relationship, and how Mac had died with Chelsea's address in his pocket, and how it took a long time before Gran found the letter and longer yet to find that Mac fully intended to contact Chelsea three years earlier. I told her that Gran was not able to travel due to illness, but she felt so emotional about fulfilling Mac's last wish that she wanted it to be carried out in person, not impersonally by mail.

All of this took some time to tell, and Chelsea listened without a word. Scott didn't interrupt either. I kept talking and talking and talking. And Chelsea kept rocking the stroller with a rhythm that must be instinctive in a parent. And in the middle of my story telling, it hit me that Chelsea finally had been able to have a baby, or perhaps had adopted.

When I first started talking, Chelsea was looking at her hands pushing the stroller, as if hypnotized by the motion, but eventually I noticed that her eyes shifted to me, listening almost without breathing. She never interrupted me, never questioned. She simply listened, drinking in my story.

I wanted to remember this part of the day to report back to Gran when I saw her again. I tried to make mental notes while I was talking, understanding that the story had become such a part of my psyche over the weeks of travel that I felt more emotional about it than Chelsea showed right at this moment.

But when I brought out a photo of Mac and handed it to her, she took one hand off the stroller handle and reached for it, and her hand began shaking so hard she almost dropped it. Without thinking I grabbed her hand and held it firmly in mine, squeezing it gently until it stopped shaking so wildly and she could hold the photo and look into the eyes of her father. Then she began to cry.

Scott and I both sat there, letting this moment happen. There were other people surrounding us but they were busy with their computers and their conversations, and I felt we had a little bubble together: the two of us, Chelsea and her sleeping child, and Mac was with us in spirit, too.

We stayed in that moment until the baby started crying, and Chelsea immediately became an attentive mother. She carefully put the photo into her purse, and reached to pick up the child. I don't know enough about little ones to gauge ages, but I'd say he was not a small baby but was not yet talking. The boy was flushed on one cheek from sleeping against the side of the stroller. His hair was light with a touch of red in it, curly. He was textbook adorable. As soon as Chelsea took him in her arms he quieted and started burbling at her. She got out some little crackers and he reached for it and took it clumsily into his chubby hands and shoved it more or less accurately into his mouth. Content as he mushed it up, he turned his eyes to us and gazed curiously. Scott and I both smiled at him and said hi, in that goofy way strangers do with babies.

Chelsea bounced him on her knee and wrapped her arms around him as if to share some of her emotions with him.

At that point, I mentioned that we had some items to share with her but, and I looked around the coffee shop, "I'm not sure this is the best place to do so. Is there someplace more private or at least that has more space to spread out?"

She cleared her throat. We had hardly heard a word from her, wouldn't have recognized her voice yet at all. "My house is kind of a mess, the baby, you know..." She left that thought out there loosely but then went on. "It's not just the baby. I'll be honest with you, I've been kind of depressed, post-partum only, I hope, although that is bad enough, I know, but my husband—he's an attorney—just got back from a work trip, and he was sleeping in this morning, and well, I don't have much to offer, but I would like to invite you over."

We nodded sympathetically. And she added, "Can you give me an hour or so to do some tidying up?"

Scott snapped back into the conversation. "Chelsea, how about this? You go home and do what you want to do but Liz and I don't care what your house looks like, so don't feel like you have to knock yourself out and please don't feel ashamed. We'll go get some takeout food and bring it over and we can have lunch together with no cooking for you. Okay? What kind of food do you and your husband like?"

Scott can do this. He'll seem completely like background scenery and other times like a nerdy, socially inept fellow, and then suddenly he is on top of it, compassionate but firm. And it apparently was just what Chelsea needed.

She nodded and pointed across the street. "We both love that Indian restaurant and haven't found anything we don't like on the menu."

Then she added, "Thank you."

Scott stood up. "Of course. Just tell us your address and we'll be there..." He looked at his phone for the time. "At 12:30."

She stood up then, too, and put the boy back into the stroller with another cracker. "My house is the yellow one, just around the corner, 48 Linden Way." Then she looked at me and asked, "May I keep this photo?"

"Of course, and we have more for you when we get to your house."

We watched her walk around the corner. I picked up

Mac's bag, and sitting where I had not moved in the last hour, I held that bag on my lap and hugged it to me just as Chelsea had hugged her child to her. I looked up at Scott who looked right back at me.

He cleared his throat. "Good work, Elizabeth."

I looked back up at him, standing there tall before me. Everything we had shared over our whole lifetime was culminating in this moment outside a coffee shop in the city of Peterborough, Ontario Canada. I loved this guy! "You too, Prescott." I grinned, and he reached down and patted me on the head.

30

It went well that afternoon, I suppose, but it felt fragile to me. Chelsea greeted us at the door and behind her stood a blond man who was as tall as Scott, wearing glasses and an old tee-shirt with the blue Maple Leafs team logo on the front. He was holding the adorable Robbie in his arms, who was busy pounding a rubber toy on his father's head.

The house was not at all the mess Chelsea had described. Or perhaps she had gone home and spent an hour in a frenzy of cleaning. It felt comfortable, much like a house where any of our friends might live. We sat at the dining room table and ate the Indian food, which might have been tasty but I was too distracted to taste anything. But even Robbie enjoyed gnawing on a piece of naan bread, his big eyes taking us in.

Chelsea's husband was named Robert and he wanted to hear the full story. Chelsea said she had tried to repeat it for him but finally decided that she would ask me to retell it over again, if I didn't mind.

So, over lunch I did, as best I could verbatim to my first telling to Chelsea. Robert listened carefully, but he also kept looking over at Chelsea as if to check on her.

And then I asked if they wouldn't mind telling us more of their story so I could tell Gran. After a long pause, Chelsea talked. Robert helped her out from time to time, and he also amused Robbie so Chelsea could talk. What a good daddy, I thought. And what a good husband.

Chelsea had had four miscarriages, including one after she had written to Mac, and they decided they would try only one more time. They just couldn't go through any more disappointment and grief. If she lost one more pregnancy, she would throw herself into her jewelry-making, and go back to selling at craft fairs. She was not interested in complicated and expensive pregnancy interventions, and she did not want to adopt.

That one last try was the miracle and she conceived Robbie. They held their breath through month three and four and five, and finally at about six, just as she began to be hopeful, her doctor ordered her to go on bedrest. How awful that had been, to not only be inactive, but to try to deal with her worries so they wouldn't carry over to the baby. Robert took on so many home tasks that he missed a work promotion. It had been a long haul.

But then Robbie was born, healthy and almost full term, he was the sweetest baby on the whole earth, they both agreed, and it was not just them talking. She said that everyone who ever met the baby thought he was special.

Chelsea's eyes spilled over at this point and I felt tears well up in sympathy.

Then I asked more about her early life. She told us she was adopted as a newborn in Scotland and brought to Canada at the age of two. Her adoptive parents were also Scottish. She had no siblings and had experienced a lonely childhood despite her parents' good care. Her desire all her life was to be an artist and to have a house full of children, but the last part of that dream had been dashed. Although they were blessed with Robbie, they didn't know if they should push their luck further or not. They were ready to think of something else besides pregnancies and babies; perhaps it was time for both of them to enjoy their son and focus on their careers and interests.

Robert chimed in. "Chelsea is incredibly creative. I'd love to see her get lost in her work again. She can make anything, not just jewelry but paintings, sculptures, fabric art."

Chelsea looked at him gently. "I think it would be good for me to get back to all of that. I am so grateful for Robbie. But, dear child, he will grow up to be an only child, too, just like me." She gave a rueful laugh.

"And like us, too!" I spoke up. "Scott and I are only children. We are cousins and grew up together. Our moms are sisters and very close. We grew up seeing each other almost every day. But we are only children."

"How did you like it?" Chelsea asked. "I used to long for other children to be with. Our house was so quiet and so adult."

"Well, like I said, Scott and I played together every day, so I never felt alone."

Scott added his thoughts. "I agree, we had each other as cousins, but still, I know what you mean, Chelsea. When you are an only child, your parents focus on you and you alone."

And then Chelsea said with some bitterness, "At least you knew who your birth parents are. I always wanted to know."

The room grew quiet except for the babbling of Robbie.

Robert said to her, quietly, "And now you do know who your father was, Chelsea. This is the gift you have been searching for as long as I have known you."

Chelsea sat lost in her own thoughts. Finally, she said, "I apologize, I'm being selfish. I guess I have been depressed about so much. And I'm being a drag on Robert, and on everyone around me, and on myself. I want to be a different person. I'm trying, I am." She looked up beseechingly, mostly at Robert, and apologetically at me.

It was time for me to share Mac's things.

"Chelsea, I have some things to show you. Can we make some room on the table?"

Scott got up and started clearing off the food. Robert got up, too, and said he would take the boy to bed, Robbie having quietly fallen asleep in his father's arms.

When we four adults were back at the table, I opened up the bag, tempted to tell her about how the kayak bag saved everything during the rain storm but decided it would lead us too much off topic for this moment.

I laid on the table in front of her the box of photos of Mac. "These are all for you, Chelsea. You can take your time to look at them after Scott and I have gone. But let me show you what my Gran carefully picked out for you; all these things were Mac's." I noticed Chelsea's eyes take in the decorative features of the painted box.

Next, I pulled out the bag of tools. "Your father was a master carpenter and craftsman and here are a sample of his tools, tools he used with his own hands."

Robert leaned forward and squeezed her arm. "Maybe that's where you get your artistic skills, babe."

Chelsea picked up the hammer, and unconsciously caressed the worn wooden handle.

I took out the kilt and spread the kilt out on the table. "This is your family plaid, or whatever they call it in Scotland. Gran says your dad actually wore this sometimes when he wanted to party." I laughed. "Gran says he was one handsome, kilt-wearing, wild and lively Scottish man."

Chelsea gave a dazed half-smile.

I pulled out the tape that Gran had made. "This is a video that our Gran made for you just before we left on this trip. It's on an old-fashioned video tape. Scott offered to just film her with his phone, but she is kind of old-fashioned, and she insisted on using Mac's old video camera to shoot the tape. I sat in while she did it, and I can tell you it is definitely worth finding a digital transposing service so you can see it. You can see some of the house that Mac and Gran built, a lot of it with their own hands. And best of all, you'll hear Gran share her memories of Mac."

Scott kind of chuckled then and we all turned to look at him. He looked embarrassed. "Sorry, it's just that when she was talking about Mac, I said to her, 'Gran, this guy sounds like a saint. No one is that amazing.' And she gave me The Eye, as Gran can do so well, and she said, 'Even when Mac was bad, he was the very best at it. He was no saint, thank God, but he was magnificent!'"

"So, there you go, Chelsea. This tape holds more even

than these photos about the man who was your father," I concluded.

There were of course two things left in the bag that I hadn't put on the table yet. The photo of her possible/probable mother and Mac's journal. I told myself that Chelsea looked overloaded. I didn't want to add even more to her basket. And that might have been an honest concern on my part in terms of the photo of the infamous Marlena. But in truth, I was selfishly finding it hard to let go of the journal.

I leaned forward and asked her point blank. "Is this too much all at once?"

She squeezed her hands together around the hammer, not yet touching anything else that I laid out in front of her. "I feel overwhelmed, but please understand it's not bad. It is just so much of what I've always wanted to know. I want to lap it all up and learn more. And then I feel angry that life has cheated me out of knowing my father. I used to be angry that he had abandoned me. I have spent a lot of my life going back and forth between that anger at abandonment and guilt at not appreciating what I have been given. Sometimes it feels like I get whiplash going back and forth between those two emotions. When Robert and I, and now Robbie too, are together just being a family, I feel most balanced. But since I heard from Scott about you two coming all the way out here to tell me things about my father, I struggle to get back to that balanced place."

Robert pulled her close to him.

"Everything you say makes so much sense," I told her. "We don't want to make things harder on you. You wanted to know about your father. Gran wanted to do the right thing for the man she loved. We wanted to help her make that happen. And yet I can see it is all monumental, all this information and what it means to you. Wow."

We all sat there in silence for a short time, not knowing what to do. Scott told me later he was wondering if I was going to do anything about giving Chelsea the journal and the picture of her possible/probable mom.

I made a decision. "It feels to me that this is enough for tonight. I think we should go. Remember you don't have to look at any of this stuff right away. It's in your hands and that is all Gran asked of us. It is now all yours. I think that in time, whether that is tonight or ten years from now, you'll figure out what to do with all of this. Maybe today is the first day of putting all the pieces together."

I spoke into silence but at last Chelsea choked out what was clearly brewing behind her teary eyes. "Elizabeth, I'm sorry I don't have the wherewithal to thank you properly. I just don't. You'll have to take my word for it. But there is one thing…"

Chelsea lifted her arm up and rubbed her dark-circled eyes and face hard. I admired the tattoo that ran from her wrist and circled on up her forearm and disappeared under her sleeve. I couldn't make out the design, maybe something Celtic?

We waited and then she went on, sounding chipped, even bitter. "You are right that this is the beginning for me to understand whom my birth father was and that all sounds good, but you are wrong that this puts all the pieces of my puzzle together." She looked at us with a piercing gaze. And then as if we were kind of slow children, she said firmly, "I had a birth mother, too. And while I am grateful for fifty percent of the puzzle being solved, and for all of this," she waved her arm at the array of things on the table, "there is fifty percent of me, half of my DNA, much less all the information that can't be recorded on a DNA sample, that is missing."

Robert, maybe thinking that his wife was being rude to us, said, "Babe, you've been given so much tonight. We can focus on your father now and try not to worry so much about your mother."

Chelsea didn't look pacified and ignored his gentle plea.

I looked at Scott and he shrugged; clearly, he was going to leave it up to me to decide what to do.

I took a deep breath. "Chelsea, there is one other thing, and I was going to wait until tomorrow, but since you brought the subject up, I do have something to show you."

She looked at me dully.

I took out the envelope with the two photos that Gran thought might be Marlena. Her eyes followed my hands.

I thought this was risky, too much uncertainty. Too many words like *possibly, probably, Gran thinks, Mac alluded to, the dates might match*, and so forth. Could this be the wrong thing to do? But didn't Chelsea deserve to have every bit of information she could get? I wish Gran had told me, do it, give it to her regardless. Instead, she had said, "if she is worthy."

I looked at Robert, as if begging him to understand the tenuousness of this moment.

"Chelsea, are you able to hear one more thing tonight? It might be a huge thing, or it may be nothing, but I don't want to bury you in information that may not even be accurate."

I waited until Chelsea nodded. Then I held up the thin envelope that held two photos. I remembered looking at them and tried to bring the face of the woman in the photo to my memory as I looked right at Chelsea, assessing her feature by feature, expression by expression. I sighed. I don't think I was doing well at this.

"Mac made reference to a woman he had an intense relationship with back before he left Scotland for good. He was apparently with her for several weeks, and perhaps he had known her for some time. He never discussed this woman with Gran, and certainly never indicated he had a child or left anyone pregnant. Gran said Mac would have been open about that sort of thing. They had no secrets and each had had their share of flings in their earlier lives. But the timing does seem to make it possible that if this woman was pregnant with Mac's child, it could be you. You were born about nine months after Mac left Scotland for good.

"Remember this is all totally circumstantial, totally shaky, evidence. Please remember that. But after Gran realized all of this, she spent hours looking through old boxes of Mac's photos taken before she had met him, and she came up with a couple of photos, that..." Chelsea had not moved but her eyes burned into me, and I quickly went on. "Mind you, Chelsea, this is only a very wild guess. Gran found a couple of photos that are not dated, but she judged by styles of hair and clothing that they are of the same era..." I became acutely aware of Chelsea's agitation, and rushed on, "...none of this may mean anything, but Gran felt, and we do too, that you deserve to have anything possible that might bring you some resolution or at least even... even a scrap of possibility, because all this is amounts to is a possibility..."

Scott burst out, "Oh for God's sake, show her the photos, Lizzie."

I stopped abruptly, took out the photos and handed them to Robert who was sitting closest to me.

He picked up the first one and gave a jerk. "Shit" is all he said at first. He looked at his wife and then back at the photo. He handed the photo to Chelsea and her reaction was not nearly as visceral as Robert's. She just looked back and forth between the two pictures with interest, but I sensed that her expectations had been flattened a bit, like she expected to see a woman with a sign that said, "Hi, I'm your mother."

Robert sat staring at Chelsea and the photos. I wanted to know what he was thinking, but before I could ask, Chelsea spoke up, sounding like an attorney herself instead of a slightly depressed, confused, overwhelmed artist and young mother who was absorbing the news of her birth parents for the first time.

She said forcefully, "How do you know all of this?"

She had me. I swallowed and said, "Because of this." And I pulled out the beautiful bag containing Mac's journal. I took out the book and held it reverently in my hands, stroking the cover. "I was going to wait and give this to you tomorrow, because there was just so much going on here. And because this is so special. So special." My breath was tight.

"This is yours, and in my opinion, this is the most important legacy anyone could ever leave their child, especially since he was never able to know you and be with you when he was alive. It's the story of a big part of his life, written out. And it's beautiful." I actually wiped my eyes, that's how intensely I felt.

Get a grip, I told myself. It's time for you to hand this over to Mac's daughter and let her be the owner of all of this. I had become bewitched by the man Mac, by all this drama. It hit me at that moment as I held that leather journal in my hands for the last time, that while the drama was all true and real, it wasn't my drama. It was Chelsea's and her family's, and of course to a degree Gran's, but it was not mine. I had been merely the caretaker and the messenger. It felt honorable to me, but I also knew that it was time to turn it over to Chelsea.

I could feel Scott's eyes on me. I reached across the table and placed the journal in front of Mac's daughter. She didn't say anything but finally released the hammer and touched the book lightly. I imagined I saw the same respect that I had seen in Gran's hands and had felt in my own. Mac was only a man, a flawed and bigger-than-life man, but even dead, he made a huge impact.

It didn't occur to me at the time, but later I realized that Mac's words were only as powerful as how they were received and valued, by Gran, by me, and now, I hoped, by Chelsea. On its own, the journal was only the jottings of a man. In Gran's hands, and in mine, it became a story.

We took our leave then. I wanted to hug Chelsea but she

seemed to be fastened to her chair. I simply said, "You have everything now, Chelsea. We don't need to return tomorrow, but you have our numbers and Gran's so feel free to be in touch if you like." She nodded and exchanged a glance but didn't move.

We left her with Mac's stuff spread out on her dining room table. Front and center were the photographs of the dark-haired woman right next to the photograph of Sean MacIntosh.

Robert walked us to the door. I realized when we got there that we had not taken a photograph of Chelsea for Gran, but I figured Gran would just have to understand. As we said goodbye to Robert, Scott said. "Robert, what did you see when you looked at that photo?"

Robert looked over his shoulder but Chelsea was out of hearing. "That woman, she had the same expression, the very same way of holding her head and smiling that Chelsea does, or did anyway when I fell in love with her. Chelsea has not been herself recently but I hope that once she starts to learn more about her dad, she can regain some of her former spirit. And that woman in the picture, if that isn't Chelsea's mother, well, I will never cheer for the Maple Leafs again." He smiled to lighten the mood.

He continued as we walked down the steps. "Hey, thanks so much for all you've done for Chelsea. And thank your grandmother, too. Someday I hope Chelsea can be in touch to thank her. This is monumental, and it may take some time. Hope you understand?"

We said goodbye and went back to where we had left our

car. As we walked, Scott grinned and pointed out that I was clutching the empty kayak bag. I guess that was what was left for me out of this mission.

Before he opened the door of the Explorer, Scott looked at me and smiled, saying, 'Well, I guess you decided she was 'worthy' after all."

I got in and sat down then explained. "All of a sudden it was clear to me that Gran was wrong, or maybe she was right but just used a strange word. It had nothing to do with whether Chelsea was 'worthy' or not. It had everything to do with the journal being Chelsea's to have and cherish, or ignore, or discard, or hate. Mac was her birth father and that journal is the closest she will ever come to having that father in the flesh. Daughters normally have the opportunity to hate their fathers, love their fathers, be snotty, be kind, ignore or be devoted, and maybe most daughters do a little of all those things over the years. Chelsea now has a chance to have some semblance of that experience with her birth father, who is bigger than life in her mind, but who also without knowing it, abandoned her. Scott, it is really complicated, and also, it's her choice. Not mine. Not Gran's."

Scott pointed his finger at me as if to affirm my words. "Good work, Elizabeth," he said for the second time that day.

31

That night I slept as if I had spent weeks rowing across the ocean. Silly of me to feel so drained. I had not done anything to merit such a reaction, but there it was.

I woke to the ping of a text message. It was Scott.

Awake?

Just.

How you doing?

Feel… can't explain.

Makes sense. You are bereft.

That was a big word for so early in the morning.

You're right. How about you?

There was a pause and I closed my eyes, falling back asleep when the ping came again with one word:

Liberated.

I thought about that. I could see it. I didn't feel that way yet, but I thought I might in time. Scott was just ahead of me.

He sent another message.

Going out for coffee. I'll bring you tea and eats. Back soon.

Thirty minutes later he was at the door. I was still in my pajamas when I opened the door for him and pivoted right back to plop carefully on my tangled sheets with my tea in my hand.

Scott dropped a paper pastry bag in front of me and pulled up a chair next to the bed, swinging his feet onto the bed and taking a huge bite out of an apple fritter.

I peered into the bag he brought me and smiled. "Oh, Scotty, you scored big time. Bear claws!"

I took a large bite and closed my eyes. "Good one. Great bakery. Good find," I mumbled with my mouth full.

Scott nodded and changed the subject. "Your flight is in three days?"

"Yep, day after the day after tomorrow."

I thought about how he was probably chafing to get on the road up to the French River to see Gina. "Listen, you can drop me off in Toronto and I'll manage until my flight. No sense you hanging around waiting for my flight."

"Thanks. But I've got a plan. I've never been to Toronto and I was reading about all the great breweries and things to do. I'm going to be out in the middle of nowhere soon—okay, in the middle of nature's heaven according to Gina—but I was thinking, what if you and I enjoy some city time for two days, then I'll drop you off at the airport the morning of your flight and I'll head up north?"

I felt a lightness inside. I guess I was not quite ready to spend a couple of nights by myself in a new city, not with so much still ricocheting around in my brain about Chelsea and Mac and Gran and all. Two days jamming in a new city with Scott sounded like the perfect antidote for me before we parted ways.

My mouth was full of almond paste and crust but he saw my thumbs-up. "I've been doing some research, and why don't we start with..." He pulled out his phone and proceeded to lay down a full schedule of Experiencing Toronto in Forty-Eight Hours.

Before we left the hotel, I thought long and hard about calling Gran. Tibby had conveyed an explicit message, though: Don't call. Come see Gran when you get home. While that seemed odd, it dawned on me that Gran might be one of those people who were uncomfortable with phone calls, so I simply sent Tibby a text telling her when I would be back in California.

We drove to Toronto, found a place to park our Explorer, and ran ourselves delightfully ragged in those forty-eight hours, walking, eating, drinking, walking some more, drinking and eating some more, and also seeing some of the major sights of this humming, diverse city. Our pace kept us too busy to give Chelsea another thought. It also kept us from thinking about saying goodbye or what came next. Both being a good thing. It kept us from getting maudlin and we had a blast exploring at least a small portion of the most populous city in Canada. Our memories of Toronto will always be happy ones.

We dropped into bed each night happily exhausted, and on the second night, I made us both set our phone alarms for fear I wouldn't wake up in time to get to the airport. It was a flurry but we arrived in front of the airport with an adequate window of time for me to get through customs before my flight. You know how airport drop-offs are: I had to jump out of the car, grab my bags from the back of the Explorer, and give a quick hug goodbye, with no opportunity for awkward farewells. Just that quick hug, then Scott ran back to the driver's seat while the airport security guard motioned vigorously for him to move on and let the next car in.

I stood there on the curb, my suitcase handle grasped in one hand, my carry-on bag tightly held over my shoulder, and I watched the back of our silver Explorer disappear down the multi-lane airport highway, just one of hundreds of cars heading out and away to someplace else.

"Good luck, Scotty," I said to the air around me. "Good luck."

Then I turned and walked into the confusing maze of the airport, relying on the kindness of strangers to guide me through each step of my departure process. By ten a.m. I was in my window seat and Toronto stayed behind as my plane soared away, leaving Scott, Gina, Chelsea and her family all behind me now. Mac and his journal were in the right hands at last. I was heading home, feeling like a different Elizabeth Kuiper than I had been before I looked into the one good eye of my Gran late last spring. It was now early August, and my school year would start soon. Only a short time had passed, yet I felt transformed.

I closed my eyes but I didn't sleep. I sat and let it all course through me. Then I opened my computer and started typing furiously. When I stopped a moment to gather my thoughts, I happened to glance over at the woman sitting next to me. She was looking at me and smiled, her book closed on her lap with her finger holding her page. She reminded me of Nellie but when she spoke, her English was vaguely accented. Nonetheless, what she said was so Nellie-like. "When you have a lot to think about, it is such an excellent idea to write it down. Yes?"

I had to smile. Was I that obvious? Once again, I was in the presence of an observant older woman.

I said to this stranger with the nice face, "There's just so much going through my mind right now, and I'm not sure about the future. I thought that if I write down all that has happened and how I'm feeling before I get back to my daily life, I will have a better idea of what's next."

Her voice was kind. "Maybe you will. But don't think that you will always know whether this or that is the absolute right thing to do, or the right direction to follow. You might make a mistake, but that's okay, because if you are looking, you will find the way. And then you will find the next step to take, too. Don't get yourself backed into a corner like so many people are these days. Don't defend some stupid idea to the death, just because someone with a platform yells it out loud enough." Her voice amped up several levels.

She put her hand over her mouth as if to zip it up and I heard the laugh from behind her hand. "Listen to me! I just spent a week with my sister who has profoundly different ideas about life than I do, and I am heading home to try to wash some of the toxicity out of my head. I love her, after all, she is my sister—goodness, we shared a bed when we were children—but I find it hard to come up with topics that we can talk about, you know? Everything seems so inflammatory these days. I keep thinking that we have to keep open minds or we will all be at each other's throats."

I could see the pain in her eyes. "I'm sorry you and your

sister have a barrier between you now, after all your shared experiences." I stopped myself from saying "at your age."

"It makes me sad, too. It is like a civil war inside families now. Fortunately, I have two other sisters and this breakdown has not happened for us. Next time I will visit them second instead of first—they live in Toronto—so I can fly away with happier thoughts in my head."

"I thought Canadians were progressive in their thinking," I said, remembering all the diverse and open people we had come across on our romp through Toronto.

"There is a Canadian demeanor, eh? As a people we are little different than Americans. Much has been made of that. There is some truth to it, but don't be fooled, closed-mindedness and fear can be found in the heart of people anywhere. We have to guard against it intentionally."

"Are you Canadian? You said you were going home now."

"I'm an American citizen now, I live in San Francisco, well, in Marin, but I was born and raised in northern Ontario and a part of me will always be Canadian, of course. And you?"

And that's how I told her a snippet of my story and mentioned that my cousin was going to go up to the French River area to meet up with a woman who was studying beavers.

Like Nellie, this woman was an attentive listener. She knew the French River region very well and told me some stories from her childhood. She told me that as a young woman working as a waitress at a fishing camp cafe, she had discovered Joni Mitchell's music and fallen in love with the singer's voice and lyrics. That had motivated her to move to Toronto, and from there she and a girlfriend got a wild notion to go live in San Francisco and she had been there ever since, going back and forth to Ontario and Quebec every year to see family.

"Now the only family left in my home town is my youngest sister and my visits are getting edgy as she is embracing so-called news sources that are nothing but false and ugly!" She sighed. "I don't think these are really Vivian's values, but she spouts other people's hateful opinions non-stop as if they were God's truth."

"Maybe it's a passing phase," I said unhelpfully, trying to be encouraging because the woman looked so very sad. "But you can only do what you can do and stay true to yourself."

It sounded like the cliché it was when I said it, but my seatmate brightened. "Wise words from a young woman. And here's the truth: you can live a long time, as I have, and just when you think you have it all figured out, there are new problems to confront. And new prejudices to discover within our own minds. But…" Here she tapped her glasses against her book she held on her lap… "that is what makes life interesting. It's never boring, not unless you are sleepwalking. Never do that. It is better to have problems and questions to wrangle with than to be asleep, or dead to life."

With that she put her glasses back on her face and picked up her book. "And now, I have taken enough of your time. Get back to your writing, figure out where you have been, think about where you want to go, and enjoy the journey, and for the sake of all the Goddesses in the Universe, don't be afraid to make some mistakes along the way!" She smiled then, a smile that convinced me she was Nellie's twin sister, or perhaps I just missed Nellie after all these weeks apart.

I went back to my computer, opened it up and stared at what I had written. And then suddenly I didn't feel the need to write anymore. I closed it up, settled my head against the window and promptly fell asleep.

I was heading home.

Part 5
Back Home

32

No one met me at SFO. That was all my doing, but nonetheless I felt a little forlorn.

I had not given my parents a definite arrival day; I was not ready to go into superficial travel chatter for them. This could have been seen as ungenerous, even unkind or elitist, but I knew it was good self-care.

I also didn't share my specific flight details with Jerry or Tibby or Gran. Gualala was much too far away to ask anyone to do an airport pickup, especially since I had no idea what my possible relationship with Jerry might be. I didn't ask any friends to come all the way from Davis to the airport because I had not corresponded with any of them all summer and felt disengaged, whether temporarily or permanently I wasn't sure. And I knew Nellie wasn't confident to make the drive to SFO, although for me she would have done it. I told her what day I was flying in, but I assured her I had my ride covered. And of course, my usual ride, Scott, was now with Gina, hopefully ensconced in their own little paradise.

Therefore, I took BART from the airport all the way out to Antioch, which was a long ride. For the most part it was fine, only a few sketchy folks—and I kept my eyes staring out the window, not really registering the scenes of home rushing past. Then I arranged for an Uber to take me home from

Antioch, which was costly, but I had already racked up quite a credit card bill over the summer, so what was a little more? I had written off money concerns for now, just put it all out of my mind. If Gran came through and paid for some of it, that would be sweet, as long as she could afford it, but I had savings and was probably too frugal anyway.

In truth, the impersonal nature of BART and Uber was just what I needed.

The Uber driver was a woman who clearly would have welcomed a chat to pass the time; she started out telling me that she lived near Davis herself and had three kids. She was anxious to get home to make sure they did their homework and had eaten the dinner she had laid out before she left early that morning to drive Uber in the East Bay.

Reflexively, I remarked that I was sure her children would benefit from her diligence in helping them with their homework. At that she began to tell me all about her life. I'm most often quite interested in the stories of other people, but today I was too tired to even feign politeness, so I did something I rarely do.

"Please forgive me, Connie (she had given me her name), but I am falling asleep. I've been traveling a long time today, and I'm going to nod off here. Not trying to be rude but need to warn you." And I laughed self-deprecatingly.

She stopped her story abruptly. I hardened myself not to avoid feeling like I had an obligation to listen.

I closed my eyes, opening them only from time to time to see where we were, and let my body and mind relax. When we drove up to Nellie's house, I thanked Connie profusely for the drive, tipped her generously, said I hoped her kids would do well in school and that she would always be safe on the road. She looked a little mollified and even said to me, "I know how it is to be so tired you can hardly keep your eyes open. Happens to me sometimes, and I have to get more coffee and slap my face to stay awake. That's one of the reasons I like to talk to my passengers."

This didn't exactly make me feel better about safety on our roadways, but at least I was home now. I pulled my suitcase over to my stairway and popped my head inside Nellie's kitchen door to announce I was home.

Nellie had old rock-and-roll music on high volume, drowning out my voice. She was down on her hands and knees looking into a low cupboard in her kitchen. When I called her name a second time, she looked up and for a split-second Nellie looked her age. Then her face lit up and beamed at me and ten years dropped off. She slowly pulled herself upright on the chair and once she was up, she came hurrying over to me and gave me the hug I wanted at the airport. I was home and I was loved. It was so simple with Nellie and me.

Fletcher came into the room. I'm sure he had been deep into a post-dinner doggie nap on his soft bed by Nellie's chair in the living room. His welcome was equally warm and unconditional.

After she turned the music off, Nellie put her hands on my arms and looked at me intently. "Welcome home, Elizabeth dear. I have missed you every single moment and I'm so happy for your adventure. But no talking tonight; all those good stories will come out one by one, over the days and weeks. Your face tells me all I want to know, that you are glad you went. Right?"

"Oh, definitely, yes. I'm so glad we went."

"And Scott?"

"With any good fortune, he is safely in the arms of the woman with whom he is smitten, and at this very moment they are doing it next to the waters of northern Ontario," I said laughing.

Nellie laughed too. "I will hope so with all my heart. Go after it, Scott!"

Then Nellie became businesslike. "I put some minestrone soup and cheese and bread in your kitchen, and a bottle of that red wine you like, plus some eggs for breakfast. So, unless you need to do a debriefing right now, go upstairs and take your travel clothes off and have some alone time. Tomorrow is soon enough to talk."

It sounded like heaven. I didn't even feel like talking with Nellie right now. Once I got that hug, I was good to go for a few days. Stories would come later.

I kissed her cheek and went out the door to grab my suitcase when I stopped and hit my hand against Nellie's doorframe. "Oh, damn it! What was I thinking?"

"What is it?" Nellie asked from behind me.

"I told my teaching colleague, Lupe, that I'd go to an art exhibit in the City tomorrow. What was I thinking?"

"I can't imagine what you were thinking, but then I am an old woman who spaces out my outings several days apart in order to recover in between. You are young. If it is important to you, just do it. Keep going. Where is it? And do I know Lupe?"

I thought maybe Nellie would have fussed over me and told me that of course I should stay home and rest up and that an outing the day after returning home was ridiculous. But instead, what had she asked? Did I really want to go? And yes, I did. I loved the Museum of the Legion of Honor. And although Lupe and I had only had a few outings together (all to other art exhibits), I had enjoyed each one. Lupe did not waste time on frivolous talk but she spoke intently about art. She was the other art teacher at my school and was a very dedicated and valued teacher, but she didn't socialize much because she had a young daughter and lived with her mother who had some health problems. And the thought of spending the day with her, even in my post-trip exhaustion, was a pleasant one.

I explained to Nellie. "Lupe's never been over here, but I like her, I like her a lot. And I do think it might be the perfect way to spend my first day back home!"

I grabbed my suitcase and moved towards the stairway. "Thanks for encouraging me not to take the easy way out and beg off."

Nellie chuckled. "I hope I have never tried to get you to take the easy way, Elizabeth. If you were crazy enough to set up this date, then you can be crazy enough to follow through, and not make Lupe try to get someone else at the last minute."

I nodded. I know Lupe didn't go out much, so I was honored that she had thought of me, and the first thing I did when I got upstairs after heating up the soup and cutting the bread and pouring a glass of wine, was to call Lupe and finalize our plans. We'd drive to the closest BART station, take the train into San Francisco and the Muni bus to the Museum, and there might be time for a walk along Land's End. I was home.

The next day was perfect. Lupe was focused on the art and wanted to talk about the show. She also filled me in a bit on the changes in our school over the summer—there always are some—staff changes, curriculum changes, and more. But over lunch she asked me directly about the trip. I found myself telling her more than I thought I might. And she listened calmly without commenting. No "oh wow" or "oh no," and no advice or sidetracks. She just listened and finally, when the waiter walked away with our credit cards to pay our bill for lunch, she smiled her unruffled smile and commented, "And now you can find out what your trip was all about and what comes next."

I just said, "Yes." And that was that for the rest of the day. We went back to discussing the art and school. I felt that a bond had been created. I felt safe with Lupe.

So that was the day after I got home.

The following day, I texted Scott for the first time since he had driven away from the airport. Just a brief message:

I'm home. All is well. You?

After a few hours he wrote back.

Connections bad here. Everything else is fucking amazing. Talk next week

Then I sent a text to my mom and dad and Scott's mom and dad, saying simply:

I am home, tired, but it was a wonderful trip. Scott is with Gina and all is well. I've got a lot to do to get ready for school, plus some dentist appointments, etc. But I'll come over soon and will share more about the trip.

Then I added another note.

Dad, the Explorer was perfect for the trip. Thanks. Scott will drive it home.

It wasn't much to offer to our parents after everything that had happened, but I was avoiding them. That is not a good thing about me. I should be more delighted to be with them. I wrestle with some guilt, because I had nothing specific to complain about, but there was never the ease in communication that I felt with say, Nellie, or the day before with Lupe, or with Gran and Tibby, for that matter.

I called Tibby and told her and Gran that I was home and would look at my calendar to find a weekend to come up to see them and tell them everything. Tibby welcomed me home, but didn't ask many questions on the phone, simply assuring me that they were looking forward to our in-person conversation.

And then there was Jerry. I didn't know what to do. He knew I was home. I had told him I had landed and was home, and he had responded with

Happy the flight went well and that we are now in the same state again.

In between my routine appointments and an informal meeting with my principal, I received a couple of invitations, one from my hiking friends, and one from the book club group to join them in Carmel for a weekend. I politely declined both for reasons I officially put down to time constraints.

But through all the busyness, despite my compartmentalizing, Jerry kept coming back into my thinking. Just wondering. Wondering what we had. Wondering what I wanted to have or do. Wondering what I wanted him to want or do. And really not knowing what to do about it.

There were voices in my head, mostly the voices of older women, I realized. Who else did I listen to these days, anyway? The most persistent voice said, "Do something." Sometimes this voice was followed by the words, "What are you afraid of?"

Since texting had been our exclusive mode of communication all these weeks, at last I wrote Jerry a text saying,

I'm not quite sure what to do about you? Any ideas?

I wasn't sure what that sounded like, what it might mean to him, but I was tired of trying to decide and just hit send.

There was an immediate response.

Yes.

That was it for a time, but I decided to let him finish his thought.

Two hours I waited. Then:

Sorry, customer came in. Very busy. Everyone's car needs work and they need it yesterday!!

This was followed by a second text:

Would you be willing to meet me at a coffee shop in Jenner, part way for both of us?

This was immediately followed by:

They have tea, too, of course!

I answered, also simply,

Yes.

Great. I can get away on Thursday. You?

Yes. What time? And where?

So, he told me where and when, and then one more text from him.

I really want to see you.

I felt my throat constrict. I loved that statement.

Yes.

I answered and then changed it to

Yes! See you very soon.

I sat there for a while, then went down to see if Nellie was around, feeling like I wanted to tell someone, but she was out. So, I went to school to drop off some items in my classroom, and as I was walking back to my car, kind of floating along, a voice said, "Liz."

Unguarded, I turned around and there was Lupe. She laughed at me. "You look happy." That's all she said.

I walked over to where she was putting materials into her car.

"Well, Lupe. I'm opening a door to a possibility. Might be crazy, might be wonderful, might lead nowhere, and don't even know what I want, but I have to try it."

She acted as if this nonsensical statement was perfectly rational. She gave me a hug—a first from Lupe. "That's the best we can do. Nothing ever happens if we don't try. You'll figure it out."

I smiled and absentmindedly waved to a staff person across

the parking lot. Then I looked back into Lupe's deep brown eyes. "You're right, Lupe." I said, remembering the woman on the plane. "And if I make a mistake, I'll deal with it when I know it. In the meantime, I am pushing that door open a little bit more so I can see in."

"And when is it that I should think of you and say some rosary beads for you?" She laughed. Lupe had a devout Catholic upbringing and was living in a house with her mother who still followed the traditions of her childhood. Lupe is comfortable living half in and half out of the beliefs of her heritage. I think she is the most secure person my age I have met yet.

"Thursday," I told her.

"Gotcha covered, my friend."

And we both drove away.

33

Thursday came. I drove to Jenner. Having ridden twice with Scott, I had some familiarity with the drive. I held the steering wheel tightly in nervous excitement.

I found the coffee shop. I didn't see Jerry anywhere, so I went in and ordered myself a cup of black tea with foamy milk and wandered outside to find some wooden Adirondack chairs facing the water, where the Russian River runs into the Pacific Ocean. I sat down, perching at the edge of the chair, and worked on unwinding the tension that ran through me. I noticed my hands were shaking so I practiced calming them. I tried not to keep checking for messages from Jerry; he told me that when he was driving down Highway One, he does not text even if he has coverage. He also said that he might get held up at the last minute by a talkative customer. Having faith in the man who provided us with blankets and ropes, I sat and waited.

In front of me, a couple and their dog left their chairs and walked away. Like a vulture to the kill, I quickly slipped into the space they had abandoned directly overlooking the river. Beautiful. I made myself ease back into the long, low chair and breathe. For the next half hour, I hugged my jacket around my shoulders when the clouds covered the sun, and then shrugged it off my shoulders when the sun came out full and bright. After having done this several times, I felt someone standing by me.

He was looking at me, smiling with that crinkle in the corners of his eyes that I remembered. Should I hug him? I started to stand up but he said, "You've got the best seats in the house, so don't give them up. I'll go get my coffee and be right back. Do you need anything more?"

I shook my head. "No, I'm fine for now."

"Well, I'm very aware that I have promised you a cup of tea, so perhaps a little later." He grinned and walked back to the café to order his drink.

Despite the initial awkwardness, now that I had seen him, I felt peaceful. And when he returned and slipped into the other chair, situated about a foot away from mine, I calmly asked him about his drive down from Gualala.

"Every RV in the state was in front of me and didn't have the courtesy to pull off when they could do so. Happens sometimes, although not usually mid-week. Not much you can do but relax. I just didn't want you to be worried if I was late."

"I was early because I left plenty of time to get here. One never knows about traffic."

Then he told me about his day at the shop, and I asked about Gran and Tibby and he filled me in on those two old friends taking care of each other. Gran looked good he said. He asked me about Scott and I told him what I knew, which was not much.

Jerry laughed. "Scott was keeping in touch with me during

your trip, but since the day he went north to see Gina, I haven't heard a thing."

I changed topic to something I had wondered about. "Jerry, Gran told me once that you had been 'raised by the village.' And I always wondered what she meant by that."

"She's right about that, and she and Mac, and Jim and Tibby, were all part of the community that took care of me."

He stopped a moment. "I'm only thirty-two years old, but my life has had a lot of twists and turns. The broad strokes are these. I was born in San Francisco, but my parents raised me on a communal type of farm outside Point Arena. Brought me there when I was a baby. And yes, they named me Jerry Garcia on purpose because they were Deadheads. And no, I don't mind for the most part. I have come to consider it a legacy from them; you see, my parents died."

I made a sound of concern, and he acknowledged it but went on with his story. "I'll tell you the facts, and leave out the emotional fallout, save that for another time. They took a vacation to Yosemite. They wanted me to go along, but I was ten years old and much more excited about spending the weekend with a friend for a birthday party. I think we were going to do something exciting like have pizza and a sleepover and play video games. I stubbornly threw such a fit that my parents gave in and let me stay home with my friend's parents and they went to Yosemite by themselves.

"It was a warm day, and my mom went wading in the Merced River, just calf-deep, not far, but she slipped on a rock and fell into the river and the current swept her downstream. My dad jumped in to help her, and he too was swept away. They both drowned."

"Jerry, I'm so sorry. So sorry," I whispered.

He kept going. "Like I said, this is the facts, and I won't slow down the story by going into the sad, lonely after-effect. I lost my parents at age ten, and of course I felt guilty, as if had I been with them, I could have rescued them. I carried that burden for years. What happens to a kid left an orphan at age ten? Well, I had very few relatives. Both my parents were not connected with their families, and Social Services had trouble getting in touch with anyone to take me in. And before they did finally reach an uncle who showed at least minimal interest in having me, my community, my village if you will, rallied around and went to bat for me, dealing with Child Welfare. The communal farm I grew up on was disbanding. But a local family offered themselves as foster parents for me, going through all the training and rigamarole involved in getting that certification. I didn't fully appreciate it as a child, of course, but I have spent my adult years grateful for what these folks did for me.

"I spent four years living with my friend's family, the ones whose son's birthday party kept me from being at the river with my folks that day, which could well have saved my life. The Edwards were my foster parents, in essence my parents, although there was never formal adoption work. And they helped me start to work out the guilty fantasy I had that I could have rescued my parents. They also drove long distances to make sure I got swimming lessons, not that it helps someone caught in the current of the Merced River. But it did help me deal with the nightmares I had about my parents drowning, and it enabled me to be able to go out fishing here off the coast, although I have yet to go to Yosemite. I just haven't been able to face that." Jerry swallowed and then went on. "They were good to me, the Edwards family."

"Did you stay with them until you graduated from high school?"

"No, my foster dad got a job transfer that he couldn't pass up because it was in Santa Rosa where his mom was in a nursing home, so it was decided that their son Peter and I would live with our neighbors while Peter's parents would move to Santa Rosa. It was close enough that we could visit often, but Peter and I could still go to school with all our friends in our home town.

"So, we moved in with the Baxters when I was a freshman in high school. Peter did too, but by Christmas time he decided to go live with his family in Santa Rosa. I didn't want to leave. The Baxters were amazing. They had grown kids who were lots older than me, so they were more like grandparents to me, but I was very happy there and I loved my home town. It wasn't just the Baxters and the Edwards who took me under their wings. My teachers did, and so many people around town, including your Gran and Mac. Everyone looked out for me, giving me part time jobs, including me in events."

"Did you ever think of leaving town?"

"I planned to go away to college. I thought Sonoma State would be a good fit for me. But then life intervened. Mr. Baxter—Oscar—owned the local garage. He taught me everything I know about cars. I helped him in the garage all during high school. He and Helen encouraged me to go to college. They never tried to keep me in Gualala, mind you. But my senior year, Oscar got sick, and he just couldn't work enough to keep the garage open. It came down to this: he would need to sell the garage or I could stay after graduation and work it by myself under his guidance. I just couldn't leave them and force them to sell out to someone else. These folks had given me everything for four years. The town had supported me since I was a scraggly little kid with the funny or iconic name (depending upon your perspective) who lost everything. I thought about it for about ten minutes, tossed out my college admission papers, and told Oscar not to worry, that it was my turn to take care of them."

My eyes misted. "What happened to them, the Baxters?"

"They stayed in Gualala for a few more years, which was good because I still had things to learn from Oscar about mechanics and from Helen about business management. But then Oscar got sicker and they moved to San Rafael because their daughter lived there. Oscar passed away five years after I graduated from high school, but Helen still lives there, ninety-five now and in assisted living but very sharp. I bought the shop out from their estate in a generous deal for me. And I've been on Main Street ever since."

After listening to Jerry's story, even minus the deep emotions that every part of the story surely had brought to bear, I felt I not only knew him, but I also felt more connected to the community, to Gran's village.

"So that's my story, Lizbeth Kuiper. A long story but I can't tell that story in snippets."

"No, you can't, Jerry, and thank you for it. It's a story that is sad but also redemptive. I'm wondering a couple of things."

"Yeah?"

"One, did you ever have regrets about not leaving town or going to school? And two, tell me more about what's happened in the past ten years."

"College? Of course, it's crossed my mind, and on long hard days in the garage, I fantasize about having a desk job! But when I weigh my life choices and outcomes, I find the scale is much fuller on the side of my life in Gualala than any imagined path elsewhere. I never felt anything but gratitude to Oscar and Helen and the life skills, work skills and security they gave me."

"That is why you seem so grounded," I mused. "But there was the girlfriend…"

"What?"

"The girlfriend who loved the sun more than life in Gualala."

Jerry threw his head back and laughed. "You want to know something, Lizabeth? From the day I first saw you sitting in Scott's little Karmann Ghia, looking for all the world like young Linda Ronstadt with your big brown eyes and bewitching smile and saucy talk, I have not had a thought about Miss San Diego!"

I felt a wash of happiness come over me, body and soul.

We smiled at each other, and as if choreographed each took a sip of our cooling beverages.

"Linda, huh? Sorry to disappoint you, Jerry. I can't sing, except in the shower."

He just grinned at me.

Then he changed the subject.

"Well, you traveling woman. I'll be honest, I had more than a tinge of envy for your trip. Maybe I need to make that kind of thing happen for myself someday. I couldn't help but try to read in between the lines of your phenomenal text messages; they were like poetry, or super short stories. I hope to hear everything you want to share about what happened, from the day you two drove away from Gualala until you got home. I'd like to have the opportunity to let those stories unfold at leisure."

He spoke deliberately and I was very much aware that he had placed his hand on my arm. Suddenly nervous, I said flippantly, "Oh, I'd just bore you."

I hated the way my voice sounded, so fake and flirty. So ungenuine. His touch on my arm had unnerved me.

He didn't move his hand, but he shook his head, maybe understanding that I didn't mean what I said. He replied kindly, "I don't think I need to tell you that you could never bore me, never, ever. And furthermore, the Elizabeth who just said that is not the Elizabeth who sent me those beautiful messages from the road."

It was a rebuke, but it was gentle, and deserved. I liked that he cared enough to call me out on my stupidities. "I'm sorry, Jerry. I'm sort of nervous about... all of... what this means, what I feel, what you feel, if this is anything… and then babble comes out of my mouth."

He grabbed my hand and held it in his, resting our hands together on the broad arm of the wooden chair. "I don't have any answers. Believe me, I realize that I could say or do the wrong thing, too, because I don't know exactly what is going on with you and me either. But let's just be real with each other, okay? Maybe together we can discover what's happening."

He paused. "Will you look at me a moment?" I tried but my eyes couldn't quite meet his.

He went on anyway, "Let's just tell each other what we are thinking, without judging each other or worrying whether what we each feel matches up with the other. I'd like to have that level of trust, whether this is the beginning of something deep or whether we are going to simply enjoy each other's company from time to time."

I did look right at him then, right into those dark eyes, those eyes I had been afraid of thinking about too much, much less looking into, because I knew I wanted to do a deep dive into this man.

My words came tumbling. "Jerry, I've been thinking along those lines, too. I don't want to play games with you, nor you with me. So let me start. Let me tell you what has been going through my mind all summer. Okay?"

Jerry nodded. I began to talk, and out poured all the things I had not been able to put into words before and now as I stumbled and stammered, my usual verbal adeptness failing me, my patient listener gave me time and held every word I said safely. I talked about my tendency to worry about the future and what this might mean, wanting to have all the pieces of the puzzle in place, and how I was trying to let go of that need to be in charge. I told him how I had been unleashed in my college years and how out of control I had felt, how it had backfired, and perhaps that is why I had lived such a settled, routine life ever since. On and on I went, not sure if anything of what I was saying was making any sense.

"Jerry, that is me, my proclivity, and you might as well know it. But I am digging deeper into what really feels right to me, what feeds me, what serves me, and I know that letting go of this need to control and plan everything is where I need to go. When I do that, it is initially terrifying but then I feel so much more powerful or free, a feeling that I can make all kinds of changes and take on all sorts of problems.

"And it may sound like I am not talking about you at all here, Jerry, that I am only talking about myself, but when I think about wanting to try a relationship with you, I have to look at myself and at my past practices and where I hold myself back. Maybe having a relationship is really about two people taking on their own issues in order to have a giving relationship with someone else."

I slowed down for a breath. "Does this make any sense? I guess it doesn't tell you how I feel about you. Just a bunch of words. Self-analysis."

I sighed. "Jerry Garcia, let me tell you this... I felt your presence with me every single day of our trip, and not just because of the obvious things like your blanket and your rope. It was something more intangible. And I held that feeling in a special guarded part of my heart all the way. And now here you are right next to me and I'm spilling my guts to you, absolutely incoherently, but as honestly as I can."

I stopped, and Jerry pulled my head over on his shoulder and caressed my face. Neither of us spoke for a very long time. Finally, he lifted my head and turned his body sideways in his chair so he could look fully at me. "Elizabeth, when an absolutely coherent person like you becomes incoherent and is so achingly vulnerable, well, you have just given me the most beautiful gift of my life. It makes it possible for me to feel some clarity, and I have one thing to tell you."

He stopped and cleared his throat. "I'm scared to say this. But although we have never touched each other more than this, and have only known each other a very short time, and we mostly have a text message relationship so this is totally crazy… how do I say this? Elizabeth, I am falling in love with you."

I stared at him. I honestly didn't know what to say, but I had no inclination to flee, so that told me something.

Jerry looked at me like perhaps he was expecting me to pull away. He shook his head. "I never in a million years thought I was going to drive down here to see you, on this a first date, and tell you that I love you, in fact, I wasn't even sure of it myself before five minutes ago, but there you go. It's out in the air now, and it does not imply any expectations or behavior or actions. It is just my truth. I'm sorry if it puts pressure on you. There are no requirements, Elizabeth, except to be honest with me. And I promise to do the same."

I began to shake a little. It was getting chillier; a lot of time had passed since we had sat down and started talking. Our hot drinks were drunk hours ago. I stood up and held my hand out. "Let's go for a walk, Jerry." And we did, we walked all around, and I put my arm around his waist and he put his around my shoulder. Neither of us said much more.

Finally, he said, "We need to both get on the road, I know. How are you feeling?"

I leaned back against my car door, and pulled Jerry close to me. "I'm full of wonder, Jerry. I can't wait to see where we go with this. I trust you."

Kissing Jerry was just what I thought it would be. No surprise but brand new, unique. That is not an oxymoron.

Later I had to wonder how either one of us drove home safely, but we did, both of us, he back to Gualala and me back to Davis. My body was throbbing like it would never stop.

34

I slept with Jerry three weeks later. Let me just put that out there and then not say more, because it is deeply personal, even sacred, and yet also the simplest, most natural act. A combination of passionate physicality, of course, but also of compassion, of connection, all equaling up to soul-level satisfaction deep under the natural chemical high.

I think that sums it up, and that is all I will say.

Except to say that it was completely different than my frenzied college entanglement with Aiden which was all hormone-driven sex at a time when I had absolutely no sense of who I was. With Jerry I feel completely accepted for exactly who am.

I can't resist explaining that while I have been profoundly gratified by our love making, so many other changes had to come about before this satisfaction could ever have been possible. And that truly is the last I will say because the more I try to put it into words, the more our relationship sounds like a romance novel.

Therefore, no more words.

Although I think it's important to add that joy flooded over me like a very high tide, and as the saying goes, a high tide floats all ships. Therefore, along with my happiness with Jerry, everything else in my life also seemed to thrive as well.

We were not an island. Jerry's life had never been an island, and my private life with Jerry was something celebrated and integrated into the community around us.

On the same weekend I first stayed with Jerry, I went up to see Gran and Tibby. They sat side by side on the couch, motioning me to the chair where Gran usually sat. The two friends held hands while I talked. I had not noticed that level of affection between them before, although I knew they had been devoted friends for a long time. But now I sensed a shift into a more intimate relationship between them.

Gran didn't interrupt me once as I told of the meeting with Chelsea—that's what she wanted to hear about first, of course. When after telling her absolutely everything I could remember about our day with Chelsea, I apologized for not having taken a photo. "It just wasn't a time to pull out my phone and say, 'Smile, everyone.' It was all very emotional."

"You've described it so well that I feel that I can visualize everything, Elizabeth."

Gran didn't ask whether Chelsea would be wanting further contact. I wondered if she would be expecting something from Mac's daughter. As if reading my mind, Gran gave a contented sigh. "Thank you from the bottom of my heart, Elizabeth, and I'll tell Prescott the same thing. Now I can rest and know that I did my best for Mac. Whether Chelsea makes any attempt to get in touch with me or not doesn't matter, because I am completely at peace. I have no expectations. Thanks to my grandchildren, I have done the right thing, at last. I wish that young woman well."

Then Gran wanted to know about the rest of our trip.

"Just start from the beginning, Elizabeth, so you don't forget anything." I began and went back through our journey, day by day, leaving nothing out: the car going off the cliff, the threatening man with the dogs in Wyoming, the wonderful time with the Andersons in Nebraska, our fabulous week in Chicago, the rain storm in Upper Michigan, and all the more mundane experiences along the way. I told Gran of reading Mac's journal and my growing fondness for the man she had loved.

Gran took it all in and nothing surprised her. Her face noticeably softened when I told her how much I had loved reading Mac's journal. And Tibby absolutely hooted when I told her about her kayak bag saving everything from ruination in the rain storm.

The best news from Gran was that for the time being, her cancer was in abeyance and she was able to enjoy her days, walking along the bluff, going to town (although she had retired from working at the market), and having dinners with small groups of local friends.

As for Scott, he was back home, with Gina. They had driven very directly home, sharing the driving, and making it as quick a trip as possible. They both had work obligations to get on with. Gina did not move in with Scott, possibly her pet dog was a sticking point for them, but they spent as much time together as her busy graduate student life would allow. They seemed happy. I wanted him to be happy, and this was the best relationship he had ever had.

Gina was often busy with her work, so often on weekends, Scott drove up the coast to see Gran accompanied by only me. I was grateful to be once again sitting in the passenger seat on my way to be with Jerry while Scott drove Hwy One.

On his first visit back, a surprise awaited Scott at Gran's. Her excited face belied her usual matter-of-fact demeanor as she led him to the garage, and for the first time, Gran showed Scott the classic cars she had in her garage. I swear his eyes danced as he took in what had been hidden in the old stone and wood MacIntosh-Templeton garage. One was none other than the 1969 VW bus that Mac had driven across country all those years ago. Its blue paint job was fading but the license plate still declared the name, "Mr. Mac." Parked next to the old bus, the other vehicle that Gran proudly unveiled for Scott was the opposite of the faithful chugging continent-crossing Mr. Mac. The second car was a muscle car (I know that because both Scott and Jerry told me), a 1967 yellow GTO.

Scott was in gearhead heaven, and as the weeks went by, I could see him wrestling between time in Davis with Gina and time on the North Coast with his hands on these two old cars. Both cars needed work. A lot of work from my viewpoint. But I always thought that for Scott, it was the process he loved and not just the restoration completion. In his own suburban three-car garage at home, besides his new electric Volt and his restored Karmann Ghia—a project that he spent most of his twenties to complete—Scott had a bug-eyed Sprite that was in the very early stages of work. Now with Gran's cars, Scott was in a mechanic's paradise with projects that would absorb him for decades to come.

Naturally Jerry couldn't resist popping in on Scott as he

worked away in Gran's garage. Two happy men. But most days it was Gran who sat and watched Scott. I have no idea how much they talked or whether their talk was about anything other than the cars. Gran was not a mechanic but she knew her old cars with stats and detailed knowledge that Scott and Jerry both found impressive.

Right after he returned home, Scott washed and detailed the Explorer and filled up the tank, and together we drove the car back to my dad and gave him a gift of a bottle of Scotch and new barbecue sauce, at a loss of how else to thank him. To his credit, in our presence, Dad didn't even look out at the car to check for any damage. We had a retrospective dinner with our parents in Dixon that same night, the usual six of us outside by the pool while Dad grilled steaks and our mothers stretched out their legs in the chaise lounge chairs, admiring their new pedicures and drinking cocktails. Uncle Ryan kept one eye on the football game on the outdoor television screen. They listened to the story of our trip, and Dad asked a few questions about places we had visited. No one probed further about my emotional response to Chelsea and to the story of Mac. The conversation was in the here and now, all business. One critical comment was made about Scott's hair having grown out over the summer and another about my choice in shoes, but otherwise our moms were pleasant enough until we made mention of Gina and Jerry.

Regarding our new loves, our parents were somewhat interested in Gina—she is pretty—and seemed impressed with her being in a doctorate program, but this interest was fleeting when they heard her subject matter. It seems they had no curiosity about her outdoorsy research project and no way to inquire for more details. And as for Jerry, I could see my mom's face when she heard I was dating a mechanic who was from Gran's town. My dad happened to call us to the table at that point, and my mom shut her mouth, but I caught the look she exchanged with Mandy. I found it didn't bother me at all.

Gran recently told her daughters that she was recovering from surgery and doing fine, and that she would let them know if she needed help. With this downplay, I could understand that our moms were not jumping to drive to Gualala and find out more. I felt a little guilty that I knew more than our moms did about Gran's health, but I had promised not to tell them, and a promise is a promise. I couldn't see what telling our moms would do to help the situation at this point. Gran assured us that if she took a turn for the worse, she would inform her daughters and invite them to come up and see her if they wanted to.

And finally, my teaching was full of life. Instead of a sloppy classroom performance you might expect given the time-consuming distractions of love and constant travel up to the north coast, I found myself having the best teaching year of my career. My classes were sailing along, both the art classes and the history, and I helped some interested students get an ecology club off and running. I dropped back to being assistant coach for cross-country and track in order to be free on weekends, but I still was out there with the girls every day after school, running with them, working on training, and at the same time burning off some of my own extraordinary energy.

And while I had almost no social time with my past acquaintances, I did spend whatever free time I had with Lupe, and this most often meant going to her house for dinner with her mother and daughter. The food, the conversation, the affection, and the laughter among the three generations of women were exactly what I craved.

Jerry and I traded traveling weekends; I went north one weekend, and he came south the next. His shop was always busy on Saturday, so he came on Saturday night and left Monday morning.

It was quite a madcap ride we were on and we were flying high.

Even Nellie, whom I felt I was neglecting a bit, happily encouraged me to be open to all the abundance that life was offering me.

What else is there to report about this happiest of times, this Idyllic Interlude?

I would be remiss if I didn't mention Chelsea. We had fulfilled our mission to her for Gran and for Mac, and after getting completely wrapped up in Mac's story and Chelsea's, I was now totally absorbed in my own busy life. But about six months after we had been in Peterborough, Gran got a letter.

Gran invited us to dinner at St. Orres that night, the same place where we had been given our quest assignment so long ago. I was at Jerry's and Scott was with Gran already in her garage, and so we all met for dinner under that majestic dome of a ceiling.

Once we ordered our food, she lifted her glass in a toast, and she said, "To friends and family far and near!" She was certainly in a good mood. Tibby was buzzing too.

Then Gran reached into her bag and pulled out an envelope. Inside was a card, a letter, and some photos. "It's from Chelsea." Gran was beaming. While she always maintained that it never mattered if she heard from Mac's daughter, deep down she must have hoped that Chelsea would respond.

Chelsea thanked Gran for all that she had given her, most importantly, "her dad." She apologized for taking so long to write, but she said she had been so overwhelmed that she had let one day slip by after another. Now she was feeling better, stronger, and more ready to get on with life. Her little boy and her husband were fine. She was starting to make jewelry again and attending crafts fairs.

She told Gran she especially treasured the journal and had spent the last six months reading and re-reading it. Now she felt she knew her father well.

(When I heard this, I shuddered to think what would have been lost had the journal been reduced to a soddened mass of ink-smeared pulp.)

The letter went on and on. Gran held it up to us and we could see it was pages long. Gran said she had read it four times already. Chelsea said she would write again when she had time. And at the end she mentioned the photo of the dark-haired woman. She said that her husband was convinced that the woman must be her mother because of something in the woman's look, but Chelsea did not see the resemblance, although her hair was the same dark color.

She said while of course she would like to know about her mother, she didn't feel obsessed with finding her anymore. Having found her father now felt sufficient.

Tibby kept saying, "Mac would be so happy!" And Gran wiped away a tear.

During these months of joy and adrenalin-laden verve, I was never surprised by all the good things that kept happening. I was doing and having it all. My metabolism was running at high speed and I needed little sleep. Life was glorious. Serendipity abounded.

Yes, all my boats were floating high and steady. I was happy. Everyone I loved and cared about was as happy as their life circumstances allowed. Everything in my little world was thriving.

35

Why did things have to crumble? What was wrong with a full and happy life for everyone in my embrace?

As Lupe and I walked out of our Thursday afternoon staff meeting together, I turned the airplane mode off on my phone. Immediately, my phone came alive with all the messages on hold for me while in the meeting.

Text messages and phone messages, three of each from Scott.

My heart began to race. Scott and I never contacted each other in the middle of our work day, ever.

Lupe saw my face. "Everything okay, Liz?"

"Scott needs me to call him. I hope it's nothing." I grimaced. "I'll let you know tomorrow."

Lupe was running late so she touched my arm and then left.

I went out to the picnic table outside my classroom and called Scott.

"Where were you?" he demanded.

"Working, Scott. In a meeting. What do you think?"

Not liking the tone of his voice, I added "What's wrong?"

"Come home. I'll meet you at your place in twenty minutes."

I started to tell him how much work I had yet to do in my

classroom. Instead, I agreed to meet him as he asked. Something was definitely wrong.

He was in his car waiting for me when I drove up. Nellie wasn't home I noticed, but Scott still didn't want to deal with Fletcher on his own, not if he didn't have to. He didn't say anything to me, but his face was like thunder waiting to release its clap.

Once inside my apartment, I dropped my book bag on the coffee table and started to sit down, but Scott arrested my movement. "Liz, get your birth certificate."

"What?" I replied dumbly.

"Your birth certificate. You do know where it is?"

"Ah, uh, I suppose. Why?"

But clearly, he was not going to tell me. I had to stop and think about where I would find such a thing in my apartment. I wondered if it could be at my parents' home, but then remembered a box of "important papers" that I kept in the closet so I dug it out and placed it on the kitchen table. While I stood there and went through it, Scott waited, also still standing. I could feel his impatience and it made me edgy.

Then I found an envelope, still sealed, that said Birth Certificate written on the outside. I held it up to Scott.

"Open it," he ordered.

I wanted to give him a dirty look for bossing me around, but there was something going on. I looked for a knife to open the envelope. The envelope was one of my mom's business envelopes, I noticed. That reminded me. My mom had ordered my birth certificate when I got my passport back in college. She had done all the paperwork for me. Being in the middle of finals, I had been happy to have her help. I had noticed when Scott and I entered Canada that my passport was approaching expiration, so I suppose I would need to order a new one. Maybe it was fortuitous that I had come across my birth certificate. But why did Scott want to see it?

I opened it up and laid it out on the table. Scott walked up and laid a page next to mine. I saw that it was also a birth certificate, his.

Scott bent over and read mine. He looked at me and said, "See?"

"See what?" I picked up the paper and read mine. I hadn't really looked at a birth certificate before, but it seemed to say the important things. Name, date, hospital, size, mother, father, even a doctor's signature. I looked up at Scott quizzically.

Impatiently, he pointed to a space I hadn't noticed.

It said, "Twin."

It took a few seconds for that to sink in. I just stared. Then I looked up at Scott, completely bewildered. "What...?"

He handed me his birth certificate, and I read it quickly. I first looked at the same spot and it also said, "Twin." I grabbed his arm and looked at him. "What does this mean?"

"Liz, read the whole page. For God's sake, don't be so dense."

And then I did. And what I read on Scott's birth certificate made me sit down hard.

Scott's name: Prescott Thomas Sullivan. Birth date same as mine, time of birth ten minutes after my birth. Hospital the same, doctor the same. Parents, Celine Kuiper and Matthew Kuiper.

My head was spinning, I could not think clearly but I had to know more. "Scott, how did you find this?"

He said dully, "I decided to get a new passport; I got one when you did in college thinking I might travel, but didn't. I've never used it all these years but when I got it out for Canada, I noticed it was about to expire. Gina has some trip plans coming up and I want to have the option to go with her. I couldn't find my birth certificate and didn't want to bother our moms, although it was my mom who took care of it for me last time, so I just ordered another birth certificate. It came in my mail today and I looked at it this time. I actually read it this time. And I read it twice and three times and then it hit me that what it looks like might be true. That's when I called you."

"What do you think it means, Scott?"

He looked at me hard. "I think we need to hear it from our parents, and we need to find out what this means, right now."

He pulled out his phone and sent a text to all four of our parents. I figured the likelihood of catching all four of them home was slim, but luck was with us and they were just gathering for a drink before going out to dinner. They tried to put Scott off but he just fired a text back at them. "No, now. We'll be there in thirty minutes."

Like a zombie I went to the bathroom and looked into the mirror and wondered what was going on. Surely there was some rational explanation for what we had just seen.

Scott drove us to Dixon and we walked in the door. Our parents' greetings were cut short by Scott's glare and my stunned face, I guess, because they froze silent. Scott told them to sit down. They obeyed, drinks held tightly in their hands. As usual, our moms sat together on the couch and our dads sat on side chairs slightly behind their wives. I didn't know what to do, so I just stood there next to Scott, my hands in my pocket to tame their shaking.

He looked at them all like they were strangers. I kept repeating to myself, there is a logical explanation. There surely is.

Scott held up his birth certificate and mine, which he had grabbed from the table. "We need some clarification and we need it now."

They all looked at the papers as if they had no idea what he was talking about, but their looks were fake. The air was pulsating with guilt, and suddenly I knew no explanation existed that would keep our lives proceeding as they had for our first thirty years.

Scott spoke slowly and with barely controlled anger. "Is it a clerical error that lists not just me as a twin, but Elizabeth as a twin as well? And is it another rather big clerical error that lists my mother as Celine Kuiper and my father as Matthew Kuiper, yet shows my last name as Sullivan?"

He left it at that. I guess they could have tried to bluff us, but first Aunt Mandy began to sob. I'd never seen her cry, but now she couldn't contain herself. My mom put her arm around her sister and looked away, unable to meet Scott's eyes or mine either.

My voice sounded shaky, not strong like Scott's. "Someone, one of you, talk to us!"

It was my father who finally spoke up because the moms were unable to and Scott's dad was slinking into his chair as if he wanted to disappear. No blustery Irishman left in him.

My dad said, "Liz, Scott, you do deserve to know the truth." He leaned forward to the moms as if to turn the matter over to them, saying to them. "If you don't speak up now, I will, right now. This is enough."

Our ever-competent moms were unable to make a sound, other than the choking noise of Mandy's sobbing. So, my dad took it on.

"Over the course of several years, Mandy and Celine both tried to get pregnant, and then finally with the kind of synchronicity that we had come to expect from these sisters, they both got pregnant at the same time. The due dates were just two weeks apart. We were thrilled, all of us!"

He looked around and as if listening to a story they both yearned to hear but didn't want to acknowledge, the other three parents looked captivated. That's how it struck me.

"Everything was perfect for six months until Mandy's baby was stillborn. It was devastating. Celine felt guilty for having a healthy pregnancy, which by this time we knew would be twins, fraternal twins. Mandy was crushed. It is hard to explain if you weren't there.

"Celine told Mandy that she would give one of our babies to her and Ryan to adopt and raise as their own. She never asked me, just did it, but after my first shock, she convinced me it was a noble gesture. I own up that I did nothing to try to stop this from happening. It took a little convincing for Ryan as well, but in the end the anticipation brought Mandy back to life. We were all very concerned about how depressed she was. We thought we might lose her."

Neither Scott nor I gave a response. I'm guessing my dad was trying hard to paint the picture as they had rationalized it, but surely as he laid out the story in words spoken aloud, he could see how horrendous this sounded to us.

"And so that is what happened," he finished quickly.

Scott looked incredulous. Then lashed out. "And tell me, in all this wonderful, loving charity, how did you decide which baby to give away?" He addressed this directly to my mom, who refused to look at the venom that flooded his face, causing my dad to once again speak up.

"Uh… The arrangement was that the second born would go to Mandy and Ryan, and Celine and I would keep the first born. And Elizabeth was born ten minutes before Prescott."

It was stunning. They believed this was a creative arrangement. Like a great philanthropic event. I felt like a pawn, like a token, like a plaything so our moms could play house, play motherhood, and everyone could be happy.

"And the hospital just went along with this?" I sputtered.

"They were busy that day, and they didn't seem to notice that we had put Sullivan down for last name—although the staff filled in all the other details, they just accepted what we told them for names. And it was not a surprise that a woman's sister would help her take twins home We had an attorney, friend of mine who played golf with me back then, who set up the adoption." For whatever reason, my dad added, "He's since passed away."

My curiosity almost got the better of my rising anger. "And how about your friends and neighbors? Someone must have noticed this strange arrangement?"

My dad looked at the others, but clearly, he was the spokesman so he ploughed on. "Mandy was home, like I said, depressed for months after she lost her baby, and no one really knew about it. We didn't tell, and when we made the decision to do this, we all decided to move from Pleasant Hill to Dixon so we could essentially start over."

What Dad didn't say was that our moms had very few friends, beyond each other.

Scott looked at Ryan, trying to pin him down with his eyes and words. "So how about that, Dad, no wonder I never looked Irish! All this blather about being Irish and it turns out I have the same DNA as Elizabeth."

This was followed by another bitter laugh. "And, Dad, no matter how hard you tried, you never could make me love sports, could you? Just wasn't in my DNA!" Every time Scott said "Dad," it reeked with sarcasm.

Uncle Ryan pulled out what I guess had been the rationalization the menfolk had hung on to all these years. "Celine just wanted to help her sister, my lad. They are such good, caring sisters."

The whole reality of this was starting to sink in. Scott and I were not cousins. We were twins, siblings, sister and brother.

Of course, as bizarre as this all was, there was something

bigger here. Something that was really bothering me, and I'm sure Scott, too.

I said it. "How could you have kept this secret from us? We are thirty years old. It's weird enough in itself, but the secrecy? I feel betrayed." My hands were clenched into fists as I burst out, "I feel like an idiot."

My mom spoke up at last, blurting, "Oh, Elizabeth, dear, don't feel bad, we chose you, we kept you."

The sting of that remark hit Scott fully. He threw his birth certificate, mine too, on the floor in front of our moms and walked out the front door. I followed.

The last thing I heard before I shut the door behind me was my dad saying to the room, "I told you this would happen someday. I told you we should have told them when they were eighteen. Remember? I did my best to convince you…?"

36

Scott did not look good. I was too shocked to know what I felt, but I knew for sure life was not going to proceed on its merry way. As we drove up to Nellie's, it was clear to me what we had to do.

"Scott, I'm going in to pack some clothes for the weekend. You go home and I'll be there in a half hour to pick you up. You are definitely not driving; you're in worse shape than me. But we both need to get out of town, immediately. We'll go up to see Jerry and Gran and Tibby."

I must have sounded convincing or Scott wasn't thinking straight because he just nodded and drove off. I noticed Nellie wasn't home yet, but I didn't know how to tell her all of this anyway, so it was just as well. I packed automatically. Over the last months I had learned how to pack very quickly. I left Nellie a note under a rock by her door. She didn't always remember to use her phone and besides I didn't want to invite conversation right now. I just wrote, "Something's come up. Gone for weekend. Love ya. Lizbeth."

I picked up Scott. He had a backpack only.

"Where's Gina?"

"She's in Monterey at a conference."

"Did you tell her?"

"No." He looked out the window. "It's a real important conference for her doctorate. I don't want to bother her."

"Okay." I wondered about that. When your life as you have always known it crashes, wouldn't you want to tell your girlfriend? Wouldn't your girlfriend want to know? I myself was running to Jerry. I knew that. Yes, Gran was there too, but I was running to Jerry because I couldn't think of anyone who could comfort me more. I sent him a text while I was waiting for Scott to come out to the car.

Something very big has come up. I need to be with you. I'm driving up. Leaving now. Scott is with me. Will tell you all soon.

He wrote back immediately.

I'm here of course. But it's king tide—be careful of flooding.

He didn't demand an explanation or try to talk me out of coming. I liked that he trusted my instincts because it was certainly was out of character for me to drop everything on a school night and do something so crazy.

School? I hadn't even thought about it. I reminded myself to call for a sub when we got to Gualala.

I drove through rush hour traffic. Scott said almost nothing and I couldn't formulate words either. A timelessness settled into our car. It was familiar, to be driving somewhere with Scott, only this time we were in my little Honda and Scott was not driving. It actually helped me that I was forced to focus on driving. That Scott let me drive was a sign of how messed up his mind was.

It was February and dark. I don't like driving at night, but I had become more accustomed to doing so. And everything went fine at first, even with rain off and on. I held the steering wheel firmly, kept my eyes on the road as much as I could within the beam of headlights from my little car. Then we were off the freeway, in the middle of a peaceful rural area, an area I had driven through many times by now. We were quite a distance from the ocean or any noticeable river, so how was it possible that signs began to warn of flooding?

It took several more miles of splashing through sporadically flooded parts of the road before I remembered Jerry saying something about king tides. Could this be part of what he was warning me about? Fortunately, with each enormous puddle, there was enough high road to make it through. There were only a few cars that passed by going the other direction, but to my increasingly frightened eyes, the other vehicles all looked much bigger than my car. I flashed back to our Explorer and how much higher it was off the road. But the Explorer made me think of our parents and I pushed that thought away. I had to focus with all my might. There was no distinction now between road and fields because it there was only water. My hands were gripping the steering wheel as though I could, by sheer strength of my hands, keep us moving through the water and the darkness. Turning around was not an option at this point, but stopping seemed dangerous in the middle of the waters that rushed around us. I concentrated on going forward.

And then we hit a section where I felt certain that our wheels were not touching the asphalt anymore. I could feel us starting to float like a boat, out of control. The wheels and the engine of my little car were helpless in the face of the water that surrounded us.

I could feel Scott's presence beside me. "You're doing great, Lizzie. Keep going," he whispered.

And I did. Well, I don't know that I did anything to make it work, but I didn't freak out. I held my breath and somehow my car made it through the small lake we had been fording that spread out into the fields around us and covered the highway in a foot or two of water. I kept driving. The rain kept falling, but at last I could again feel my tires on solid ground beneath the churn of the dark water. My teeth clamped down on my lower lip, I followed the wake made by a Fed Ex truck down the wet road for what felt like endless more miles, the windshield wipers providing a steady rhythm until we arrived in Bodega Bay. All this while neither of us said a word.

I pulled into a gas station where I had stopped before on my travels back and forth, on all those previous innocent drives during daylight hours when the world was my oyster.

Everything in my life was restructured that night. I felt like I was going to fall off the edge of the world.

But Scott was with me. I shut off the engine and turned and looked at him. My eyes were so very tired and my shoulders were tightly hunched as though they would never relax. He was looking right at me, and obviously he was not thinking of our parents in the moment. He reached out and gripped my shoulder. "You're a trooper. You got us through."

"Scott," my voice was trembling, "was that as scary as it felt?"

"Yep. Could have been bad…." He stopped and then added, "I don't want to think about it right now. You didn't lose your cool; you did it. I'll drive the rest of the way. You deserve a break and I am totally focused now. Don't worry."

Not much was open on that rainy Thursday night, but Scott got a super-sized gas station coffee and bought me a giant bag of M&M's, and we got back on the road. Fortunately, the rain was now light and intermittent and we drove up the windy road all the way to Gualala in alert silence. We were in a little world of our own, lost, yet together, and heading to safe territory.

37

It was pretty late by the time we splashed and crunched up the gravel drive to Jerry's house. He had turned on all the lights in the house to guide us in the pitch dark, and the brightness reflected in the puddles surrounding the house and glistened on the wet trees. When he saw us drive in, he came out the door and down the stairs. I got out of the car and stumbled right into his hug and didn't let go of him for a long time. Scott pulled himself out of the driver's seat. His long legs must have felt cramped in my small car. He walked around the side of the car, opened the trunk and retrieved both of our bags and only then walked up to where I was locked in a sustaining embrace. It hurt me to think that I was receiving comfort and Scott was not. With that in mind, I released Jerry and he me.

Without asking for any explanation from us, Jerry reached out and took one of the bags from Scott and we all turned and walked into the house. It felt like an oasis in the storm. Jerry went around and turned off all the excess electricity that had guided us to his door, and what remained around us was a soft glow of scattered lights and the cracking fire behind the glass door of the woodstove.

Jerry offered Scott a beer, and I went to the bathroom. I found myself afraid to meet my own eyes in the mirror.

When I returned to the living room, Scott was ensconced in the big chair, legs stretched out in front of him and a beer in his hand. His eyes were closed, and I guessed it was less fatigue than emotion. Jerry hadn't asked me, but by now he knew me well and held out a glass of dark wine. I fell into the sofa where I had sat many times with him.

Those happy days of cuddles and conversation seemed like a lifetime ago. I tried to count how many hours it had been since Scott called me at school. That had been about 4:00 that afternoon. It was now midnight. Eight hours? How quickly a life could turn upside down.

Jerry asked whether we had eaten and whether we were hungry. We both shook our heads to the last question. He put his hands on his hips and looked at both of us, then quietly sat down next to me and held my hand. I knew we had to tell him something and soon; it wasn't fair to just keep him sitting there, but how to start?

"We got caught in flooding east of Bodega Bay."

"I hoped you would get through. Those king tides with heavy rains can make a flood out of that drive. How did it go?"

"I was scared to death. That's the truth. I was driving and I thought we might float away. I'm so relieved that we made it through. I didn't know that could even happen."

Scott came out of his funk long enough to say. "Liz did an awesome job of keeping her head. She got us through it. It was fucking disturbing."

Jerry squeezed my hand. "Really, really glad you made it okay. I've been caught like that… and it's dangerous."

He paused a moment. Then he added tentatively, "I'm a little surprised you were driving and in your car. Usually, Scott likes to drive his car."

I nodded, choked up, and couldn't say more.

"And I'm surprised you are here on a Thursday night and sort of out of the blue. That's not really like either of you during the work week…"

That reminded me. "I have to call for a sub tomorrow," I said, pulling my phone out of my pocket to call the sub line. It involves several steps so we all sat there and listened while I went through the whole process. I rarely called in sick so I barely remembered my employee ID number and the answers to the questions, but I finally completed the call, then put my phone away.

Jerry got up and got Scott another beer. Scott nodded. Jerry sat back down and finally said. "I can see that whatever is going on, whatever happened, is hard to talk about, so I'll not push it until you're ready."

And then I was ready. I wanted to share this new life-changing news with someone safe. I thought that maybe if I verbalized it, heard the words come out of my mouth, that it would be so preposterous that we would all laugh because, of course, it could not be true. We must have misunderstood something, I thought, despite my mom's words ringing in my ears. "Elizabeth, we chose you."

And so, without looking at Scott, I told Jerry what had happened. In fact, I told it to the fire; I couldn't look at Jerry either. His kindness was so huge. The lovely normalcy of our relationship up until this day was too much of a contrast to this creepy shift in our family dynamics. But he had to know. We had run to him for sanctuary. He deserved to know for that reason alone. But there was more. He was the one I wanted to share the good and the bad with. And this was the bad, the worst.

After I had told everything, I snuck a look in his direction. He was watching me intently. I looked at Scott finally and he was staring at the fire, seeming to have sunk even further into that big old chair. His second beer was long empty.

Jerry was gregarious, could hold conversations with strangers at the garage, at a bar, anywhere, but he did not say anything now. After a few quiet moments he pulled me into his chest and hugged me again. I felt then that as long as I could be with Jerry, I could survive this. In fact, some of the shock had already started to dissolve. It would come back and hit me like a wave. I don't mean I had gotten over this bombshell by any means, but I was surprised to have been hit with the most outrageous and painful news of my life only to find that there was a resiliency already beginning to stir within me. Maybe it was shock but I felt a calmness. There was no doubt that a new life had begun for both Scott and me only that afternoon. But for some reason at that moment, I knew already that I would be okay, that I would absorb this, that I would be angry and sad and grief-stricken and confused but that I would be okay.

Maybe it was the powerful hug I got from Jerry. But somehow it seemed like more. It felt like a part of who I was. It dawned on me that my happiness in life did not stem from anything other than from within me. Even something so monumental as my parents' deceit couldn't shake my inner core.

But Scott, now Scott I was worried about. Scott's identity had been shattered and he bore the pain of knowing he had been given away, of not being the one chosen by his parents. No matter how close we were, he would carry that burden alone.

The new reality that we were twins, not cousins, was staggering. But somehow it didn't faze me. I had stopped shaking. My head was not spinning. And in fact, I felt like sleeping, like sleeping a long, long time and I suppose that made sense as sleep is my coping mechanism.

I felt my eyes close and if I hadn't trusted Jerry, I might have thought he had dropped a sleeping pill into my wine. Jerry stood me up and walked me to the bedroom, got me undressed, and put me under the covers and pulled up the blanket. That's all I remember. But I gathered later that he went back out into the living room and stayed up several hours with Scott.

38

In the morning, Jerry was in bed with me and when I opened my eyes, he was awake and looking at me. "How you doing?"

I blinked a few times to bring myself back to reality. "I slept so well that I almost forgot about everything. How can that be?"

"Your body's response to shock. A good reaction I would say. Sleep is powerful medicine."

I turned and looked to the bedroom door. "How's Scott?"

"Screwed up. Unfortunately, sleep has not been his friend. I think he finally dropped off about 4:00 in the morning."

I looked at the clock. It was 8:00 a.m. I jolted, thinking of my first period class, and then relaxed remembering I had called a sub. But Jerry? "Should you be at work? You always say that Fridays are an extra busy day."

"Should be, and I will need to get off soon," he agreed but didn't move. "Sweet Lizbeth, I'm honored that you came to me last night. Just saying that."

"Where else would I want to go? Where else would I feel so safe?"

"Well, maybe Nellie, but if you didn't want to stay in town, you might have gone to Gran's."

"I only thought of coming to you. My first and only thought, Jerry. You are the one I trust. But I'll see Gran today. I have to find out if she knew of any of this or even had a guess. I hope not. I hope she would have told us and not let us be ignorant. That is part of what is tormenting us, that we could be thirty years old and be so in the dark about something so central to our identity, to everything."

Jerry nodded. "The Grandin Templeton I have known all my life has been a handful at times, but she has always been a straight shooter. I'd be disillusioned if she knew and had not told you, especially now that she knows you as adults."

He jumped out of bed. "I'm going to shower and get dressed. Let's not wake Scott. Let him keep the lights turned out for a little longer. I can tell you something, Liz." And Jerry leaned over me on the bed and spoke very seriously. "I know it is a fresh and horrendous shock, but Scott is smoldering, he's really angry."

I blinked away a tear. "This is going to resonate inside us for the rest of our lives. I'm not sure what to compare it to, but it's a loss of trust, and it isn't something to get over quickly, or say, hell, it doesn't matter. I'm going to hope that both of us will emerge someday with something hopeful, or happy, or, well, I don't know. Something."

Jerry and I both showered and then we slipped out the door quietly, leaving Scott a note by the coffee maker saying we had gone out for breakfast and Jerry would be going to work and I was going to Gran's but I would be back by noon to see if he was up. Over a quick bagel at a shop near his garage, Jerry told me that he had a full day of work but would check in with me throughout the day to see how I was doing.

I kissed him goodbye and got in my car to drive towards Gran's, wondering what I would learn. I wished Scott was with me. I must have wished hard enough because in a live-zone, a text came through saying he was up, hadn't been able to get back to sleep and wanted to go see Gran with me. I swung around to pick him up. He looked like something vital had been stripped out of him. My poor cousin. How long would it take to think of him as my brother? I reminded myself that it was not yet even twenty-four hours. But the sense of time was meaningless.

Tibby and Gran were out in the meadow looking at some old artwork from years past and with the wind and the waves, they did not hear us approach until we were ten feet away. The look of surprise on their faces was genuine, and their cries of delight let me know that there was no way our parents had called to let them know about what had transpired.

For a moment I wondered what our parents had done last night after we had stormed out of the house? But I found myself caring very little. A part of me was proud of my dad for having the courage to set the record straight when no one else did. Then I remembered that he had been part of the coverup. In fact, his deception hurt me the most. Maybe I had higher expectations of my dad.

Gran and Tibby's joyful surprise quickly changed to worried looks once they saw our faces, and they hurried us into the house.

Gran, although she looked more tired than usual, took charge. Before she was settled in her chair she demanded, "Something is very wrong and I want to know what it is."

There was no patient waiting for us to be ready to talk, not like Jerry last night. I started to tell the story and then stopped. Scott needed to share this burden. I needed to stop being the spokesperson. I looked at Scott and waited. He pulled himself together enough to tell the story from the time he opened his birth certificate until the time we stormed out of our parents' house, leaving our moms and dads behind.

When he finished, he leaned in and pointedly queried Gran. "What we need to know, Gran, is whether you knew about this."

I watched Gran carefully. And she replied with great dignity. "I am as stunned as you are, Prescott. I had no knowledge and never even guessed such a thing. And if I had, I would have told you the minute I found out you were in the dark. I would have done that without a second thought. I saw your moms when they were newly pregnant and then not for another year when they met me in Sonoma and showed me their babies, you two."

She stopped, and wiped her eyes, took Tibby's hand and held it. Into the quiet of the room, she added. "It is ghastly, abhorrent."

We didn't say anything. But Gran wasn't through. "It is reprehensible."

Tibby squeezed her arm and said nothing.

Finally, I broke the silence. "Gran, we drove up last night. We had to get some distance. And I wanted to see Jerry. We didn't talk about it, but I know both Scott and I needed to find out if you knew, and if not, we wanted to have a sanity check with you."

Gran looked at me. Not a hint of a smile, but her look buoyed up my heart. There was strength in her presence.

"I'm very glad that you wanted to come here. I'd like to believe that you would never think I would keep such a secret from you, but I can understand that you needed to know for sure. I'm certain that your sense of trust has been smashed to pieces."

After a few minutes of contemplation for all of us, Gran asked us. "What is going through your minds?"

Scott shrugged, which I knew to mean that he needed some time to think, so I tried. "Gran, I instantly felt like I was not a real person to our moms and dads. The image that keeps coming into my head is that we babies were pawns in their game of playing house with matching infants, and I can't shake the feeling that even as we grew, we were pawns. I think even babies need respect for their personhood. And also, I feel a total loss of trust. Our parents gave us everything money could buy but I will never trust them again. It's a huge slam against us. I mean it was a weird enough thing to do, to give one of your babies to your sister, and I know that through human history that sort of thing has been done, but by far the worst thing was to never tell us. To let us go on all our life thinking we were cousins, when in fact we were twins. We shared the same prenatal space. We are brother and sister."

When I said those last words out loud in a shaky voice, it really hit me. Scott being my brother, my twin, was not a bad thing. I had a sibling! Could we ever see that as a happy realization? Now it was simply unnerving, because moving from cousinhood to siblinghood was not something one can do overnight.

Gran had been listening intently and she murmured, "Yes, the act of commission and then the sin of omission." Then she turned to Scott. "Prescott, I would very much like for you to tell me what is going on in your mind right now."

It was not a request; it was a demand and only Gran could get away with that.

Scott did tell her. Staring just over her shoulder but in her general direction he said, "In only a few short minutes, I lost my identity. Gone. All that Lizbeth says is true for me too, but something has happened to me that has not happened to her. She has the same parents, the same father and mother, that she always knew she had, but I don't. The woman I called Mom and the man I called Dad are not my dad and mom. They misled me to believe that they were. They lived a lie and made me live a lie all my fucking life, and that is all I can think of."

Gran nodded. "You are angry deep to your core."

He nodded. "And it is more, Gran. It is not just anger. But it is also an emptiness, that lack of identity. That feels like the worst of it, but the anger keeps playing tug of war with the emptiness. I can't describe it very well, but you asked, and that is how I feel."

He said another thing before he retreated into silence. "I can't get over how stupid I feel. I mean I work for Ancestry.com for fucking sake, and I am now thirty years old and I just found this out. I mean don't they advise every adoptive parent to be straight with their children and tell them they are adopted?"

Gran looked at Scott with tenderness. "Prescott, I won't mince words. From my perspective, you and Elizabeth have been treated with contempt. An insult to your personhood, as Elizabeth so aptly said. And if I am not wrong, what makes it even more complicated, is that your parents have given you everything money could buy, and they have raised you to be good human beings. They have done some things right, but they have made a huge moral transgression and now the chickens have come home to roost, as we used to say. Oh, dear ones, I am so very, very sorry.

"You know you are always welcome to stay here with us while you sort things out."

I shook my head. "Thanks so much, Gran. We know Jerry would also shelter us as long as we need. But I have dozens of students whom I won't let down. I think they will be good therapy for me. Many of my students have endured so much, some have violent home lives, some are refugees, and even with this shock, my life has been easy street compared to many of them. I'll be back in my classroom on Monday. What I do about our parents going forward, however, I have no idea."

I had one voice message from my dad, which I deleted before listening to it. I was determined to take care of myself and of the innocent students who were in my charge. That much I knew, and that provided purpose and action, something to hang on to.

Gran nodded. Then she looked at Scott. "Prescott, what does Gina think?"

Scott's frown deepened. "Actually, I have not talked to her at all. She is in the middle of a big conference that is important to her dissertation and I don't want to bother her. She'll be home Sunday night, that's tomorrow, so I suppose I should go home and tell her about this. I hate to spoil her excitement about her conference."

Gran almost spat out her answer. "Prescott, you either have a relationship that puts first things first, or you don't. If she is the woman for you, then she will be affronted if you don't share such a wounding experience. And she will not mind putting her research in perspective!"

Gran was livid at Scott for his self-effacement, and I was glad she spoke up because I felt the same way, but I didn't want to poke at Scott while he was so demoralized. I wondered. Was it a problem with Gina, or was the problem with Scott? Or was it just a great miscalculation on Scott's part and Gina would be able to walk with him as he got past this great injury?

Then Gran softened her words. "Okay, dear ones. Go on home but come back soon if you can. You're safe here. You can vent and decompress, curse up a storm, rant and rave or weep if you like. This house has seen a lot of all those things. And it's a good place for it all, including happiness." She turned to Tibby. "Right, dear?"

Tibby agreed but added, "Injustice hurts so badly. I know it sounds trite, but love carries us along."

The knock at the door surprised us. Jerry came in and

gave Gran and Tibby hugs first, then a kiss to me, and then turned to Scott.

"I can't stay long I'm afraid, so busy today. Scott, I was wondering if you could come back with me and help. I'm swamped, and if you come, we all can have time for a good dinner tonight. Otherwise, I'll be working late into the evening."

Scott shrugged but he rose up and said, "Yeah. If it's not over my head."

The guys walked to the door, with Tibby behind them asking if they needed something to eat. Jerry responded, "Thanks, Tibby, but I'm short on time and I'll order out some sandwiches for our lunch."

And they were gone. I hadn't moved from my seat and neither had Gran.

Gran looked at me then. "Work can be a prudent distractor!"

I was pleased that Jerry thought to grab Scott to do something other than sink into his horrible morass, although it occurred to me that Jerry really did need the help and that our arrival, and in fact our relationship had taken considerable time that he normally gave to his garage. I felt a twinge of guilt, thinking of the weekends he drove down to Davis to see me, and the time he spent with me when I came his way, hiking, talking, cooking together, and having such very good sex that we sometimes had trouble walking afterwards. I laughed to myself; Jerry did not look like a man who was suffering. We were both running on adrenalin or whatever the chemical was that love and sex brought alive in the brain.

Now we had been hit by a punch to the gut, but life had to go on, for Jerry at the garage and with me teaching. Of course, I really wanted to go on in idyllic innocence, our relationship life untouched by trouble, but I would be forever touched and Jerry would share the fall-out.

Restless, I told Tibby and Gran that I would make some tea for us.

"I'll float away," Gran said at the same moment that Tibby said, "Oh, that would be lovely, dear."

We all laughed. We knew it wasn't about the tea. It was about having something to do and about something that represented comfort to us all.

I heard the murmur of their voices as I prepared the tea in the kitchen, and when I walked back to them with a tray in my hands of pot, cups, and cookies, I stopped just shy of the doorway because I heard my name.

Tibby said, "Are you sure this is the right time to tell Elizabeth? She's just had such a shock. Maybe we should wait until her next visit, and when Scott is here, too."

Gran replied, "Life doesn't wait around and neither does death. Elizabeth is old enough to know that sometimes hits come in clumps and who knows how fast this thing is going to go. I think it's the right time to tell her now, and we'll tell Prescott when we feel it is the right time, too."

And Tibby answered, "It's your decision, Grandin. If you feel it is the right time, do it. But remember you've just had yet another blow regarding your daughters, and you must be feeling pretty low right now."

I rested my shoulder against the doorframe, afraid of what was unfolding.

I heard Gran's reply, "My girls have been on a different path for so long, I'm unfazed by what they do, except for how they have hurt my grandchildren. That sounds cold and detached, but it is the damn truth. Tibby, I don't have time or energy to give to those two right now. My time is so precious that I'm saving it for those things and those people that have meaning to me."

I couldn't eavesdrop any longer so with a cheerful, "Okay, here's a fresh pot and I found some of your wonderful lemon cookies, Tibby," I set the tray on the coffee table and began to pour some tea for Gran. When I handed the cup to her, I saw that my hand was shaking.

After Gran took the cup, her hand much steadier than mine, our eyes locked and I started crying, silently, but tears streamed down my face.

Gran cleared her throat. "Elizabeth, I'm guessing you overheard us talking." She looked at Tibby. "I told you that your hearing needs checking. We were talking too loudly."

I'd never heard Gran be annoyed with Tibby before.

"How long have you known, Gran?"

"Got the latest scan results just this morning," Gran replied. "But I have not felt well for a couple of weeks now."

"Elizabeth, dear girl." Tibby stood up and put her arms around me, guided me to the couch and sat down next to me. She stroked my hair.

I couldn't believe how Gran could be so steady under the

circumstances, but at this moment I took comfort from her spirit as much as from Tibby's physical compassion.

Choking up I said, "Gran, isn't there something more they can do for you?"

"Of course, Elizabeth. There is a lot that could be done to me and I'm grateful for the medicine and the possibilities and the doctors and all of that. Please don't think I am scoffing at science! We have enough of that in this country, people with no knowledge of anything being distrustful of science. But in my situation right now, yes, there are chemo infusions I could endure, but the potential benefits versus the adverse effects of the treatment need to be carefully considered. The fact that I would have to be away from home for those treatments tipped the scale in my decision making. Elizabeth, we may not have much say over our birth experience, as you have now found out with brutality. But I have been given the opportunity to have some control over how I pass from this world, and I choose to let my life end without intervention except for pain medication, and I will stay in the environment that has given me so much comfort and pleasure all these years. Not everyone is so fortunate."

She gave me an intense look. "And I demand that you and Prescott not waste my limited time trying to persuade me otherwise." She paused a moment and then added, "Dear Elizabeth, if I were your age, I would take every treatment offered to me and fight like hell to stay alive. But it feels very different now for me, and I guess it is true that there is a season..."

I had stopped weeping. Some of Gran's peace wafted over to me.

Tibby asked me, "You doing okay, Elizabeth?"

And I actually felt okay, well, sort of okay. I felt sturdy anyway. Here, I'd had two world-shaking hits in twenty-four hours, and how I could say I felt stable at all was astonishing to me. I felt sad about Gran. I felt sad for Scott, even more than for myself. I felt confused about how I was supposed to feel about my parents. I felt that some very serious losses were descending on me. Yet I didn't feel like I was going to fall apart.

"Gran, have you always felt this calm?"

"You mean about approaching death? No, not when I was younger. But things have changed for me. Handling Mac's death was far, far worse for me than facing my own. It was such a shock. My world changed so radically. Mac was such a vital and large presence in my life that his sudden absence devastated me."

"And so, you go out to the cliff and scream at the ocean." It slipped out.

Gran looked at me and then I think she smiled a little. "You caught me?"

I nodded.

"It is amazing how much that helps with the pain. You ought to try it sometime."

Tibby looked bewildered and Gran confessed. "I haven't done it since Tibby has been living with me here. I've been so much happier." She gave Tibby a luminous smile and explained to her what I had witnessed that first night at Gran's.

Tibby smiled back. "Now, Grandin, that sounds like something Mac would have done when he was drunk with joy or glee, or maybe when he was furious out of his mind."

Gran agreed. "That's how I learned to do it. We used to do it just for the pure pleasure of releasing our energy. But when he died, I found myself out there one night and had to let out my agony somehow. I even considered jumping off the bluff, but then I started screaming instead, and by God, it kept me from jumping."

39

So, counting up the hits that pounded me in rapid succession—Gran's terminal illness on top of learning of our parents' deception—the third was losing my dependable friendship with Scott. All the years of our lives when we were "only" cousins, we had been effortless best friends. Now that we were twins, a great unlabeled wall stood between us. I am not sure what I would call the thing that was causing our new uncomfortable disconnect—but it was strangling us.

To be honest, for some months, Scott and I had already not been spending the time together we once took for granted. Some of that disconnect started around Gina's presence in his life. When they first arrived back from Ontario, I deliberately gave them more space to spend time as a couple. And, who am I kidding? My life had been a whirlwind of activity with my involvement with Jerry and all the traveling our relationship entailed. But this new lack of ease between Scott and me was about far more than just Scott and Gina, or Jerry and me.

I hoped that this break was temporary because I missed him like part of me had been amputated; he had been my constant companion in life. Now I didn't know if our relationship would ever be the same, but maybe we could someday take a stab at recreating something new and sustaining.

When I did talk to Scott, I found that any mention of Gina, no matter how carefully I worded my comments or questions, was met with evasion or defensiveness. I began not to ask about her at all on the increasingly rare occasions we got together. And despite Scott having the treasured vintage cars to work on in Gran's garage, he was now disinclined to make the trek up the coast with me. My guess was that he was uncomfortable with both me and in his own skin.

There was a fourth blow that descended, and it happened on the very same momentous weekend. I dropped Scott off at his house that Sunday night, and then parked in my own driveway. It seemed quiet at Nellie's. No Fletcher ran out to greet me. I looked at her doorway and the note I had written her on Thursday night was still there. Alarmed, I took out my key to her place and went inside. Everything was as always, nothing amiss. No sign of anything wrong, but no Nellie or Fletcher to be seen.

I locked up and went upstairs to my place. First, I picked up the note I had left for Nellie Thursday evening when I had driven away with Scott and stuffed it into my pocket. After putting my bags inside, I went back outside to water a plant by my door that was drooping, desperate for a watering. And there behind the pot was a note from Nellie. From the looks of the paper, it had been there for a while.

It was dated (Nellie always dated everything) Thursday noon and it read, "Elizabeth, I have to go to Petaluma to help my sister. She's in the hospital. I've taken Fletcher of course. Be back Sunday night I hope."

I walked back inside thoughtfully. Nellie was not a fan of

texting or calling. She'd rarely answered the texts I sent her while on the road. She was an old-fashioned paper and pen woman who preferred in-person time. In the rush with Scott on Thursday night, I must have overlooked her note or perhaps the wind had blown it away from the doormat.

I was relieved there was a logical reason for her absence. I had met her sister before, a retired doctor who had a sprawling home outside Petaluma. She, like Nellie, had been widowed early on and had no children. Also like Nellie, she was an avid gardener. The sisters were close but sometimes rubbed each other the wrong way, competitive in a sibling sort of way, Nellie explained to me.

I cut some bread and cheese—my kind of dinner—and opened up my lesson planner to try to get my head back into teaching. Then Lupe called. When I explained that some very enormous changes had happened for me, and that I wanted to share with her, but this was not the time, that I had just got home and needed to try to get myself ready for school, she simply said, "Stay the course, Liz. We'll catch up when the time is right. Is there anything I can do to make tomorrow easier? I have a great new art lesson that I could come in and do with your first period class—that's my prep period."

Normally I would never have let her do this. Prep periods are too important to a teacher. But when I hesitated, she laughed. "That pause tells me a lot. Don't plan anything for first period. I'll be there. And you can repay me someday if you want or pay it forward. Sleep well and I'll see you tomorrow."

I could have kissed her had she been in the room with me. One less period to worry about for the next day. I spent another hour getting everything else in shape and about that time, I heard Nellie's car return. I heard the car door slam and Fletcher's collar jangling as he ran out into his own yard.

I came down the stairs and under the overhead light, I saw Nellie struggling to get her suitcase out of the trunk of her car. I ran down to help her.

"Oh, Lizzie, good to see you. Such a long drive back in the dark with all that traffic. I just don't like driving at night anymore. It saps my strength, can't even get my bag out of the trunk. What a wimp!"

Her laugh was not very convincing. She looked so tired.

"Nellie, I'm glad you got home safe and sound. Come inside and I'll make you something."

"Thank you, Elizabeth. It is nice not to come home to an empty house tonight."

As she settled herself in her easy chair and I bustled into her kitchen making her some tea and a sliced apple, she closed her eyes. When she saw me come in, she perked up and said, trying to be cheerful, "Well, dear, I hope you had a wonderful weekend. Wasn't this the weekend you had tickets to that concert in San Francisco?"

Oh, lord, I had entirely forgotten. Well, that was over $200 dollars down the drain. And Jerry had not even brought it up even though we had planned to go together because it had been his weekend in Davis, a weekend that had turned out very differently than planned.

In response, I just smiled and said, "Oh, I didn't go after all, but tell me how is your sister? What's going on?"

"Oh, Elizabeth, this tea is just what I needed, and maybe a little later some of my brandy?" she said with a smile. And I went to retrieve the bottle and her brandy glass.

"Sheila had a stroke."

I must have looked shocked because Nellie quickly said, "She's going to recover for the most part. It is hard to know with strokes, but they can do so much to treat them now. I was in the hospital with her all weekend and soon they will move her to a rehab center for six weeks or so, and then she can go back home, if there is someone there to help her. And that is the catch."

Nellie looked at me sadly. "Just like with me, there is no one to help her. She doesn't even have a kind upstairs neighbor. She is truly alone. Oh, she has some friends. But she will need someone close by all the time."

She took a sip of her brandy and let the warmth slide down her throat. With her eyes closed with fatigue and worry, I saw a different Nellie.

She went on. "Liz, over this weekend, it wasn't just my sister whose life has changed, but mine has as well. And now I have to have the courage to take action."

When she paused, I encouraged her. "Well, Nellie, when haven't you taken action? Action is your middle name."

"I know what you are saying, and I know what I'm like. I am all go, go, go, but that's on my terms. Now I have to make a move for Sheila's future and for my own. It's clear to me now. Clear as a bell. But oh, dear, Elizabeth. It is going to mean a big change."

She looked at me with tragic eyes. I waited.

"Sheila has a lovely house and it's all one level. She has a guest house in the garden that's attractive and comfortable. I can live there and be close to the house to take care of her and keep her garden going. It will give us something to argue about.

"And she likes Fletcher so I can take him with me. To move into her brand-new guest house is in every way a sensible solution, and it's luxurious compared to my dear old house here. I have already talked to her about it. She can think clearly; she just can't walk or speak very well. When I told her my plan, I saw the fear leave her eyes, and that is what will keep me going now. While she is in rehab, I'll have to move quickly. I need to go through my belongings and get rid of things. I have to back out of all my volunteer activities."

Nellie looked at me now, almost apologetically. "I will put my house up for sale. Liz, I am so sorry. I will miss you so much, but I will make a clause in the bill of sale, I think you can do that, to make sure that all new owners will let you continue to rent upstairs as long as you like, the rest of your life if you want."

She looked anxious, and I had no choice but to reassure her that I was fine with that, that I was happy that she had a chance to help her sister and find a nice place to move to, and that of course I would help her with whatever she needed.

She looked only a little more relaxed from my reassurance.

As I was leaving her to get ready for bed myself, she asked, almost as an afterthought, "And how are you doing, Elizabeth?"

For the life of me I could not tell her. I have always bent Nellie's ear with my issues, with the details of my day, the trivial and the troublesome. She has always listened to me and affirmed me. She has been more of a mother to me than my mom has ever been. Nellie has been my rock all through my twenties, and I now understood that the conversations had been lopsided most of the time, meaning they had been Nellie listening to me and encouraging me, and not the other way around. I felt like some rite of passage had just occurred in the hour we talked.

"I'm fine, Nellie. I think your garden needs some watering. You'll want it to look its best for selling purposes. Let me help you after school this week. Now I have to get upstairs and go to bed before my alarm goes off in the morning. Rest well, you deserve it. And don't worry, we'll have you in that new garden cottage by the time your sister gets out of rehab."

So that was blow number four. My beloved Nellie was moving out of town and her house would be owned by someone else who may or may not be happy with their upstairs neighbor. But more than the house and any of that, it was that I saw that my rock, my Nellie, was making plans for her elder years. She, the invincible woman, was actually mortal. The changes kept rumbling along.

I walked up the stairs with another thought. Before this weekend, Nellie would never have believed me when I said I was fine or that my weekend was uneventful. She would have seen right through those lies. Now she either was too tired or too preoccupied to notice or too overwhelmed to care.

I felt a little orphaned. Or maybe I should say, a little more orphaned. Then the awareness and the shame of my self-absorption hit me like a one-two punch as I realized all that Nellie was losing.

40

If it sounds like everything in my life was falling apart—and I surely felt that way at times—that is not completely true. I often wallowed in my sadness, most often while lying awake at night, but I also began to be able to visualize all the things that were going well in my life and I saw that the picture painted in my mind was an intricate tapestry of grief and joy, strength and humiliating helplessness. It was not a totally dark canvas. Instead, it made a picture that was captivating and multi-dimensional. My life was a good life after all, although now colored with a reality not entirely of my choosing.

Things with Jerry were deeper than ever. For a relationship that relied on weekend visits back and forth from the North Coast to Davis plus phone calls and text messages, it was the best thing in my life, ever!

My friendship with Lupe was also better than I could put words to. I was part of her family, her three-generational family of women. Our time together was often talking at her daughter's soccer games and school band concerts or over tamales in her mother's kitchen. Sometimes I took her mother to doctor appointments when Lupe had meetings. Occasionally Lupe got away from family responsibilities and we hung around my apartment like college buddies, eating pizza and ramen noodles and drinking good wine, this frugal girl's one luxury. Our occasional outings were always to art shows, the one luxury Lupe gave herself. We had a friendship that became more rock solid every day. I thought of Tibby and Gran and recognized what was happening in my life, knowing I could look ahead to the sustaining power of just the right women friends.

My teaching was feeding me. When I had been in the interlude time of the first passion of love, my teaching experience excelled, and now that life was a much more complicated existence, my teaching not only didn't suffer, but buoyed me. Perhaps I had some exceptionally good students that year, but I also knew that I had matured into someone who knew a little more about the bad and the good of humanity and could put that multidimensional spirit into my teaching, not relying solely on my youthful energy or positive but naïve intentions. My students sustained me. I think sometimes they were my teachers in the business of life, and I was the student.

There was much that was distressing, however. Gran grew weaker and was experiencing pain. I saw her on my weekends up the coast. I tried to be in the moment with her and not shield myself in busyness. I wanted to be strong for her but I had never been in this situation before and had no background experience from which to draw. The hospice nurses were very kind and I tried to follow Tibby's lead who told me to just be myself and not to worry about saying the wrong thing. She reminded me that this was still Gran and she wanted me to be myself. I tried. Scott began to come to see her, still simmering in his funk of resentment. The best times for those two was when he would go to her garage and work on her old cars. Gran would make her way to the garage and sit on an old canvas chair as long as she was comfortable and watch him. I suppose they talked but mostly I stayed away and let them have this time together.

Scott refused to see or talk to our parents. I went out for a dinner with my dad one night at his invitation. It was awkward, well, how could it not be? I explained that I hadn't written them off forever, but that I needed more time to figure out how to go forward. My dad told me that they all felt shattered by the experience. I was not sure what he meant by that; did he mean that they were shattered by our finding out, or that they had not been honest sooner, or that they regretted ever making the decision to give the second-born twin to his aunt? And was my dad really speaking for the other three, or just himself? He looked wasted, not like his normal preoccupied, smooth self. Until (and if) I came to more clarity on the whole mess, I needed to keep my distance. I told my dad I was grateful for all they had provided throughout my life but my sense of trust had been severely damaged. We didn't hug. Neither of us could bridge that gap, however, I was glad I was able to remain free of overt hostility.

I didn't try to speak for Scott. And that was something new, after a lifetime of shared reactions and responses, particularly regarding our parents, we now were not one hundred percent united in our painful experience.

Downstairs, Nellie was packing and throwing things out. Some of the volunteers she had worked with over her many years in Davis came over and helped, which was great since

I could only do so much. She was so busy we rarely had time for our tea-time talks. In time I did tell her about our parent's deception and she was flabbergasted (her word). She was also saddened by the word of my Gran's progressing illness. But it was clear that she was overcome with her own task and her sister's recovery. I had to accept that, and not expect her to think about only me. I felt a great loss when I looked at Nellie and the flurry of activity around her house and garden. She had spoiled me of course, being such a confidant and a mother figure who had always put her own needs on the back burner to support me.

Perhaps she realized this, too. One day as we were busy sorting through clothes, she stopped, wiped her forehead and said to me. "Lizzie, once I get this move made and my house sold, I want to get back to my old lifestyle, even though I'll be basing out of Sheila's cottage in Petaluma. It's right on the way of your drive north. I want you to stop and see me whenever you pass through so we can go back to our nice long conversations."

I smiled and assured her that I would love that. But I wondered. The reality was that I stayed up north as long as I could each visit, eking out as much time as possible with Jerry and Gran. And then I rushed back to Davis to make sure I was ready for teaching on Monday morning. It was a crazed life, but I was making it work. How in the world was I going to cram in a leisurely stop in Petaluma to see Nellie?

One day a realtor came looking around the house, and at Nellie's request, I let the realtor come into my apartment. I saw the woman look at my brightly painted walls, and having heard it from my mom and aunt all through the years, I knew what the realtor was thinking. I felt protective of my walls!

Nellie and I had one more good talk before she left for Petaluma. In the middle of her moving frenzy, I popped in on her one afternoon and found her sitting on the floor where she had been sorting through her extensive library of books.

She looked up when I walked in the room. "Ah, you caught me! What time is it? I've lost track. Thomas Hardy always does that to me, although look how old this book is. It's a Penguin classic, just about falling apart. Cost me seventy-five cents!"

"Which one are you reading? I like Hardy too, although it's been a while!"

"Jude the Obscure." Nellie moved slowly. "Dear girl, please help me up. I sat so long my leg is asleep and I'm totally stiff."

"That's the sign of a good book," I said as I carefully helped her get up.

"And, Elizabeth, I was thinking of you, although this isn't completely relevant, but he writes here that it doesn't matter whether a child is yours by blood or not, that all little ones are the collective children of all the adults in our society."

I stopped and thought about that. "Nellie, that is something Gran believed when she was a young mom. And I agree that all of us as adults are responsible for raising the children. It's the village concept. Mr. Rogers would surely believe that. And Scott and I owe gratitude to our nanny Cozy. But that's not what is so hurtful about finding out what our parents did. It's that we were never told the truth, that it was deliberately hidden from us and that we were shared around like objects instead of children who had feelings and minds and futures."

"You're right, Elizabeth. But I do like the concept of bloodline being not near as important as guidance and love."

"Well, that was certainly the case for Jerry. He lost his parents when he was a boy, and the whole community came together to give him a home and guidance. He never feels sorry for himself. He is only grateful to everyone."

"That says a lot about the community that sustained him, and also a lot about that young man's character," Nellie said robustly. She liked Jerry.

She looked at the book in her hand. "Well, Mr. Hardy. You have given me hours of enjoyment and edification, but I know for certain that my sister has this same book on her book shelf, so you will have to go." And she put it in the box for giveaway and moved on to the next book on the shelf.

As I walked back up my stairs, I thought about how much I would miss the interesting conversations Nellie and I had shared over almost a decade as neighbors and friends.

While all of this was going on, Gina and Scott parted ways. Scott was distraught enough one night to call me and talk. He admitted that Gina had not been able to handle his brooding countenance and—as she called it—his obsession with his parents and what they had done to him. She had left and I wondered if Gina had simply not been sympathetic enough, or whether Scott had truly become impossible to be around. As much as I loved him, I would have found it hard to be around the angry Scott for very long, that I had to admit. While I had often questioned whether Gina was as devoted to Scott as he was to her, even during the happy-go-lucky days of the past summer, I couldn't cast blame on the woman now. I wished her well. Meanwhile Scott, my twin, that tall version of me, was miserable. He settled only when he was working on cars, whether in his own garage or in Gran's. It was something at least and I was happy for those moments. Somehow, he kept his job; that was another good thing.

I got a phone call from Nick in Chicago one day asking about Scott. He was worried about him. He said he would keep calling, no matter how long it took Scott to rebound. I was glad for his optimism, that Scott would rebound. It was not easy to be patient and not worry. Jerry felt that Scott was too good a man not to return to some form of happiness and move on. But it sure hadn't happened yet.

One weekend when I was in Gualala with Jerry, I got a call from Scott. I didn't like the voice I heard. It went from anger to depression, that hopelessness that he occasionally reached.

After he hung up, I kept fretting, and finally Jerry asked, "Isn't there someone close by who could go check on him?"

Who would I trust? A few of his old drinking buddies crossed my mind. No, I thought. They don't know the scale and complexity of Scott's situation. I finally thought of Lupe. She was the one I would trust. She knew Scott, certainly knew all the issues involved. I trusted her like no one else. The problem was that she had her hands full with her life, her family, her teaching. There was no husband at home to help out. Lupe's boyfriend had left them before her little girl was born. I hated to bother her. It seemed like too much to ask her to go over to Scott's house and say I'm here because Elizabeth is worried that you are too depressed and might do something stupid.

Yet, I couldn't let go of it. I called Scott back and he didn't answer until I called three times. Then he did. He didn't want to talk. He wasn't rude. He didn't get mad at me, but he just didn't want to talk. At that point, I called Lupe. I felt caught between not wanting to ask too much of my friend and not being able to sleep for worry about Scott.

One thing I thought as I waited for Lupe to answer the phone, at least Lupe lives only a short distance from Scott. That eased a tiny bit of my hesitancy in asking her to help.

I should have known. Lupe said immediately she would go over. And I heard her mom in the background saying, of course I will watch Marta. I told Lupe everything I was worried about and she listened some more and then said, "Let me get going, Liz. And listen, if you don't hear anything from me, that means things are okay, or at least that nothing bad is going on. Okay? So, get some rest and I'll definitely be in touch in the morning or whenever I can. Don't go around waiting for my call, okay?"

And then she added, "And stop feeling guilty about calling on me to help!"

Lupe knew me. Still, I never would have sent her had Nick lived within twenty miles of Davis.

I didn't hear from Lupe that night or the next day. I trusted her and that came with a sense of relief. I had always felt that I was the one to take care of Scott, and no one else could be or should be entrusted. I wondered, did he feel the same way about me, or did my ten-minute advantage in the birthing order make me take on the responsible role of the older sibling, despite his height advantage and his very obvious competencies in life?

On Monday at school, I heard what happened from Lupe, and this is what she told me. She arrived at Scott's door Saturday night, and even though she lives close, she took her car just in case she needed to drive him somewhere. He took a long time to come to the door but she just waited and kept knocking every few minutes. When she saw him, she guessed right away that he was not drunk but that he was depressed. Lupe has had a lot of experience in all sorts of situations, and maybe that is another reason why I trusted her to go check on him.

He didn't even ask her why she was there, but she invited herself in and said she and her mom had made some fresh tamales and wondered if he liked them as much as Elizabeth did. He didn't say anything, but he let her come in and stood there while she bustled around his kitchen, acting, she said, like she knew where everything was. She put a plate of food in front of him, and as she suspected, he took a bite just to be polite (she thought that was a good sign, that he could do that) and then—well, these tamales are the best in the world in my opinion—he kept eating and ate the whole plate. She gave him a diet soda and he drank some of that.

And then, she said, he started talking and he talked and talked. And she told me, "I was not overly sympathetic, but I was also not 'get over it and get on with life either.' Clearly the guy is hurt so badly that he can hardly function. He is not at all the same guy I met before."

She said he talked about Gina and about our parents and about this big dark hole he felt he was in. Lupe asked him if he wanted to get out of that hole or whether that hole was comfortable to him. He said it was comfortable because in it he didn't need to do anything big or bold. But he said that he knew he was just stewing in his angst—his words—and that he shouldn't stay there, that he should be more like Elizabeth and get on with things, but then he repeated that Liz hadn't been as jilted as he was, that at least Liz had the same parents that she'd always had had. That seems to be a theme for him, and he said he knew he should get past that but he just couldn't do it.

Lupe also told me, "I asked him how he felt about Gina leaving, and he just shrugged. Said it didn't surprise him, that things hadn't been going well anyway even before, that he didn't feel she was really interested in him, that it was always him dancing around her life and her wants and needs. He admitted that their relationship had always been one-sided. He said that when he sees the relationship you have with Jerry, he knew he didn't have that with Gina, but he didn't have the energy to take the steps needed to fix or end the relationship. Plus, he had been so gaga over her that he didn't want to let go of that feeling."

Lupe caring for Scott brought a lump to my throat and I left my sandwich uneaten.

"Liz, he talked and talked. He made me coffee in the middle of it all. Really good coffee, too."

I listened to Lupe, amazed. "Lupe, you are an angel!"

She shook her head."Liz, I'm no therapist and didn't try to be. I believe he was ready to talk but couldn't get over the hump to get started. I probably surprised him into it by showing up at the door out of the blue, with tamales in my arms."

I laughed. "Your mom's tamales would make me sing like a canary in any situation! But do you think he knew I had called you to go over?"

"Oh, sure. In fact, at one point, I told him that. I don't believe in playing games. He's depressed, but he is as bright as anyone I have met. I told him flat out that my friend Liz needed me to check on her brother, and I used that word. And then I told him that I really enjoyed talking with him and would like to do it again, but my little girl wouldn't be able to go to sleep without a kiss from her mama, and so I had to go. But if he wanted more good food, we only lived a few blocks away and my mama would love to cook for him."

"And then he said, 'Liz told me that your mom is sick. But she sure is a great cook.'

"And I told him I would pass the compliment on to my mama who had health issues from time to time but was currently doing okay."

Then Lupe grabbed my arm and became more emotional in her tale. "And, Lizzie, he asked what my daughter's name was. Which I thought was a huge deal!"

I nodded vigorously and let her finish the story.

"Anyway, I gave him my phone number and address and

told him that dinner was usually about six but if he stopped by anytime, he would probably be overwhelmed with food.

"Then he asked if there was anything he could do for me. I thought quickly and said my car had been making a weird sound and I wondered if he could listen to it sometime and tell me if I should take it in to the shop or not. He said he'd be happy to do so, maybe the next day."

Scott came over the very next day, and her mom had made him some good (Mexican, of course) food, and he had listened to Lupe's car. Although the car didn't make the noise when Scott was listening, he told her to let him know if it ever did it again.

By the time Lupe finished my mouth was gaping.

"Do you think everything is all better, Lupe?"

"Oh, of course not, Liz. What kind of wonderland do you live in? He's still wrestling with anger at your parents, wondering about his identity in life, and still wanting to return to that deep, dark, safe hole, but I think it might be a beginning. Marta was charmed by him and he lit up when she charmed him right back. And my mom doted on him. I think for my mom it was like my brother was back in the house."

I thanked Lupe for helping me. But she stopped me.

"Liz, I went over there for you, of course. You'd do the same for me should I be lucky enough to have a brother still living." She stopped for a moment and I knew she was thinking of her only brother, who had died of an overdose eight years earlier.

"But honestly, I really like Scott and it was nice to get to know him for himself, not just because he is your cousin… ah, I have to get used to this… your twin."

Then she added. "I'm no therapist and I will never fall into that role. When the time is right, soon I think, I will suggest he see a therapist for the issue with his parents. The Gina thing, well, he will get over that. He fell for her, haven't we all done that, and it didn't work out. it's over now. Pride hurt. Dreams dashed a bit. Temporary. But this business with your parents. That is darker and more serious stuff altogether. He is hurting and hurting bad, Liz."

It was a moment that I started to believe in miracles. Not the abracadabra type, but the kind that stem out of the best of human connectedness and resiliency.

41

Now Gran was fading away. She had hospice care to guide and assist Tibby. When I was in Gualala, I would help out, too. Jerry and many others from all over came around to give Tibby a break when they could and to share a little time and a few words with Grandin Templeton.

Gran instructed her daughters to come for a farewell. She wrote to them to tell them that she was dying, in those words. She gave them a date to come. She told Scott and me that she required that we be there because she had matters she needed all of us to hear. It was not a request.

Mandy and Celine dutifully showed up. Scott and I too. We all sat around Gran's bed. I felt like we were in some sort of movie scene, had to pinch myself that this was real, and this was me sitting on a chair directly facing Gran at the foot of her bed. Scott sat on one side of me, slightly behind me, refusing to even look at our moms who had pulled up two kitchen chairs to the left of where Gran lay. Whether they realized it or not, they were sitting as close together as if on a short bench. On another kitchen chair, near the doorway to distance himself from the family but to be available if needed, sat Larry Phillips, Gran's attorney. And sitting right next to Gran, who was propped up on the bed, was Tibby. Our dads had not made the trip, which was wise; the room felt crowded as it was, or perhaps it was the hostility from Scott and the tension from our moms that filled the space making breathing difficult.

I tried to focus only on Gran. She was getting sicker by the day, and I wanted to be present with her in each moment she had left. When I tried to envision life without her, I only saw a blankness.

When we had all sat down, Gran began to speak. Her voice was tight. She was holding things together.

"I have some things that are important for me to say and I have been saving my energy up to talk to you all. I'm in quite a bit of pain but I wanted to make sure I was cognitively intact to see and talk to you today. After this I will be upping my morphine doses and who knows how coherent I will be. Frankly, I hope to sail away in an ultimate foggy bliss with Tibby by my side. But for this day, the pain sharpens my thinking and keeps me alert. Are we good on that? No interruptions?" She glared around the room and we all nodded.

"It seems that I have been given the opportunity to die at a pace that allows for summing up and saying goodbyes and wrapping up my business. I don't know if this is good or bad—Mac certainly didn't have that opportunity, and perhaps he was the lucky one—but since this is the card I have drawn in life and death, then I want to do it right, or at least do it my way. I realize that some of you may not think I have done much of anything right all my years, but you can't deny that I have done things my way."

She didn't address this to anyone in particular, and although I didn't turn to look at them, I wondered if our moms were squirming or nodding in full agreement. I was focused on Gran, but also aware of Scott and his unhappiness next to me.

I felt like I was in the middle of an inedible sandwich.

"It is amusing to me," Gran went on, "that after being a lowly grocery clerk and amateur artist who barely paid my bills most of my life, I have ended up with assets enough to give away, and given how ugly things can get in families when there are assets to divide up, I put some thought into this and Mr. Phillips here has drawn things up for legal purposes."

Gran shifted in bed, wincing, and Tibby pushed and pulled some pillows to make her more comfortable. Gran turned to share a thankful pause with her friend.

"So let me get to it. Only in the last six months, I learned that when my parents left the Piedmont house to my brother forty-five years past, they wrote in the will that it was to be my brother's as long as he lived but when he passed, which he did last year, the house was to be fully mine, lock stock and barrel. I don't imagine his son was happy about that, but so it goes. He is not hurting financially, I've heard.

"The Piedmont house being mine is very interesting to me. I have happy memories of growing up in that house. My parents were good people. I was a difficult daughter to handle but they loved me and I always respected them. I know they left the house to my brother because they had confidence he would care for it better, and he did. It is a beautiful house, last time I saw it, and the realtor assures me it still is. I will never see it again, and I leave it in my will to my daughters Celine and Amanda, and, yes, I use your new names.

You have chosen your own names and I will honor that. So, you two may do with the house as you wish. You can move into it; you can sell it. It's yours and I give it to you without any sentimentality attached. I feel compelled to remind you that it will be the second home I have written over to you. Selling the first house in Benicia allowed you to start your business life, and now this one should be very profitable for you to share. You have done well in business and I admire your brains and skill. And it is because of that admiration I have for you and not out of any guilt, that I bequeath you the Piedmont house."

I did turn slightly and look at our moms now. They looked stunned, also pleased. Clearly, they had not known about the Piedmont house. My mom started to say something but Tibby held up her hand to stop her because Gran was pushing on as if she had to get through this soon.

"Our house, mine and Mac's, is in my name only and it is paid off. I'm leaving it to Elizabeth and Prescott. They can split it any way they want. I know they will work together on this. And this house includes the garage, the cars, and the acreage. Larry will give you all the details, but it is my hope that it is a blessing to you both, and not an albatross around your neck. If it is a problem, or doesn't suit your lifestyle, then sell it. No matter how sacred this place is to me, in the end, everything is transitory except true love, and that lasts forever across time and space and eternity...." Gran almost let down her guard but she steeled herself and continued.

"So please, my dear grandchildren, do not let my sentimentality keep you from making the right decisions for your lives, both of you. Live here, sell it, split it, do whatever you need to enhance your lives. I know you will honor this space whatever you end up doing.

"I have just one stipulation, one caveat, about your possession of this home. Give Tibby time to decide when she wants to move out or move on."

Gran took Tibby's hand in hers and spoke with tenderness. "Tibby and I have been friends since before I moved here. In fact, she is the reason I came. Our friendship and our love are not something I can talk about easily, but now that Mac has been gone these years, no one on earth is more precious to me than Tibby. My first inclination was to give everything I own to my Tibby. However, she has brought me to my senses by reminding me that she needs for nothing materially. However no matter how long Tibby may live, I don't want her lost or forgotten or alone without anyone to care for her.

"And I don't know how to make sure that doesn't happen. Tibby repeatedly tells me not to worry, that she's a big girl and will take care of herself. She and Jim did okay and she owns her own home, which she is now renting out to the family that is taking care of her animals. Therefore, it is not material support that concerns me, but I want her to not be alone. She has taken care of me, but who will take care of her? That is what concerns me more than anything else these days."

Gran wiped her eyes and Tibby squeezed her hand, her eyes cast down. Tibby, better than anyone, knew when to honor Gran's request for silence. I'm betting they had discussed this matter many times privately.

Without realizing it, both Scott and I raised our hands at the same time and pointed to ourselves, without speaking, of course. Gran knew what we meant because her whole face relaxed. "I was hoping that you two would agree to that. I trust you."

She cleared her throat and went on. "And to Chelsea, Mac's daughter, I am leaving a sum of money that Mac had in a brokerage account that I never touched. It would have made him happy to do that."

We all sat silently then. Gran called over to Larry Phillips. "Larry, have I forgotten anything important?"

He looked at his hands and, as discreetly as possible, offered, "Nothing of legal interest, Grandin. I can go over all the particulars with both your daughters, and your grandchildren, as well as with Tibby, of course." He turned and looked at Scott and me. "Your Gran has a lot of faith in your good will, but we can take care of things in more detail when… when the time comes," he ended awkwardly. "And the same for you two about the Piedmont house." He added to our moms, "It's empty now but is being maintained.

"But, Grandin, you did ask me to remind you that there were a few things you wanted to say if you felt up to it."

She stared at him for a moment as if trying to remember, and then Tibby bent down and whispered into her ear, and she nodded as if remembering. "Thank you, yes, I do feel up to this one last thing."

"My girls." She addressed our moms. "I mentioned that

I admire your business acumen and I do, although it has not been the path I ever wanted to follow. But I admire you having the smarts and determination to create your own path and make it work for you, despite our rocky mother-daughter home life. We were not a good fit, me and you two. But at least you had each other.

"The gift you gave me and the world is your children. I know I would never win a good parenting award, but let me say this bluntly, your secrecy was a horrible mistake, caused lasting harm, and you are reaping the outcome of that now. Prescott is deservedly angry, and Elizabeth is as well. All of you are damaged, including your husbands who are just as guilty as you are in your decision and your secrecy. I must address this before I die. It was so wrong. Secrets almost always are. I made many mistakes, you might scream, but I know that secrecy was not one of them.

"Ironically, however, I do at some level understand the intensity of your love for each other that led you make this pact and give the ultimate to each other, your child to Amanda, Celine, and you raising your sister's child as your own, Mandy. And I understand that it is painful to have it out in the open. But when I see my daughters' families broken by what they have brought on themselves, and even more when I see my beautiful grandchildren slammed with this deceit, I feel I must speak up. This may be the only time you will all be in a room together and I want you to sit and listen a few more minutes."

Everyone sat still. The air in the room remained unmoving.

Gran's voice raised a notch. "I don't know if Prescott will

ever be able to forgive you, both of you, any of you. I don't know if any one of us could make that leap of forgiveness, not so much because of what you did, which was done out of phenomenal sisterly love, twisted as I believe it was, but because of the bigger issue, the breach of trust."

She looked directly at Scott now. "But, Prescott, I hope in time you can move on in your life, freely and without the hate that I see in you now. You are justifiably angry, but you have only one life to live, and whether or not you can ever have a relationship with any of your parents again, that is not for me to say. Only you can call that one. You might be right to stay detached forever, and your parents are just going to have to accept that, but for your well-being you must release that smoldering resentment and make room for happiness in your life. Let someone or something in to create happiness with you, Prescott. Let nature or music or car maintenance or something, maybe even love, into your heart and find contentment. You will never be the same carefree young man, ever. I can guarantee you that. But it doesn't mean you have to cancel out happiness."

Gran looked so tired I wanted her to stop talking and rest. But she had one more thing to say, and it was to my surprise, to me. "Elizabeth, I'm glad you have found love and that you have been embracing change. Don't stop. But remember, you have to give Prescott time to figure things out. He will do it. And you don't have to be the bridge for him or for anyone else. Let people figure out how to solve their own shit. It's not your job to fix things. Don't take that burden on because trying to do so will hold you back and you can't do it anyway."

She closed her eyes then. And we wondered if we should all leave. But of course, Gran had one more thing to offer. She opened her eyes and grinned a lopsided smile before saying, "Damn, I have sure gotten smarter in my last years. Why in hell didn't I know all of this earlier in my life? Maybe I would never have caused myself and others so much trouble."

Then she turned to Tibby and said, "Tibby, I'm finished."

Immediately, Tibby left her silent pillow-propping role behind and stood up and told us all it was time for us to go. When we hesitated, she said, "Now." And we of one accord got up and filed out of the room. The hospice nurse came in then to join Tibby with Gran.

We stood in the kitchen, unsure what to do next.

Scott gave me a brief sideways shoulder hug and then left, walking out the door and across the meadow to the garage. Whether he left completely or just went into the garage and closed the door, I could not tell.

I looked at our moms but I didn't know what to say, and they were momentarily quiet as well. Finally, my mom said, "Did you know about the Piedmont house, Elizabeth?"

I just looked at her. Was that really what she wanted to talk about or was that the only level our conversation could be right now? I wasn't angry, more annoyed.

My aunt added, "You seem to have been on the inside about so many things that we didn't know about."

I thought that was a very tacky response but maybe I should also give her the benefit of the doubt that she was stressed and tacky things were coming out of her mouth, too. But I felt doubly irritated now.

I replied, "I had no idea. I didn't even know there was a Piedmont house in the family anymore. Gran never talked about it."

Our moms accepted that, and then my mom turned to Larry Philips, who was standing discreetly near the door. "Mr. Phillips, are you free to meet today, since we drove all the way up here?"

Larry Phillips looked embarrassed. "Ah, this would be premature to discuss, ladies. I mean…" And he looked towards the bedroom door where Gran was slipping away from us. "I mean, Ms. Templeton is still with us," he finally managed to conclude.

Our moms almost looked mildly contrite. They shook the man's hand and slipped him their business cards with comments about looking forward to meeting him in the near future, and then they turned to me and both came over and gave me a small hug and a kiss that barely tickled my cheek. My mom said, "Come for brunch when you are home next, Elizabeth."

"Tell Dad hello from me," I said, making no promises. Exchanging a look but making no comment, our moms made their way down the steps. Standing in the doorway watching them, I noticed that neither one gave a glance to the ocean, where the sky and water were giving Gran a farewell display, mixing their colors in the evening light to create a vision no painting could match or camera could capture credibly.

I stood there wondering how anyone could not notice that view!

Larry Phillips stood beside me then, both of us gazing at the spectacular scene, thinking our own thoughts. Finally, some tattering of social protocol came over me and I thanked Larry for his presence there that day and offered him a cup of coffee or tea.

"Thanks, Elizabeth, but no, I need to get back to the office." He hesitated. "Are you doing okay? I know I'm just here for legal purposes, but clearly there is a degree of discord in the family. You seem to be balancing in the middle. That can be a tough place to be."

"I'd rather things not be like this, sure." I squeezed my hands together. "Not sure whether this schism can be healed, or not, or what the right answer is for all of us, but Gran sure made a valiant effort. I believe Scott and I will be solid, the rest I don't know. But for the present time, I have only one priority, and that is to be with Gran every day I can be with her. The details will all work out eventually. And I thank you for your help. I promise you that we—Scott and I—will work with you as smoothly as possible and that Tibby will always be in good hands."

He smiled and reached out to shake my hand. "I don't know you much yet, but I trust anyone who has the trust of Jerry Garcia and Grandin Templeton! Take care, and call me if, you know, anything changes here."

I made myself a cup of tea and took it out to the porch. I texted Jerry just to say the meeting was over and that I would fill him in on everything that evening, and that I was just taking some alone time to process things. He replied,

Take your time. Love you.

About an hour later, Tibby came out and sat beside me on the porch. She looked exhausted.

"Tibby, let me get you a cup of tea."

"Thanks, Elizabeth, that might be nice, but I'm so tired I am not sure I could even drink it!"

I got her one anyway, and she held it in her hands as if huddling around a camp fire, so it served a purpose.

"How are things?" I asked gently.

"All that really exhausted her, and she doesn't know if she did the right thing to talk so openly and directly, but she figures she'll never get another chance, so like she always has done, she jumped in and did it."

"That's what I love about Gran." I smiled despite the sadness of the moment. "Tibby, I regret with all my heart that I didn't have more years to know my Gran. All I had is this short time." This had been bothering me a great deal. This regret.

Tibby gave me a hug with her tired eyes. "I know what you are saying, Elizabeth, but look at it this way, far better for you to have had a short but meaningful time with her than a lifetime of knowing her without the powerful relationship you have grown. And you have done the ultimate task for her."

I thought. "Taking Mac's things to Chelsea?"

"That's the visible part of it. But that act, that's all wrapped around you being willing to do it, and you caring enough to get to know Gran, and for her to feel kinship. That's not something she has ever had with her family, not her brother or sister, not her daughters, only with a few—Mac, me, you and Scott."

I felt that too. That kinship. So, I was able to accept what Tibby told me.

I wanted to ask if Tibby had any idea how long Gran had to live. But then I thought what Jerry had just said the night before when we lay in bed and talked long into the night. That we have to relax and let life and death work itself out for each person. We can't predict and we can't wish for either a quick release or to keep someone we love with us for as long as possible. That it was up to the person themselves as well as to that mysterious force of spirit, or God, or whatever merging with the soul and body of the dying person.

That's what I love about my Jerry; how he thought deeply about all these things and was willing to try to articulate his thoughts. More than one observant friend had called me an old soul, but I knew for sure that Jerry was one, too. When I told him that, he had laughed and said the secret of a good life might be to have an old soul as a young person and a young heart and spirit as we age. I'm looking forward to that, with him.

42

I was in Gualala for the summer when Gran died. We scattered Gran's ashes out to sea near where Mac had been swept off his little boat. Our moms and dads came to the house for a short memorial where Gran's closest friends gathered, but they declined to get on the boat that took Scott, Tibby, Jerry and me out beyond the rocks where Mac was swept overboard. Instead, they met with Mr. Phillips for the rest of the afternoon, leaving without coming to the after-party we held out on the meadow in front of Gran and Mac's house. They called and said that they had to get home before dark because one of them—I don't recall which one—had an appointment the next morning.

I believe that the party was just what Gran would have wanted. I baked a huge cake that read MacIntosh and Templeton. People brought food and drink. Tibby sat quietly in a chair attended to by ever-changing friends from the loyal community that had encircled both her and Gran over the years. No one left her to sit by herself.

After the cold morning, it was a perfect coastal day that ended with the wind picking up about the time people were leaving. Jerry and Scott and I cleaned up and we insisted that Tibby rest. She didn't argue. In fact, she said very little all day long. Her face held a timeless, gently ravaged grief. That's the best way I can describe it.

Back in the Bay Area, Nellie made the move to Petaluma and was adjusting to a new location and to daily life with her recuperating sister. I stopped by briefly to see her home. It was new and pristine, as she had told me. As she walked me out to the car, however, she minced no words. It was not an easy transition and she missed our old house, but she did not second guess herself for a minute. Speaking directly to me with her hands on my arms in her familiar style, she admonished me that I shouldn't cling to the past; that I should never be afraid to move on. I hadn't given up my apartment in Davis quite yet, but the new owners moved in downstairs the day I left for nine weeks in Gualala. I introduced myself to them on the very day I drove north.

Things were changing rapidly. Besides the privilege of being with Gran in her last weeks, I was in heaven being with Jerry, day after day, night after night that summer. It was luxurious to not always have on our mind that in forty-eight hours or less, we would be back on the road apart from each other. From this perspective, the pace I had kept over the last year began to loom as crazy, whereas when in the midst of it, I had felt capable of doing it all. Adrenaline was quite a chemical. I knew I was being spoiled by waking up next to my Jerry, day after day, week after week.

To suddenly not have either Nellie or Gran in my life made me feel a like a lost child. Fortunately, that hole in my heart was soothed by Jerry and of course Tibby's companionship. And as for Scott, he was spending most of his time at home in Davis, and more and more of that time was with Lupe and her family. Lupe joked that she thought Scott was in love with her mother and daughter, as much as with her, but I know that it was Lupe who made it all happen, that it was Lupe with whom Scott, without fanfare, had slipped into love. Lupe had been right. Gina was a non-issue with him.

As for our parents… it has been a tough dilemma for me. I feel no hate, but I feel such nothingness towards them that it scares me. How can I feel this way when these people raised me, fed me, sheltered me, drove me to tennis tournaments, helped me with homework, and took me to doctor appointments? And yet, I really have no idea what to say to them now. In fact, I had never known what to say to them.

As soon as Gran died, our moms were off and running with the Piedmont house. I went over to see it because I wanted to see where Gran had grown up. It was a beauty, a large two-story house with a cupola, surrounded by towering trees. A classical house that required a great deal of money to keep looking so historically grand on the outside as well as functioning so perfectly inside. That it was so well-maintained was due to the money Gran's brother put into the house over the decades. Now Gran's daughters were enjoying the payoff in the outrageous housing market. A very desirable home by current standards, you could easily imagine a family in the early 1900s running in and out of the house and up and down the wide stairways. It was Gran's last gift to her daughters, and it was a gift that met them exactly where their values stood: a good business venture. Gran knew her daughters and maybe ultimately, she accepted them for who they were, expecting—and getting—nothing in return.

I stood at the bottom of the stairs, my hand on the newel post, imagining the young Grandin Templeton running up the stairs laughing and calling to someone, a friend, perhaps her brother or sister.

I said to my mom, who was briskly hustling around making plans for upgrades and sale, "I was just thinking what a wonderful home for Gran to have grown up in. So much character and history here. Just imagine what Oakland was like back in that time period."

My mom sniffed. "Elizabeth, you always were too sentimental, too caught up in…" She seemed not to know what to express whatever it was she was thinking, but finally added, "Gran always caused trouble and I'm sure she caused trouble here in this house, too."

The bitterness of that comment pierced me. I felt it was an arrow shot through both me and Gran, all in one or two sentences. Well, another way to look at it was that Gran and I were stitched together, of the same fabric!

My mom walked away, busy with her plans. Our conversation was over for her. But this time I didn't let it pass. My grief-filled thoughts came pouring out to her—beseeching, pleading, yet angrily demanding, "How can you not spare one minute to imagine your mother as a child in this gorgeous home? How can you not hold some love for the child your mother once was? Can't you dig down and come up with on speck of grief in your heart? If not for yourself or for Gran, but then for me? You must know how dearly I came to love Gran and how much I miss her." I started to add, "how much her death hurts me," but choking back a sob full of anger and sadness, I decided not to be that vulnerable in the face of my mom's indifference.

All I got from her was a pause, not even a glance. Was there a moment she was processing what I said? I'll never know because she didn't say a word, just pulled out her phone, and while I'll never know for sure, she pretended to be taking an incoming phone call, as she bustled off up that grand staircase leaving me to watch her smart heels click on the old wood floors and her trim bottom move efficiently from side to side as she climbed and turned out of sight down the hallway.

I didn't go back to Piedmont to see the house again. Not too much later, my mom proudly sent word of the selling price. I didn't hear a word of thank you to Gran. But I knew Gran wasn't expecting it, even in her new stage of life as part of the ocean waves, where she was mingling with Mac for eternity.

As for my future, it was dangling. I knew I didn't want to be running back and forth between the North Coast and Davis forever. It would wear me out. I knew I wanted to be with Jerry. I knew my apartment would never be the same without Nellie. But I loved my school and my students. And Scott and Lupe were in Davis, and at last Scott and I were growing closer again, in a whole new, more separate style. For a time, I continue to dangle, knowing some change would happen or, more proactively speaking, that I would make some change happen eventually.

43

All was wine and roses when we celebrated Jerry's birthday a few weeks after Gran's passing, but the next day something was amiss. My even-keeled, attentive, supportive, understanding, contented boyfriend—a man who actually had been known to whistle while he worked—became moody, detached, uncommunicative. Every day he was more withdrawn, and when I inquired if he was feeling okay or if something terrible had happened down at the garage, he either shrugged it off or acted like I was imposing upon him to ask.

This continued for a week and then it was ten days. I examined everything I might have done to offend him. I lay beside him in bed at night knowing he wasn't asleep either, but a barrier existed that was impenetrable. I spent most of the first week in angst, which slid into agony about how our beautiful life had disappeared. I was too upset to talk to Lupe or Scott about it, it felt too personal. Then about the start of the second week, I pulled myself up short and decided to get out of my head, to stop thinking it was all about me. Instead, I looked at Jerry and realized he was in misery. When I started focusing on his pain—whatever the hell it might be or what was causing it—it took the pressure off myself. It was still a horrible way to live, but instead of hating myself or resenting this man I loved, I now felt my heart go out to him.

I figured that time would alter the situation one way or another, and I needed to be patient a little longer. It took ten days. Ten extremely long days, no joke.

It was a Friday evening. Jerry was sitting at the table having just picked at his dinner. I walked by on the way to the stove and since I had no idea what words to say, I gently caressed his shoulder. When I made contact, he stiffened, then stood up, grabbed his jacket, and headed out the door making some comment about not waiting up for him. I heard his car drive off.

For three hours I fought the emotional swing between anger and worry, hating both him and myself at either of those points. All the while I alternated furiously between riding the exercise bike and baking three different cookie recipes. Finally, towards midnight, I lit the fire and made myself sit down with some tea, not trusting myself with alcohol, and began counting my breaths in and then out. I heard a car drive in, a door slam, and the car drove away. I sat still. Jerry walked in the house.

Our eyes met. It was a very long look, and unlike the last days, he did not look away this time. He came and sat down by me and brushed the hair back over my ear like he so often had done in the past. I couldn't help it; a tear ran down my cheek. He touched my cheek and then put his finger to his lips, tasting my tear drop.

"Who brought you home?"

"Paul," he answered and then added, "He thought I

shouldn't drive. I don't think I had too much but he thought I shouldn't drive," he repeated. Jerry didn't seem drunk, but he was talking very slowly and deliberately so perhaps Paul had been right. I was grateful.

Jerry gazed at the dying flames in the wood stove and then looked back at me. "Lizzie, I'm going to quit being a jerk and talk to you tomorrow. I promise. I'm sorry. But tonight…" His voice trailed off. "Right now, I think I better go to bed."

He got up and wandered to the bedroom and by the time I shut up the fire and double-checked the doors and walked in the bedroom, he was asleep on the bed with one shoe on and one off. I took off the other shoe and his cap and threw a cover on top of his snoring form. I got undressed, grabbed several blankets, returned to the couch, and managed to fall asleep myself.

In the morning, I woke up to Jerry's touch on my face. He was bending down to me. Showered and shaved, dressed, with a cup of coffee in his hand, jacket zipped up. He smelled like coffee and peanut butter.

"Umm. How are you?" I asked.

"I've felt better, but also felt worse. Listen, Lizzie, unfortunately, I have two cars that I need to service this morning, so I'm off but I'm putting up the Closed sign at 12:00 and I'll be home. I promise. Can you hang in there with me a few more hours?"

"Yeah. Did you get something to eat?"

"Peanut butter and jelly."

He got to the door and then stopped. "My car."

I sat up. "I'll take you to get your car. Where is it?"

"St. Orres."

I stumbled to the bathroom, then threw on some sweats, grabbed my keys and walked out the door, too sleepy to think of suggesting he take my car and we could retrieve his car later. I sensed he wanted to get his car back sooner rather than later. And so, I drove him without any words to where his car sat all alone in the parking lot. Before Jerry got out of the car, he turned to me and stroked my hair out of my face. I must have looked a mess. His look was tender and after ten days of no affection on his familiar face, I was happy to see it. But he had some real explaining to do, something shouted in my mind.

"I promise. Home by noon."

Back at the house, I got in the hot shower and cried a little, not knowing what might come when Jerry got home. The fog began creeping in, making everything outside gray and gloomy and cold. The summer gift to the North Coast. I decided soup would be the right thing for lunch. Concocting a new recipe kept me occupied that morning while I wondered what was coming next.

I heard Jerry's car drive up the driveway at 11:30 and I put two steaming bowls of soup on the table with a loaf of bread in the middle. Then Jerry was in the house, washing his hands in the mudroom sink. He stood in the kitchen door, taking off his work shirt, standing there in his tee-shirt and jeans and looking at me in a way I couldn't describe. And despite my frustration and worry, at that moment I thought he was the most desirable man I'd ever seen.

As I motioned to the table, he simultaneously pulled me to the old couch that lined one wall of his kitchen. He sat me down and he sat next to me.

I couldn't hold back anymore. "Talk to me, Jerry."

"I want to, Elizabeth. I mean, I don't want to admit what a jerk I've been, but you deserve to know it."

My heart was pounding out of control and I struggled to soothe it. "Just talk to me, Jerry. Just talk to me."

His voice was soft as he began but gradually became clearer. "The evening of my birthday, I got a text."

He stopped. I thought I was going to have to pound on his chest to get him to keep going, but I made myself just say gently, "A text from whom?"

"From Kelsey."

"Kelsey?"

"San Diego Kelsey. Ex-girlfriend Kelsey."

"Oh." What could this mean? "And she wrote what?"

"Happy birthday, Jerry."

"That's it?" I didn't know whether to laugh or worry that there was more to come.

"I know, stupid, huh? 'Happy birthday, Jerry.' Not a big deal, except, Lizzie, we have had no communication from the time she left. All I knew is that she moved to San Diego."

"Jerry, you are going to have to help me out here. I don't know what went on for you when you got this text that has changed everything about you. Please help me out."

"I'm trying. It's complicated for me. So, when I read her three words, it was like a force was unleashed in me. Just like that. Just like that. I got it. I got what a jerk I was then and how I have kept this truth not just from others, including you, but from myself, from acknowledging it myself."

"What truth, Jerry?"

"Lizzie, when Kelsey and I got together there was a frenzy of excitement and attraction enough to last through some wild dating and convincing Kelsey to move here and buying that house in Sea Ranch together. Between some money she had inherited from her grandfather and her savings of her own, she had enough for a down payment, and I convinced her, or perhaps we agreed in a state of infatuation to buy that house together. I just wanted to possess her, she was so beautiful.

"But then the frenzy kind of wore off and we settled into life here. I was doing what I had always been doing here in my home town, the town where I belonged. My friends, my shop, my surroundings, my bar, my ocean, my fishing buddies, my grocery store and art center, you know, my corner of the world. My place. But Kelsey was in foreign territory. And she did not fit in at all and didn't know how to try to fit in either.

"And here is the part where I was so wrong, Liz. And this is what hit me like a brick when she sent me that text. I did nothing to help her belong here. I did nothing. In fact, in time I think I… What's the word I'm looking for? Oh yeah, I sabotaged her chances of learning to become comfortable or to find her niche here. I knew she was increasingly miserable and lonely and out of place, and I ignored that and I ignored her silent or not-so-silent pleas to listen to her. God, I was a jerk, Lizzie!"

He looked at me with such pain that I could hardly bear it, but I said nothing yet.

"Not only did I not help her, I can see now, but what I never saw before is that I actively began to belittle her in my eyes and in the eyes of my friends. I did that, Liz. I did that to her!"

"Why do you think you did that, Jerry?" It was hard to believe Jerry could ever be cruel, but here he was telling me that he had been. "And how did you last so long together, what, three years?"

He laughed bitterly. "Sex, I guess. We both loved it, and between the sheets, as they say, we came together very nicely."

"Jerry, did you love her?"

He was quiet for a long time. "Fair question. I was clearly *in love* with Kelsey. But I have to question how much I knew how to love someone. I sure didn't love her with my behavior or my thinking."

I thought about my tumultuous relationship with Aiden. I think I knew what Jerry was talking about. But I was curious. "Do you think Kelsey loved you?"

"You ask difficult questions, Liz. Honestly, it's a topic I have not allowed myself to consider over the years. Perhaps I didn't want to face the truth because I think she loved me more than I loved her. At least she was willing to sacrifice more for me than I did for her. Her hard-earned money bought the house in Sea Ranch, for one thing, to say nothing of several years of her life given to our relationship."

He went on as if determined to answer all my questions. "As to why I did it? I think I've figured it out at last."

He stood up, agitated, and then sat down again.

"I am ashamed to admit this to anyone, to myself much less to you, Lizabeth. I don't want you to be disgusted with me or, worse yet, distrust me. But I need to share this. We pledged each other honesty. You know, my community has always meant the world to me. These people have given me my life, and in return I have always been reliable. I've been a part of this place, someone that everyone can count on, and not just for their car repairs, but for everything, for… for… you know doing my part to make this place a good town, a place where others could belong, just as I belonged. I guess that at some stupid level I felt a sense of pride at being the person I have always perceived myself to be and that others have perceived me to be. Except your Gran."

He gave that bitter laugh again. "Your Gran, she was at the shop one day with her car and she heard me talk to Kelsey on the phone. After I hung up, she gave me that Gran glare and said to me, 'Jerry, you treat that poor girl like shit. You should think about why you do that.' I blew her off, but obviously not really, because I still remember what she said."

I knew that Gran glare very well. "So, Jerry, did you figure out why you were treating her like shit?" I said more gently than my Gran had.

"Oh, not at the time. I'm a slow learner, I suppose. You see, when the glamour of our infatuation started to wear off, I could see how Kelsey did not fit in, and I was running scared. I was afraid that she would try to talk me into moving somewhere she liked better. And deep down I knew that it would be the decent thing to do, to try to find out what she was feeling and work together on where we could both be happy. But I didn't want to accept that reality. I was never going to move after all. Gualala is where I belonged and I would not consider any other place to live. She was going to have to accommodate me. But I wasn't going to make any efforts to help her because deep down I didn't think she would ever fit in. If I did make an effort to help, it would be softening myself to her needs, and I would be put in a position of having to meet her halfway. And I was adamant about staying here. Underneath I was frightened to even think of leaving the coast. If that makes any sense."

I just nodded although it was kind of convoluted logic to me, but clear to Jerry.

"So not only did I not support her or listen to her or try to understand, but I outright sabotaged any small attempts she did make to get to know people, like trying to be part of the Art Center. And I began to make little snarky comments about Kelsey being not just Miss San Diego but in particular Miss La Jolla, implying that she was superficial, a real rich bitch, pardon my language, and she could never make it up here in the rugged North Coast. And, Elizabeth, I played it perfectly, put myself into the role of good old Jerry, local boy, being stuck, victimized if you will, by this Southern California bubblehead blond. Never overplayed it, as to be obvious or garner any sympathy for Kelsey. And again, the only ones who caught it or at least called me on it, were your Gran and Mac. Each one separately let me know what I was doing. But I ignored them.

"I didn't hear or understand what Gran and Mac were

telling me because honestly, I was mostly oblivious to what I was doing. Isn't that fucking amazing? I realize now that it was all because I was simply scared that if I dealt with Kelsey, I would have to deal with something I never wanted to think about—possibly leaving my town, the only place I ever felt I belonged. This was big, deep, existential agony that I just stuffed, and instead I let Kelsey take the brunt of it all. And of course, when she finally left me, I played out the role of shafted Jerry and I got a lot of 'Jerry buddy, she wasn't good enough for you, she wasn't one of us, good riddance, come have a beer!' And I got to play out the lucky survivor."

He looked at me. "Proud of me now, Liz?"

"But you sounded genuinely hurt by the breakup when we first talked," I said, remembering that first conversation.

"There was some truth to that. I was a hurt soul, and some of it was genuine, like missing the great sex, and hating all the turmoil of having to sell the house I could no longer afford, and I think now there was also the unacknowledged guilt over my role in the whole debacle! I played the victim role perfectly here in my comfortable place where everyone knew my name. I convinced even myself. I am after all, a child of Gualala. Raised by so many here and no one wanted to see me other than as a good guy."

He sighed. "My God. What a jerk I am."

He started to say more, but I stopped him. "Hey, fellow, if I hear you call my boyfriend a jerk one more time, I am going to spank you and send you to bed without your lunch."

Jerry stopped mid-breath, so caught up in his self-flagellation that it took him a moment to tune in to me and my words and my smile. When he did, he leaned in and breathed, "Elizabeth, you vixen!"

I put my arms up around him and pulled him to me. Around my kisses I said to him, "Jerry Garcia, I'm following you all the way in this revelation, but we have lots of time to figure out how to deal with this huge load of guilt that's rolling around in your head and gut. But right now, I just miss you so badly that I think we should take a break and continue this heavy discussion later."

It took him about thirty seconds to move from his mindset to mine, but he made that adjustment with enthusiasm. Sex in the kitchen is just as uncomfortable as advertised even with an old couch conveniently located there, but it was well worth it. Afterward as we relaxed in relief and happiness, both of our stomachs growled in unison.

I jumped up and reheated our soup, and we sat down together and ate with such gusto that we had to each wipe tomato soup off each other's chins. Oh, it was good to be back.

The fog had only thickened while we had talked and loved each other. So we turned off our phones, went to the fire and, wrapped in blankets together, we launched into phase two of the unveiling of the flawed life of my lover. The theme was general variations on the earlier confession. It was eye-opening to Jerry, and for that reason I was right there, sympathetic with him in unpacking this new view of himself. But it was also strangely reassuring to me. Jerry had been so absolutely perfect all along, and while I had no complaints and was over my head in love with this man, I knew of my own imperfections, and as I told him partway through the afternoon, I now liked and loved him even more knowing he hadn't been perfect along the way, even subconsciously.

For dinner we had some leftover spaghetti and meatballs with a bottle of wine. We sat by the fire and stuffed our faces going back for seconds and even thirds.

Finally he said to me, "I've been wondering what prompted Kelsey to send me a birthday text. And I have been wondering if I should call Kelsey and, you know, apologize or make amends or something. What do you think?"

I thought for moment. "Well, that depends. For so long you let Kelsey take all the blame for your relationship failing. And now just out of the blue, you have taken it all on yourself with overwhelming self-blame. If your purpose in calling her is to just take that enormous guilt-ball and try to throw it back to her for your absolution, then I think that is a terrible idea, simply not fair. If, on the other hand, you genuinely want to acknowledge that you bear responsibility for hurting her, and you have no expectation of her response, understanding she might rightly hate you, then it could be the decent thing to do. It is curious why she reached out to say happy birthday after all these years. You haven't responded, have you?"

"No. I hear what you are saying. I'll think about it. But here is another thing that occurs to me. And I think it's big. What happened this week is more than about Kelsey and me, I think. I honestly think..." Jerry's voice wavered. "I honestly think that I have grieved for my parents this week, more so than at any time since they died. And how is that related to my being a jerk…?" He stopped for a moment. "…to Kelsey? I think it all has to do with this sense of belonging that I have in Gualala. Life took my parents but gave me a community to love and raise me. And unlike most people, it is not just a family that gives me a sense of my belonging but it is a place, a place full of people, but still it is a place. It's been my identity and I've clung to it desperately. Oh, I know I never have looked desperate, but I believe I have been. And that is why I fought off any sense of responsibility to my girlfriend to consider that perhaps this was not the only place for us to live. I couldn't give up my community because I would be losing my parents again in the process."

Jerry looked at me. "I don't think I am explaining myself exactly logically, but then our minds don't always follow a logical thinking pattern, do they?"

I agreed with that, and kissed him tenderly.

Then I pulled back and looked him straight in the eyes. "Any feelings left for Kelsey, Jer?"

"No, only guilt and a sad feeling that I wasted her time while I didn't even learn a lesson at the time, took me all these years. Ha, I should have listened to Gran and Mac, of course."

There was one more thing I had to know. Why not, I thought. "Has your sense of belonging to Gualala changed any? How does it relate to our relationship?"

"That's another thing I have been wrestling with all these days, Lizzie, sweet Lizzie. First of all, my relationship with you is so much deeper and stronger than it ever was with Kelsey—if I even did love her—whether it was Kelsey who made the difference, or whether it was who I was at the time and who I am now that makes such a drastic difference. But my love for you is beyond words, although I try, and beyond my feeble actions, although again, I try. I am humbled to find that you are able to love me despite my shortcomings. I didn't knowingly try to put up a persona for you, Liz. I thought I was exactly how I have always seen myself and been seen by others: reliable, calm, steady, and loyal. I think I had a certain point of pride in being that strong, perfect man and couldn't see my own weaknesses." He grinned ruefully at me. "Now layers have been peeled away for me, all because of a nice gesture by my ex-girlfriend. Fucking crazy, isn't it, Liz?"

He squeezed my hand. "Going forward for us? First and foremost, I need to belong to myself and in my own skin and head regardless of any history. But, Liz, don't you think we humans need to also belong to something bigger than just ourselves? What do you think?"

"Um, I think you are right." I thought some more. "All my life, I felt I belonged with Scott. He was my grounding point. I am sorry to say I never felt I belonged at any deep level with my parents, although of course physically they provided for me. And when I met Gran, I felt an instant sense of being at home with her, like I was part of her family embrace. But I also felt that comfort with Nellie as my neighbor and I feel it now with Lupe. As for you, Jerry Garcia, I feel that I belong with you more than anyone else." I paused and went on. "And here's what is funny. When I am teaching, I feel that I belong with those young students in a very important way and that they belong to me, but of course that is transitory, changing every year. I liked my Davis home, but the closest I have ever felt to belonging to any one physical place is when I arrived here on the North Coast the first time. This place calls to me."

I thought about what he said about his parents. It hurt my heart to think of my young Jerry becoming an orphan. "Jerry, your situation is different than mine. Your place and the people in it have blended together, grounding you in life and purpose, helping you live out your grief when as a kid you really didn't know what grieving was all about. You had no idea how to face your loss, and your community got you through it. I think it's brilliant that you have figured this out now."

"I don't know about that, Liz. I haven't felt anything but stupid and unlovable this week. But just by calling it out into the open I am losing my fear. I want to move on. I love watching you just slip right into life here. You make it look so effortless and it's been so much fun sharing what I love about my home with you. But I also see you looking comfortable back in Davis, so I think you are much more fluid in your attachment. You are more secure with life and relationships than most people, despite your crazy parental situation. Certainly, you are more secure than poor old Scott ended up feeling. It's awesome that you love it here in my home town, but to go back to answer your question, I know that you being drawn to the North Coast is not the critical factor in our relationship. I want to be with you, and if that is here, fantastic, but if that needs to be somewhere else, then, honey, I am ready to work with you and figure that out, and yep, even make a move. With you is where I belong. I know that now."

I felt like we had crossed into a new dimension.

Then Jerry mused, "Does that mean I have finally grown up as any normal boy would have if he hadn't lost his parents when he was ten?"

We let that question float out in the air as we succumbed to what appeared to be a never-ending fiery yearning for each other that had overtaken us since that afternoon. Who's to argue with the body needing a respite from the overexertion of the poor mind and soul?

44

I was abruptly awakened out of deep sleep by a memory. It was 4:00 a.m. and Jerry's arm was still laying over my breasts weighing heavily, too heavily. I gently pushed it off and he rolled over never waking up.

As this particular memory grew stronger, it hit me for the first time how powerful the subconscious can be, connecting the dots behind our awareness.

In my careful reading of Mac's journal—before it became Chelsea's to hold—I had been perplexed by the lack of entries for one particularly year. It was during the middle of the big house project. Uncharacteristically for the usually fluent and loquacious Mac, the journal pages for this particular year were mostly empty of commentary or thoughts. All that was written was a few cryptic sentences, and read something like:

Gran and I have been having some tough times and it's all my doing. I've been a real fuck up and don't deserve her good loving. She's too good for me. What's wrong with me? What a bastard I've been. Scum.

Back on the north coast one day, I impulsively asked Gran why Mac had written those words and little else that year. She became very quiet before finally saying, "Well, we were very busy that year. Mac simply didn't have time to write."

I stared at her. Everything about Gran's demeanor was oozing with the falsehood of what she had just said. She who always spoke her truth! Sure enough, in the following breath she changed course.

"Elizabeth, that is a lie, a flat-out untruth. The truth is kind of painful to remember but so it goes. Life is not for the faint-hearted."

Here she stopped what she was doing as if frozen in another time. "It was right in the middle of our house building time. I came across Mac flirting outrageously with one of the young women who was helping us with our project. When I confronted him about it later, he was at first embarrassingly full of excuses. When I didn't say anything and just looked at him, he finally confessed that he had slept with her three times and was miserable about screwing around with her. He said she meant nothing to him. That gave me mixed feelings. She was after all, a human being and one of our neighbors. But I suspect he was relieved to have it out in the open and thought that was what I would want to hear.

"Mac promised it was over and that he must have been out of his mind, and then he proceeded to beat himself up, calling himself all sorts of degrading names, many of them Scottish, and just generally said he was not worthy of me, and on and on and on. Really pathetic I remember thinking at the time.

"I was, of course, devastated on the one hand, and disgusted on the other. For several weeks we were in a state of impasse, neither one of us knowing what to do, and here we were in the middle of building our dream house and living in our tiny garage apartment. Our bed was a small one and we had no sofa, so every night we had to sleep next to each other, but we couldn't bear to touch each other. I couldn't even tell Tibby because it was so personal, just between Mac and me."

Gran straightened up taller then as if she was recalling a turning point in her memory. "I realized one day that on top of the cheating, what had been bugging me ever since he had confessed was that he kept overly dramatically flogging himself to try to get my sympathy and forgiveness." Gran looked right at me. "I tell you I was relieved to at last understand what was annoying me about the whole mea culpa crap."

"I'm sorry, but I am a little confused about what bothered you so much about that, Gran. He wasn't making excuses or blaming someone else, was he?"

"Not exactly, Elizabeth. I know it's ironic. But think about it this way. He was making himself the focus, almost like he was the victim instead of the perpetrator, and in doing so, he was making me the oppressive voice of his conscience. He had hurt me, but he didn't directly acknowledge that. He just made himself the center of all the drama. The spotlight was all on him, not me, and I felt he was not taking responsibility for hurting me and lying to me. He was wallowing in his badness like he was the class hellion and I was the school teacher who needed to console and reassure him after catching him behaving badly.

"I know it sounds counter to common thinking, but I finally figured out how to articulate this building sensation I was feeling. I said to him, 'Mac, all I hear from you is what a rotten man you are, how you are not worthy of me, how you are disgusted with yourself, how weak you are, blah blah

blah! And I'm sick of it. And you want to know why?' He was speechless. So, I told him, 'This is not all about you. It is not even all about you and her. This is also about me. And it is definitely about our relationship. Have you stopped to think about that? Have you stopped to think about how this hurt me? About how I am going to have trouble trusting you again? I'd love to hear just once that you are trying to comprehend how I feel. I am not a goddess-like figure that you have transgressed against. I am me. A real-life woman. Your lover and best friend. And I am hurting. I need to know that you understand and care about me.'

"And then I added, 'We are not some sort of casual hookup. Once we made a commitment to each other, I became fully committed to you, to be truthful and faithful, and it is hellish for me to not be able to trust you. It's going to take time, and you have to give me that time. I want to be with you the rest of my life, but I will tell you this and you can take it to the bank. If I ever find out that I can't trust you again, I will be seeing you only at the market when you come by my check-out line as you buy your groceries for a dinner that does not include me, and that's it.' Well, Elizabeth. That stopped him cold. He gradually changed his I'm-such-a-terrible-weak-brute laments and focused on doing what he could to rebuild my trust and ease my pain. But it took the better part of a year. It took a lot of relearning of behaviors and reactions and old practices, for not just Mac but for me, too."

Gran relaxed then and smiled at me. "Obviously it all worked out pretty damn good!"

And that is Gran's story that woke me up at 4:00 in the

morning the night after Jerry came home and confessed his self-deception and his lack of honesty.

I thought about how I had responded to Jerry. Had I been so famished for his love, wanting only to move back into our dreamy lover's state of being, that I gave up my own perspective? While I was somewhat relieved that Jerry was not a flawless man, now I couldn't help but wonder whether there were other hidden stories he had not shared of this magnitude or perhaps even bigger potential earthquakes. It was not an affair like Mac's, but it was nonetheless something Jerry had hidden from me. And from his former girlfriend, as well as from himself.

There was more, however. It was actually not the content of his confession that bothered me; I immediately loved him all the more for admitting to being so fallible. No, what had really hurt was the ten days of withdrawal and silence. I realized now, in the clarity of the morning's dawning light, that I would carry the pain of that withdrawal a lot longer than anything he had actually told me. And in his continual self-berating, just like Mac, he put the focus on himself, leaving out any direct recognition of how this had wounded me during those excruciatingly long days while I waited for him to stop freezing me out as I tortured myself wondering what I had done wrong. The million-dollar question, I realized now, was how could I be sure this wouldn't be a pattern in the future?

I knew I had two choices right then. One—the easy way out—I could simply celebrate being back in Jerry's good graces with his usual kind and easy-going loving. But there was a danger in that. It wouldn't be fully honest, and my suppressed feelings might very well come back to bite me, or us. Or, two, I could gather my courage just like Gran had done so long ago with her Mac, and try to explain to Jerry how this was hitting me, how I felt a lack of respect for my experience and how this worried me for our future.

Well, I'm not Gran and I cannot speak with her arrow-sharp authenticity, but I managed to hold my own in the face of my sexy, sleepy Jerry, who woke up about seven, wanting to have some morning loving. He was surprised when the woman who had passionately jumped him the day before had been doing some thinking overnight and was in a different frame of mind.

To give him credit, he didn't get pissed. He didn't sulk. He didn't retreat. He hung in there with me, and as I told him that I could not tolerate being frozen out and given the silent treatment ever again. It was too painful. I explained as best I could that what he thought was his total remorse had a double-edged effect and that self-flagellation is not the same as making amends. I was not entirely coherent—it felt strange to be criticizing how he was showing his remorse—being a novice and not having Gran's piercing clarity and strong will, I struggled and I cried, and Jerry got frustrated and weepy, too. But we hung in there with each other; in retrospect, it was the beginning of the next phase of our relationship: the realistic stage.

Jerry finally ran his fingers through his hair and admitted that though he didn't fully understand yet, he was hearing me and wanted to learn more. I admitted that I had a lot to learn too, but that I wanted to not live with resentments that would poison us. And as the morning sun was well up and burning off the fog, Jerry scrambled to get ready for work. I had a moment of chagrin at how our relationship had impacted his business hours and I said this to him.

He came over and kissed me and said, "I wouldn't have it any other way, Lizbeth."

He headed out the door and I brewed my tea, saying out loud into the kitchen air, "Thank you, once again, Gran."

The next day, Jerry called Kelsey, managed to catch her out on a run along the San Diego waterfront. She told him that she had sent him a happy birthday text because for the first time she realized she didn't hate him anymore. She could now think of him kindly and wanted to simply send genuine good wishes for him. She was doing fine, working hard, making money, learning to sail and was planning to sail to Mexico soon with a new boyfriend.

Jerry shook his head when he told me about it. "We talked for five minutes, and we sounded like two mature people with no blame and no shame. Amazing."

45

Scott sent me a text.

Wrote Ryan and Mandy a check for $50,000 to pay back the house deposit. Now at last I feel free.

Before I could absorb this and respond, he sent a follow-up text, as if for dramatic effect.

They cashed it the next day.

While one might be able to come up with some logical reasons why they so quickly cashed the check without responding to Scott, even I didn't want to rationalize this. As I told Jerry at dinner that night, "Well, that certainly puts more nails in the coffin!"

I did a good job—I think I did, anyway—of just accepting Scott's actions and not trying to fix or analyze anyone's behavior or thinking. But I do admit it was on my mind for many days, making me a tad restless. So, the next Sunday, Jerry suggested we get out of town for the afternoon and see where we ended up. And soon we found ourselves sitting at the same Jenner coffee shop where we had first touched each other.

I was watching some kids nearby, "my age kids," I thought, thinking of my students. And as if it was a brilliant thought, I realized that there were "my age kids" all over the world and that while I would miss my school, and especially Lupe, I could make a change, teach in a new school anywhere.

I looked at Jerry—that mind reader— and he looked at me and said, "Are you thinking what I'm thinking?"

"So now you're psychic?"

He replied, "I think so."

He reached over, lifted my hand to his lips and said, "I'd like to marry you, Elizabeth Rose Kuiper. And as far as I'm concerned, the sooner the better. And I'm hopeful that you want that, too. It's very simple to me, except perhaps deciding where to live."

I didn't need to analyze anything. It was also simple for me, including where to live. "The answer is yes, Jerry Garcia. And honestly, we can live anywhere as long as we are together."

He smiled at me, that great smile with crinkles around his eyes.

"I'm in agreement. For you, and a life with you, I would go live anywhere. And I don't even feel I'm having to be brave to make that statement."

I knew how much he was grounded in his town and how the North Coast was in his blood. But I also knew how much he loved me. I also believe that if I had at that moment said, Jerry, let's go live in San Francisco, or in Nebraska (at least we would have friends there), he would have been right beside me.

But for now, at least, I had no interest in any place but the North Coast. It was Jerry obviously, but it was Gran and Tibby and the big old house plus the whole environment, and of course the pounding surf on the rocky bluffs and the ever-changing forever sky. And there were kids and schools on the North Coast. I would find my role there. And maybe Jerry and I would have baby and there would be a little one in the world from our union, a child with equal Mexican heritage from each parent. Did Jerry's one-quarter plus my one-quarter equal one-half? What was the genetic math? I felt both calm and giddy at the same time.

Our future seemed abundant; anything was possible. And we did not waste much time on a long engagement.

We were married on the meadow at Gran and Mac's house, the same setting where they said their vows. We were surrounded by the people we loved as well as the community that had first embraced Jerry as a boy and now me as well. We did not invite our moms and dads. Scott and Lupe came, with her mom and daughter, and Scott was grinning the whole time, Marta holding his hand and chattering happily as they looked out over the ocean. And much to my delight, a package arrived the morning of the wedding: a set of first-class linens for our bed, sent with warmest wishes, from Susan and Jacob and the whole Anderson family.

Of course, there was a party. It looked like half the town came—everyone knew Jerry from his garage—and they all brought food so there was plenty. The local bell-ringers—a group that once included Gran—stood on the steps of the porch and rang us down the steps and into our marriage ceremony where we exchanged our vows amidst tears and laughter. The bagpiper came in memory of Mac and the dancers came in memory of Gran and we all danced to a local fiddler band. Tibby cried a never-ending stream of tears, but her face afterward was full of more smiles than I had seen since Gran died. Johnny, who was now Tibby's faithful companion pressed his furry body into Tibby's leg to comfort her.

We wanted no honeymoon; we knew we lived in our own paradise. That night, after the chilly fog chased us inside, I looked around the scene in Gran and Mac's cozy living room and found that it embraced our little community of family and friends. Tibby and Nellie were deep in conversation as if they had known each other forever. (Scott and Lupe had rented a van and picked up Nellie on the way up the coast so she wouldn't miss the wedding.) Lupe was sitting in a corner reading a chapter book with her daughter, who was trying hard to stay awake. Lupe's mother was sitting on the couch, feet up on the ottoman, her head back and quietly snoring. In the kitchen, still in his wedding clothes, Jerry was on the floor fixing the dishwasher that had picked our wedding day to malfunction. Scott looked restless, so I motioned for him to come outside with me. The truth was that I could never get enough of being outside here on the coast. I grabbed a blanket off the couch to wrap around my wedding dress because the fog was thick and the sunshine we'd had earlier was only a nice memory. Now it was dark and gray.

Scott and I made our way over to the edge of the cliffs. In their endless pattern, the waves crashed and thundered below us. No moon nor a star was in sight.

"Hey, Lizbeth, do you remember that first night. Remember how freaked out we were when we ran into that fox?"

I laughed. "Yeah, and we were sure we would be attacked by a bear. I think Gran enjoyed scaring us."

This let loose a string of "do you remember" questions and although we knew it was formulaic, we were both happy to be back in touch with each other, talking and remembering. We talked about the trip, the Andersons, Chicago, the rain storm, Chelsea, all of it. Everything we could possibly remember. We were both so happy. Scott even made a lighthearted comment about Gina.

Then I laughed about sheltering in the car during the rain storm. Immediately I could have kicked myself that I mentioned the Explorer, because that led to thinking about my dad, and then of course our moms and our new reality. And then our mood was subdued once again.

Scott kicked at a rock near the cliff edge. It went over the side and was lost to the waves far below. I wondered how long it took to fall so far. I shivered thinking of falling down so far to certain death. The cliffs were mesmerizing, staggering in beauty and also in danger.

Scott said to me, "Elizabeth, I don't know what you are going to do going forward, but I will not have any connection with our parents, ever. A complete and final break. I need that clarity to go on."

I wrapped the blanket around my shoulders a little tighter. "You have my support whatever you decide to do. Actually, I envy you that clarity. It more complicated for me. I can't get past feeling that there is some obligation on my part towards our parents. Then I get all confused."

Scott's calmness transformed to anger. "You tell me, Liz,

you tell me one thing that our parents did that wasn't motivated by their own self-centeredness. Tell me one thing and maybe I will reconsider my decision."

It was a challenge. I was quiet for a long time, just living with his question. But then one single incidence came slamming into me and I couldn't shake it.

I looked away from him. I didn't want to spoil the certainty of his decision. He had worked so long and hard to know what to do. He hadn't been this healthy since the day he opened up his birth certificate. Lupe would kill me if she knew I undid any of the good work Scott had done towards healing.

"See, you can't think of any, can you?" he threw at me confidently.

The image that had come to me would not go away.

"One. Scott. But… your clear decision is surely the best one for you to hang on to."

He stared. I looked out to sea. Oh, I wished I hadn't thought of this memory, because Scott was doing so well, being happy with Lupe, happy with his life minus our parents. I wished I hadn't said anything. Maybe he would agree, best not to hear it.

But that wouldn't be Scott. He would need to know and even now, even when I warned him not to make me tell him, he did and of course I did tell him, with great trepidation, but it felt like the only fair thing to do, because after all, most people are not totally bad or totally righteous, are they?

With us both standing there, staring out to the waves, with the pounding of the surf drowning out any other sound around us, I relived my memory of the day the dog attacked Scott.

We were playing out in front of our house, about five years old, maybe four, but old enough to remember. Our moms were up by the porch talking about painting the house. Scott and I had been out near the street. It was a cul-de-sac so we often played near the street, it being fairly safe. I had gone up to my mom to ask for a popsicle. It was a hot day in Dixon. My mom kept putting me off because she and Auntie Mandy were trying to decide what color to paint the trim. I kept bugging them and they kept telling me to wait. While I was standing pulling at my mom's shirt to get her attention, out of nowhere the dog showed up. We never knew if Scott did something to provoke it or whether the dog was just an aggressive beast, certainly not from our neighborhood, and none of us saw any tags. The next thing we heard was Scott screaming and when our heads flew around to look, we saw the dog's teeth sunk into Scott's arm. Then our moms were running out to the street and my mom grabbed a solar lamp that was stuck into the ground to use as a weapon, but it was stuck, and she had to pull it a couple of times to get it out of the ground. Meanwhile Scott's mom went running ahead up to the dog and yelling at the top of her voice, she reached to pull the dog off Scott. In the process, the dog released Scott and went after my aunt, sinking its teeth into her hand and not letting go before my mom got there with the stick and pounded on the dog until he released my aunt and ran away. I stood there screaming, Scott was sobbing his eyes out, and Aunt Mandy was bleeding like crazy. To this day my aunt can't move her right hand freely. She had to relearn to write with her left hand. To this day she bears the scars of that dog.

So does Scott. Inside and out. Even though he doesn't talk about it.

I've never heard Aunt Mandy discuss or complain about her injury, either. And that is probably more remarkable than the fact that she rushed in to save her child, something most adults would have done.

To my mind what my aunt did for the boy she called her son was a purely unselfish act. And it was even more unselfish in light of all the complaining she did about us over our lifetime, that she never mentioned what happened to her hand. That's all I am saying. It doesn't mean I think my aunt was or is a good mom. She is superficial. She never understood Scott or me. And she deceived us both for thirty years. But she did one valiant heroic action that saved Scott's life and suffered the effects for the rest of her own life.

Even though I didn't want to, I dared to remind Scott of all of this. I didn't want to spend the rest of my life walking carefully on ice around my brother.

Scott stared at me as I spoke, and then started pacing back and forth along the meadow edge. He looked out over to the ocean, almost hidden by the fog, and he lifted his fist into the air and turned to spit something back at me. I couldn't make out what he said. The waves muffled even the loudest noise.

Scott came back to me. "Damn it, Liz. You and your fucking ambiguity! Your need to always be fair and just and see all the nuances of every single thing.... How can you do this to me?"

I didn't know how to answer that. I could have left well enough alone, but there it was. Once that scene had come back to me, I couldn't put it out of my mind but I should have left my mouth shut tight.

Miserably, I tried to sooth the situation. "It doesn't have to change anything at all for you. You have made a well-thought-out decision and I support you one hundred percent. I only want you to be able to go on with your life and, like Gran said, let happiness in. Just because I remembered that moment twenty-five years ago doesn't mean you have to change anything. All it means is that at least for one critical moment, Mandy did behave unselfishly.

"Most of us, have a little good and bad mixed together. Somehow, somewhere, you and I learned to love, and learned what was right and wrong, and we also found ways to express our creativity. We had to have gotten that from somewhere. We didn't go to church. We didn't have grandparents or extended family. We had school, but I can't believe we learned all our values and picked up our core self-worth there. I find myself searching my memories. We must have got something from our home."

Scott scoffed, "I'm not ready to accept that. I know Gran implied something like that, but other than a work ethic, I think maybe we got our values despite our home life, not because of it!" His voice remained defiant. "Maybe we got it from each other. Or maybe from Mr. Rogers. Or maybe we got it by osmosis."

He looked at me, wild-like, then more calmly said, "Cozy. That's where we got love. From her."

I thought, "Yes, he's right about Cozy, but I'll leave the door open to other influences."

I sighed. "I don't know. I answered your question about naming one unselfish behavior, Scotty, but I certainly didn't mean you should change your decision. You have to take care of yourself! That's what you have to do. Do that first."

He looked at me. "Tell me honestly, Lizzie. Have you forgiven them?"

I didn't know. "I have moved past a lot of the hurt. I have let happiness and doing things my way be central to my focus, so that the anger doesn't have much room to grow. I try not to feed it. I'm uncomfortable around our parents, but I don't know what that means. I just don't know what to say to them. How to act. Do I act like nothing happened? They have not reached out to have a big talk-it-out session. Dad has told me he is very sorry. But I have not heard that kind of talk from any of the other three. Is it my job to try to rebuild, or truthfully to build, a relationship? The truth is I never felt connected to them before, and so what's different now?

"They deceived us. But I think there is more to this disconnect than just one egregious act and the coverup. I keep coming back to the concept of connecting or belonging. It's what has been missing in terms of family our entire life. And now? I don't feel that they hold any power over me. That is really important to me. Does that mean I have forgiven them? I have no idea, Scott. I am pretty sure I don't hate them anymore, but I don't feel love either."

I thought and then repeated, "That they don't hold any power over me anymore feels liberating, but I also don't know how I will be handling this a year from now, or ten years, or if they get sick or die…." I shook my head. "But, to answer your question, I don't understand fully what forgiveness entails. That's a lot of blather but I guess the short answer is, I don't know."

Scott was calm again. "Maybe that is as good as it gets. Maybe that is what it takes to move on."

He came over and put his arm around my shoulder. "I'm happy for you, my Lizbeth. You are a gorgeous bride and you couldn't have found a better man. I'm sorry to bring up the bad shit on this great day!"

"Oh, it's okay. No day is safe from memories of bad shit, as you say. It's not like trauma disappears. It dances in the back of my head even when it doesn't have any lasting power over me. I figure it will be part of who I am for the rest of my life. I think it is more how you look at it, so when it pops up, I just try hold it for a bit and then put it in perspective, and it generally fades away, pushed out by awareness of all the good that is in my life. I am over-the-top lucky."

"Big sister, you are one cool, calm woman," Scott said to me.

"Oh, yeah? Well, how cool and calm is this?" I dropped the blanket, grabbed Scott's arm and raced to the cliff edge. Lifting my arms up to the misty sky and facing the ocean, I started yelling at the top of my voice. It's not something we do very often in life, and it's scary to let out the sound at first, and then it's exhilarating. I was channeling Gran at that moment. I figured she was with us in spirit. I'd felt her during the wedding and I think she was still with us on that cliffside. I had been wanting to do this ever since the night I witnessed her releasing her grief for Mac out to the universe.

Scott jumped back startled, but when he saw me turn and smile at him mid-scream, he stared and then amazingly, the man who had always been so chill and rational (unless there was a dog around) began to shout at the night sky with me. Together we shook our fists and raised our voices until we were spent. We collapsed on a large boulder, laughing through tears.

The fog became thicker, the waves muffled in the denseness of the wet air. Looking towards our own crazy house, we could barely see the lights on in the downstairs, but I knew that inside it held our community, our family of choice if not of blood.

When I could collect my breath, I said to him, "Gran taught me that display of mania, in case you wondered."

Scott jumped up and smiled straight at me, hands on his hips, glasses misting with the heat of his breath in the chilly ocean air, his hair disheveled, his thick parka open to the wind. My brother and my friend.

"Figures," he laughed. "Gran knew how to live, and how to die."

He wrapped me in a warm hug and, resting my cheek against him, I let him hold me. Being in synch with each other was where we belonged, and I was so glad to be back there.

"Yeah," I murmured.

Epilogue

I received a text from my dad. It came as I was approaching my thirteenth week of pregnancy, finally leaving the daily nausea behind, starting to feel some of that famous pregnancy glow I had heard about.

It was such good news that I was feeling solid again because in two months I would stand as maid of honor for Lupe as she and Scott would be married. The wedding would be held at a brewery, no surprise, and my quietly gregarious brother would have many friends attending from across the country, including Nick and Arturo. Scott would no longer rattle around in his four-bedroom home as a single man. He would be joined by not just Lupe but her daughter Marta and her mother, the maker of the excellent tamales and more. Not only did this invading female contingent not faze him, Scott could not have been happier. Lupe herself was glowing, looking years younger. It was the radiant effect of love, although it could also be her new hairstyle, her long dark hair now in a ponytail much of the time. As for me, I am thrilled. I will now have a sister who will always be my best friend. And I almost cried when Scott told me that Marta had asked him if she could call him "Daddy." He said he didn't hesitate a second before telling her yes, of course. And her next question for him, said in all her ten-year-old innocence, was that since there would be a large fenced yard, could they could get a puppy. And Scott just smiled at Marta and said, "Christmas is coming…" As Nellie proclaimed when she heard this story, "Wonders never cease!" I had more than one reason to be leaving the world of morning sickness behind me.

I am aware that some women get pregnant easily—Lupe, Susan Anderson, to name a few—I somehow thought that I would be like my mom or like Chelsea where pregnancy came only after years of trying. But Jerry and I had barely made the decision to discard our birth control and "see what happens" when Baby happened. So, my thoughts of applying for a teaching job in one of the schools up and down the coast went on hold. And when I was hit with constant nausea and fatigue, I also put aside my plan B to substitute teach and to remodel Gran's house to make it more "ours." Everything would wait until Baby made his or her appearance. We were living in Gran's house, renting out Jerry's place to the family who had been living in Tibby's house. Tibby moved back to her place, but we insisted she keep a room at Gran's house as hers and she, accompanied closely by Johnny, came over several times a week.

Gran's place had some deferred maintenance we had never noticed until we moved in, but we just could not resist the location and the view from the Templeton & MacIntosh home. We worked out a financial deal with Scott, who was half owner, and moved in. I am fairly certain that Baby was conceived on our first night in our new abode. We were thrilled with our future, but it did alter many plans, including me moving on to the next phase of my career.

I was not entirely comfortable with this pause in my life. I expressed my frustration with Jerry, who listened and then replied in a straightforward manner.

"Lizbeth, you have always worked hard and you will always work hard. You'll have many more students in your future. But for this year, you don't have to be busy all day just to prove that you are hardworking. Your body is doing some phenomenally hard work right now. Rest and relax, and use this time to slow down. You are worthy of it. Look at the big picture."

It wasn't easy but I tried. Having a house that was mine helped. And now, it was great to be feeling not just normal, but sort of super-normal with a new life—a baby boy we had just found out—asserting itself within me. That Sunday I took my usual afternoon nap but felt I didn't need it as much and found myself actually thinking some erotic ideas. I got up and walked into the living room and whispered into Jerry's ear as he sat in his chair with the remote poised in outreach position in front of him.

"Holy cow, you are feeling better!"

"Well, you got anything better going on?"

"Right now?"

"Yeah, right now."

To his credit he didn't miss a beat. "Okay, let me save the 49er game for later and tell Paul not to stop by. I'll be right with you."

"Oh, dear, I'm sorry. The ultimate sacrifice for a Sunday afternoon!" I teased him.

"Hell, I'd say the 49ers can win or lose without me!" He laughed as he sent off a quick text to his friend.

I smiled at him. "Yes, I am starting to feel human again. Maybe I'm over the worst of it. And for dinner tonight, I don't want toast and soup. I want something real, maybe some pasta? And I can at least help cook for the first time in three months!"

Yes, it was great to be feeling robust once again.

When we were contentedly enjoying our meal later, I remembered. "Jerry, guess what? I got a text from my dad this morning."

He looked up at me, mid-bite. "It's been a while, right?"

"We haven't had any communication for months now. Before I got pregnant. He sent a card with a check for our wedding. Funny that it came from him and wasn't signed by my mom. In fact, I heard nothing from her, and I figured she was mad that we didn't invite her to the wedding."

"You regret that?"

"Not at all," I replied immediately. "It was the right thing to do, I'm sure of that. We had the folks there who are really happy for us."

"What did he say?"

I pulled out my phone and read it to Jerry.

I am driving up to Gualala this weekend, Saturday, and hope to see you. I have something to tell you. If you are willing, please send your address.

"You'll see him?" Jerry put his napkin down and watched me.

I hesitated but said, "Yes."

And then added. "Jerry, will you be with me?"

"You need me to be a buffer or what?"

"No." I smiled at him. "I'd like to have you bear witness and be the outside observer to give me feedback. Do you think I am missing something or acting too defensive or too conciliatory or guilty or too cruel or what? I just want your outside opinion."

"Hardly outside, since you are my wife and my beloved and the mother of our child." He reached out and rubbed my hardly visible baby belly. "But I understand what you mean and I will be with you and give my feedback if that's what you are asking."

"Yep, that's what I'm asking."

When Jerry returned from the kitchen—he had been doing all the cooking and cleanup these last three months, something that needed to change now that I was feeling a better—I snuggled up to him on the couch.

"Jerry, do you know what wacky thought came to me the other day, a day when I was so miserable and exhausted?"

"I imagine there were many thoughts, such as 'I'm going to kill the man who got me in this predicament.'" We both laughed.

"No, no. I'll just hold that idea in abeyance for the rest of our lives whenever I think you are getting too full of yourself!!"

"Okay, what did you think about?"

"I thought of my mom. I wondered, well, I figured, she may have well been just as miserable as me in her pregnancy with Scott and me. And while that doesn't change how I feel about our relationship now, it does give me pause to relate to her at least on one level. While I will never understand how my mom's mind works, and I have often wondered where her heart is, at least I do know how her body might have felt once upon a time!"

Jerry looked at me a moment and then hugged me. "I love you, Elizabeth Kuiper. For so many reasons."

Later I wrote back to my dad with address and directions. I did find it odd that he couldn't get it from my mom and that he hadn't remembered from Gran's memorial service.

He said he would be there about 5:00 so I decided that if it felt okay in the moment, we could invite him for dinner and maybe even for night. And if it felt weird, we would direct him to lodging and a café in town.

Dad didn't arrive until near sunset. I sat in Gran's old porch chair, which, although falling apart, I had not been able to discard yet, and watched as he emerged from behind the garage. I could relate to him standing a moment to blink his eyes with the dazzling sun setting over the ocean. I watched him walk halfway across the meadow on the path and then just stop in his tracks. He was taking in the ocean and sky. He stood there for almost five minutes, perfectly still.

I loved him for that. Despite all the water under the bridge. I did.

Then I saw him turn and look all around until he spotted the house. He walked about twenty-five feet and as he got closer, he stopped again. And I knew the architect in him was taking in the sight of Gran and Mac's house. He looked at it as if it were the first time. And then I remembered, Dad had not made it to the memorial service. I had been caught in a blur that day and had not interacted with our parents. I had been only vaguely aware of their presence and their quick exit. But now I remembered, my dad had not been there. For the first time, I wondered why.

He was still gazing at it, feature by feature, occasionally looking out to the ocean view and then back to the house. I imagine he was thinking about how the view was framed from various windows. Finally, I stood up and walked to the top of the steps and called out to him.

He jumped and then came walking up towards me. He looked up at me. I almost didn't recognize my father. It wasn't so much that he had aged, but his demeanor had changed. His hair was different, longer, and he had a small beard. He wore glasses, which I rarely saw him wear. He always wore contacts. I can recall my mom harassing him about it when he tried to wear his glasses around the house on a weekend. She thought he looked best in his contact lens. But it was more than physical changes, it was something below the surface.

"Hi, Dad. Welcome to our little corner of the world. Come on in. Jerry will be here shortly. He shut down the shop early today so we could be together. In fact, there he is." Jerry came striding across the meadow to the house.

Dad looked at Jerry and then smiled at me, and I liked the smile. He walked up the stairs. He carried no bag. Just a jacket slung over his shoulder. When he got to the top of the stairs, he reached for me and before I could decide to hug or not, he pulled me into a hug, not a needy hug but a genuine one.

Then Jerry was up the stairs and shaking Dad's hand.

As we walked into the front door, Dad asked to use the bathroom and I directed him. As he walked away, I suggested, "Drinks on the front porch?"

He stopped and thought, and then said, "Liz, how about some wine?"

I was surprised. Dad was a gin drinker, or whisky or vodka, one or all of those. He had never been a wine drinker when given a choice. "Sure," I said.

I got out some hummus and chips, a bottle of white wine and a glass of white grape juice for me, and headed out to the front porch. I was still getting used to being the host in Gran's house. It would take more time to make the full transition. I still thought of it as Gran's.

We sat on the porch, the three of us, and we tipped our glasses to each other, he took only one sip before he cleared his throat and started to say something the same time as Jerry made a polite inquiry about his drive up the coast.

Dad quickly said, "It was fine, but before we talk about anything else, there is something I want to tell you. I've put it off long enough so don't want to waste any more time."

My heart started to beat. Don't tell me, Dad, that you are sick. That's what I was thinking. I didn't want any more of that kind of sadness.

Still holding his glass, he began to talk. "I have left your mom, Elizabeth. We are in process of divorcing."

He let that sink in, as if glad to get the preliminaries out of the way. I was silent. Surprised, yet more curious than saddened. When he didn't immediately go on, I prompted him.

"Tell me about it, Dad."

"From the day you and Scott burst into our house with your birth certificates waving, mad as hell, as you rightly should have been, something shifted for me. I had been sleepwalking from the moment your mom told me she was going to give one of our babies to Mandy. I froze up then, and by not acting or speaking, I was complicit with the whole plan. You know what they say, by not acting you are acting. I was frozen for thirty years. I knew it was wrong and I didn't stop it, and I have lost my son, and perhaps my daughter as a consequence, and I deserve it. For thirty years it has tortured me to see my son living in another home, not that they treated him badly.

"Celine and Mandy were inseparable. Those sisters care about each other far more than they care about their husbands. Ryan could never relate to Scott, and I wasn't able to acknowledge Scott as my son, only as my nephew. That was so painful. Instead of confronting the situation and insisting that you two learn the truth, I took the cowardly way out and removed myself from active participation in both of your lives, especially Scott's. I lived for my work and my golf game, and isn't that a pathetic and cliched existence for a father?"

Dad was speaking calmly, looking at his hands holding the undrunk wine the whole time. Behind him the sun disappeared in splendor while this agonizing confession unfolded. I sat still and listened. Jerry sat and watched both of us as our solar lights began lighting up.

"About my behavior all these years… I am ashamed, I am revolted, I am guilty as hell. I expect no forgiveness, that's not why I am here. I am here to tell you my story and just ask you to listen. And I am here to tell you that although I am all of the above, guilty, shamed, horrified at myself, I am no longer depressed as I was for all those years, all the years of your growing up, dear Elizabeth, and Scott's as well."

"Over the last year I've felt huge anger, at myself and at Celine and the others. I asked Celine if she wanted to go see a therapist. She looked at me as if I were crazy. Maybe I was. So I went alone. And it has helped me to find myself again, realize what I can do and not do. Eight months ago, I moved out of the house and started the proceedings."

He stopped, paused really, and looking at his wine he took a small sip. I wondered if he was going to AA and needed to ask for amends, but my dad had not really been a heavy drinker, just a regular drinker.

I asked him, just to get him talking again. "Where are you living, Dad?"

"I've been living in Sacramento, near my office. Got a small studio apartment. I don't need much. Just my computer and my golf clubs, but I find I am not even golfing much. I've been walking a lot, hiking in the mountains and also just walking streets."

He stopped and for the first time really looked at me, and then turned and looked at Jerry. "You know what's funny? I feel better than I have felt in years, thirty years to be exact. I have all this miserable history, all the years where I cheated myself and my children, but I'm taking some baby steps towards trying to like myself. And every tiny bit of liking myself is better than a full scale hating myself. I mean I figured I had the choice. Hate myself so much that I throw in the towel and kill myself one way or another, or I could have swallowed the pain and disgust and kept living my life as I had been, in a joke of a marriage and completely estranged from my children. Or I could at least salvage some of my sense of life and selfhood. Start over, you know, on my own."

There was a silence then. I didn't know what to say, and my dad sat in quiet, not with the nervous energy he had always exhibited as a constant, having to be doing something, anything except connecting with me or anyone else.

At last Jerry said to my dad, "Starting over is a difficult thing to do, but the alternatives are bad. Sounds like the best choice."

Dad gave Jerry an appreciative nod.

All I could say was "Dad, thank you for coming to tell me. It means the world to me that you have come, and… and, you know what? I look forward to getting to know my real dad, flaws and pain and all."

His voice was gruff. "Lizzie, thank you for those words. I will hold on to them, and to yours too, Jerry, in the next stage of my life. Leaving the marriage was actually the easiest part. I feel free and like I can be myself. But it is the self-loathing

I experience when I think of what I gave permission to that keeps me awake and tormented at night. Ha, during the day too. Working and walking, that's what keeps me as sane as I am. But I need to do this alone, Lizzie. I am going to drive away tonight and I will leave you and Jerry to your happiness in this gorgeous place. Maybe someday I can come back feeling a little more like a lovable man, although not worthy of my children's respect. That I know will never happen."

"Dad, why do you think that couldn't happen? I think it is possible."

He shook his head. "Not yet, my dear. Not yet. You are a compassionate young woman, and I'm not sure where you learned that. There wasn't a lot of kindness in our home. You are a wonder to me. But thank you for keeping the door open to the future. Maybe. In case you are wondering, I accept that Scott will probably never be able to look at me again. And Lizzie, it is not your job to try to help him accept me." He looked at me sternly. He knew me after all.

"Dad, I am no longer connected at the hip with Scott. Ironically, once we found out we were twins, I learned that we were separate beings and he was not tasked with taking care of me or me of him. Our experiences are different. I can tell you that Scott is moving along and he is letting happiness into his life. You can know that your son is a great guy who is doing well."

Dad listened carefully. "Thanks, Liz. That's important to me." He changed topics. "You haven't said one word about your mom, or asked how she is doing with all of this."

To be honest, there was a part of me that wished I could

care more or believe I could miraculously change things and find the mother I wished I had been graced with in the beginning. But that was magical thinking. I didn't want to waste my time trying to squeeze myself in where I didn't belong. I looked at my father and was able to say, without rancor, "I am certain that outwardly she has not changed a bit. She is unflappable and relentless. And inside she is so disconnected from her emotions that I doubt anything could shake her. I've seen her at the Piedmont house once, but she has not approached Scott since the initial night."

Dad nodded. "I'm afraid you're correct, Liz. I believe in some way she feels the pain of losing her children, but she will never show it. I really think that the only thing that will shake her is if something happened to Mandy. Her sister is her lifeline."

I thought about that for a moment and agreed with him.

We stood in silence for a time, the three of us there on Gran and Mac's front porch. Not uncomfortable but there seemed little more to say. We could not get Dad to agree to have dinner with us, much less stay with us. And when we gave him names of cafes and inns in Gualala, he declined. "Thanks, Jerry, Liz, but I am a restless and ever-moving man these days. I find that my adrenaline keeps me moving, and for now that keeps me steady." He did say that he would like to someday come back and study the "interesting" architecture of our house and soak in the ocean view, which he said was "soul stirring."

I looked at Jerry and then back at my dad. "Well, I hope that you will be ready for your 'someday' to come and visit us about six months from now. Meanwhile, start practicing your Grandpa Matt routine."

I swear it took my dad, that bright man, a full minute to understand what I just told him. Then he grabbed me and hugged me tight, then broke away and hugged Jerry even tighter and longer. I had never seen my dad cry. I had never seen him overcome with joy.

After we answered a few of his garbled and delighted questions, we tried once again to get him to spend the night, but he insisted he was on the right track to just keep going. The only thing I could get him to promise to do was to send me a text when he arrived back in Sacramento or wherever he decided to spend the night.

"I'm a bit of a rolling stone right now, Elizabeth. I haven't been this loose since my college days before I met your mom. She was so beautiful, I was hooked, but I let her pull me into her orbit of control within her ideal lifestyle. It was insidious. But finally, I'm back to being myself again, only I have this terrible burden to process. But your news has given me all the fuel I need to fire myself up to achieve some level of broken recovery."

And he laughed as he started to hand me his almost-full glass of wine, then turned and gave it to Jerry. "I guess you are the only one drinking right now, right? I'm not drinking tonight because I knew I would be driving and these roads you have up here bear paying attention."

I know there was a lightness to my dad's step that had not been there when he arrived. Jerry walked with him out to the car. When he came back Jerry took me in his arms and held me close without talking. But then he laughed.

"What?"

"Guess what car your dad was driving, Lizzie."

I looked at him. "Not the Explorer?"

Jerry nodded. "Only it now has California plates."

I smiled. I had good memories of that vehicle. "But, Jerry, here I am worrying about my dad driving all the way back to Sacramento in the dark when for months he was out of my mind most of the time. I guess when you love someone, that's when you start worrying about them."

We walked down to the cliff to say goodnight to the waves, arm in arm. Jerry said, "Looks like Baby Kuiper-Garcia may have a real bloodline grandparent after all."

"That would be nice, Jerry. A real nice plus. But our baby will be well-loved regardless."

"What do you think about Scott, you know, in relationship to your dad?"

"I'm someone who likes to fix things, but I am not going there. Scott is happy now and he may never get past the betrayal that my dad silently supported. But then again, time and time and more time may help. I'm keeping an open mind about everything these days."

The End

Author Notes

Through the centuries storytelling has often been based on the premise of a trek or a journey, driven by a quest to fulfill a mission, reach a goal, and perhaps through the help of a talisman, deliver a message. These are usually exciting sagas replete with physical perils where a hero (or anti-hero) overcomes many obstacles and grows into full maturation in the process, such as in *The Odyssey*, or *The Wizard of Oz*, or *Lord of the Rings*.

While I don't write action-adventure books, I challenged myself to tell a story where everyday people take on a mission and in less dramatic style, learn and change as they wrestle with their pasts and their circumstances, ultimately altering the course of their lives and others. Out of this musing, ***Belonging: The Journey*** was birthed.

I believe it was inevitable that someday I would write a story set in one of my favorite places on earth, the wild and glorious Mendocino and Sonoma coasts, and when Gran called out to me from the front porch of her amazing and whimsical house sitting on the bluff over the ocean, I was ready to start.

In writing my stories, it is always a marvel to me how the first sentence falls in place and the characters show up. And once they show up, they tell me their stories which I dutifully bring to life. Eventually, one thing became clear to me: this is a story about finding our place to belong. ***Belonging: The Journey*** is about how our place of belonging may require a journey to understand, and when we find it, we may see that it comes in many and evolving forms and in surprising places.

It was in September of 2023 while staying for a month on the Central California coast, when I began to write of a trek: Elizabeth and her cousin Scott's mission for Gran. I added chapter after chapter each day in an industrious and engrossing writing splurge. Then near the end of our coastal stay, a writing disaster occurred. One morning I found that my emerging manuscript had not been saved in three weeks. No amount of computer sleuthing could bring it back. It was simply gone. I kept reminding myself to keep this loss in perspective, but it was a sickening blow.

I took a pause, doubting for a time whether I would have the heart or the skill to rebuild the story. Just in case, I jotted down every scrap of lost detail and event I could remember, and finally one day I had the courage to start again. I picked up after the first three chapters which miraculously had not been lost, and with that running start, climbed back into the flow of the story. Gradually the trek within the story and the trek within my writing process came to completion. I will never know how the second version compares to the missing version.

Beyond their California coastal experiences, Elizabeth and Scott drove the interstate and backroads, through many states and into Canada; every place they traveled is vividly familiar to me. However, none of their experiences are mine. Every trek is unique.

The cities of Davis and Dixon, and those along the Sonoma and Mendocino coast are all real, including Gualala and the beautiful St. Orres restaurant and lodge. However, all the characters in the book are completely fictional as is Gran's house. I've heard there is a trusted mechanic in Gualala but I have never seen or met him.

With ***Belonging: The Journey***, I honor the value of strong love relationships, good friendships, and particularly the wisdom and resiliency of older women through the characters of Gran, Nellie, and Tibby. Our American culture often makes older women invisible and without merit. I know differently and whether you call women of a certain age crones or sages or elders or simply by our names, we carry a wealth of living inside our bodies and hearts and minds. Lucky are those who, like Elizabeth and Scott, run into such an elder and stick around to love and learn.